picks
& shovels

also by cory doctorow

cory doctorow
picks
& shovels

HEAD
of ZEUS

An Ad Astra Book

First published in the US in 2025 by Tom Doherty Associates / Tor Publishing Group

First published in the UK in 2025 by Head of Zeus,
part of Bloomsbury Publishing Plc

This is a work of fiction. All characters, organizations, and events
portrayed in this novel are either products of the author's
imagination or are used fictitiously.

9 7 5 3 1 2 4 6 8

A catalogue record for this book is available from the British Library.

ISBN (HB): 9781804547830
ISBN (XTPB): 9781804547847
ISBN (E): 9781804547823

Printed and bound by CPI Group (UK) Ltd, Croydon, CR0 4YY

Head of Zeus Ltd
First Floor East
5–8 Hardwick Street
London EC1R 4RG

WWW.HEADOFZEUS.COM

For the Homebrew Computer Club, the WELLbeings, Barlow, Gilmore and Kapor, Woz and Tom Jennings and Tim Pozar and The Little Garden, the alt.* hierarchy and FidoNet, the hardware hackers and the dip switchers, bunnie Huang and Seymour Papert. For Claire Evans, and her magesterial Broad Band (without which this book would not exist). And of course, for my parents, who raised me right, with an acoustic coupler and a teletype terminal on the kitchen table.

picks
& shovels

prologue

There was never any question but that I would become an engineer.

So naturally, I became an accountant.

My old man was a mechanical engineer, dragged me and my mom around the country from job to job. His big brother, my uncle Ed, left home at seventeen to be an air force mechanic, spent four years in Europe with the USAF, then a decade more with Boeing, servicing Stratocruisers at Heathrow for Pan Am, United, and BOAC. He came home for my fifth-birthday party in Disneyland. He gave me his air force mechanic's cap, green and faded with old grease stains and a couple of darned-over rips. I still have it. It fits me better now than it did when I was five.

Uncle Ed went to work for Rohr Aerospace in Chula Vista, doing field repairs on test rockets. Dad followed him as a consulting engineer, and we had Sunday dinner every week, sometimes with one of Uncle Ed's glamorous girlfriends in attendance. Uncle Ed would rib my dad about engineering's design defects that kept him and the other mechanics busy. I hung on every word.

Dad moved us to Ohio in my last week of junior high, then again to Escambia County, Alabama, in 1977—my junior year—for the oil boom. We felt like the only Americans thanking OPEC for the embargo. Dad made more money in the next two years than he had in the previous decade. They were so goddamned desperate for oil in those years that they recruited *Black people* to come to *Alabama* to work as *managers* in the fields. I survived two years of that. That was two years of high school with townies who hated us boomtown from-aways with a seething resentment that often boiled over into lonely-road beatdowns. I hated every goddamned thing about my life: Alabama, my school, boomtown living, and my father.

We were all ecstatic when I got accepted to MIT for electrical engineering. My dad was visibly relieved by the fact that I was going far, far away. He was only too glad to part with tuition and living expenses. With all that oil money sloshing around, he barely noticed. Anything to get me out of the house and end the constant screaming matches that left us both shaking and my mother in tears.

I was a prototypical MIT fuckup. I had a *lot* of hobbies. I wasted my time with the Tech Model Railroad Club, which led me into tabletop war-gaming, and from there into steam-tunnel exploration. Some of my circle overlapped with the anti-war movement, and I had a four-month-long intense romance with Dominique, a French anti-nuclear-proliferation activist who was doing a poli-sci degree at Harvard.

But it wasn't the railroad or the war games or the steam tunnels that accounted for my terrible first-semester grades. It wasn't even Dominique's fault, though there were months there where we kept each other up late every night, arguing politics and being horny teenagers.

I got straight Fs in my first semester because of an Altair 8800 kit that I bought the second week of school after seeing one at a Tech Model Railroad Club meeting with money I was supposed to spend on furniture, textbooks, and meals. I ran out of money the same week the provost wrote to my father to tell him that I was failing every class. The two letters arrived the same day. I got a message from the RA to call my father urgently. I called the operator from a pay phone in the lobby and inquired about the long-distance toll, added up all the money I had left, shrugged, and called collect.

"Martin," he said, after he'd told the operator he'd accept the charges. Even over the long-distance line, his voice was heavy with barely controlled rage.

"Hey, Pop," I said, trying to keep it light. I felt like I was about to puke. Then I had a sudden epiphany about a hard programming challenge that I'd wrestled with on my 8800 all afternoon and I was so distracted that I missed whatever he said next. "Sorry, what?"

"Martin Harold Hench, get the shit out of your ears." My nausea returned. My father abhorred "low language." The only other time I'd ever heard him say *shit* was the night Nixon resigned. My mother had sent him for a walk around the block and told him not to come back until he'd mastered his sensibilities.

"Sorry, Pop," I said. "It must be a bad connection. Can you say that again?"

"Son, I have spent the past three hours on the phone with the provost, begging—*begging*—him to give you a chance to bring your grades up next semester. I told that man that you are a brilliant scholar, a *prodigy,* and that you had merely stumbled because of a lack of structure in your life. Now, as it happens, I don't actually think you're as smart as all that, but I by God know that you're smart enough to pass freshman physics, algebra, and chemistry. It goes without saying that you are smart enough to get a passing grade in freshman Introduction to American Literature. There are *toddlers* who are smart enough to pass a literature-review class."

He paused long enough that I knew I was supposed to say something. I knew what I was supposed to say, too. I said it: "Yes, sir."

"'Yes, sir,' is right, you little shit." My stomach did another slow roll. "Because this isn't just my faith in you talking. This is a—" He choked momentarily, his anger so close to the surface. I flinched involuntarily, because my autonomic nervous system couldn't understand that he was thirteen hundred miles away and could not smack me around, no matter how much he wanted to. "This is a . . . *fucking*"—I jumped at the word—"ultimatum. You have one more semester to pull your grades up, and if you fail to do that, then you will wash out of MIT.

"And listen carefully to me, you shit, you little *shit,* if that happens, you will not be coming back here when they sling your ass out of that dorm room. Am I being very clear?"

"Yes, sir," I rasped. It was the swearing. My old man *never* swore. The words were like blows, conjuring the same feeling in my chest as I'd felt when he would come into my room, hands clenched into fists.

"I hope so, son. I truly hope so. Because I am as serious as a fucking heart attack. You hang up this phone, you go back to your dorm room, and you hit your goddamned books. You get one more semester to sort yourself out, or you can find someone else to call 'Dad.'"

"Okay," I said. My voice was barely a whisper. "I mean, yes sir."

"Goodbye, Martin." I stood there holding the receiver for so long that the operator came back on and asked me if I wanted to be reconnected. The thought literally jolted me, and I barked *"No!"* and racked the handset.

I was all the way up six flights of stairs to my dorm room when I realized he hadn't said anything about the money.

My second semester was an even bigger disaster.

I'd like to say that I tried, but it would be a lie. It wasn't that I wasn't putting in any effort: I was. At no time in my life have I ever worked harder. I broke up with my girlfriend and lived on noodles and free Hare Krishna temple lunches or forgot to eat. I'd taken up smoking in my first semester. I quit—not (just) because I was broke, but because I resented leaving my desk to go to the store for a fresh pack.

I worked until I couldn't keep my eyes open anymore, then I

keeled over and dreamed about work for a few hours until I got back up and worked again.

I was learning. God, was I learning. Every day came a new epiphany, sending me off on a new research angle, yielding more insights. I burned through whole sections of the MIT library and then started in on journals, looking for more current sources than the slow-motion world of book publishing could provide.

The problem was, I wasn't learning anything related to my classwork. I was learning to program a computer.

The Altair 8800 was made possible by Intel's 8080 chip, the first low-priced microprocessor powerful enough to do useful work. My kit came with a 4K BASIC module, and I traded a night's typing work to a kid I knew for a second 4,096-byte memory board and a copy of 8K BASIC.

A plug-compatible PROM from IMS—bought as-is cheap from a guy at a swap meet and rehabilitated with a soldering iron and some schematics—gave me another 4K of memory. By historical standards, my dorm room was now a supercomputing lab.

But I needed more. I was teaching myself to hack, first using the switch plate on the front panel to code in assembler, laboriously toggling the Enter switch after each eight bytes. After more swap meets, more soldering, more scrounging, I graduated to a keyboard and BASIC, a printer and reams of fanfold paper that had only been printed on one side and could be fed backward into the machine.

God, I wanted a screen!

I didn't encounter the word "toolchain" until many years later, but that's what I was making: programs to help me write programs that would help me write other programs. I'd never heard of a debugger, but I created one of those, too.

One cold February night I was contemplating one of the

administrative building's dumpsters, looking for more printer paper—the dumpster had better hours than any office-supply store in town—and I ran into a fellow traveler.

Even by Cambridge standards, Art Hellman stood out as an eccentric, even at two in the morning, even in a dumpster. He was barely five feet tall (later, he'd swear he was five one, and only terrible people called him on the lie), with a head of wild red curls that both shot a foot into the air and crawled down over his back and shoulders, sometimes getting in his face. What he lacked in chin, he made up for in nose, and he had the bugged-out eyes of a ceramic frog statue.

He wore a snowsuit under a parka—he ran cold and found eastern winters almost physically intolerable—and he was waist-deep in a dumpster, holding a big three-cell flashlight in one hand and awkwardly sorting through trash with his free hand.

"You look like you need someone to hold that light for you," I said, and he just about leaped out of the dumpster, eyes rolling and hair flailing.

"Jesus, man, *don't sneak up on a guy,* would you?" He shone the light in my eyes and I shielded them.

"Sorry," I said. "Get that out of my eyes, okay?"

He didn't move the light. "You a cop?"

"Yeah," I said. "I'm a seventeen-year-old cop offering to hold your flashlight for you. Cut it out, dammit."

He clicked the light off. Green blobs danced in front of me.

"Sorry," he said. "You scared me, is all."

"Don't mention it. What are you after?"

"Anything, you know? If it's any good, I bring it to the Free Store. I got everything I need. Last year's move-out date was a record-breaker: bed, dresser, sofa, even a TV."

"Color?"

"Shit yeah, color. You a freshman?"

"I told you, I'm seventeen."

"Well, you could be a prodigy. We got seventeen-year-old seniors here. Are you a prodigy or a freshman?"

"I'm not a prodigy," I said, and vaulted into the dumpster. The cold kept the smell down, but there was definitely a sour coffee-and-spoiled-milk odor. "I'm Marty," I said.

"Arthur Hellman," he said. That was how he always introduced himself, even though every person on Earth, from his professors to his mother, called him Art. We shook. "What are you looking for, Marty?"

"Computer paper, you know, the kind with the perforated sprocket holes on the edges? For computers?"

"I am familiar with the article in question," he said. He shone his light around the dumpster, looking for something. "This box," he said, kicking a cardboard carton. I opened it up and squinted at it in the darkness. It was filled with reams of printer paper, at least two bales' worth—that is, twenty reams or five thousand sheets. I checked a couple of the reams—they were all blank on one side.

"Perfect!" I said. I hefted the box, then balanced it on a corner of the dumpster, vaulted out, and set the box down on a dry patch of parking lot. Then I hopped back into the dumpster.

"What, that's not enough paper for you?"

"No, that's plenty," I said. "I don't think I could carry more than that, anyway."

"So what are you doing?"

"I said I'd hold your flashlight."

"But you found your paper." He sounded bemused.

"But I said I'd hold your flashlight."

"Where are you from, Marty?"

"All over. Last place was Alabama."

"Alabama."

"Yup."

"What's your last name, Marty? You're Marty what?"

"Marty Hench."

"Marty Hench from Alabama. You're a mensch, Marty Hench. Hench the mensch. Here's the flashlight."

He had a much bigger haul than mine: a perfectly serviceable tool chest, a box of hanging files, a pile of mismatched plates and cups, and a toaster oven he hypothesized came from one of the break rooms. Then he moved on to the next dumpster, and the next. It was 4 a.m. by the time he was done, and the pile was taller than him. He'd told me repeatedly that I could go, I'd done enough, but I was spellbound, watching him work, helping out with my free hand. I'd always been so focused on printer paper that I'd never noticed all the great junk around it.

"Now what?" I said. "You're gonna have to make what, fifteen trips to get this back."

He snorted. "This won't even fill up half my van," he said, and took off around the corner. "I always park on a side street so a passing cop doesn't wonder why there's a mysterious van in the parking lot in the middle of the night," he called over his shoulder.

It was a Chevy 108, mostly rust-colored under the yellow streetlight. He unlocked it and then slid across to unlock the passenger-side door. I was just about to get in when I had a moment of serial-killer anxiety. I was literally getting into a strange guy's van in the middle of the night on a lonely street. I didn't know *anything* about this Art Hellman.

But it passed. Right from the moment I'd spotted him in the dumpster, methodically one-arming through the trash, I'd known him for a kindred spirit. He'd dropped some hints that he knew a thing or two about computers, too. Besides, he was a squirt. I had a whole head on him. I could take him.

I got in the van. It smelled of crusty road salt and dirty ashtrays with an undercurrent of BO, your basic *parfum de Boston winter*. He fished around in the ashtray for a half-smoked butt, lit it with the push-button lighter, turned over the van's frozen engine with a series of asthmatic revs, threw it into gear, and drove back to the dumpster.

"I can drop you off," he said. "Maybe you want to get that second box of printer paper?"

I helped him load up, using dirty quilted movers' blankets to back up the fragile pieces. I offered to help him unload his stuff first, and he grinned at me. "A mensch," he said, and gunned the van through the Cambridge dawn.

The Free Store was a cramped storefront next to a package liquor store and a disreputable Chinese restaurant near the Alewife T station. He drove around back and unlocked a loading door and I helped him empty out his finds, along with several bags of day-old bread he'd picked up from a bakery dumpster at the start of the night. He offered me as much as I wanted, so I kept a couple of loaves of dark rye for myself and mentally filed away bakery dumpsters as an adjunct to free Krishna temple dinners.

When we got to my dorm, he insisted on helping me carry up my printer paper, and told me to balance the rye loaves on his box. We had to stop twice in the stairwell, and drew stares from some student athlete types on their way to morning practice.

He set his box down on my bed. I was suddenly self-conscious about the dirty laundry and dirty dishes, but his attention was riveted by my Altair. He shucked out of his coat and sat down in my desk chair and started running his fingers over the faceplate, toggling the switches, checking out the burns where I'd gotten careless with my soldering iron, tracing the wires to my cassette drive and flipping through my box of tapes, puzzling over my handwritten labels.

"What's 'Essay Magic 2.1'?"

I blushed. "It's what I call my word processor. I based it on

Electric Pencil, a little, and I had an idea that it would help me write better term papers."

"Did it?"

I shook my head. "Not really. I spent so much time debugging it that I blew all my term paper deadlines."

He nodded. "That happens. Show me."

So I did, bootstrapping the Altair and feeding one of the reams of cold paper we'd just hauled up the stairs into my printer. I loaded the tape into the drive and loaded and ran the program. Once I had my editor prompt, I typed "The quick brown fox jumps over the lazy dog," toggled the edit mode, and changed "lazy" to "crazy," as the printer chattered beside us.

"May I?" he said, commandeering the keyboard before I could answer.

"Sure," I said. "I followed Electric Pencil's command structure and—"

But his fingers were already clattering over the keys, sending blocks of type to the printer and then editing them. He broke out of the program and listed it out, peering at the printer, killing the listing to follow my gosubs, then jumping back. His finger traced the odd line, and he made little grunts of satisfaction.

"This is cute," he said. "Really, really cute. I like it."

I grabbed a binder off a shelf. "Want to borrow the whole listing?" I said.

"I want a copy of the tape," he said. "And the printout. This is *seriously* cute." He peered at the paper. "Got a toaster?"

"A toaster?"

"For the rye. I'm starving."

So I made toast and found some peanut butter for it, and he got crumbs on my desk and peanut butter on my listings, and then he came to a part of the program I'd really sweated over, a way to swap whole paragraphs in and out of the text buffer without long lags, and he stabbed it with a finger and sprayed crumbs as he began to talk around his food.

"Swallow," I said. "I can't understand you."

He chewed impatiently and swallowed. "This is bullshit," he said. "God, why would you do it that way?"

I wasn't even angry. This chinless, all-nose redheaded clown was criticizing *my* code? Especially *that* code? Let's see him do better. "How would *you* do it?"

He rolled his eyes and wiped his hands on his snow pants and grabbed the keyboard and loaded up the relevant section of my program and started to code, freehand, right over my own code. I started to object, then my attention snagged on the code pouring off my printer and I stopped. At first I couldn't figure out what he was doing, then I got the general shape of it, and then it just *snapped* into place and I saw that he was right, my painstakingly worked-out solution sucked, and his was a million times better.

I made more toast.

"I think you'd better start coming to our user-group meetings," he said.

"What user group?"

"The Newbury Street Irregulars."

I'd never heard of them. I agreed instantly.

Though it's possible I'd have flunked my whole second semester on my own, once I joined the Irregulars that possibility became a certainty. Formally, the group met on Tuesdays and Sundays, but you could show up at the clubhouse—underneath a record store on Newbury Street—at any time of day or night and you'd find our members, mostly guys, mostly undergrads, but there were a few graybeards and a few high-school kids and even a few young women who must have felt very isolated and weird. Looking back on it, I think they must have loved computers a hundred times more than I did, because they ended up putting up with a hundred times more shit than I did, and still they showed up, wrote code, soldered, designed, argued.

Oh, how we argued. The walls were papered with annotated program printouts that were scribbled over with comments and suggestions and rude criticisms. There were three dumb terminals with acoustic couplers that could be used to dial into one of the electrical engineering department's DECs or even the IBM 360, if you were lucky enough to have a login.

There were dues, and a roster of people who hadn't paid them, but some of the kids came from money and would quietly kick in a few extra bucks to float deadbeats like me for another month. The best of these patrons expected nothing in return; the worst of them acted like I owed them endless debugging work in exchange for their charity. Art told me to tell them to go fuck themselves, but the truth was, I *liked* debugging, liked solving the mysteries presented by gnarly, chewy problems.

I saw my first Apple][+ when someone brought theirs into Newbury Street and immediately grasped its importance— not just the elegance of its hardware design, which was on fine display in the schematics that shipped with the machine, but in the RF modulator that let us connect one of Art's curbside-rescue TVs and conjure up programs that could be endlessly revived without finding more paper or ink, without waiting for a printer to laboriously output its text.

I wanted one of those computers more than I wanted anything in my life. The system was the plaything of one of the rich boys, Nick Cassidy III of the Louisville Cassidys, who had a seemingly unlimited budget courtesy of his spectacularly wealthy parents. He was one of the guys who expected debugging work from charity cases like me, and it wasn't even interesting debugging work because (a) none of the programs he wrote were very interesting and (b) all of the mistakes he made were very obvious.

But that didn't matter. Fixing Nick Cassidy III's awful computer programs meant time with his wonderful Apple][+. I just about moved into his house—no dorm for him, he had a three-bedroom place all to himself, with one room designated as a "study" and the other as a "guest room"—and hogged his Apple machine. Working with a screen was . . . transformative. It was like I'd been learning to hit a baseball blindfolded, or dance in cement shoes, or . . . Well, it was like I'd been doing something I loved in a very hard way, and now I was doing it the easy way. I'd programmed on glass teletypes plugged into a mainframe or minicomputer before, but to have this window into a computational world I controlled, a computer that was right before me, for me alone, it was *incredible*. I didn't hear the word "cyberspace" until well into the next decade, but the minute I heard it, I knew where it was—it was the place I went when I was working on that computer.

The provost called my dad halfway through the semester, when our midterm grades posted. My dad left a message for me at the dorm. I didn't return it. He left another message the next day. And the next.

Nick Cassidy III had a girlfriend visiting from back home, so I was stuck in the dorm, and that meant I was in the lobby when he called for the fourth time. The dorm monitor grabbed me.

"You'd better talk to him. I'm not an answering service." He had a point. I liked him. He was doing grad work in anthropology and spent a lot of time in the monkey house and often compared the dorm to his primates. It was a good bit.

"Hi, Dad."

"Son." It wasn't the stony voice I'd been expecting. It was choked with emotion.

"Dad?"

"Listen, Marty. You're a thousand miles away. I can't be there to sit on you and make you go to school. I tried threatening you. It didn't work. You are going to flunk out of MIT. Nothing short of a miracle will prevent it at this point. Even if I hired you half a dozen tutors, you cannot pull your grades up high enough to pass any of your courses. None of them. It's a mathematical impossibility. Does that mean anything to you, Marty?"

It pulled me up short. Look, I was seventeen, I was in love with computers, drunk stupid love, and nothing else had mattered. But MIT was in Cambridge and Cambridge was where the Newbury Street Irregulars were and the Newbury Street Irregulars knew more about computers than anyone else who was willing to talk to me. They were my co-addicts, my technological family. I would have bet that not a single person in Escambia, Alabama, owned a personal computer. I couldn't go back.

The realization pulled me up short. I mentally recited the six-year-old's catechism: *make it didn't happen.* But it had happened. I'd made my bed. I'd shot myself in the foot. I had no one to blame but myself, and I knew it, even as the six-year-old inside me was saying *why didn't anyone tell me?* They had. My father had. I wasn't angry at him anymore.

"I'm sorry, Pop." I really was.

He didn't say anything, and he didn't say anything, and he went on not saying anything for so long that I finally asked if he was there.

"I'm here, Marty."

"Okay," I said.

"Marty, what's done is done. You have options. You don't have to get a degree, and if you do, you don't have to get it from MIT. You can do what your uncle Ed did, join the air force, get trained, do a degree when you muster out."

"I don't think I want to join the air force," I blurted. I thought about what my girlfriend—the one I'd gone on so many anti-war and anti-nuke demonstrations with—would think about me joining up. Then I wondered what *I* would think. I wouldn't like it. I definitely would not.

"That's fine. From what Ed tells me, it's not for everyone,

that's for sure. But Marty, you need a trade. You can't just drop out of college and push a broom around. You need a marketable skill. You need to be able to stand on your own. Someday you're going to want a family, kids. You'll want to support them."

I was seventeen. I knew that all that was theoretically true but in a distant way that was as remote as a comet in the Oort cloud. "I guess so."

"I know so." He took another deep breath. "Marty, you know I love you. You know your mother loves you. This thing that's happened, it's not the end of the world. I'm sorry I blew my stack before. So you're not going to be an electrical engineer, so that's fine. But you gotta learn a trade.

"The provost gave me a number for a student counseling center. There's people there, they can help you figure out what's available. Maybe there's a trade school, some place where you get a one- or two-year certificate. Plumber. Electrician. Metal-worker. Nothing wrong with any of those things. Get your plumber's ticket, you'll be able to work anywhere, anytime you want, as long as or as short as you want, and you'll earn a good living. It's dirty work, but it's *clean* dirty work. Without plumb-ers, the world wouldn't be a very nice place."

I laughed at that. Who was this guy and what had he done with my dad?

"That sounds good, Dad. I'll talk to them. Where did you say they were?"

I borrowed a pencil and some scrap paper from the monkey guy and wrote it down.

"Thanks, Dad."

"Your dorm is paid for until the end of the semester; your meal card will be good in the cafeteria until then. You've got one of the country's great cities there at your feet, you've got some of the greatest institutions of learning, their libraries and lecture halls, all there for you to visit and use as you see fit. You use the time you've got, figure this out. I know you can do it, Marty. I have faith in you. Your mother, too. We both know you will be a great man."

I hung up in a daze and handed back the monkey guy's pencil. He handed me a tissue and I noticed there were tears on my cheeks. My old man and I butted heads a lot, but there were also lots of good times—tossing a ball, arguing about science fiction novels, watching *Star Trek* together, going for hikes in the hills or swimming in the Pacific before we left San Diego. Sure, he made me angry as hell, and I clearly disappointed and frustrated the shit out of him, but he was my dad. I loved him. He'd just done me a solid, giving me time and space to "find myself" as my flakier classmates would have put it.

The thing is, I *had* found myself. I was a Computer Person. I wanted to compute with every hour that God (or whoever) sent, and then I wanted to do some more. Forever.

With that in mind, I went to the student career counseling office and spent a couple of hours with a very attractive and extremely cheerful senior from Louisiana with an accent that just *melted* me, and emerged having decided to become an accountant.

Why an accountant? Well, there were the practical reasons: Accounting was like plumbing—everyone needed it and they'd pay for it. I could do a two-year associate's degree and walk out into a job, and then upgrade that to a bachelor's degree while on the job. I could work for just about any big company—even a hardware or software company, because they needed accountants, too—or for an accounting company, or just set up a one-man shop doing work on word-of-mouth.

Those were the practical reasons. I could reel them off easily. None of them mattered worth a damn, though.

Here's why I chose accounting: UMass Boston had just opened up a new two-year associate's degree program that was taught on Apple][+ computers running a new kind of program called a "spreadsheet," dubbed "VisiCalc" that had just been released by two Boston-area hackers who'd actually demoed the program for the Newbury Street Irregulars a couple of weeks before. I'd been trying to convince Nick Cassidy III to shell out the ninety-five dollars for a copy of it for his Apple. For a guy who had a lot of money, he was monumentally disinterested in financial products (I'm sure his old man would have been more interested).

If I could spend the next four years just hacking away on an Apple][+ doing *anything*, I'd be a happy man. Spreadsheets, though, were fascinating, and I'd had so many ideas for how I could build on VisiCalc. Sitting opposite that wonderful older girl from Louisiana, I realized that if any of my courses had involved a computer, I'd have gotten an A+ and maybe been promoted to teacher's assistant. I would ace this accounting thing.

"Uh, Martin, you don't think accounting's a little, well, *boring*, do you? I mean, I don't want to discourage you, but if you're going to succeed at this, it's going to have to be something that really captivates your attention, you know? Obviously, after your last academic year, that's something you really should be considering. That's what I think, anyway." She looked worried, like she'd offended me.

"Thank you, Marion, I appreciate it. But to be honest, I don't think accounting is boring *at all*. In fact, I'm more excited about this than I have been about anything for months and months."

She smiled and unconsciously smoothed her feathered hair, smiled again. "That's grand, Martin, and I'm glad to hear it. I wish you all the best. You've got all the application paperwork, right? Be sure to call on us if you need any help with it, and feel free to come back if you change your mind or just to tell us how it's all going."

"I will, Marion." It was like I was emerging from a trance, the months I'd spent with my face in my computer, with the other Computer People at the Newbury Street Irregulars, all fading away like a dream. I hadn't thought about girls, romantically, I mean, for *months*, whereas before I'd discovered the Altair 8800, I had thought about almost nothing else.

I'd noticed that Marion was attractive as soon as we'd met, but it was just a fact, disconnected from any emotion, like I'd noticed that she was wearing a dun-colored turtleneck and brass bangles on her wrists. Now, though, I was remembering what it was like to think about women as possible romantic interests. How had I forgotten that? My cheeks were hot, and I knew I was blushing. I stammered a goodbye and went away, my mind swimming, the application paperwork for UMass Boston in my backpack.

The old man approved. Accounting was an honorable trade, tuition was half of what I'd been paying at MIT, and Art Hellman's roommate was graduating so I was going to take over his room at half the rent of the MIT dorms. What cinched it, though, was when I told him about the spreadsheets. My dad believed in computers, and he could tell that I was on to something, or at least that I was thoroughly hooked and would be committed to my coursework in a way that I hadn't been at MIT.

My acceptance came through before the term ended. By then, I wasn't even pretending to be enrolled at MIT anymore, except to use a computer lab where undergrads weren't technically welcome, but where no one asked any snoopy questions if you only used the terminals after midnight. I flipped to nocturnal without a moment's hesitation. They had a half dozen PDP-11s, and I was teaching myself assembler by creating my own version of Spacewar! that could support up to ten players and multiple planets with their own gravity challenges. They had unlimited printer paper and I brought home program listings for Art to mark up in red pen, not even minding his sarcastic notes in the margins.

I even started dating. I found that nocturnal existence lent itself to dating girls who were attending class. When they were in school, I was asleep. By the time they got home and did their homework, I was up and fresh and caffeinated and ready to go for dinner and a movie, or to a weird live theater show or a terrible gig with a local band. I was up for anything. It made me a pretty popular guy.

I even went out on a date with Marion from the counseling center. We ran into each other at a midnight pancake dinner (student events often felt like someone had generated them by rolling dice) and got to talking. It turned out that she was finishing a chem degree and I'd just attended a Newbury Street Irregulars session on food chemistry—two riveting hours on how to cook the perfect juicy burger, and what made it so perfect—and she was delighted to tell me all the ways that I'd misunderstood the speaker, and even more delighted that I was happy to be corrected.

It was my first experience with shutting up and listening to women who weren't afraid to show me they were smarter than me. I am embarrassed that it took me nearly eighteen years to try it, but in my defense, many of my contemporaries *never* tried it. Meanwhile, I benefited immensely from learning that lesson before my eighteenth birthday.

Marion took me to a party that some of her chem buddies were throwing, the kind of party where the party favors came dropped onto sugar cubes that you let dissolve on your tongue. It wasn't the last party like that I attended, but it *was* the first, and you never forget your first. Marion and I spent the evening giggling at each other and wandering around the student house that had been commandeered for the occasion and generally enjoying the hell out of ourselves. She gave me a chaste kiss the next morning as we watched the sun rise and thanked me for a lovely evening and asked me to write to her in Louisiana and tell her how accounting school was treating me. She'd graduated and was heading home for the summer before starting work in a refinery come September.

Accounting school was a homecoming.

From the way I fucked up my first year at MIT, you could be forgiven for thinking that I am a slapdash, chaotic sort of person. But you'd be wrong. I am the most plodding, methodical, careful fellow you could meet. It was just that computers offered me more opportunities to be precise and careful than any mere coursework. There's a reason I was happy to get work debugging other people's code.

Accountancy was pure catnip for me. I was born to practice the ancient and noble Venetian technology of double-entry bookkeeping, checking and cross-checking debits and credits and making all the numbers balance perfectly.

Accounting was fascinating enough, but the fact that we were doing it in VisiCalc spreadsheets made it all-consuming. Automating the tabulations made it possible to automate errors, to commit them with a scale and velocity that mere pen-and-paper accountancy could not have hoped to match. Tiny errors in formulas could cascade through sheets and workbooks, creating subtle, compounding errors that were nearly impossible to catch and even harder to root out.

I *loved* it.

It was all I wanted to talk about, in such loving detail that I even managed to bore Art, one of the human race's most patient and engaged listeners. It got so that I agreed to go help Nick Cassidy III with his homework again, something I'd halted during the summer of PDPs and girls, and not had any inclination to take up after I started classes again in the fall.

Nick Cassidy III was no more interested than Art was, but he'd let me run my mouth while I fixed his buggy code, something I could easily do while telling war stories about subtle calculation errors.

It was Nick Cassidy III who suggested that I give a workshop on spreadsheet debugging for the Newbury Street Irregulars. In retrospect, I think he was hoping that I'd find a kindred spirit who'd listen to my stories so he wouldn't have to. Whatever the motivation, it was a fantastic idea.

By that point, there were half a dozen Irregulars who'd bought Apples and copies of VisiCalc, and we set up a regular hackers' night, styling ourselves SIG-SS, the special interest group for spreadsheets. Thereafter, Wednesdays at the Irregulars' basement clubhouse were given over to spreadsheets, the core group of six expanding to ten or even twelve on a busy night, working in pairs to figure out ways to wring performance out of them.

It was an innocent and wonderful time, one of the most creative and exciting in my life. It was a moment that captured the excitement of my solo hacking in my dorm room during my first semester, but with a side of intense sociability that just *fizzed*, as ideas bounced from person to person, each of us adding something more to the pot until we had a stew of indescribable deliciousness.

It wasn't to last, of course.

Spreadsheets are a form of science fiction. All those novels we loved in the Irregulars' clubhouse, passed hand to hand until their bindings broke and their covers fell off, they all asked some variation on *what if* or *if this goes on* or *if only*—and that's exactly what a spreadsheet was for.

Spreadsheets could break down a complex system as neatly as any engineering process diagram, but unlike a diagram, a spreadsheet was *alive*. I could cram a whole chemical factory into a spreadsheet—all its machines and its workers and its raw inputs and its batch times and QA inspections. Then, I could *change* it. What if we find a process improvement that makes this machine 10 percent faster? What if we schedule a third shift—will the additional outputs pay for time-and-a-half for the night crew? What if they just do this part of the job, increasing the productivity of the day shift?

What if we save 2.63 percent in production by buying a machine that costs $47,342.87, and we have to take out a loan at 8.2 percent interest to pay for it—when does that machine pay for itself? Is there a different machine we could buy that would pay for itself faster? People have been solving those kinds of min-max problems for years, but pencil-and-paper finite mathematics is tedious—"fiddly," as my Veddy English algebra prof put it—whereas with the spreadsheet, it was instantaneous.

Being able to alter my assumptions and having them instantaneously ripple through to a conclusion in the future made me feel like a science fiction hero, like Asimov's Hari Seldon, or better yet, like a science fiction *writer,* like Heinlein constructing one of the future-history timelines that my father and I had puzzled and argued and delighted over for so many happy hours.

I loved building these models, these science fiction stories in formula form. Doing so scratched an itch I'd never known I'd had. It was an art form combining meticulousness, puzzle-solving, and imagination. It engaged my whole mind. It turned out that when my whole mind engaged with something, I was *good* at it.

My first inkling that I could do something with all this was thanks to Marion. She came back to Boston for a visit—I later learned that she was there to pick up a quart of liquid LSD to bring home to Baton Rouge, and she generously shared some of that with me—and we had dinner.

She made the mistake of asking me how I was liking accounting school and so I told her . . . and I told her . . . and I *told* her.

The waiter came and took her plate away and asked if she wanted dessert and that's when I noticed my cold hamburger and fries and realized how long I'd been talking.

"Shit, I'm sorry, Marion. I've been blabbing. Shit! I'm so sorry—it's just that I don't have anyone to talk to about this, not really, and I'm just *digging* it so much and—"

She snorted and put her hand on my arm. A summer in Louisiana had left her with a dark tan, and the time away from college kids had made her seem really grown-up, like a genuine adult, maybe a patient and kindly aunt. Who was also gorgeous. I was confused.

"Marty, it's okay, honestly. I'm interested. In fact—" She took a sip of her martini, another sign of sophistication in a town where putting salt in your beer was considered the mark of a true cosmopolitan. "In fact, I'm *very* interested."

Marion's oil-refinery job wasn't exactly glamorous, though it paid well. She was an assistant to a couple of junior chemists, really nothing more than a bottle washer, but they'd been charged with assessing a new sulfur-removal process that some of the other refineries had adopted. Her boss was convinced they'd fallen for a trendy gewgaw, but he was nagged by the worry that he was missing the boat.

"So I'm thinking, this is exactly the sort of problem you're solving with your models, correct?" She took a kitten-sized lick at the vanilla ice cream on her spoon, and I melted more than it did.

"Are you kidding? Yes, that's exactly right!"

And so I spent the next day in heaven—which is to say, in Nick Cassidy III's "study," with Marion at my elbow, as we built a dynamic process model on his Apple machine, while III peered in from time to time, befuddled by the whole affair but enchanted by Marion in a way that she studiously failed to take notice of.

It only took a day—in truth, I could have done it in less, if I'd understood the process she wanted me to model—and then I presented her with a floppy disk and fifty pages of printout showing different outcomes based on a range of assumptions. She offered to pay for the floppy disk, but I insisted.

Instead, she took me out for dinner and gave me another one of those warm and sisterly kisses on the cheek and slipped me a stoppered vial, whispering, "One *small* drop, no more, if you want to see God. No more, otherwise you might start thinking you *are* God. I've seen it and it's not pretty."

"Roger that," I said, pocketing the vial.

I walked home carefully, convinced I was going to crack the vial and also unable to stop thinking about Marion and most of all unable to stop thinking about the model we'd built together. I was just slipping the vial inside my thickest pair of sweatsocks when Art appeared at the door of my room.

"Man, you're finally home. The phone's been ringing off the hook for you."

"For *me*?" I got a cold feeling. The only people who ever called me at home were my parents, and if they'd been calling over and over, it could only mean that something really terrible had happened to one of them.

"Yeah. Your Richie Rich bougie shithead friend, Mr. Number Three."

"Nick Cassidy the Third?"

"Every fifteen minutes." On cue, the phone started to ring. Art shook his head, sending his red curls every which way. "It's for you."

I walked to the kitchen and picked up the phone. "Hello?"

"Jesus, you're finally home. What took you so long?"

"Nick—"

"Shut up, it's fine. I just have something I need to talk to you about."

"Uh, okay," I said. "I just got through the door though, and I was going to make a snack and grab a beer—" Yes, I'd just had dinner, but I was eighteen and I was perfectly capable of eating six meals a day. My metabolism was a furnace back then.

"Fine, do that. I'll be there in fifteen minutes."

"Here? I thought you wanted to talk on the phone—"

"This is too big for a phone call, Marty. Fifteen minutes." I'd gotten a ride home with him a couple of times in his metallic red Trans Am, and it had never taken less than twenty minutes. But he was ringing my bell in fifteen, and I swear I could see the car tires smoking on the curb when I went downstairs to answer the door. As we climbed the stairs up, he was trembling with excitement. I started to get worried that he was having a mental breakdown, or that he'd gotten into some rich-kid trouble by snorting too much coke and was about to suffer a complete break.

I sat him down on one of our ratty living room sofas and cracked him a beer. He drained half of it in one swallow and then said, "Marty, I've got a business proposition for you."

It turned out he'd been paying very close attention to me and Marion and our model-building, and he'd talked to his dad about it, and they were both convinced that there was a product there.

"Don't you get it?" Beer-spittle flecked off his lips and he sloshed more beer on our floor as he waved his arms around. "There are a million broke grad students within a couple of miles of this place. Every one of them knows how some kind of factory or plant or process works. You sit down with them for a day, build a model, and then we market it to business owners who own that kind of plant."

Art wandered in, wearing baggy gym shorts and a sloppy T-shirt advertising Talking Heads, a band he hadn't shut up about since he'd seen them play at the Orpheum the month before. He'd tied his hair into a ponytail, which only highlighted the patchiness of the tragic beard he'd been failing to grow for weeks.

Nick Cassidy III eyeballed him, then shrugged.

"Don't mind me," Art said, and sat next to me on the other sofa. We exchanged a look.

"Nick," I said, "I can see this is exciting for you, but how many chemical refineries or potato-chip factories are there? How many of them even have Apple machines that can run VisiCalc? How many copies of each model can you possibly sell? Even if you charge twenty bucks a pop for models—"

He laughed so hard beer came out of his nose. Nick wasn't much of a beer drinker. I got up and handed him a kitchen towel and relieved him of what was left of the beer. Once he'd finished gasping and snorting, he said, "Are you kidding? We're not going to sell this for twenty bucks a pop. More like five grand."

Art and I exchanged another look.

"Nick, VisiCalc is only ninety-five dollars," I said. "Who's going to pay us five grand for a floppy disk that spares them a day's worth of VisiCalc work?"

He began to pace. "Marty, no offense, but you aren't seeing it. You're not a businessman. Here's what we are going to do: we're going to sell these factories and plants a complete *system*. An Apple machine, a screen, two floppy drives, a copy of VisiCalc, a customized model, and a technician to show them how to use it. This isn't going to be something they try once on their kid's toy computer—it's going to be a key piece of serious business equipment, something they keep in its own *room,* for whenever they want to evaluate any business plan."

Nick Cassidy III was spoiled, sheltered, and obnoxious, but he wasn't necessarily wrong. Art and I exchanged another look. Then another.

Art said, "Where do you get these technicians? What happens when the factory setup changes and the model is out of date?"

Nick grinned. "Where do we get technicians? Friend, we've got a clubhouse full of them, down there on Newbury Street. You think there's a single Irregular who'd turn up his nose at a hundred dollars a day and a plane ticket to some exotic town where he'd get a chance to explain the ways of the modern world to old engineers, staying in the local Hilton and drinking on an expense account?

"And as for when the factory changes, man, that's just another chance to charge them *again,* send out another one of our trusty minions to spend a couple days adjusting the model, charge them a cool thousand dollars."

"What makes you think any of this stuff is worth all that money, though?" I asked. "I mean, they could hire someone themselves, buy their own Apple, get their own copy of Visi-Calc—"

"They could, but they *can't.* These guys have *no idea.* You know how I know? My old man. *He* has no idea, and he runs the biggest printing house in Kentucky, prints everything from grocery store circulars to the programs for the Derby. He's got four hundred employees, three plants the size of football fields, a fleet of trucks and the teamsters to drive them, and he has *no idea.* No idea. None. He can't tell you which press makes him the most money. His foreman draws up the shifts on paper every Friday afternoon. He buys new equipment when something breaks, or wears out, or when a fast-talking salesman convinces him he has to. He doesn't know what to buy, he doesn't know what to use. The only reason my old man isn't a pauper is that no one else knows anything, either.

"That was what got my dad so excited. Once I told him how this worked, what we could do for *him,* for *his* business, he started to think about what he could do for everyone else. He's the chairman of the Louisville Chamber of Commerce, and he reckons we could close our first fifteen sales just by showing up at one of their monthly meetings and doing a demo."

Fifteen times $5,000 was $75,000. Less the cost of the computers and software, a hundred bucks a day for one of the Irregulars to set it up—that was still more than $50,000. For five days' work, assuming I could build each model in a day. If we split that three ways, I'd be making $17,000 or so. That was more than Marion was making in a *year*.

Art was better at arithmetic than I was. I could see that he'd come up with the same numbers. We exchanged one more look.

We founded Process Engineering Models Ltd. that afternoon, in Art's and my beer-spattered living room, sending out for vegetarian pizzas in deference to Art's dietary preferences, moving the whole project to the Dewey Library so we could burrow into the reference stacks to figure out which industries were concentrated where, which processes they used, what their gross margins were, and how much capital they needed. I'd always thought of Nick Cassidy III as a half-wit but it turned out he was really good at this kind of work, especially with Art and me as his willing research associates, dashing to the card catalog and then to the shelves, going through indexes and bookmarking pages for him to look at and jot notes about on his yellow pad.

We were still at it when they closed the library, so we checked out an armload of heavy reference books using Art's library card and Nick Cassidy III drove us back to his house, where we converted his study into a war room, taping up sheets of yellow lined paper and using string to connect the sheets. Finally, I had the idea to fire up his Apple and create a VisiCalc spreadsheet to track it all, and we stayed up well past dawn, filling in that sheet, creating the whole business plan for Process Engineering Models Ltd. and using a ream of his virginal fanfold printer paper—paper that had never seen the inside of another printer, let alone a dumpster—to create five copies of the plan, which we hole-punched and clipped into colored Duo-Tang folders from Nick Cassidy III's generously stocked supply cupboard.

Those folders went off to Nick Cassidy III's father by special messenger, and he circulated them to a few trusted friends. A week later, we had a $20,000 check, articles of incorporation, and a board of directors, none of whom I'd ever met. Art, Nick, and I each got a 20 percent stake, while our investors took 40 percent, which everyone assured me was normal and fair.

I wasn't all that worried about it—I had other things on my mind, like keeping up on my schoolwork while building our first five models, while Art flew to Louisville to explain how this stuff all worked to our commissioned salesman, a fellow named Paul Stockton, "who could sell ice cream to Eskimos" according to Nick Cassidy II (III's father). Stockton was apparently much prized across the South for his ability to sell heavy machinery of all kinds, and his client roster was—according to Cassidy II—going to land us a string of sales that would keep us busy for months to come.

He wasn't wrong. Stockton closed two sales in the first week, and I flew down with Art on a Thursday night, with the plan of working through the weekend, flying back on Sunday, and being in class by Monday.

I hated it. I was terrible at it.

My client was a cement factory where all the foremen were white and all the workers were Black. It took me less than an hour to figure out that none of the foremen had any idea what their workers did, and that the real brains behind the operation were the Black guys out on the floor, none of whom I was permitted to talk to.

I spent the day gamely taking notes on one of Nick Cassidy III's yellow pads, clipped to one of his clipboards (clips and

Nick Cassidy III's things were a theme—I was also wearing one of his clip-on ties, at his insistence). I figured out that if I played stupid enough, the pig-eyed ruddy foreman I was interrogating would heave a great sigh and walk me out onto the floor to show me a machine or process, while narrating its significance in a blustering voice. By listening to the foremen and carefully watching for when the eavesdropping workers scowled or rolled their eyes, I was able to determine which parts of the system the foremen were absolutely clueless on.

Art and I were staying at the Cassidys', in a house that could only be called a mansion. I was staying in the guest room while Art had Nick Cassidy III's mother's sewing room, one of several bedrooms that had been given over to specialized tasks—study, gun room, hobby room, games room. Nick Cassidy III told me that it had been built by Nick Cassidy I, who had taken the money from the sale of the family plantation and built the house to raise his seven children in. The kitchen china, gilt mirrors, and formal dining room set had all come from the "family place."

We ate with the family that night at the formal table, served by the cook—Ruby—and the maid—Leora—both of whom were Black. It was a hushed meal, complete with an opening prayer, which Art giggled at, drawing a glare from Nick III. Try as I might, I couldn't figure out how to bring up the situation at the cement factory, especially not with Ruby and Leora around. Maybe born Kentuckians are able to talk about race relations in the presence of Black people who are serving them, but just the thought made my mouth run dry and swelled my tongue to unsuitable girth.

But when the endless dinner was finally behind us and we were invited onto the porch for brandy, I took my shot.

"I don't think this is going to work," I said. "Today was a goddamned disaster." Cassidy II glared at me and Cassidy III elbowed me, and I rewound what I'd said and found the blasphemy. Jesus, was I going to have to avoid *blasphemy*? "Sorry," I muttered.

Art rescued me. "What went wrong?"

I told them. "None of these guys have the slightest idea. It's not like with Marion. She was deep into the processes—they'd turned her loose to actually run most of those machines when she was starting out. I get the feeling most of these guys got their jobs because they're someone's nephew or college buddy. If I have to rely on them, I'm not going to get *anything* useful."

Cassidy II took a moment to light a small cigar, ponder the twilight across his rolling lawn, and blow a stream of smoke into the night.

"Son," he said, and with only a single word managed to convey that he and I would never, ever see eye to eye about anything. "You are not going to make any progress so long as you go in there disrespecting those men. They are your customers, you understand? You aren't in a position to tell them what to do. They pay the piper, they call the shots. I know you Boston boys want to make everything about race, but it just ain't so."

I opened my mouth to tell him I was from Alabama (most recently, anyway), but Cassidy III made a small, urgent hand gesture where the father couldn't see it and I shut up.

Cassidy II was just warming to his subject anyway. "I have a prediction for you, young man. If you go back in there tomorrow with respect, with *humility,* with the recognition that you're just a teenager and these men have been working on that floor for longer than you've been alive, and you open your ears and shut your damn mouth, you will learn something, and not just something about how that big old factory works. You might learn something about being a man."

My years in Alabama taught me that when an old, powerful man gives you a lecture like this, you say "Yes sir, thank you sir," and shut your mouth. It took everything I had to say the words, and I almost didn't manage it, but I reminded myself that I was planning to spend the night in this man's house and I was depending on his money to fly back to Boston on Saturday night.

The next morning, as Cassidy III drove me back to the factory, he tensely explained that Cassidy II was a major investor in the factory and that three of the foremen were cousins of his.

That about set the tone for the next two years of my life. I spent them ping-ponging between Boston and cities down the Eastern Seaboard, as Stockton's silver tongue closed deal after deal. It felt like I spent eight hours a day fixing models that had gone wrong because our client didn't understand their own systems; eight hours a day writing new models for clients who refused to admit they didn't understand their own systems; and eight hours a day doing coursework for my accounting degree.

With the remaining eight hours, I slept.

If the only issue had been Cassidy II, we might have made it work. He was all the way in Louisville, 950 miles from Cambridge.

The real problem was Cassidy III: instead of managing his old man's anxiety and keeping him off our backs, he tried to manage *us* to get his dad off his *own* back. Within the first three months, word got around to all of the Irregulars that it was absolutely not worth $100 to go be a "field sales engineer" for our company, and even putting the rate up to $150 didn't bring back our workforce, so it was Art and I who flew around and around the country, getting to know the check-in clerks at Logan on a first-name basis.

We had fights. Oh, did we have fights. The initial $20,000 disappeared in an eyeblink, spent on God knows what. I was half an accountant but I never did get a look at the books. Cassidy III muttered about how much Stockton's commission ate up, how much all those airfares and hotels were costing him—him, not us, him. He told us we ate like hogs on the road. We sometimes got salaries, but it was never clear how much we were supposed to get.

Two years later, I graduated and barely noticed. I was broke, exhausted, and I couldn't even attend my own graduation party because we had six customers demanding cleanup work.

At two in the morning on the night I graduated, I looked up from my Apple machine. We'd gotten a reseller license from Apple, and our apartment had become a warehouse for Apple systems, stacked to the roof in our living room and bedrooms, and we had plenty of systems to work on whenever we needed them.

I was in the living room, using a door balanced on two un-opened Apple boxes as a sawhorse desk. Art was on the other side of the desk, our knees threaded between one another's in the narrow space. His hair was lank and greasy and his skin was gray in the light of his monitor, his freckles washed out to pale brown, a scattering of angry red acne across his forehead and cheeks. The red of his zits matched the red of his eyes.

He looked up from his machine, too.

"Are we going to keep doing this?" he asked.

"No, of course not," I said. "Why the fuck would we keep doing this? This is bullshit. It's going to kill us. Fuck that."

When you wake up from a nightmare, there's a minute where you're still terrified and miserable, still living in that reality. Then, something delicious happens: you realize that none of it was real. You don't have to solve the impossible problems of your nightmare. Those problems don't matter. They're not your problems. You can just forget about them. The burden is lifted. The way is cleared.

I laughed.

A snort at first, then a giggle, then a guffaw, and Art joined me and we just kept on laughing until Art staggered into the kitchen and grabbed us a couple of beers. He came back and placed one finger dramatically on his Apple's power switch. Just a tiny bit of pressure and it would snap off, and all the work he'd done since he'd last saved would disappear.

I took a beer in one hand and a church key in the other and we locked eyes. I opened the beer and he snapped the computer off. Then he stretched across the desk to rest his finger on *my* machine's power switch. I was terrible about saving my work—something about saving while the code wasn't working felt *wrong*. It was stupid, but it was just one of those programmer superstitions I couldn't shake. I tried to remember when I'd last saved. Hours before. The panic I felt at the thought of his finger flipping that switch was both real and distant, like someone in another room was telling me about a feeling I was having in my own body. Much closer by was my excitement at what it would mean.

Click.

The TV screen I used for a monitor flipped from glowing green characters to static. I popped the top off my beer. We clinked them.

Cassidy III wasn't angry at first. He was disbelieving. Literally, he just didn't believe we were quitting. Art and I had stayed up until 4 a.m., laughing about the absurdity of the years we'd given to this foolish endeavor, and then we went to bed. I had the foresight to take the phone off the hook.

He started hammering the buzzer shortly after ten. I got up and pissed and ground my fists into my tired eyes and shuffled to the intercom, the buzzer blatting the whole time.

"Yeah."

"Marty? Let me in." It was his usual impatient, imperious tone, the *I'm the boss and I know things you'll never understand* voice. Normally it put me on edge. That morning, I was bemused by it. I buzzed him in and put a pot of coffee on.

He knocked a couple of minutes later.

"It's open."

I heard him let himself in, heard him make a disgusted grunt at the mess in the living room. It *was* disgusting, but only because he'd been working us so hard we didn't have any time to pay attention to hygiene.

He let himself into the kitchen as I was rooting in the fridge for some milk. I sniffed it. It had turned. I couldn't remember the last time I'd gone to the corner store for groceries.

"Hello, Nick."

"Is your phone broken? I've been calling all morning."

I poured a cup, black, and pointed at the phone on the wall, receiver dangling from its curly wire. "Needed to sleep," I said. "Coffee?"

He scowled. He was a handsome kind of blond person, the sort of guy someone could call a "chap" without failing the giggle test, dressed in preppie loafers and a golf shirt, his hair wavy and carefully arranged. He was good at scowling. It came naturally to him.

"How much of the DePaul Plastics model did you get done? Can I courier a floppy disk to them tomorrow? Stockton's worried they're going to ask for a refund if we can't service them."

I sipped my coffee. I felt as light as a cloud. "I'm not doing that," I said.

He cocked his head. "When *are* you doing it?"

"I'm not doing it," I repeated.

"You can't just take the day off without discussing it with me, Marty. We have commitments to customers and—"

"I'm not doing it ever, because I don't work for Process Engineering Models Limited anymore. I quit."

"Be serious." He had a new scowl, one I hadn't seen before, like maybe he was smelling something really terrible.

"I'm serious. Coffee?"

"Fine," he said, twisting his face out of its sneer with an obvious effort of will. "Take a day off if you need it. But we've got deadlines, Marty. I did my job, now it's time to do yours."

"I don't have a job anymore," I said, rinsing a mug under the tap, shaking the water off and filling it with coffee and holding it out to him. "I quit."

He didn't touch it. "Stop *saying* that!"

Art shuffled into the kitchen, clad in sagging underwear, his Talking Heads shirt, and a huge, irregular halo of tangled red curls. "You guys are loud, you know that?" He took the coffee I was holding out for Nick Cassidy III. "What's all the shouting for?"

"We've got *deadlines*," Cassidy III cried, in tones of pure anguish.

Art sipped his coffee, then set the cup down on the counter. "No," he said, very carefully. "*You've* got deadlines. *We* quit. Let us know when you're going to pick all this stuff up." He gestured at the stacked Apple boxes visible through the door that connected the kitchen to the living room.

"What the hell are you guys talking about?" he said. "Come on, what is this bullshit?"

"It's not bullshit," I said. "I mean, it *is* bullshit, but the bullshit part is this—" I gestured at all the computers. "It's the long hours and the stupid customers and the fact that it's all, you know, stupid. I don't want to do this for the rest of my life. I don't even want to do this for the rest of the week. I'm twenty years old and I'm not going to spend the rest of my life making spreadsheets for cement factories."

Art slurped his coffee loudly. "What he said," he said, and shuffled back out of the kitchen. "Bye, Nick." A moment later his bedroom door closed.

Cassidy III looked like he wanted to cry. He whispered something to himself, too quiet for me to hear. Then again, and this time I read his lips: *He's gonna kill me*. Yeah, Cassidy II was no fun at all and he was gonna take this hard.

"Why didn't you talk to me if you were so unhappy, Marty? We're friends!"

Even at the age of twenty, I had the sense not to rise to this bait. We'd never been friends, and it had been at least a year since we were even *friendly*. "Sorry this didn't work out, Nick. Let me know if you need some help getting this stuff out or what. I'll pack up the systems we were using so they're all ready to go today."

He looked hunted now, eyes darting back and forth like he didn't know where the next blow was going to come from. I actually felt kinda sorry for the guy. Not sorry enough to ever work for him again, but sorry.

He didn't say another word, just left the apartment and pulled the door shut behind him. My coffee was lukewarm. I took another sip and then poured it out in the sink. I decided I wanted to have a decent cup of coffee and a big diner breakfast to go with it. What the hell, I was celebrating. Art and I showered and dressed and went to Henry's, a student place that we'd gone to all the time back in the Newbury Street Irregulars days, and then afterward he told me he had a big baggie of magic mushrooms he'd been saving for a special occasion and that took care of the rest of the day.

Movers rang the doorbell the next morning at 7:30 a.m., and I struggled to focus on what they were trying to convey to me but eventually figured out that they'd come on behalf of Nick Cassidy III and Process Engineering Models Ltd., and I showed them what to take and they lugged it down the stairs. The place seemed huge without all that junk in it but I was barely able to keep my eyes open and almost collapsed on the sofa but managed to get back into bed.

It felt like I'd barely closed my eyes before the buzzer rang again. I stayed in bed. Let Art answer it. The buzzer rang again, and then again. I looked at my alarm clock. It was 8:30 a.m. I'd had three hours' sleep—not counting the interruption for the movers. Call it two and a quarter. I put a pillow over my head. The buzzer rang again. And again. Art could sleep through anything.

Bzzzt.

Bzzzt.

Ten minutes went by, according to the alarm clock. My eyelids started to droop.

Then: *Bzzzt.* Bzzzzzzzzzzzzzzzzzzzzzzzzzzzzzzt.

I dragged myself to the intercom and thumbed the talk button.

"Fuck," I suggested.

"Courier."

"Fuck," I asked.

"Courier, sir. I'm sorry, I'm not allowed to leave until—"

"Sixth floor," I said, and unlocked the door.

It takes a long time to climb six flights of stairs, but not so long that it was worth getting back into bed. I stretched out on the sofa and put a pillow over my face. After a short eternity, someone knocked on the door.

I moved the pillow so my mouth was uncovered. "It's open."

The door creaked open. "Sir?"

"What?"

"Courier, sir."

"Fine," I said.

"Courier. I need a signature." I moved the pillow off my face, struggled to focus on the kid who was standing in my living room, radiating the cold of a Boston autumn off his parka and boots. I held my hand out and squinted at him.

He was young, but surprisingly nonchalant about the fact that I was just wearing boxer shorts and a pillow. He extracted a clipboard from a shoulder bag and then a pen, and put the former under my hand and the latter in my hand. I scrawled some lines. He gently placed a cold envelope down on my chest and let himself out of the apartment. I was asleep again in an instant.

I woke to Art Hellman in a pure redheaded fury, stalking back and forth in the newly emptied living room, cursing under his breath and running a carpet sweeper over the grimy, newly exposed parts of the landlord's threadbare green broadloom.

The blinds were up, revealing a gray winter sky that could have been noontime or three in the afternoon or 6 p.m. I sat up and he dropped the carpet sweeper and picked up the sofa cushions I'd vacated and viciously beat the dust out of them, creating clouds that glowed in the weak light.

Once he'd replaced the cushions, he gestured impatiently for me to move so he could attack the ones I was sitting on, and I took that as my cue to go for a piss and run a washcloth over my face. The bathroom was sparkling. The mirror was sparkling, cleaned of its layers of spattered toothpaste spit, and the rim of the toilet was white for the first time in my memory—it had been nearly brown with dried piss when I'd moved in and no one had cleaned it in the years since.

I crept into my room, half expecting to find it spotless, but it was the same comforting nest of scattered laundry and take-out containers. I got into a pair of shorts and a half-clean Escambia County High School gym shirt and cautiously braved the living room again.

Art had shaved and pulled his hair back into a ponytail and he was wearing a pair of clean jeans and a polo shirt that I'd never seen before, which must have been dredged from the bottom of some drawer. An overflowing laundry hamper sat by the door, waiting to go to the laundromat.

I stared at him until he stopped muttering and wiping at the window with a dishcloth and acknowledged me.

"Art, everything okay?"

He squinched his eyes shut and made fists, then took a deep breath and relaxed it and said, "That courier envelope I found on your chest? It was addressed to both of us, so I opened it. It's on the kitchen table."

He'd made a fresh pot of coffee, so I got myself a cup and picked up the papers and tried to make sense of them. They were written in highly obfuscated legal gibberish, and as I puzzled over them, he came and read over my shoulder, literally breathing down my neck. I gave up and handed him the papers.

"Why don't you translate? It'll be faster for both of us and I get the feeling you aren't in the mood to wait around."

He took the papers and glared at them. "It's from a law firm in Newton," he said. "Apparently it's Process Engineering Models' law firm, though I never heard of them, but that's the least bullshit part of the letter."

He stabbed at a paragraph. "This one says we never vested our shares, because we didn't stay for the full thirty-six months, so we own exactly zero percent of the company."

"Fucking outrageous," I said, "but Art, it's just symbolic. Process Engineering Models doesn't have a business. It's dead and it just doesn't know it yet. There's no way they'll be able to turn a profit. One hundred percent of nothing is nothing. Who cares?"

"If that was all, I'd agree with you," he said, rattling the papers and stabbing the next paragraph. "But then there's this: they're treating all the plane tickets and hotel stays and meals on the road as taxable benefits and reporting them to the IRS."

That I understood. Two years of accountancy school had included four semesters on U.S. tax law and tax preparation. "We're going to have to pay *tax* on the plane tickets?"

"And the meals, and the taxis, and the hotels. All of it."

I shook my head. It was unbelievably petty. "Well, the good

news is that we made so little money this year that our tax bracket is going to be next to nothing—maybe 17 percent? I can get my textbooks and verify it, but—"

He silenced me by rattling the papers again, shuffling through them and pointing at the final paragraph. "Did you notice that we signed noncompete clauses with all the paperwork? No? Me neither. But apparently we did, and these motherfuckers say that this means we can't do anything related to computers in Massachusetts for the next *three years*."

I opened and shut my mouth. Then I did it again. A day before, I'd been ecstatic at the thought of leaving Process Engineering Models, but I'd never doubted that I'd end up doing something else, with a better company—Lotus was hiring.

"It's bullshit," I said. "That can't be legal."

He laughed darkly. "Welcome to the Bay State, pal. This is one of the most noncompete-friendly states in the union. We're fucked, brother. Nick Cassidy III owns our asses for the next three years. If we make a single nickel working on computers, his old man will pay these Newton lawyer motherfuckers to ruin us. Bury us. *Bury us*." He threw the papers down in disgust and started taking dishes out of the cupboard and stacking them on the counter, then he got up on a kitchen chair and attacked the shelf paper with our last clean kitchen towel.

I drank my coffee and stared at the papers. I was an accountant. I could go to work for a CPA for a couple-three years, continue to play with computers as a hobby, maybe go to night school to upgrade that associate's degree to a bachelor's. It would pay reasonably well and I could do the job in my sleep. It would leave more time for RPGs, the Newbury Street Irregulars, maybe even dating again. The last time I'd been out to dinner with a girl was, what?

Two years before.

Jesus.

"What a prick," I said.

"I want to murder that motherfucker," Art said. "Kill him. Shoot him or run him over or—"

"Forget it," I said. "They'd give you a lot longer than three years."

"Maybe I'll egg his house."

"That's a far more reasonable plan," I said. "Add TP for a winning combination."

He smiled a little. "Fuck that guy so much."

"Amen."

We were saved by *Creative Computing.* Even before long work hours kept us away from the Newbury Street Irregulars' clubhouse, we'd bought a subscription for the apartment. The Irregulars' copy was the subject of fierce contention, and anyone who paused to savor an article was likely to be accused of "hoarding" an issue. The Irregulars' archive of back issues was in very sorry shape, covers taped on and pages curled and torn from so much handling. Buying a separate sub for the apartment was the smartest thing we ever did. *CC* was just *great,* a magazine whose contributors could somehow channel our wildest fantasies and favorite musings about computers and turn them into fascinating articles, guides, and interviews.

CC was proof that we were part of something bigger than what was going on in the Irregulars' clubhouse, and that computers were destined to be far more exciting than anything Nick Cassidy II and III could ever dream up.

So naturally it saved us. It arrived in that day's mail, slightly damp from the slushy outdoors. I picked it up from the mailbox in the lobby and made a beeline for my bedroom so I wouldn't have to share. Immature, I know, but a couple of hours alone with *CC* was a pleasure to savor.

But I was only twenty minutes into it before I rushed into the living room.

"Art, listen to this."

He looked up from his book—*The Green Ripper* by John D. MacDonald, which we'd both been waiting for all year and wanted to read badly enough that we got it in hardcover when it came in at the Coop—and said, "Is that the new *CC*? When did that get here? Did you sneak it into your bedroom?"

"Yes, just like *you* snuck it into your bedroom last month. Shut up and listen, okay?"

He used the dust-jacket flap to mark his page and put the novel down. "I'm listening."

"Though many U.S. states' laws allow for these clauses, one state's constitution actually forbids them: California." I did a little jig.

"What are you talking about?" He was tired and irritable, at the tail end of a shitty day, and I could barely control my excitement enough to explain it.

"It's a history of Fairchild Semiconductor," I said.

"O-kay," he said.

"Remember when they got bought out by Schlumberger last year and everyone made a big deal out of it, like this pioneering American company that invented microchips was now going to be owned by Germans?"

"Sort of," he said. "I didn't really pay attention. It was more of a business story than a computer story, you know?"

"I know," I said. "But it turns out it's really interesting. It turns out that Fairchild *wasn't* the first microchip company in Silicon Valley. That was another company called Shockley, and they never managed to make a working microchip, which is why no one's ever heard of them."

"No offense, Marty, but I wouldn't call that 'really interesting.'"

"That's not the interesting part, asshole," I said. I sat down next to him on the sofa and held the issue of *CC* where he could see it. He made a grab for it, but I didn't let go. "The interesting part is *why* Shockley never made a working chip. The guy who started the company was a complete psycho. That was Shockley, William Shockley, the guy who won the Nobel Prize for the silicon transistor. He's why it's not called Gallium Arsenide Valley."

"Ar ar nerd humor," Art said. "So he won a Nobel but he was bugfuck, huh?"

"Seriously bugfuck. He was obsessed with eugenics and used his Nobel Prize money to offer cash to Black women who'd get their tubes tied."

"Ugh."

"Double ugh. And it wasn't just that he was a racist creep. He was also on the road half the time, promoting this Nazi garbage. And he was seriously squirrelly, paranoid to the max, with wiretaps on all his employees, even his family members. So no one could get any work done, and they never made a microchip."

"Which is why I've never heard of them."

"No, you haven't. But you *have* heard of Fairchild Semiconductor, I take it?"

"I think we established that already. Great American company, now a mere division of Schlumberger, a company that is not only German—and who won the goddamned war, anyway?—but also has a name out of a Don Martin *Mad* magazine gag."

"That's Fonebone," I said. I had over two hundred *Mad* magazines stashed in my closet in Escambia. "Here's the thing. Shockley's eight top engineers quit on him to found Fairchild. They called them 'the Traitorous Eight.'"

"This *Mad* magazine gag just became a spaghetti western."

"Shut up, okay? So the question is, how did the Traitorous Eight manage to leave behind the company founded by a Nobel Prize–winning Nazi and start Fairchild? And while we're at it, how did Fairchild employee Gordon Moore and all their top Hungarian engineers quit Fairchild to found Intel?"

He tried to take the magazine from me.

"Ah-ah! No peeking," I said. "Besides, I'm not done with this ish. You'll get it when I'm through. Back to the question. How was it that these guys were able to quit and start these other companies without getting sued into oblivion by their vengeful, wealthy, powerful, unhinged Nazi ex-boss?"

He got his concentrating face on, the one that he got when he was hacking on some genuinely gnarly program. It was a face like a bulldog chewing a wasp and it never failed to bring a smile to my face.

Eventually, I couldn't help giggling. "Enough, pal, you're going to break something, I'll tell you. *The Constitution of the State of California bans noncompete agreements.* They can't be enforced there."

"Seriously?"

"Seriously. You quit on Shockley, you can set up shop next door to him the next day and compete head-to-head and he can't do a thing but gnash his teeth and stamp his tall leather boots and polish his monocle."

"It's funny because he's a Nazi."

"Come on, Art. This is amazing. It's the answer. All we need to do is get jobs in Silicon Valley and pick up and move out there and there's not a goddamned thing that Nick Cassidy III can do about it."

"Except gnash his teeth and stamp his tall leather boots—"

"And polish his monocle. Yeah! You get it? California! Land of my birth! Palm trees! The Pacific Ocean. No winters, ever!"

"Swimmin' pools, movie stars."

"That's Los Angeles. Nothing there but fake cowboys and failed starlets. No, I'm talking about San Francisco. Open up those golden gates! Fleet Week! Alcatraz!"

"I thought you were from Alabama. Did you just say you're from California?"

"Born and raised. San Diego. The old man dragged us to Alabama in junior high."

"And you're seriously thinking of going back?"

I gestured at the slushy gray night outside the window. "Are you kidding? Why wouldn't we? All I want to do with the rest of my life is screw around with computers. What better place to do it? I'll be thousands of miles from Nick Cassidy III, I'll never get a boot full of slush again, and I'll be able to get Mexican food whenever I want."

"How's the pizza?"

"Terrible. But the burritos are amazing."

"You're saying I'd have to give up pizza?"

"No, just *good* pizza. Trust me, there's more important things in life. They're starting new businesses out there like crazy and every one of those little companies will need an accountant."

"So what, get on a Greyhound, get off, and start ringing doorbells until you get a job?"

I shrugged. "More or less. Why not? We're young, we understand computers, and we've got nothing better to do. Alternatively, we could stay here and *not* work with computers for three years. Or maybe we could ask Nick Cassidy III for our jobs back."

"Jesus, no. Okay, this is actually exciting and now I'm hungry. I think I was so angry at Cassidy III that I forgot to eat. Let's eat."

"Nothing in the kitchen."

"Forget that, let's go out. I'm buying."

"Sold. Chinese?"

"Fuck no. Pizza. Last chance!"

He got a job first. One of the Irregulars had gone out to Santa Clara to work for a company making backup tape drives and they were hiring anyone who could hack anything, hoping to ship a working product before they ran out of their investors' money.

"You're starting when?"

"Day after tomorrow," he said, continuing to shove clothes in his suitcase. "Anything you don't want, just have the Free Store people come by and pick up."

"What the hell are you talking about?"

"I'm flying out today. I'm going to stay with Grant until I can get a place of my own. They're paying me a hiring bonus and they bought me a plane ticket. They're in a hurry."

"What about the apartment?"

"First and last is paid. Take a week or whatever to pack it up and then drive the Chevy out with anything you want to take with. Landlord can keep the deposit. See if any of the Irregulars want to take over the place, or just stay here for the last month."

"Art, what the fuck are you talking about?"

He stopped packing and gave me a you're-being-deliberately-obtuse look. "Marty, I'm flying to San Francisco to take a new job. You don't have a job there yet so you're going to bring my van across the country and use my hiring bonus to pay for gas and hotels and meals on the way."

"I am?"

"Of course you are. That'll give me a couple of weeks to scout a decent place for us and maybe find you some work, and then we'll have wheels when you get there."

I snorted. "Why don't you just sell the van and I'll fly to California like a normal person?"

He slammed his suitcase lid down and stared at me in disbelief. "Marty, are you *kidding* me? I'll give you three reasons. First, that's not just any van, that's a 1969 Chevy 108 with the three-speed TH-350 Turbo-Hydramatic automatic transmission and roof-mounted, body-integrated air-conditioning. It is a palace on wheels.

"Second of all, you are heading for gold rush country. The only difference between the slave-driving bullshit that Cassidy III put us through and the work we're going to be doing out there is that Cassidy III was an idiot and nothing we did for him was worth shit, while the work we're going to do out in California is going to turn the fuckin' world on its head. You are going to be chained to a computer for the next five or ten years, maybe even twenty years, and this is your chance to see the whole god-damned country, the U.S. of A. in all its roadside glory, before you disappear into technology's salt mines for the remainder of this dying millennium.

"Third and finally, you aren't going to fly to California like a normal person because *you are not a normal person.* Normal people are well-rounded. You are thoroughly spiky. You are a hundred miles deep and a single nanometer wide. You are a freak. I know because *I* am a freak. If you were a normal per-son, I wouldn't be trusting you with my beloved and cherished 1969 Chevy 108 with three-speed TH-350 Turbo-Hydramatic automatic transmission and roof-mounted, body-integrated air-conditioning."

He stared at me, his eyes bulging with intensity. I held back my laughter for as long as I could but then I lost it and before long we were both holding our guts and laughing and slamming our hands on the drywall and the dusty carpet.

"Are we doing this? For real?" I asked.

"Brother," Art said. "*I'm* doing it. It was your idea, so I as-sume you're doing it, too. You don't have to. You can get another roommate, get some accounting work—whatever you think is best for you." He clapped me on the shoulder and stared intently at me. I remembered how short he was then: he had such a big presence that I often forgot that I had a full head on him. "But I hope you do, Marty. You're a hell of a friend and we're a hell of a team. This is a moment, you feel it? Something big is about to happen. Hell, it's already happening. I'm going to go where it's happening and be a part of it."

"New York, New York?"

He smiled. "No, Marty. Nothing wrong with New York. But I'm going to San Francisco."

"Do you seriously think the Chevy will make it?"

He blew a raspberry. "You kidding me? The 108? That thing is a beast. It's unstoppable. A monster. You're going to have the drive of your life. Just make sure if you pick up any serial killer hitchhikers that they don't get blood on the upholstery."

He was right, it was the drive of my life. I picked up hitchhikers (none of them were serial killers, most of them were very nice, and only a couple were weird and broken, but it was clear that they needed protection from the world rather than the other way around). I ate some terrible food and some transcendent food, including a roadside Mexican meal in Oklahoma at a place that was just closing when I arrived, so I ate with the owner/chef and his family, who put me up for the night and showed me how to cook huevos rancheros the next morning.

The Chevy broke down in Nebraska (thankfully I was close to Omaha and a garage that could service a three-speed TH-350 Turbo-Hydramatic automatic transmission) and then again on a mountain road in Colorado where I was stranded overnight before someone went for a tow and then I dry-docked in a ski resort while they fixed the radiator; and then again in Nevada, just outside of Reno. I got a cheap hotel room in a casino, saw Earth, Wind & Fire play a passable set, discovered that I was better at poker than anyone else at the table that night, got to sample seven different Scotches of varying vintages at the pit boss's expense (and promptly lost my poker winnings), and then I was back on the road the next morning, with a new fan belt purring in the motor.

My last night on the road, I stopped at a motel outside Sacramento and walked to a bar down the road and asked if they had any of the Scotches I'd developed a taste for in Reno (I'd made a list in a spiral-bound notebook I'd used to keep track of expenses on the trip). They didn't, but the bartender introduced me to good bourbon—Four Roses, better than the Jim Beam my old man drank—and I watched a ballgame and sipped it and felt a great and expansive feeling.

I had driven across the whole nation, from a frozen city: a place of ice and snow, a place where the law let Nick Cassidy III freeze me out of the thing I loved best in the world. I had met hitchhikers and solved technical problems and found a place to rest every night and places to eat during the day. I'd done it on my own, without my parents' guidance, without a friend or copilot.

I was one sleep away from pulling into the Bay Area, a place I had never been, where I was going to start a new life doing something that absolutely consumed me and took me to places where I felt things I'd never felt before.

I sipped my bourbon.

"Well, you look like a happy son of a bitch," came a voice from my elbow. She was in her thirties, lots of smile lines, big glasses, a messy pile of hair under a kerchief. She reminded me of my great aunts, when I was a kid—these mysterious, competent, benign women who had lots of things to do but also always seemed to have an eye on me. She was wearing a faded Beatles tee and a pair of jeans with bell-bottoms that had been fashionable six or seven years before.

"I guess I am," I said. As I said the words, I felt the smile on my face. It was a big one, all right.

She took a pull off her beer, a Bud with half the label picked away. "Now, I just have to know what you're smiling about. Normally I wouldn't ask, but normally I don't get to see anyone with a smile like that—you looked like a baby who just found his toes for the first time."

I laughed aloud and choked on the bourbon. She thumped me between the shoulders and finished her beer while I coughed it out, signaling the bartender for another. I managed to raise my empty glass and point at it while I caught my breath.

"Sorry to make you squirt bourbon out your nose," she said, when the new round was in front of us.

"Not at all. Thank you for the thump," I said.

"So tell me, young man, what has you so cheerful? I'm not gonna lie, I could use some cheerful news."

So I told her. It came out in a bit of a jumble, but not a total mess, because I'd told parts of it to various hitchers I'd given rides to on the trip, polishing up the tale.

She was a good listener. I know, everyone says that about other people, but she really was. In the days that followed, I had a lot of chances to mull over the way she listened, and what I've decided is that she listened like she was glad I was talking. Grateful, even, making these little noises and nods that made it clear she was following and enjoying it. Being listened to like that felt *wonderful*. It was a new experience for me. I'd never felt *valued* like that. It made me want to keep talking.

More than that, it made me want to be a good listener, too. To be grateful for the things people told me and to let them know it and make them feel special and valued the way I felt then. I decided to cultivate that, not fake it, but mean it.

As it turned out, that decision was even more consequential for my life than the snap decision to leave Boston and move to California.

So I told her more than I'd intended to, backtracking to my boyhood in San Diego, our move to Escambia for the oil rush, my loneliness in Alabama and my excitement in MIT, then on to how I got captured by computers, totally devoured by them, meeting Art in a dumpster at 2 a.m. while looking for printer paper for my Altair 8800, discovering my fellow obsessive tech freaks at the Newbury Street Irregulars, falling so far down the computing rabbit hole that I flunked out of MIT.

About my old man, and how angry he was at me when he realized I was failing, and then how kind and even gentle he became when he realized I had failed, when he realized that kicking my ass wouldn't get me back on track because there was no track to get back on.

I told her about meeting Marion at the school career-counseling office, and how she helped me find a two-year associate's degree program in accounting that was built around VisiCalc and its revolutionary spreadsheets, and how I'd figured that I could go to school for two years, learn a trade I could get work in everywhere, and do it while spending every hour God sent in front of a computer.

I told her about my asshole "friend" Nick Cassidy III, who'd convinced me and Art that we'd get rich by starting a company called Process Engineering Models Ltd. that his father would invest in. How I spent the next two years juggling accounting classes and flying back and forth to the southland to try to build optimization models for white factory bosses who had no idea how their factories actually worked and wouldn't let me talk to the Black workers who *did* know.

I told her about the night that Art and I had looked at each other across the door-balanced-on-boxes we were using as a desk and realized that neither of us wanted to work for Nick Cassidy III and *especially* not Nick Cassidy II, and how we'd turned off our computers without saving our work and eaten a bag of mushrooms to make it official.

I told her about how Nick Cassidy III had disbelieved us at first, then been outraged, then had begged—and then had couriered over a bowel-loosening lawyer letter telling us that he had slipped a noncompete clause into our contracts, and how that meant the Commonwealth of Massachusetts would lend him the full power of its system of civil justice to render us a smoking ruin if we had the audacity to work in any technology-related field for the next three years.

I told her how we'd found an article in the new issue of *Creative Computing* that told the history of the failed Shockley Semiconductor, whose Nobel-winning founder had never made a working chip because he was too obsessed with eugenics and paying Black women to get their tubes tied to lead his company. So his eight top employees quit and founded Fairchild Semiconductor, and they *did* ship a working chip, and then *their* top engineers quit and founded *Intel*.

"It was all because California doesn't allow noncompetes, and that's why we're here. My roommate got a job straight off, one phone call, bam. He's a programmer, got the degree and everything. I program a little but I'm trained as an accountant, so that's the work I'm looking for. I drove his van here from Boston, saw the country, and I made it after every kind of adventure and whatnot. Tomorrow I'll finish my drive and I'll give Art his van back and crash in his spare room in Mountain View and start the next phase of my life and yeah, I'm pretty happy about that. That's what the smile was about."

She had a gorgeous smile, lopsided and warm with one crooked tooth and two dimples on one side. "That's quite a story, Martin," she said. No one called me Martin, except my dad, and then only when he was pissed at me. But hearing the name out of her lips was fantastic, like she was talking about someone new, the person I was about to become. "Living out here in the back of beyond, we don't get much more than rumors of the Great Awakening out there in Silicon Valley.

"But I'm familiar with the shape of your story, Martin. When I was your age, I made the big cross-country move, from Milwaukee to San Francisco, for the Summer of Love and all that it supposedly entailed. It permanently changed my life, mostly for the better, even if it wasn't the great and epochal moment I'd been anticipating.

"Sitting here on the trail between the real world and the fantasyland, I've seen plenty of pilgrims. First, the latter-day hippies. Then it was the lovely gay boys and those lesbian ladies off to San Francisco to finally be themselves. A lot of them stop here outside Sacto, like they're standing on the diving board and taking a couple test bounces before they make the leap. They often have a smile like yours, though I must say, you have an *excellent* specimen of the type." She reached out and tapped my upper lip with the tip of her index finger and a thrill ran down my spine.

I had been practicing listening the way she had, and it was so different from how I usually listened. For one thing, I could see where her attention was—when she looked at me dead-on and looked away, a whole layer of meaning that I'd been missing out on. Between the bourbon and the finger on my lip and the listening and the moment, I felt so very . . . *alive.* The moment seemed to crackle.

What would someone who was a good listener say to this woman? "May I ask you your name?"

She laughed so big I saw her back molars, then seemed to catch herself a little and ran her fingers through her hair. "Would you get me?" She held her hand out. "It's Lucille," she said. "Very pleased to meet you, Martin."

I shook her hand. Her fingertips had thick calluses on them but her palms were soft and warm. "Very pleased to meet *you*, Lucille." She raised her bottle and I clinked my shot glass against it. We drank. I only had a sip left and I saw that her bottle was nearly empty.

"Another?" I said, pointing at it.

"What a grand notion," she said, and signaled the bartender.

It was Lucille ("Not Lucy, please, I've had my fill of *Peanuts* and *I Love Lucy* jokes, thank you") and she was a third-grade teacher who played guitar in a folk band that sometimes played gigs in Sacramento and toured the festivals in the summer when school was out.

She was single and very emphatic about it: tapped her ring finger, "See, no tan line." She grew up in Wisconsin. She'd spent a whole year taking acid and following the Grateful Dead. She cooked. She'd grown up in Milwaukee and then lived in San Francisco for half a decade before landing here in "the back of beyond" and she loved it.

"No privacy," she said. "I know just about everyone in this bar. Some of 'em have kids in my class, other ones I've taught now and again."

"And you're not worried about what they'll think of you for being in a bar and talking to a strange man?" By this point, we'd established that she was actually having the kind of conversation you could fairly describe as "talking to a strange man."

"They're in a bar, too," she said. "Sorry, that's glib. They know who I am. They know the kind of people I talk to. That's the thing, I am who I am here. They see me. Some of them don't like me and I know it. Some of them, I don't like, and *they* don't know it. In the city, I never knew where I stood. There was so much uncertainty."

I thought of my excruciating years in Escambia, the glory of Cambridge and Boston and their endless variety. "But didn't cities also give you, you know, *pleasant surprises?*"

Even on my third drink, I was practicing my listening skills, so I glimpsed the fleeting wistful look that crossed her face, though it was as quick as a flashbulb. "There were many of those, yes. But I never knew when they would happen. I couldn't control them. Here, I can manage it. When I am in the mood for a surprise, I come here, buy a Bud, sit at the bar, and wait to be surprised. It doesn't happen every time, but you'd be surprised at how many surprises I can expect when I come into this place. Like I said, this is the way station—the top of the high dive, the place where people stop and ponder the drop. It can be awfully nice to contemplate it with them, especially when I know I'm not going to be making the leap myself."

"I like how you talk," I said. "And I like how you listen. Lucille, I like you."

She slipped her hand around mine. "I like you too, Martin." She sprinkled a wave with her free hand at a booth in the corner. "A parent," she said. "Had his daughter two years ago, got his son this year. Daughter number two is coming up right behind him—Irish twins. Nice family."

"And that doesn't make you self-conscious? It makes *me* self-conscious and I don't even teach that guy's kids."

She waved at him again. "I'll be honest, it used to. I used to be much more of a sneak about things like this"—and be assured, I noticed, and thrilled to *things like this*—"but in a town this small being a sneak is a losing proposition. The only difference between sneaking around and being out in public is whether people think you're ashamed of yourself." She gave me that gorgeous, lopsided smile again. "I'm not ashamed of myself. Are you?"

"I can honestly say that I am completely unashamed of where I find myself and what I find myself doing. Now that you mention it, I'm rather proud."

That won me another laugh. The drinks were nearly done. I pointed at her bottle. "Another?"

"I've had enough, thank you."

I felt a wild boldness. "Then I'll get the tab, shall I?"

"That would be great."

The funny thing is, we mostly talked. (Mostly!) The motel room was not the worst place I'd stayed since I hit the road, but it was filthier than Art's and my place in Cambridge had ever gotten, even at the peak of our freakishly long working days and nights for Process Engineering Models. I felt a moment's obscure shame when Lucille stepped inside and I turned on the lights but she just clucked her tongue and criticized the housekeeper, whose son she had taught the year before.

"Small town, remember?"

There was one chair and the bed. I sat on the edge of the bed and she took the chair and we faced each other and we talked, and listened. I watched how she listened when I was talking, and tried to listen the same way. The world melted away. We talked about computers, and we talked about third graders, and Escambia and Milwaukee. She had lived with an egg farmer in teacher's college and she explained things about cooking eggs that I *still* use all the time and show other people whenever I get the chance.

Here is how to make a perfect hard-boiled egg. Boil a large saucepan of water. Gently lower the eggs and continue to boil for thirty seconds. Reduce to simmer, cover, and cook for eleven more minutes. Use a timer. Eat hot, or submerge in ice water and then refrigerate for up to five days. Once you've tried it, you'll never cook eggs any other way.

And eventually she came and sat next to me on the bed.

The last time I'd kissed a woman was more than two years before, at the end of a date with a woman I'd met during college orientation week. It wasn't much of a kiss (it hadn't been much of a date), and shortly thereafter, I fell into a black hole of doing my associate's degree while building the models that Nick Cassidy III demanded of me as my contribution to Process Engineering Models. I'd thought about women and kissing and sex over those two years, but always in an exhausted, abstracted way, the way I thought of faster-than-light travel or what I'd do with one billion dollars.

By contrast, kissing Lucille after all that talking was very concrete and here-and-now. I felt her lips configure themselves into the smile I'd admired so often that night, and I raised my fingers to her face and stroked the place where I knew I'd find her dimples. She got her arms around me and got her fingers into my hair and then touched the cords that ran up the back of my neck to my skull, tracing them up and down. No one had ever done that before. It felt amazing. I made a noise I'd never made before.

We stopped kissing after a while and she took my hand and looked into my eyes.

"Well," she said. What a smile she had. I loved that crooked tooth.

"Well," I said. I squeezed her fingers a little.

"That was something really fine," she said. "Practically perfect, I'd say."

She smelled good—the smell of beer, the smell of her hair and her laundry detergent, and something else, her, I suppose. A warm smell.

I leaned forward, and she kissed me again, just for a short while.

"Practically perfect," she said. "And you have a long day tomorrow, a big day, jumping off that diving board and making the long drop. And I have a day tomorrow, too, twenty-five eight-year-olds that need corralling and nose-wiping."

She stood up and the spot next to me that had been very warm with the radiated heat from her body went instantly cold. I stood up, too.

"Is everything okay, Lucille?"

She smiled. Lopsided. Crooked tooth. Lovely. "It's fine. Like I said, practically perfect. This was enough. I made a friend, I think. I don't really need any more than that. Not tonight, anyway. Maybe the next time you're passing through town."

She squeezed my hand. "What a face. Sorry, Martin. It's not because you did anything wrong. It's because I've gone as far as I want to go for now. But I'll give you my phone number." She picked up the pen beside the bedside phone and wrote a number out on the pad next to it. "And I'll wish you the very best of luck and ambition and love and happiness down the road in fantasyland. I have no doubt that you'll meet great people and do great things." She leaned in and placed one soft kiss on my lips. "Good night, my friend."

Part of me wanted to sulk, or beg, or whine. But she was

right. It had been practically perfect. I'd thought the kiss was the start of something, but it was the capstone. That was okay—it was the capstone of the whole journey, my life up to that point, flunking out of MIT, the chaos of accounting school, the grind of Cassidy III's stupid business, the miles and miles of America I'd just crossed. That lovely, warm kiss was the perfect ending to that long trip, a send-off before the start of what was to come.

"You're right," I said. "I have to do some driving tomorrow. Big day."

"Big day," she agreed.

The hug was almost as good as the kiss.

I thought I'd lie awake, horny and frustrated, but after I brushed my teeth and slid between the sheets, I dropped off like a stone.

In the morning, I drove the rest of the way to fantasyland.

1

Fidelity Computing was the most colorful PC company in Silicon Valley.

A Catholic priest, a Mormon bishop, and an Orthodox rabbi walk into a technology gold rush and start a computer company. The fact that it sounded like the setup for a nerdy joke about the mid-1980s was fantastic for their bottom line. Everyone who heard their story loved it.

As juicy as the story of Fidelity Computing was, they flew under most people's radar for years, even as they built a wildly profitable technology empire from direct sales through faith groups. The first time most of us heard of them was in 1983, when *Byte* ran its cover story on Fidelity Computing, unearthing a parallel universe of technology that had grown up while no one was looking.

At first, I thought maybe they were doing something similar to Apple's new Macintosh: like Apple, they made PCs (the Wise PC), an operating system (Wise DOS), and a whole line of monitors, disk drives, printers, and software.

Like the Mac, none of these things worked with anything else—you needed to buy everything from floppy disks to printer cables specially from them, because nothing anyone else made would work with their system.

And like the Mac, they sold mostly through word of mouth. The big difference was that Mac users were proud to call themselves a cult, while Fidelity Computing's customers were literally a religion.

Long after Fidelity had been called to the Great Beyond, its most loyal customers gave it an afterlife, nursing their computers along, until the parts and supplies ran out. They'd have kept going even then if there'd been any way to unlock their machines and use the same stuff the rest of the computing world relied on. But that wasn't something Fidelity Computing would permit, even from beyond the grave.

I was summoned to Fidelity headquarters—in unfashionable Colma, far from the white-hot start-ups of Palo Alto, Mountain View, and, of course, Cupertino—by a friend of Art's. Art had a lot more friends than me. I was a skipping stone, working as the part-time bookkeeper/accountant/CFO for half a dozen companies and never spending more than one or two days in the same office.

Art was hardly more stable than me—he switched start-ups all the time, working for as little as two months (and never for more than a year) before moving on. His bosses knew what they were getting: you hired Art Hellman to blaze into your company, take stock of your product plan, root out and correct all of its weak points, build core code libraries, and then move on. He was good enough and sufficiently in demand to command the right to behave this way, and he wouldn't have it any other way. My view was, it was an extended celebration of his liberation from the legal villainy of Nick Cassidy III: having narrowly escaped a cage, he was determined never to be locked up again.

Art's "engagements"—as he called them—earned him the respect and camaraderie of half the programmers and hardware engineers in the Valley. This, in spite of the fact that he was a public and ardent member of the Lavender Panthers, wore the badge on his lapel, went to the marches, and brought his boyfriend to all the places where his straight colleagues brought their girlfriends.

He'd come out to me less than a week after I arrived by the simple expedient of introducing the guy he was watching TV with in our living room as Lewis, his boyfriend. Lewis was a Chinese guy about our age, and his wardrobe—plain white tee, tight blue jeans, loafers—matched the new look Art had adopted since leaving Boston. Lewis had a neat, short haircut that matched Art's new haircut, too.

To call the Art I'd known in Cambridge a slob would be an insult to the natty, fashion-conscious modern slob. He'd favored old band T-shirts with fraying armpit seams, too-big jeans that were either always sliding off his skinny hips or pulled up half-way to his nipples. In the summer, his sneakers had holes in the toes. In the winter, his boots were road salt–crusted crystalline eruptions. His red curls were too chaotic for a white-boy 'fro and were more of a *heap,* and he often went days without shaving.

There were members of the Newbury Street Irregulars who were bigger slobs than Art, but they *smelled.* Art washed, but otherwise, he looked like a homeless person (or a hacker). His transformation to a neatly dressed, clean-shaven fellow with a twenty-five-dollar haircut that he actually used some sort of hairspray on was remarkable. I'd assumed it was about his new life as a grown-up living far from home and doing a real job. It turned out that wasn't the reason at all.

"Oh," I said. "That makes a lot of sense." I shook Lewis's hand. He laughed. I checked Art. He was playing it cool, but I could tell he was nervous. I remembered Lucille and how she listened, and what it felt like to be heard. I thought about Art, and the things he'd never been able to tell me.

There'd been a woman in the Irregulars who there were rumors about, and there were a pair of guys one floor down in Art's building who held hands in the elevator, but as far as I knew up until that moment, I hadn't really ever been introduced to a homosexual person. I didn't know how I felt about it, but I *did* know how I *wanted* to feel about it.

So Art didn't just get to know all kinds of geeks from his whistle-stop tour of Silicon Valley's hottest new tech ventures. He was also plugged into this other network of people from the Lavender Panthers, and their boyfriends and girlfriends, and the people he knew from bars and clubs. He and Lewis lasted for a couple of months, and then there were a string of weekends where there was a new guy at the breakfast table, and then he settled down again for a while with Artemis, and then he hit a long dry spell.

I commiserated. I'd been having a dry spell for nearly the whole two years I'd been in California. The closest I came to romance was exchanging a letter with Lucille every couple of weeks—she was a fine pen pal, but that wasn't really a substitute for a living, breathing woman in my life.

Art threw himself into his volunteer work, and he was only half joking when he said he did it to meet a better class of boys than you got at a club. Sometimes, there'd be a committee meeting in our living room and I'd hear about the congressional committee hearing on the "gay plague" and the new wave of especially vicious attacks. It was pretty much the only time I heard about that stuff—no one I worked with ever brought it up, unless it was to make a terrible joke.

It was Murf, one of the guys from those meetings, who told me that Fidelity Computing was looking for an accountant for a special project. He had stayed after the meeting, and he and Art made a pot of coffee and sat down in front of Art's Apple clone, a Franklin Ace 1200 that he'd scored six months ahead of its official release. After opening the lid to show Murf the interior, Art fired it up and put it through its paces.

I hovered over his shoulder, watching. I'd had a couple of chances to play with the 1200, and I wanted one more than anything in the world except for a girlfriend.

"Marty," Art said, "Murf was telling me about a job I thought you might be good for."

The Ace 1200 would have a list price of $2,200. I pulled up a chair.

Fidelity Computing's business offices were attached to their warehouse, right next to their factory. It took up half of a business park in Colma, and I had to circle it twice to find a parking spot. I was five minutes late and flustered when I presented myself to the receptionist, a blond woman with a ten-years-out-of-date haircut and a modest cardigan over a sensible white shirt buttoned to the collar, ring on her finger.

"Hello," I said. "I'm Marty Hench. I—uh—I've got a meeting with the Reverend Sirs." That was what the executive assistant I'd spoken to on the phone had called them. It sounded weird when he said it. It sounded weirder when I said it.

The receptionist gave me a smile that only went as far as her lips. "Please have a seat," she said. There were only three chairs in the little reception area, vinyl office chairs with worn wooden armrests. There weren't any magazines, just glossy catalogs featuring the latest Fidelity Computing systems, accessories, consumables, and software. I browsed one, marveling at the parallel universe of computers in the strange, mauve color that denoted all Fidelity equipment, including the boxes, packaging, and, now that I was attuned to it, the accents and carpet in the small lobby. A side door opened and a young, efficient man in a kippah and wire-rim glasses called for me: "Mr. Hench?" I closed the catalog and returned it to the pile and stood. As I went to shake his hand, I realized that something had been nagging me about the catalog—there were no prices.

"I'm Shlomo," the man said. "We spoke on the phone. Thank you for coming down. The Reverend Sirs are ready to see you now."

He wore plain black slacks, hard black shiny shoes, and a white shirt with prayer-shawl tassels poking out of its tails. I followed him through a vast room filled with chest-high Steelcase cubicles finished in yellowing, chipped wood veneer, every scratch pitilessly lit by harsh overhead fluorescents. Most of the workers at the cubicles were women with headsets, speaking in hushed tones. The tops of their heads marked the interfaith delineators: a block of Orthodox headscarves, then a block of nuns' black-and-white scarves (I learned to call them "veils" later), then the Mormons' carefully coiffed, mostly blond dos.

"This way," Shlomo said, passing through another door and into executive row. The mauve carpets were newer, the nap all swept in one direction. The walls were lined with framed certificates of appreciation, letters from religious and public officials (apparently, the church and state were not separate within the walls of Fidelity Computing), photos of groups of progressively larger groups of people ranked before progressively larger offices—the company history.

We walked all the way to the end of the hall, past closed doors with nameplates, to a corner conference room with a glass wall down one side showing a partial view of a truck-loading dock behind half-closed vertical blinds. Seated at intervals around a large conference table were the Reverend Sirs themselves, each with his own yellow pad, pencil, and coffee cup.

Shlomo announced me: "Reverend Sirs, this is Marty Hench. Mr. Hench, these are Rabbi Yisrael Finkel, Bishop Leonard Clarke, and Father Marek Tarnowski." He backed out of the door, leaving me standing, unsure if I should circle the table shaking hands, or take a seat, or—

"Please, sit," Rabbi Finkel said. He was fiftyish, round-faced and bear-shaped with graying sidelocks and beard and a black suit and tie. His eyes were sharp behind horn-rimmed glasses. He gestured to a chair at the foot of the table.

I sat, then rose a little to undo the button of my sport coat. I hadn't worn it since my second job interview, when I realized it was making the interviewers uncomfortable. It certainly made me uncomfortable. I fished out the little steno pad and stick pen I'd brought with me.

"Thank you for coming, Mr. Hench." The rabbi had an orator's voice, that big chest of his serving as a resonating chamber like a double bass.

"Of course," I said. "Thanks for inviting me. It's a fascinating company you have here."

Bishop Clarke smiled at that. He was the best dressed of the three, in a well-cut business suit, his hair short, neat, side-parted. His smile was very white, and very wide. He was the youngest of the three—in his late thirties, I'd guess. "Thank you," he said. "We know we're very different from the other computer companies, and we like it that way. We like to think that we see something in computers—a potential—that other people have missed."

Father Tarnowski scowled. He was cadaverously tall and thin, with the usual dog collar and jacket, and a heavy gold class ring. His half-rim glasses flashed. He was the oldest, maybe sixty, and had a sour look that I took for habitual. "He doesn't want the press packet, Leonard," he said. "Let's get to the point." He had a broad Chicago accent like a tough-guy gangster in *The Untouchables*.

Bishop Clarke's smile blinked off and on for an instant and I was overcome with the sudden knowledge that these two men did not like each other *at all*, and that there was some kind of long-running argument simmering beneath the surface. "Thank you, Marek, of course. Mr. Hench's time is valuable." Father

Tarnowski snorted softly at that and the bishop pretended he didn't hear it, but I saw Rabbi Finkel grimace at his yellow pad.

"What can I help you Reverend Sirs with today?" *Reverend Sirs* came more easily now, didn't feel ridiculous at all. The three of them gave the impression of being a quarter inch away from going for each other's throats, and the formality was a way to keep tensions at a distance.

"We need a certain kind of accountant," the rabbi said. He'd dated the top of his yellow pad and then circled the date. "A kind of accountant who understands the computer business. Who understands *computers,* on a technical level. It's hard to find an accountant like that, believe it or not, even in Silicon Valley." I didn't point out that Colma wasn't in Silicon Valley.

"Well," I said, carefully. "I think I fit that bill. I've only got an associate's degree in accounting, but I'm a kind of floating CFO for half a dozen companies and I've been doing night classes at UCSF Extension to get my bachelor's. I did a year at MIT and built my own computer a few years back. I program pretty well in BASIC and Pascal and I've got a little C, and I'm a pretty darned good debugger, if I do say so myself."

Bishop Clarke gave a small but audible sigh of relief. "You do indeed sound perfect, and I'm told that Shlomo spoke to your references and they were very enthusiastic about your diligence and . . . discretion."

I'd given Shlomo a list of four clients I'd done extensive work with, but I hadn't had "discretion" in mind when I selected them. It's true that doing a company's accounts made me privy to some sensitive information—like when two employees with the same job were getting paid very different salaries—but I got the feeling that wasn't the kind of "discretion" the bishop had in mind.

"I'm pretty good at minding my own business," I said, and then, "even when I'm being paid to mind someone else's." I liked that line, and made a mental note about it. Maybe someday I'd put it on my letterhead. *Martin Hench: Confidential CPA.*

The bishop favored me with a chuckle. The rabbi nodded thoughtfully. The priest scowled.

"That's very good," the bishop said. "What we'd like to discuss today is of a very sensitive nature, and I'm sure you'll understand if we would like more than your good word to rely on." He lifted his yellow pad, revealing a single page, grainily photocopied, and slid it over the table to me. "That's our standard nondisclosure agreement," he said. He slid a pen along to go with it.

I didn't say anything. I'd signed a few NDAs, but only *after* I'd taken a contract. This was something different. I squinted at the page, which was a second- or third-generation copy and blurry in places. I started to read it. The bishop made a disgusted noise. I pretended I didn't hear him.

I crossed out a few clauses and carefully lettered in an amendment. I initialed the changes and slid the paper back across the table to the bishop, and found the smile was gone from his face. All three of them were now giving me stern looks, wrath-of-God looks, the kind of looks that would make a twenty-one-year-old kid like me very nervous indeed. I felt the nerves rise and firmly pushed them down.

"Mr. Hench," the bishop said, his tone low and serious, "is there some kind of problem?"

It pissed me off. I'd driven all the way to for-chrissakes *Colma* and these three weirdo God-botherers had ambushed me with their everything-and-the-kitchen-sink contract. I had plenty of work, and I didn't *need* theirs, especially not if this was the way they wanted to deal. This had suddenly become a negotiation, and my old man had always told me the best negotiating position was a willingness to get up from the table. I was going to win this negotiation, one way or another.

"No problem," I said.

"And yet you appear to have made alterations to our standard agreement."

"I did," I said. *That's not a problem for me,* I didn't say.

He gave me more of that stern eyeball-ray stuff. I let my negotiating leverage repel it. "Mr. Hench, our standard agreement can only be altered after review by our general counsel."

"That sounds like a prudent policy," I said, and met his stare.

He clucked his tongue. "I can get a fresh one," he said. "This one is no good."

I cocked my head. "I think it'd be better to get your general counsel, wouldn't it?"

The three of them glared at me. I found I was enjoying myself. What's more, I thought Rabbi Finkel might be suppressing a little smile, though the beard made it hard to tell.

"Let me see it," he said, holding his hand out.

Bishop Clarke gave a minute shake of his head. The rabbi half rose, reached across the table, and slid it over to himself, holding it at arm's length and adjusting his glasses. He picked up his pen and initialed next to my changes.

"Those should be fine," he said, and slid it back to me. "Sign, please."

"Yisrael," Bishop Clarke said, an edge in his voice, "changes to the standard agreements need to be reviewed—"

"By our general counsel," the rabbi finished, waving a dismissive gesture at him. "I know, I know. But these are fine. We should probably make the same changes to all our agreements. Meanwhile, we've all now had a demonstration that Mr. Hench is the kind of person who takes his promises seriously. Would you rather have someone who doesn't read and signs his life away, or someone who makes sure he knows what he's signing and agrees with it?"

Bishop Clarke's smile came back, strained at the corners. "That's an excellent point, Rabbi. Thank you for helping me understand your reasoning." He collected the now-signed contract from me and tucked it back under his yellow pad.

"Now," he said, "we can get down to the reason we asked you here today."

Rivka Goldman was the only woman in Sales Group One, this being the group that serviced and supported synagogues and their worshippers. She'd traveled all around the country, sitting down with men who owned garment factories, grocery stores, jewelry stores, delis, and other small businesses, training their "girls" in the use of the Fidelity system. It could handle business correspondence, company books, payroll, and other functions that used to be handled by four or five "girls"—who could all be replaced with just one.

Rivka was the only woman, and often it wasn't she who made the sale, because the men who owned these businesses talked to other men. It was her male colleagues in Sales Group One who closed those sales and pocketed the commissions, but Rivka never complained.

"She was very good at it," the rabbi told me. "She had a knack for computers, and for explaining them. The girls she trained, they learned. When they had troubles, they wanted to talk to her."

Sister Maria-Eva Fernandez led a very large, all-woman team that ran mostly autonomously within Sales Group Two, a group that exclusively serviced parochial schools across the U.S., with a few customers in Central America. She was a product of these schools—she'd graduated from Christ the King in Denver and gone straight from there into the order, doing some student teaching before finding her way to Fidelity Computing via an internal talent search that filtered down to the convent from the archdiocese.

Like Rivka, Sister Maria-Eva was a natural: she could patiently train school administrators, their secretaries, department heads, and even individual teachers on the use of the Fidelity system. A couple of schools—fat with money from wealthy patrons—had bought entire classrooms' worth of machines, creating programming labs for ambitious high-schoolers, and they were universally a success.

"We valued her, we praised her, we sent her to the national sales conference to lead workshops and share her expertise," Father Marek said. "She was a *star*." He spat the word.

Elizabeth Amelia Shepard Taylor didn't have to go on a mission, but there was never any question but that she would. Her family had been prominent in the Church of Jesus Christ of Latter-day Saints for over a century, and, as the eldest of eleven kids, she had a familial duty to set an example.

She had hoped for a posting in Asia—she'd studied Cantonese and Japanese in high school—but instead she drew San Jose, California. She staffed the Mission House, helping the boys who knocked on doors all day, serving as den mother, big sister, and the object of innumerable crushes.

She'd found a women's computing club via a notice at the local library and had taken turns with four other women—two her age, and two retirees—prodding at a pair of Commodore PET computers, learning BASIC. Her letters home to her family were filled with the excitement of discovery and mastery, the esoteric world of assembly language that she'd dived into with the help of books and magazines from the library.

When her father heard that Fidelity was recruiting, he wrote her a letter. The same day she'd received it, she'd written a letter to Fidelity Computing Ltd., typing it up on the used ZX80 she'd bought at a swap meet ("for the Mission House"). It arrived at Fidelity in a #10 envelope, three neatly printed pages with the

rough edges of fanfold paper that had had its perforations sepa-
rated. The last page was all code examples.

She was promised a job by return post, starting the day she
finished her mission, and she never ended up going back to Salt
Lake City—just got a Caltrain to the Daly City station and met
with Bishop Clarke's personal assistant, a young man named
John Garn who *had* done his mission in Taipei and chatted with
her the whole way to the office in Taiwanese, which she laboriously parsed into Cantonese.

"She whipped Sales Group Three into a powerhouse," Bishop
Clarke said, with a sad shake of his head. "We went from last to
first in under a year. Outsold the other two divisions *combined,*
and we were on track to doubling this year."

The three women had met at the annual sales conference, a huge
event that took over the Fort Mason Center for a long weekend.
Most of the event was segregated by sales group, but there were
plenary sessions, mixers, and keynote addresses from leading
sales staff that helped diffuse the winningest tactics across the
whole business.

"We think they met in a women's interfaith prayer circle,"
Rabbi Finkel said. Father Marek made another of his disgusted
grunts, which were his principal contributions to the conversation. Rabbi Finkel inclined his head a little in the priest's direction and said, "Not everyone agreed that they were a good
idea at first, but the girls loved them, and they created bonds of
comity that served them well."

"We don't have a lot of turnover," Rabbi Finkel said. "People
like working here. They do well, *and* they do good. People from
our faith communities sometimes feel like the future is passing
them by, like their religion is an anchor around their necks,
keeping them stuck in the past. A job here is a way to be faithful
and modern, without sacrificing your faith."

The bishop nodded. "When they turned in their resignation notices, of course we took notice. As Rabbi Finkel says, we just don't get a lot of turnover. And of course, these three girls were special to us. So we took notice. I met with Elizabeth myself and asked her if there was anything wrong, and she refused to discuss it. I asked her what she *did* want to discuss and she went off on these wild tangents, not making any sense. I wrote a letter to her father, but I never heard back."

"Rivka is a good girl," the rabbi said. "She told me that she still loved God and wanted to live a pious, modest life, but that she had 'differences' with the teachings. I asked her about these 'differences,' but that was all she could say: 'differences, differences.' What's a difference? She wants to uncover her hair? Eat a cheeseburger? Pray with men? She wouldn't say."

Father Marek cleared his throat, made a face, glared. "When Sister Maria-Eva ignored my memo asking her to come see me, I called her Mother Superior and that's when I discovered that she'd left the order. Left the order! Of course, I assumed there was a man involved, but that wasn't it, not according to her Mother Superior. She had taken *new* orders with a . . . fringe sect. It seemed she was lost to us."

The logo for Computing Freedom was a stylized version of an inverted Fidelity Computing logo, colored magenta, just a few shades off of the mauve of the Fidelity family of products.

Their catalog was slimmer than Fidelity's, omitting the computers themselves. Instead, it was filled with all the things that went *with* the computers: printers, ribbons, paper, floppy drives and disks, RAM and modems. Unlike the Fidelity catalog, CF's catalog had prices. They were perfectly reasonable prices, maybe even a little on the high side.

"Our computers, they're a *system*," Bishop Clarke said. "We provide everything, and guarantee that it will all work together.

Our customers aren't sophisticated, they're not high-tech people. They're people who organize their lives around their faith, not chasing a fad or obsessing over gadgets."

"We hold their hands," Rabbi Finkel said. "There's always someone who'll answer the phone and help them, whatever problem they're having. It's like a family. One of their computers breaks, we send them another one! That way, they can keep working. We know the system is important to them."

"It's not cheap," Father Marek said. "That kind of customer service isn't cheap."

"We filed suit as soon as we found out," Bishop Clarke said. "We didn't want to." He looked sad. "What choice did we have." It wasn't a question.

CF managed to fly under the radar for a couple of months. They started with sales calls, cold calls to their old contacts, their best customers, explaining that they had created a new business, one that could supply them with high-quality, interchangeable products for their Fidelity systems. The prices were *much* lower than Fidelity's, often less than half.

"Sure they were less than half," Father Marek said. "When you don't have to pay a roomful of customer-service people, you don't have to charge as much."

The customers were happy, but then a San Antonio stake president was invited to dinner at the home of a local prominent businessman, the owner of a large printshop who relied so heavily on Fidelity systems to run his business that he kept one at home, in his study, with a modem that let him dial into the plant and look at the day's production figures and examine the hour sheets and payroll figures.

The president noticed the odd-colored box of fanfold printer paper behind the congregant's desk, feeding a continuous river of paper into the printer's sprockets. He asked after the odd packaging and the parishioner gave him a catalog (CF included a spare catalog with every order, along with a handwritten note on quarter-sized stationery thanking the customer for his business).

The president assumed that this was some kind of new division of Fidelity, and he was impressed with the prices and selection in the catalog. Naturally, when he needed a new box of floppy disks, he asked one of the girls in his congregation for a box of the low-cost items—

"Why would he ask a girl in his congregation? Didn't he have a Fidelity sales rep?" I'd filled much of my little steno pad with notes by this point. It was quite a story but I wasn't quite sure where I fit in with it.

Bishop Clarke started to answer, but Father Marek silenced him by clearing his throat in a loud and pointed way. The priest stared at me for a long time, seeming to weigh me and find me wanting. I can't say I liked him, but he fascinated me. He had such a small bag of tricks, those glares and noises, but he was a virtuoso with them, like a diner cook who can only make a half dozen dishes but prepares them with balletic grace.

"Mr. Hench," he said. He let the words hang in the air. "Mr. Hench," he said again. I knew it was a trick but he performed it so well. I felt a zing of purely irrational, utterly involuntary anxiety. "We don't have a traditional sales force. The sales groups are small, and their primary role is *Empowerment*." He leaned so heavily on the word that I heard the capital letter.

"Our sales groups travel around, they meet people in each place who know their communities, people who have the knack for technology, who need a little side business to help them make ends meet. The sales groups train these people, teach them how to spot people who could use our systems, how to explain the benefits to them. They use their personal connections, the mutual trust, to put our machines where they can do the most good."

Bishop Clarke could see I wasn't quite following. "It's like the Avon Lady. You know, 'ding-dong Avon calling'? Those girls are talking to their neighbors, helping them find the right products. Their friends get the best products for their needs, the girls get a commission, and everyone is happy."

I got it then. Fidelity was a pyramid scheme. Well, that was a waste of time. I almost said so, but then I held my tongue. I didn't want to get into an argument with these men, I just wanted to leave.

"We're not a pyramid scheme," Rabbi Finkel said. Had it shown on my face? Maybe rabbis got a lot of practice reading people, hearing the unsaid words. "We follow the rules. The Federal Trade Commission set the rules in 1979 and we've always followed them. We are a community-oriented business, serving faith groups, and we want to give back to them. That's why we pay commissions to local people. It's our way of putting some of our profits into the communities that depend on us."

"That's so well said," Bishop Clarke said. "*So* well said. Perfect, in fact."

"*Perfect*," Rabbi Finkel said, with a scowl that made it clear he wasn't happy to have been interrupted.

The San Antonio girl—the daughter of a local real-estate broker—had no idea what floppy disks the president was talking about, so he showed her the catalog, and she immediately called the rep in Colma. The receptionist was on the ball and passed the call on to Shlomo, who immediately grasped the catalog's significance and approved an expensive Federal Express courier.

"Our general counsel advised us to seek an injunction and file a suit," Bishop Clarke said.

"It would have been better to talk, of course," the rabbi said. "Nobody wanted to drag those three little girls into court. They're like family, even though they left."

Up until then, they'd all been telling the same story, but something about what Rabbi Finkel said stopped its momentum. I'd been practicing my listening, trying to be like Lucille, listening with my eyes *and* my ears. The rabbi's statement jolted the other two. *Now we're coming to the crux,* I thought. *This is the part where I come in.*

"They were good at their jobs," Bishop Clarke said, almost wistful.

"They surprised us," Father Marek said.

"Perhaps we could find an accommodation," the rabbi said. The three men looked at each other. How long had they been in business together, in each other's pockets, maybe at each other's throats? The story of interfaith harmony was such a juicy one, the stuff of magazine cover stories. Was it true, though?

"They just need convincing," Bishop Clarke said. His smile flickered on and off. He must have had dental work. The standard-issue teeth just didn't come that way: shining, white, perfect symmetry. On, off. Maybe he practiced it in front of a mirror.

Discovery is the part of a lawsuit where the parties can demand relevant documents from one another: memos, contracts, correspondence.

Tortious interference is the legal offense of stepping between two contracting parties in a way that induces one of them to violate their contractual obligations. Suing for tortious interference is the commercial version of a jilted wife confronting her erstwhile husband's lover, as though his infidelity was her fault.

Fidelity's lawyers—an outside firm with a reputation for aggression and a roster of blue-chip clients and high-profile cases, including IBM's ongoing troubles with the Department of Justice over its alleged antitrust violations—had drawn up a complaint asserting that CF had induced Fidelity's suppliers to violate their confidentiality and exclusivity agreements while simultaneously inducing the company's best customers to forgo *their* contractual obligations (and semireligious duty) to buy their supplies from Fidelity and its sales agents in their congregations.

These sweeping allegations gave Fidelity's lawyers sweeping

discovery powers: all documents and accounts related to CF's manufacturing, promotion, and sales, right down to the printers who supplied their catalogs.

CF wasn't powerless in the face of this onslaught. Their lawyers—a much cheaper and hungrier firm of lawyers, without the pedigree or track record of their opposing counsel—had secured the right to redact irrelevant, sensitive material from the documents they turned over, and, more crucially, they had convinced the judge to let them do something novel.

The bishop hoisted a bankers box onto the table and set it down with a thud. He lifted the lid like a conjurer's trick and brought out two thick binders of paperwork, bristling with dividers. "This is the hardcopy," he said. "It's almost nothing. Photocopies of handwritten memos, mostly."

He reached back in and produced a mauve box of floppy disks, the five-and-a-quarter-inch kind that already seemed slightly quaint, compared to the small, rigid three-and-a-half-inch floppies that all the new computers were using. He produced a second box. A third. A fourth. A fifth. The pile grew.

"Ten boxes of floppy disks," the bishop said. "No one had ever asked such a thing of our judge, but he said that two computer companies should be able to accept electronic submissions from one another. He said it was obvious that this was the future of discovery, and that we were the perfect litigants to start with, since our dispute was about their piracy of our formats and disks, so of course we'd have compatible systems.

"Somewhere in here is the evidence that they are going to fail in court, the evidence that will force them to come back to the table and negotiate, to *talk,* the way they should have in the first place. They've found some good ways of doing things, and we're interested in that. We want to *work with them,* not ruin them. We could arrange a sale of their little company to Fidelity, on preferable terms, but with something in there to recognize their clever little inventions and innovations. They'd get something, rather than nothing." The bishop spread his hands, patted the air. *It's only reasonable,* his hands said.

"Better they get the money than the lawyers," the rabbi said.

"Something is always better than nothing," Father Marek said. "Even an idiot should be able to see that." The other two shot him looks. He scowled at them.

"We need someone who can make sense of all this." The bishop pointed at his precarious tower of floppy disks. "They thought that they'd overwhelm us with electronic records. That our lawyers were so conservative that they wouldn't be able to sort through them. It's true, they're not set up for this. No one is, but someone could be. We think that for the right kind of person, someone who understands accounting *and* computers, these records will be easier to handle."

There it was. They looked at me, three worried sets of eyes. This wasn't how they normally operated. They were taking a risk. I wondered whose idea this was. Not Father Marek: he wanted vengeance. He'd be happy to smash CF, make an example of them. Rabbi Finkel? Perhaps. I could see that he was a thinker, someone who looked around corners. The bishop? He'd done most of the talking. But I got the impression he always did most of the talking: a Mormon bishop, after all, didn't wear a dog collar or a beard and yarmulke. Mormon bishops are laypeople, after all. They look *secular.*

"You gentlemen must have customers who do accounting," I said. "They know your systems. They know accounts. Why not use someone you already have a relationship with? Someone from the family, as you put it?" I loved solving puzzles; it was what made me both a programmer *and* an accountant. I had flipped into puzzle-solving mode and was looking for loose ends where I could begin the untangling process.

The three men looked at each other, then away. This wasn't a question they wanted to answer.

"When it comes to our customers," the rabbi said, "we want

them to feel . . . safe. We don't want them to think that the business is being distracted by foolish disputes."

"We don't want them to be tempted to take sides," Father Marek said, and I thought he was being a lot more honest than the rabbi. I could imagine that plenty of people would choose three young, pious women over these three old, feuding, rich clerics.

I could tell that the bishop and the rabbi both resented Father Marek's answer and were barely keeping themselves from telling him so because they both knew it would make the situation even worse. That was okay. I had the lay of the land.

"I think I understand." They shifted, looked at each other, at me. They were worried. They thought I might say no. They didn't have a plan B. "It certainly presents a fascinating technical challenge. My only concern is that it sounds very time-consuming and I have a lot of work right now, honestly. Some days, I feel it's more than I can handle." I enjoyed watching that land, seeing their incipient panic. These three weren't so tough. After all, they'd been made fools of by three cloistered, sheltered young women around my age.

"The job is well-compensated," Bishop Clarke said. He smiled. All those teeth. "After all, the alternative is a costly, drawn-out lawsuit, and even if we win, all it will accomplish is a shutdown of CF. If you can help us bring them into the Fidelity Computing family, we'll not only save the lawyer bills, we'll all make more money. We're prepared to pay to make that happen."

"I normally bill my freelance work at twenty-five dollars an hour." It was a breathtaking sum and I'd had to practice saying it into a mirror so I wouldn't look ashamed when I named it. I watched them freeze up and do some mental math, contemplating how long it would take to review the documents on ten boxes' worth of floppy disks.

Bishop Clarke's smile strained wider, looking like it might be hurting his face. "That's a very reasonable rate, but we had something else in mind—we thought we might align all of our incentives by offering you a share of the bounty of a successful outcome."

I regretted coming. What a waste of time. I was only twenty-one years old, but I knew better than to sign up for a commission. Who did they think I was, one of the rubes they got to sell printer paper for them in return for a dollar on every box sold? I almost walked out. I didn't, though. I had to hear this.

"Could you explain how that would work?"

"You get twenty-five percent," Father Marek said, staring hard at me. "A quarter of their projected annual revenue, based on the figures you pull out of those files." He nodded minutely at the tower of floppy disks, not taking his eyes off mine. "Our sales are already down a thousand dollars a month. You figure out how much they're making every month, figure out how much they're growing every month, multiply it by twelve, and then divide it by four, and send us an invoice."

"No matter how much it comes to?"

"No matter how much it comes to," he said. "Like you said, it's a lot of work."

I mulled this over. There was a catch. What was it? I got a hunch.

"No matter what the outcome?" I asked.

They looked at each other. "No," Rabbi Finkel said. "No, the deal is for a portion of a satisfactory outcome. If your work makes us money, then you make money."

"And if it doesn't?"

The rabbi smiled. "I'm sure you'll find the information we're looking for," he said. "We know they've broken the law and we know the evidence will be in all those files."

"But if I can't find it, or if it's not enough to convince them to settle and sell?"

"You get nothing," Father Marek snapped. "Nothing. We win, you win. We lose, you lose."

I decided I liked him the best of the three. He wasn't trying to hide who he was or what the situation was. He made it clear he didn't think much of me, but at least he thought enough of me to give it to me straight. I got the impression that Bishop Clarke would knife me in the heart without losing that amazing smile, and that Rabbi Finkel would murmur reassurances as he gave it a twist. Not Father Marek. He'd give me an honest snarl as he did it.

I had been ready to do it a minute before. Now I was ready to walk. My short time in the Bay Area had made it clear that I wasn't going to get stock options in the next Apple Inc. just because I kept their books, nor was I going to be able to command giant amounts of money just for showing up and creating the foundations of some hot company's big product, like Art.

But if there's one thing I'd learned from accounting, it was that companies didn't pay you if they didn't have to.

"I'm sorry, gentlemen—Reverend Sirs—but I think this won't work out. There's just too many ways this could go wrong. I could do my job perfectly, put hundreds of hours of work into it, and you could fail to accomplish your merger due to factors beyond my control."

Their faces turned to stone. They glared at me. The rabbi opened his mouth to say something, but Father Marek silenced him with a pointed throat-clearing. Bishop Clarke turned on his smile. Father Marek gathered up his notepad and put his pen in his breast pocket and slowly climbed to his feet. He was taller—far taller than I'd guessed. He had legs like a cricket's, they just kept unfolding. I had to force myself not to flinch as he shifted toward me.

"Marty," the bishop said, "I completely understand, really I do. But there's no need to give up hope. We're reasonable people. Perhaps you would like to make a counteroffer?"

I nearly left. But for a moment there, I'd felt close to the dream of Silicon Valley—the riches, the fame, the power to change so many lives. "What about . . ." The rabbi and the bishop leaned forward. Father Marek perched on his long legs and folded his arms. "What about my hourly rate, *or* twenty-five percent of whatever I make for you, whichever is greatest?"

"What about whatever is least?" the bishop fired back. His smile never wavered.

I opened and shut my mouth. If the figures they'd discussed were real, then my billables would come out to a fraction of what I'd get if they got their way and absorbed CF. I reminded myself that I'd been ready to leave, to forgo *all* the money, just a moment before. But against that: the sense of how much I'd regret it if I took this deal, helped Fidelity Computing recapture their tearaway competitors, and picked up a mere $1,500, while five or ten times as much money could have been mine.

Imaginary regrets were no basis for doing business, I told myself. "That's a deal," I said.

Bishop Clarke clapped his hands together once. "I *knew* we could find a way to work together. How simply *wonderful*."

"I can't wait to see what you find," Rabbi Finkel said.

"We pay net ninety," Father Marek said. "The girls in payables can get you set up with an invoicing template." He cupped his chin in one hand. "Which reminds me, I don't suppose you have a Fidelity system, do you?"

"I'm afraid I don't," I said.

"That's not uncommon, for a secular person," Bishop Clarke said.

"We'll loan you a refurb," Father Marek said. "Stop by the loading bay after you speak to payables. Tell them I sent you. I'll have my secretary call down to them."

Shlomo came and got me and steered me out of executive row and back into the cavernous room where the customer-service reps murmured into their phones. They all stiffened as the door to executive row opened, and their conversations took on a hush.

I had a friend when I was growing up in San Diego, Marc Reyes. Marc's father was an angry man, the kind of person who'd shout at his wife and kids even when there was a young stranger in the house. I'd seen him punch a wall hard enough to crack the plaster, over nothing—a failure to bring in the afternoon paper.

The hush in that bullpen took me back to the Reyes household, the tense silence that would fall over it when Marc's father would come home.

I humped the bankers box full of CF floppies through the bullpen and into the accounting department, where a middle-aged Orthodox man with sidelocks and a wide-brimmed hat gave me a floppy disk with an invoice template on it. I slipped it into the box, then put the box into the back of Art's van, and drove around to the loading dock, where I signed for a quartet of battered cardboard boxes containing a Fidelity 3000 (their 386 system), a monitor, a printer, and two floppy drives.

I pointed the van back to Art's place and put my foot down on the pedal.

2

By that point, I was familiar with half a dozen different computers—the DEC PDPs that the Newbury Street Irregulars sometimes got access to by sneaking into a deserted MIT lab at 2 a.m. and the Altair 8800 I'd built in my dorm room the first week of classes, and then fallen so hard for that I flunked out of college by the end of the year. There were the Apple][+ machines that we installed across the southland for the suckers signed up with Process Engineering Models, and the exotic Apple //c systems some of my friends had. I'd spent a week on a jobsite where they used IBM PCs, and of course there was Art's Franklin Ace.

They all had their quirks. They all had their rough edges. But none of them were as genuinely *weird* as the Fidelity 3000.

The first time I booted it, it asked me for my religious affiliation, which surprised me but only for a moment. I stared at the menu, wondering whether I should choose 1. for Catholic, 2. for Jewish, or 3. for Mormon (later, when I had to set the system up again, the menu options were in a different order—there was a randomizer that changed them every time).

I chose Catholic and was treated to a full-screen, multicolor text-art image of a blocky cathedral with a huge white cross on its lawn. The computer speaker played two bars of beep-bloop music, and then it dropped into another menu, inviting me to choose from SPREADSHEET, WORD PROCESSOR, or GAME. Naturally, I chose GAME first and found myself playing a multiple-choice scripture quiz. There was no way to quit it, either, not without answering all twenty questions and receiving my score. By question twelve, I was hunting for the Break key and hammering away at the Esc key (I'd have tried Ctrl-C but there was no Ctrl key for me to C with).

When I finally escaped from Bible Quiz jail, I fired up SPREADSHEET. The load screen displayed a string of marching crosses that clicked across the screen while the floppy drive scraped and hummed.

SPREADSHEET was like getting in a time machine set for 1981 and the first VisiCalc demo I'd ever seen. Back then, I'd been blown away, but by current standards, SPREADSHEET was a blunt tool. I prodded my way through the help menus, exploring the formula syntax. After spending a couple of years hip-deep in Lotus 1–2–3 Release 2, SPREADSHEET's impoverished vocabulary was pure Me Tarzan, You Jane stuff.

How the hell was I going to analyze ten boxes' worth of floppies using this stone axe?

"What the *hell* is that thing?" Art staggered through the apartment door a little after 1 a.m., smelling of beer, cologne, and cigarettes. His hair was mussed, his collar open, and one of the buttons on the fly of his Levi's was undone.

I'd set up the Fidelity 3000 on the kitchen table; Art had commandeered the coffee table for his Ace, and the little desk in my room had been taken up by my Apple, but I'd relocated it to the kitchen table around 10 p.m. as an adjunct system.

"That," I said, "is a Fidelity Computing 3000: 64K of RAM, twin 170K floppies, eight-color VDT and, uh, that." I pointed at the printer, which was half buried under a mountain of crumpled paper left over from several jams.

He dragged over a chair and sat down at the keyboard, which

he prodded as he stared blearily at the screen. "What's with all the crosses?" he said, eventually.

"It's in Catholic mode."

"Catholic?"

"Mode," I said. "Other supported modes: Judaism and Latter-day Saints."

"You're fucking with me," he said. "I am not that drunk."

"Seriously. If I hadn't seen the whole setup with my own eyes, I wouldn't believe it."

"Do you have a pot of coffee on?"

"I drank it."

"I'll make another one. I want to hear this."

Art had choice words for SPREADSHEET.

"Brother, I hate to tell you this, but you are not going to be able to get *anything* done with this hunk of junk. I mean, I've seen some terrible software in my day, but—"

"I know. That's why I brought out the Apple. I thought maybe I could somehow read the data off these floppies, maybe write a program to convert the files to Lotus. Remember when we did that for all my VisiCalc files?"

Making the switch from VisiCalc to Lotus had been a *lot* of work, but so worth it. Three of the Newbury Street Irregulars had pitched in to help write a program to do the conversions, and afterward we'd written an article about it for *Creative Computing*. Nick Cassidy III had ordered me and Art not to put our names on it. He didn't want to get in trouble with the VisiCalc people.

"That's what I'd do. Have you tried it?"

"Yeah, that's what's been keeping me up. These floppies are really screwed up. I can't read them with any of my Apple utilities. I decided I'd try to tear apart the Fidelity disk format, so I tried formatting a blank disk in the Fidelity and it kept rejecting it."

Art sipped his coffee. He was only half sober but he was still better at this stuff than I would ever be. He went to his bedroom and came back with a big plastic floppy-disk organizer. He flipped through it until he came to some fresh, blank disks at the back. He stuck one in the Fidelity and went into the UTILITIES menu, then chose FORMAT DISK, then watched as the NO DISK IN DRIVE error popped up.

"Those crosses are really distracting," he said, removing the disk and holding it under the light. He put it in one of my Apple's floppy drives and verified that he could format it there.

It was a joy to watch Art troubleshoot the problem. He selected a couple of disks from CF's evidence box and put them in one of the drives on his Apple clone, then tried a series of utilities on them. We had all kinds of funny programs, ones designed to defeat all the copy-protection crap that commercial software companies used, which got in the way of making backups and sharing promising programs around to friends and fellow hackers. I watched as he swapped in a progression of ever-more-hardcore utilities, until his screen was full of nothing but hexadecimal notation.

"What's that?" I asked.

"Raw sector data," he said. "Look at this—" He pointed to a long string of zeroes, scrolling down to show me how far down it went. "This disk is damaged, all those sectors are gone—unreadable and unwritable."

"Shit," I said. "Well, no wonder you can't read from it."

"Yeah," he said. He flipped open the floppy drive's latch and pulled the disk out, returned it to its envelope, and pulled another one, sliding it in and closing the latch again. He reloaded his utility and we waited while the drive's read head farted its way through the first 40K of data on the disk, then the next, and the next and—

"There it is again," he said, tapping the screen with his forefinger. He grabbed for my little steno notebook and pen and scribbled the offset where the damage started. "I think that's the same as the other disk." He swapped them again. Confirmed it. Grabbed another disk. Same. Another. Same.

"Those demented fucks. They're damaging the disks *at the factory*."

It was coming up on 4 a.m., so it took me a minute for this to sink in. "Why would they do that? That would mean that only people who own Fidelity computers could use their blank disks. They're cutting themselves off from, like, ninety-nine percent of the users in the world."

Art was now completely sober and wired tight on a full pot of coffee, practically vibrating, his eyes bulged and red. He was a hacker apparition, fierce and sleepless and glowing with technological mastery. For a moment, he reminded me of my dad, back when I was little and it seemed like there was nothing he couldn't do. An unstoppable force. "No they are *not*, my friend. They're not locking other users out of their products. *They're locking their users into their products.* They've built a whole system—if you've got their computer, you *have* to use their floppy drives. If you have their floppy drives, you *have* to use their floppies.

"That's why none of my blank disks would work on that hunk of junk: it's checking to see if the disk has been damaged and if it's not damaged, the drive refuses to read it." He said so many fuck-words, more than I'd ever heard before, like a Latin student in full declension. "It's brilliantly stupid." He stared off into space. "I bet I could fix it."

"I bet you could," I said. "I mean, conceptually—"

"Yeah. It's not hard. Just a lot of tedious assembly-level work on the drivers. But I can do it. I will. Why not? I'll give it away as shareware so these religious yokels can get their data off their God Boxes."

"I think Fidelity Computing might not approve of that. Remember why they hired me? They're not the live-and-let-live kind."

"Not even the turn-the-other-cheek kind, for that matter. Fine, I won't release it as shareware until you get paid. Then you'll be fat and happy and when they try to hire you back to ruin my ass, you won't need the money."

"I would never narc you out, buddy. Seriously, though: if you can help me export all that data to an Apple system, even if you don't convert it to Lotus, it would make my life a *lot* easier. I'd cut you in for a share of the proceeds."

He waved me off. "I'd do it for the intellectual challenge. First thing tomorrow. I don't have any work for at least a week. I was planning to spend it hacking on this fun graphics problem I've been thinking about, but I'm intrigued at the thought of pitting my wits against these cultists' programmer-drones."

We both stood up and stretched and yawned. The sky was growing light through the living room window. The table was covered in coffee cups and disks and notes. "Ugh," I said, looking at the carnage. "I'm gonna clean this up before I sack out."

"I'll help," he said.

"No," I said. "Honestly, you've done so much. Go sack out. You've earned it."

"It's nothing," he said. "I live here, too. Living in a pigsty is bad for your sense of self-worth."

Art was the best roommate I ever had, honestly. What a guy. I was washing out the coffeepot in the kitchen when he called out, "Son of a *bitch*!"

I rushed back into the living room to find him holding a crumpled snake of printer paper up to the light, laughing maniacally.

"What is it?" I said.

"Come here," he said. "Come look at this."

I stood beside him and peered up at the paper.

"I decided I'd unjam your printer for you. I think I spotted the reason for the jam. Can you see it?"

I squinted and stared until my eyes burned. "Art, I don't—"

"Look at the edges," he said.

I looked. It was continuous-feed printer paper.

The edges of the paper were perforated strips that could be torn off the paper after it had run through the printer. The strips had a row of regular holes, which allowed the sheets to be pulled through the printer by wheels of plastic spikes on either side of the platen.

Nine times out of ten, the thing that jammed a printer was a problem with this hole-and-spike arrangement, so I was used to seeing paper that was crumpled from the edges inward. What was different about this paper? If Art could see it, I could. I stared.

"Do you see it?" he asked. He was still chuckling.

"I give up," I said. "We both know you're the smart one and I'm the pretty one, so why don't you just fill me in?"

He snorted and pointed to the holes. "You see how some of these are torn at the edges? And how there are these dents where the spikes missed the holes altogether? Marty, *they've got their own stupid paper and they spaced the holes out differently.* You can't use standard paper in one of these things, and the paper you buy from Fidelity won't work in anyone else's printer. These people! Holy shit. I mean, *holy shit.*"

I shared his surprise and disgust. It was a remarkable hell of a thing, to design a whole computer system so that everything was locked to everything else.

"Sir, I present to you: my clients."

"Yeah," he said. "Yeah. Yikes. Well, everyone's gotta work for someone, I guess." He crumpled up the paper. "You'd better ask them to send over a box of printer paper, though."

"When I've gotten a few hours' sleep," I said, and put myself to bed.

It took a full day for Art to write the floppy-disk routines. I got groceries, cooked lunch, and picked up a box of printer paper from the Colma Fidelity warehouse. Then I spent two more days just figuring out how to convert SPREADSHEET files into Lotus 1–2–3 files, not so much pitting my wits against Fidelity's programmers' incredible obfuscation skills so much as deciphering the cack-handed, crude format they'd pieced together.

It wasn't exactly surprising. Looking at someone else's code was like looking under the rug where they swept their dirty secrets, because every programmer has eventually hit a wall where they can't be bothered to find an elegant solution so they go for the brute-force treatment. It could certainly *feel* like the person whose creation you were wrestling with had it in for you, but it was almost always the case that they were just being frail and foolish human beings.

(Years later, Robert Hanlon submitted "Hanlon's razor" to the Jargon File: "Never attribute to malice that which is adequately explained by stupidity." Like most of the Jargon File's most memorable entries, it caught on because every hacker knew it was true.)

Once I had the format down and had written a reliable converter, it took another day of shuffling floppies to get all the data into Lotus, and then a half day to catalog all the files. I ended up with a second binder full of that odd printer paper, just listing the contents of all those disks.

By now I was four days into the project and had eaten through all the frozen food I'd bought for the sprint. Art was back on a job and I was working mostly from the desk in my room, the Fidelity 3000 a forgotten paperweight on our kitchen table, taking up one of the four placemats (even when Art had a boyfriend over, we never needed more than three).

It was early on the morning of day four—9 a.m., a mere four hours after I'd gotten to bed—when my phone started ringing. I padded into the living room in boxers and a tee, noting that Art's shoes were gone and concluding I was alone in the house (which explained why he hadn't answered it).

"Morning?" I said, trying not to sound like I was still asleep.

"Mr. Hench?" I recognized the voice, but couldn't place it.

"Yeah," I said. "This is he."

"Mr. Hench, it's Shlomo Spinka, Rabbi Finkel's assistant."

"Oh yeah," I said. "Hi, Shlomo."

"Mr. Hench, the Reverend Sirs are hoping for a progress update on your work on those files. Their lawyers have upcoming filing deadlines if they are to proceed with the case, and much will depend on how your work is going."

I yawned. "Slow, Shlomo. It's been slow. To be honest, all I've done so far is transfer the files into a more powerful spreadsheet program, Lotus, and catalog them. That's taken about fifty hours over the past four days, not counting the ten hours that my outside specialist spent working on floppy drivers so we could get the data off those disks in the first place."

There was a chilly silence on the line.

"Mr. Hench—" Shlomo began, then he stopped and took an audible breath. "Mr. Hench, I don't want to tell you how to do your business, but I can say for a fact that neither the Reverend Sirs nor Fidelity Computing anticipated that you would engage in any kind of technical espionage as part of this contract—"

"Wait a second there, Shlomo, just hold on. 'Technical espionage'? I just did some basic reverse engineering, man, and I did it so that I could inspect all this data with mature, modern tools. It wasn't easy, but it also wasn't rocket science. And I did it for you people. It's not like I've released a shareware conversion tool." *Though I do know someone who might.* I didn't say it.

He breathed some more.

"Shlomo, I want to do this job. To do it, I need good tools. The tools you guys make, they're for people keeping books, small businesses. They're not up to this job. That's fine. You're not in the forensics business. It's no slight on your products that they're not useful for me here. I mean, if I was keeping books"—*I would use anything but SPREADSHEET, but no need to say it*—"I wouldn't go through all of this rigamarole." *Technically true, because I would just start out with a decent machine running real software.*

He sighed. "All right, Mr. Hench. I'm sorry if I sounded snappish. This is an area of some commercial sensitivity for us, you understand."

"I understand." *I understand that if I went into business making floppies or drives or printer paper or whatever, I could cut into the fat margins your Reverend Sirs are shearing from their flocks.*

"It sounds like you've arrived at a point where you can start to dig into the records. With that in mind, do you think you could provide a memo detailing your progress and estimated time for conclusion by, say, tomorrow about this time?"

"I could, but it would take me most of the day to produce that estimate and put the whole project another day behind. What's more important to you, a progress report, or actual progress?"

"We need both, Mr. Hench. I understand that there's only one of you, so all I can ask is that you work as diligently and as quickly as you can. The Reverend Sirs *do* need an estimate to inform their tactical discussions with the lawyers. A memo by nine tomorrow would be very helpful for that. The law firm is sending over its team for ten."

I held my hand over the receiver and sighed. "All right, Shlomo, I'll slip something through the mail slot before nine tomorrow."

"Though the mail slot?"

"I'm in nocturnal mode. Fewer distractions. And I won't have to fight traffic at two or three in the morning."

"I see. Thank you, Mr. Hench. I appreciate your flexibility and we're all looking forward to reading your memo."

I scribbled a note to myself so I wouldn't forget and went back to bed. The sheets were still warm and my pillow was so soft. I dreamed of spreadsheet cells linked with elegant formulas, changes rippling through complex data structures. It was a good dream, one of my favorites, and I was right in the thick of it when the phone woke me up again.

The bedside clock showed a little after 10:30 a.m. I had to start taking the phone off the receiver before bed. This was ridiculous.

I cleared my throat to get the sleep out of it and answered the phone. "Hello?"

"Hello." It was a woman's voice. Young, I thought. "I'm looking for Martin Hench." Nervous, or angry, or both.

"That's me," I said, and stretched the phone cord so I could lie out on the sofa. It was so bright in the living room. I needed to pee.

"Mr. Hench," the woman said. "This is Elizabeth Taylor."

"I'm pretty sure it isn't," I said. "I know what she sounds like, and you don't sound like her."

"I've heard that joke before. This is Elizabeth Amelia Shepard Taylor, Mr. Hench. I'm one of the cofounders of CF. I believe you have heard of us?"

My pulse jumped and my hands got sweaty and I *really* had to pee. "Sorry, Miss Taylor. Of course." I swallowed. For me, Elizabeth Taylor and Rivka Goldman and Sister Maria-Eva had been abstractions. I'd mentally taken to calling them Three Foolish Women, a little joke on Fidelity Computing. It didn't seem very funny now that I was talking to one of them. I had the irrational conviction that Elizabeth Taylor knew about my stupid joke. "How can I help you?"

She clicked her tongue. "Honestly? You can help me by knocking off what you're doing now. We're not going to sell out to Fidelity under any circumstances, but from what I hear, you're good enough at your job that you might produce some ammunition that could hurt us. That would be unfortunate, because we're on the side of the angels here."

I sat up. I *really, really* needed to pee. "Can you give me a moment?" I asked. We had an extra-long cord and I could have taken the phone into the bathroom with me but I wasn't confident of my ability to pee quietly.

"Of course," she said. Her voice wasn't nervous anymore. It was frosty. I put the receiver under a sofa cushion and dashed for the bathroom, closing the door to further muffle the sound. A few moments later, I dug the receiver out and put it back to my head.

"Sorry about that," I said.

"I take it you were calling your employers on another line," she said. "Mr. Hench, I don't think there's anything else to discuss, given—"

"Wait, wait," I said. "I don't have another line." I swallowed. "To tell you the truth, I was, uh, in the bathroom."

A long silence. "I see," she said. "Well, I suppose that is reasonable enough."

"I'm not making that up," I said. "I mean, if I was going to make something up, I'd be a lot more imaginative. Truth was I pulled an all-nighter and you got me out of bed and I always have to go first thing and—"

"I understand, Mr. Hench. No need to paint a picture." Another silence. "Look," she said, and now she sounded younger and less sure of herself. "Look. We know what's going on with you and the *Reverend Sirs*"—spat like a curse; Father Marek himself couldn't have put any more bile into it. "We have friends inside the company, naturally. We aren't the only ones who hate that racket and are ashamed to have played a part in it. We're

just the first ones who left and made it stick. They have powerful ways to keep people inside the church, as it were."

"Miss Taylor—"

"It's Ms., actually."

"*Ms.* Taylor," I said, rolling my eyes, because I was a dope
back then. "I think I have an inkling of what you're talking
about. I mean, at least some of it. But all I'm doing is finding
the facts and reporting them back to my client. I don't make
or enforce the laws. If you think the facts exonerate you, then
nothing I do will hurt you. If the facts show that you're on the
wrong side of the law, then that's not my fault, is it? I'm just a
technician here. I'm extracting and presenting data that you
turned over. If I don't do it—"

"*Mr.* Hench, please. From what I hear, you've figured out
how to extract the data from Fidelity's awful formats and put
them into a *real* program. That's a major technical feat. Fidelity
has some technical staff who could manage the technical side
of that job, but a) they don't want those people to see our books,
and b) none of those people could do the accounting part. You
may not be unique in the world, but you're darned close to it,
and your choice to work with those *very* Reverend Sirs has con-
sequences. Not just for us, but for the people whose lives they've
tied up in knots—the suckers they've got on their hooks. You
may think you know what's going on here, but I assure you, it's
far worse than you imagine. I understand that you are planning
to hand them a preliminary report early tomorrow morning.
Don't you think you owe it to your conscience to meet with us
before you make that irrevocable step?"

I closed my eyes and saw Lucille's lopsided smile. Had I been
listening with all the sincerity and ardor that she'd taught me?
Not really. I'd taken a big mental step back as soon as I'd figured
out who I was speaking to and what she wanted from me. It was
self-defense. I'd already figured out that my clients weren't the
nicest people in the world. Whatever she was calling to tell me,

it wasn't going to make me feel better about this job. I thought of Lucille again and made myself review our conversation and really listen. Part of me knew that if I didn't listen hard now, I'd have to do it later, every night, as I tried to fall asleep.

"If I meet with you," and I heard her suck breath. As nervous as I felt, she was ten times worse, and the steadiness of her voice was tribute to her inner strength. I didn't want to like this woman but I was already starting to. "If, Ms. Taylor. If I meet with you, I will not violate anything in my contract with Fidelity Computing. That means I won't disclose anything I promised to keep to myself in the nondisclosure agreement and I won't withhold any facts they've paid me to discover. Facts are facts, and if they're true you should have nothing to fear."

Listening to my own voice with the intensity that I had learned from Lucille, I heard the person I was trying to be: professional, responsible, dispassionate. Competent, above all else. Everyone I knew was more talented than me. The other Newbury Street Irregulars had all managed to juggle their passion for computers and their GPAs and had graduated with math or physics or electrical engineering degrees. Art was a thousand times the hacker I'd ever be. Even Nick Cassidy III had managed to build his terrible, failing business on *my* labor, and trap me in a noncompete agreement for good measure. What did I have? A two-year associate's degree in accounting—accounting, for chrissakes!

Of course, I also had this contract with Fidelity Computing. A contract that let me feel like someone of significance. Someone whose work could alter the world. Someone with a unique skill set. That's what Elizabeth Taylor had said, wasn't it? *You may not be unique in the world, but you're darned close to it.*

"I'm sure you'll do what you need to do," she said.

What I had taken for frostiness was despair. I heard that now.

I took the address—in the middle of San Francisco, a city I'd barely ventured into apart from some tourist sightseeing in the first couple of weeks, which I stopped once the accounting work started coming in. She said they'd expect me after 1 p.m., when they wrapped up the staff lunch break.

I got in the shower and then went hunting for clothes that were as serious as this new identity I was hoping to cultivate.

3

I ended up in jeans and a white shirt with the top button undone, and a blazer that covered up the spaghetti-sauce stains on the shirtsleeve. I hoped it wouldn't be too hot in the city, as those stains were worse than I remembered.

The CF offices were in a neighborhood called "the Mission," which I'd heard was a rough part of town. I carefully mapped out a route to it before leaving, using the big street atlas that Art bought when he arrived in the Bay Area. My trip would take me through the Castro, a neighborhood I *had* visited, one night when Art talked me into going out with a bunch of his friends to gay dance clubs. It had been uncomfortable at first, but after a couple of drinks and a couple of sneaky poppers in the bathroom, I'd gotten into the swing of things. A couple of guys propositioned me but everyone took no for an answer. It had been a hell of a memorable night, the first time I'd gotten a sense of what Art had gone through before he'd come out, how much he'd had to keep hidden from his friends. I also learned that he was a hell of a dancer, and also that I wasn't as bad a dancer as I'd thought.

The Castro by day was a lot tamer, almost the opposite of its nighttime aspect, when all the shop windows were dark and all the clubs were lit up. By day, it was a strip of boutiques—florists, bookstores, clothing stores, gift shops—being patronized by well-dressed men and women with short hair and variations on a uniform of jeans or overalls, lumberjack shirts, and the odd biker jacket or fringed buckskin jacket.

I turned east on Eighteenth Street and went over one of those hills that you see in movies about San Francisco, past a multi-block-long park, past a stately, columned church, and then I found myself in the Mission. It reminded me a little of downtown Tijuana, half remembered from boyhood visits, growing up in San Diego. Lots of Hispanic people going in and out of stores with Spanish signs: groceries, clothing stores, bookstores. Like a south-of-the-border transposition of the Castro, but visibly poorer, with more check-cashing places and boarded-up storefronts. As I turned down Mission Street itself, I drove past restaurants, rodeo clothing stores, places selling confirmation and wedding dresses, storefront churches, lots of panhandlers, and a string of giant, faded movie palaces with tall vertical marquees.

One of these turned out to be the headquarters of CF, something that Ms. Taylor had neglected to mention, so I ended up circling the block twice, squinting for street numbers, before I figured it out. I had to circle the block twice more before I found parking. I locked up the car and stepped out. A young woman with a dirty face and dirty clothes approached me and offered to sell me sex. When I turned her down, she asked me for a cigarette. I told her I didn't smoke and she asked me for money, telling me she hadn't eaten in days. I believed it: she was skeleton thin, and was missing a few teeth. Blood crusted around her nostrils. I gave her a dollar. She peeked in my wallet and demanded to know why it wasn't a five. I put my wallet in my front pocket and walked away, feeling awful about the whole thing.

In the short block-and-a-half walk to the former Plaza Cinema, I was panhandled twice more and two people tried to sell me crack. I tuned them out. San Francisco had more panhandlers than anywhere I'd ever been—even Tijuana. I had a vague sense that there was something political going on behind it, but I didn't quite remember the details. Something to do with Ronald Reagan, I knew that much. Everything was something to do with Ronald Reagan in those days.

The marquee letters on the Plaza spelled out COMPUTING FREE-DOM. I'd missed that when I was looking for the place, too focused on street numbers to check out the marquees of the dead movie theaters.

Elizabeth Taylor met me at the theater doors: big glass doors that had been reinforced with steel mesh. The doorframes were painted magenta.

She was a short woman, with a big, round, apple-cheeked face and blond hair that was almost colorless, parted in the middle and gathered into a long braid that came halfway down her back. She was broad and athletic, with a hard grip and short fingernails, in matching jeans and denim jacket over a western shirt with pearl snaps.

"Mr. Hench."

"Marty," I said. Remembering our earlier conversation, and my father's endless drills on the need to treat women with formal distance: "Ms. Taylor."

"Liz is fine," she said, and led me inside.

The lobby had been turned into a loading zone. The snack bar and popcorn machines had been torn out and stacked up against the lobby wall between the bathroom doors, and the lobby had been filled with metal shelving filled with cardboard boxes of all sizes, shipping labels out.

"Thank you for coming down," she said. She still had that icy-scared tone, and I saw her hands shake before she took one in the other and clasped them over her stomach. "Please, come to the office; it's through the factory."

The factory turned out to be the old auditorium, which was filled with music and people—mostly women, with dark shining hair and dark skin. Two out of every three rows of seats had been torn out and replaced with worktables, their downslope

legs chocked up with black rubber wedges. Each workspace had
its own Anglepoise lamp and power strip. The women bent over
their work and nodded their heads to the music. I heard fast
Spanish, laughter, chatter, under the bright lights and rotating
ceiling fans.

Two of the women were joined in intense conversation, and Liz
paused to check in on them. They were bent over a deconstructed
floppy drive with its logic board exposed, and Liz joined in in
Spanish, confirming the contact points on the board. The women
nodded and smiled and said, "*Exactamente.*"

Liz straightened up. "This way."

Down to the screen and then around it, into a maze of dark
corridors and then into a converted storeroom. The office was
three chipped desks, each with a multifunction phone and a
squeaky wheeled chair, each with an outsized, caseless PC and
a monitor.

The other two women looked up from their seats when I
entered, fingers still poised over their keyboards. It was easy to
tell which one was Rivka and which was Sister Maria-Eva, even
if the latter wasn't in her nun's habit.

Rivka wore a kind of white kerchief I associated with Orthodox women, her hair contained in a net behind her neck.
She had a narrow face and lips, and a long, narrow nose that
reminded me of the faces I'd seen on oil portraits in museums. It
was a focused, serious face. One look at her and I was convinced
I wouldn't be able to bullshit her, even a little.

Sister Maria-Eva wore her dark hair short, and her eyes were
large and luminous above her high cheekbones. She wore a
small gold cross over her white turtleneck, framed by the top
button of her wheat-colored knit cardigan. She looked at me
with something between sorrow and anger, pursing her lips.

Liz slid behind her desk and gestured to one of the folding
chairs leaning against one of the scrawl-covered whiteboards
that lined the walls. I unfolded it and sat at the narrow end of

the four-pointed diamond formed by the three desks and my hot seat. Three formidable women, all young like me, looked me up and down frankly, assessing me, judging me. My job was to destroy these women, to force them back into the Reverend Sirs' arms. They had a factory floor that throbbed with merriment and music. Fidelity Computing had a boiler room of hissed conversations and ducked heads. What the hell was I doing with my life?

Earning 25 percent of CF's future revenues, that's what.

This wasn't what I had in mind when I came out to Silicon Valley.

Sister Maria-Eva took me through the business plan.

"Fidelity Computing doesn't have customers, it has hostages. Take the printer: the serial connector looks like a slightly enlarged RS-232, but inside, there's a little board that swaps the first and last bit of each byte you send to the printer. Fidelity's printer driver swaps these bits before they're sent to the printer, and that connector unswaps them. Because this driver is always resident, you can't connect a Fidelity to a regular printer or it will print garbage. Likewise, because the printer is expecting swapped bits, you can't connect it to anyone else's computer or again, garbage.

"One of our first products was a dongle that clips between that RS-232 and any printer, which unswaps the bits in each byte; that means you can connect any printer to your Fidelity. Fidelity's printers are terrible, three-year-old surplus Okidata ML-80s they put in a custom case and sell for twice the price of a decent new printer, even though all this stupid bit-twiddling slows them down from eighty characters per second to sixty.

"Our dongle lets you use any printer with your Fidelity, and if you toggle a DIP switch, it runs in reverse, letting you use a Fidelity printer with any PC. It may be a terrible, overpriced printer, but we want to make it as cheap as possible for people to leave the Fidelity cage, and if the thing that's keeping you from buying a used PC is the cost of buying a new printer, we want to take that off the table."

She offered me one of the dongles. I stood and took it from her, then retreated to my folding chair to examine it. "It feels solid," I said. "And the seams make a good seal. Too bad your logo is just a sticker, though. It'd be a lot more impressive if you had it stamped into the metal."

"More impressive," she said, compressing her lips in disapproval, "and more expensive. We'd have to charge more, and that would make it harder for our customers to afford it, and then more of them would stay stuck inside the Fidelity Computing prison, paying and paying and paying."

I shrugged. "Or maybe you'd attract more customers if you had a product that looked slicker."

"Our customers don't come to us because we're slick. They come because they're trapped and we offer to help them out. Our sales associates want to make an act of contrition for their role in ensnaring their communities in Fidelity Computing's ruse."

She delivered this in a mode I came to think of as High Nun, the voice she switched to when she was practically vibrating with righteousness. From anyone else, it would have been cornball amateur dramatics, but from her, it *blazed*.

"Okay, but if you want to offer immediate help to the poor suckers who bought those printers, you need to get them off Fidelity's stupid custom printer paper."

The three women shared a smile. Rivka rummaged in a stacked set of document trays on her desk and held something up to me. Again, I rose and took it: it was a plastic ring with rounded spikes.

"One of the first people we hired was a former Okidata repair technician; he found us a wholesaler who had compatible replacement tractor-feed assemblies." Her voice was soft and warm, her eyes liquid and compassionate. She punctuated her sentences with brief smiles. "The part is only eighty cents, but it's not easy to install. We're working on a video we can mail out on a VHS cassette along with the right tools. We think the cost of materials will come in under eight dollars, ten with shipping and packaging. We'll sell it for twenty, to cover the labor and video production."

I turned the plastic ring over in my hands. It was hard, die-cast plastic, a simple part with no moving pieces. Fidelity's version of the part would be practically indistinguishable. Somewhere, they had a factory where workers disassembled Okidata ML-80s and replaced this part, then put the printers back together, for the sole purpose of extracting profits from people who didn't know any better.

The first time I'd used a computer, that day at MIT when someone sat me down in front of an Altair 8800, the feeling was like when I was a kid and I'd push my bike up to the top of the tallest, steepest hill I could find, and then poise myself in the saddle, aiming back down the trail, knowing that the moment I cranked the pedal I would go hurtling down, white-knuckled and whooping, out of control and loving it, every part of my attention focused on steering as I sped up, faster, faster, faster.

The ensuing months had been one long hurtle down the slope, learning as fast as I could as I accelerated into a scream-ing run through programming, hardware, systems design . . . The experience of being both in and out of control, the joyous, stoned haze of all-consuming hunger to discover and master—culminating in finding my tribe of fellow all-consumed weirdos in a basement Newbury Street Irregulars meeting.

Computers were many things to me—frustration, delight, challenge, fetish. But above all, computers were a thing that I con-trolled. When a computer balked, it wasn't because it was refusing me, it was because I had failed to express myself clearly. A computer was a kind of "Sorcerer's Apprentice" machine: it would do whatever I asked of it, perfectly, until I told it to stop. If I expressed myself badly, it would carry out my badly phrased wishes forever (or until it ran out of memory, mass storage, or printer paper).

Fidelity Computing had built a computer that said no. A computer that would countermand your orders if they threatened the profits of the Reverend Sirs.

Holding that spiked plastic ring, like a punk-rock bracelet for a Cabbage Patch doll, I felt a wave of outrage and revulsion. The way Fidelity had rigged the game—it was sick. From the first time I'd touched a computer, I'd known I was touching the future. Someday, these things would be everywhere and we'd use them to do everything. Fidelity wanted that future, too, but in their version of it, the computers would give the orders, on behalf of greedy men like the Reverend Sirs, and the people would take them.

Right then and there, I realized I was going to have to switch sides.

CF had ambitious plans. They were retrofitting used floppy drives with EPROMs—cheap, programmable chips—that would cause them to register the telltale damaged sector that marked a disk as one of Fidelity's own, no matter where it had come from. They had a whole software division, working on an MS-DOS–compatible operating system that would run any Fidelity DOS application, and they were very interested in my SPREADSHEET–to–Lotus 1–2–3 conversion utility.

It took them a while to figure out that I'd come around to their cause. To me, the realization had been obvious, even inevitable. So obvious, in fact, that I forgot to mention the fact. When Liz Taylor took me through their software plans and I started to offer suggestions, she was taken aback, but Sister

Maria-Eva filled the gap with her own probing questions. Soon we were sketching on the whiteboard together, coming up with a menu-driven system I dubbed LIBERATOR, which would convert everything, all your data, and set it up on the standard applications the rest of the world used.

"Mr. Hench," she said, after we'd resolved a gnarly technical dispute about how to manage the file operations on a system with a single floppy drive, "can I ask you something?"

"Only if it's about something other than efficient RAM caching. We've established that you know more about that subject than I ever will."

She favored me with a grin that made her seem a lot younger. When she was doing High Nun, she projected age, a kind of Mother Superior gravitas. But when we got into tech, she could be one of the women in the Newbury Street Irregulars, another college kid with a tragic romantic obsession with semiconductors.

"It's not about caching. It's about your intentions."

Oh. "Oh."

"What are your intentions, Mr. Hench?"

I looked around at the whiteboards, the partially assembled hardware, the desks piled high with papers. The three women: Sister Maria-Eva, dark and stern; Liz Taylor, baby-cheeked and nervous; Rivka Goldman, long-faced and sorrowful. I realized that I'd been freaking them out, and that they had every right to feel that way.

"I'm sorry, ladies, I should have said something. I guess I got swept away in the moment. I'm not going to take any money from your Reverend Sirs. I mean, I can't, can I? We're obviously on the same side and they're obviously on the other side. How the hell could I keep working for them?" I swallowed. "Sorry about that 'hell,' I'm not sure if it's blasphemy or cursing, but—"

"You can say hell," Sister Maria-Eva said, and that wide smile came back. She had very square, very white, very small teeth and broad, full lips. It made her smile seem impossibly large, too big for her face, but in a friendly and kindly way. It was a smile you wanted to please. "You can say stronger words if you'd like. Lord knows I've been tempted. Our faith isn't yours, obviously, and I'd no more ask you to give up saying hell than I'd ask you to take Communion. We're on the same side, as you say. We three have already found a side to be on that isn't defined by our faith. How could it be?"

"Thank you," I said. "I'm sorry I didn't say something earlier, but—"

"Mr. Hench," Rivka said, her voice low but forceful. "Can you tell me what you mean about being on the same side? Forgive me for being particular about this, but a few hours ago, you were professionally engaged in our personal and commercial destruction."

Liz shot her a look, which Rivka coolly returned.

"Rivka—" Liz said.

"Liz," Rivka said. Her tone was even more stern than Sister Maria-Eva's most intense High Nun. "When we agreed to call Mr. Hench, I told you that I didn't like the idea. He's shown that he will work for bad people. Why should we believe he'll have integrity now?"

"We all worked for the same bad people, Rivka," Sister Maria-Eva said.

Rivka opened her mouth to reply, then shut it for a moment. "All right," she said. "All right, that's a good point. Mr. Hench, I'm sorry if this is off-putting, but our situation is precarious, our adversaries are powerful and cruel, and we have many people relying on us. Not just the workers out there, but the people whom Fidelity Computing has trapped in their nasty little scheme."

"I get it." I looked at her. Despite the stern tone, she was clasping her hands together hard enough to turn her knuckles white. These women were in trouble. "Really, I do. Look, a couple days ago, I hadn't heard of you *or* Fidelity Computing. I took the job because it looked like a technical challenge and it paid well. I didn't realize that the major technical challenge would come from the janky, fuggly computers those guys are peddling. Your shop here, the things you're doing to help people with computers . . ."

I shrugged. "Let me put it this way, and I'm not trying to be funny or anything, this is not a joke about your, uh, faith. Getting people using computers, giving them the power to do more, and do it together, it's, well, *holy*. I want to make a world where everyone who wants to can change their lives the way I have. The Reverend Sirs want everyone to have a computer, too, but one that *they* control. I've read enough science fiction novels to know that a world where everyone uses computers for everything but a trio of religious maniacs have administrator access over all those computers is a *very bad world*." I clapped my hand to my mouth. "I'm sorry about the religious maniac thing. Seriously. Sorry."

Sister Maria-Eva gave me a very small smile. "That's all right, Mr. Hench. For what it's worth, I don't think the Reverend Sirs are particularly religious. If they have any faith, it's a highly selective one."

4

When you're twenty-one years old, breaking a contract seems like the easiest thing in the world. I got home from San Francisco around dinnertime, with a sack of cold, but still delicious-smelling, burritos I'd bought at a place between CF's converted movie theater and my parking spot.

I owed Shlomo a report the next morning by 9 a.m. If I was going to write it, I'd need to sit down and start work as soon as I got through the door, pound on the keyboard until 2 or 3 a.m., then drive to Colma and put it through Fidelity's mail slot.

Instead, I ate burritos. Art came home and changed into tight jeans and a Crisco T-shirt that we both laughed at. He ate half a burrito and listened with interest as I told him where I'd been that day and what I'd seen that day.

"That's the craziest Silicon Valley story I've heard yet," he said. "Those women sound like they're something else."

"Yeah," I said. "They're amazing. The Reverend Sirs made me feel like I was some kind of heathen, while those women were more like an ad for how religion can make you a better person."

He looked at his watch. "Dammit, I gotta go. I'm meeting some friends at a club." He wrapped up the rest of his burrito in foil and put it in the fridge. Even half eaten, it was a whole meal. "You wanna come?" He was always good like that, inviting me out to his clubs, making sure I felt included. Sometimes I said yes. It had been weird at first, but in those days, the weirdest thing was how weird it *had* been. "Wait, you've gotta write that report for tomorrow, right?"

"Uh, no," I said. "I'm not gonna do that. I'm not gonna do anything for those creeps."

"You're quitting?"

"I guess so. I'm not doing it, so that means I'm quitting. Plus, I think I want to help those women and their homebrew gadget factory. It's pretty clear to me that they're the Rebellion and Fidelity Computing are the Empire. It's not enough to reject Darth Vader, you've gotta grab a lightsaber and fight him, right?"

Art snorted and slapped me on the back. "When you put it that way, brother, it's a moral imperative. Just . . ." He trailed off. "Just be careful."

"Careful?"

"Like, you're hitting these guys in the wallet. They don't strike me as the shy, retiring types who'll take that lying down."

It was my turn to snort. "They're clerics, not fighters."

"What does that make you? A thief?"

"No, dude, I'm a magic-user."

He laughed. "Another programmer who thinks he's a wizard."

"Naw," I said. "You're a wizard. I'm just the guy who helps with the spellbook."

He left. I finished my burrito. On my way to the kitchen to throw out the foil, I looked at the monstrous purple Fidelity 3000 and its peripherals on our kitchen table. I'd have to give that one back.

Later.

The burrito had given me the torpor, and all my missed sleep was catching up with me. I went to bed. A moment later, I got up and took the phone off the hook, then went back to bed. I was asleep in seconds.

I woke the next day with a feeling of great freedom and moral clarity, and a half-digested burrito still in my stomach. It was past noon, and Art was already gone for the day. He'd left the phone off the hook. I scrounged in the fridge while I brewed coffee and found Art's half-burrito leftover stump and decided it could keep the one working its way through my guts company.

I put it in the toaster oven and pushed down the "toast" lever a couple of times in a row until it was warm (on average— scalding on the outside, still cold in the center). I wrapped it in a dish towel and puttered around the apartment, tidying things away and bagging up the kitchen garbage.

Moving in with Art after a couple of years as roommates back east was the easiest thing in the world: we'd just picked up our old division of labor, though I'd been letting my chores slide while I crunched on the Fidelity contract. Another reason to be glad about quitting.

I forced myself to get my bankbook and my checkbook out of the side table in my bedroom and put them down on my office desk beside my computer. I'd also been slack about keeping my own financial spreadsheets up to date, and a little nagging voice in my head had been growing more insistent on the subject ever since I'd decided not to take Fidelity's money.

I fired up my Apple][+ and propped open my bankbook with a stapler and got ready to face the music, and that's when the phone rang. I'd absently returned the receiver to the cradle when I had been tidying up.

I looked at it and looked at it. It rang and rang. It could have been anyone—my dad, the landlord, the Publishers Clearing House sweepstakes—but I knew it was Shlomo.

I stared at the phone. It wasn't a sturdy Western Electric number like the one we'd had bolted to the kitchen back in Boston: it was a beige touch-tone phone I'd bought at Radio Shack the week I'd arrived, after a couple of hours perusing the shelves and exploring the exotic SKUs of the West Coast Shack. It had an electronic ringer, piercing as an alarm clock. Every time it rang, I thought about going back to Radio Shack and seeing if

I could figure out what components I'd need to make it sound less sinus-piercing.

It was ringing now, and not stopping.

Fuck it. I was twenty-one years old. An adult. I wasn't gonna duck this guy's call.

"Martin Hench," I said as I put the phone to my head. It was the first time I'd ever done that, answered with my name instead of an all-American "Hello?" I liked it. It sounded confident. Like a private eye (or my dad). Even better would have been to just say, "Hench." One syllable. Forceful.

"Mr. Hench?"

"This is Hench," I said. I *really* liked the sound of that.

"Mr. Hench, this is Shlomo Spinka of Fidelity Computing."

I sat down on the sofa, stretched out my legs, and crossed my ankles. "Shlomo, how can I help you?"

"We were expecting your report by nine a.m. today. Was there some problem?" He sounded brusque.

"There's no problem, Shlomo."

"Then when can we expect the report, Mr. Hench? Our attorneys are hanging fire on it. This delay represents a significant legal expense and business risk." He sounded pissed.

"I don't see how that's any of my business, Shlomo."

"I beg your pardon?" He sounded nervous.

"I said, it's not any of my concern. I don't work for Fidelity Computing. I decline to complete the contract."

"Mr. Hench, this is quite unprofessional—" More nervous now.

"Don't worry, I won't bill you for the work to date."

"That's not my concern, Mr. Hench. You were contracted to—"

"I've changed my mind. Something better came along."

"Something—" Scared now. Definitely scared. The Reverend Sirs were not going to like this. "Mr. Hench, we were expecting a report on your progress today. If there's been some problem—"

"No problem, Shlomo. Here's the report. I have made no

progress. I will make no progress. Report ends." I was actually enjoying this. I should have racked the phone hours ago. Quitting a job was *amazing*. I couldn't wait to tell the CF girls about it. They were gonna love it.

"Mr. Hench." His voice turned husky now. "I don't think you appreciate the gravity of this situation. You have a legal duty to this firm, you signed a contract. We have remedies in the event of the breach of that contract."

"Oh, I know," I said. "I read it carefully. If I'm in breach of the contract, I'm supposed to return all the money you've paid me to date. That won't be a problem, seeing as how I haven't billed you yet. As I recall, I have forty-eight hours to return your equipment. You can have a courier come and get it anytime. I'll give you the address. Do you have a pen?"

"Mr. Hench, this is a very serious matter. I urge you to think about your actions carefully and govern yourself accordingly."

I made a note of that phrase, "govern yourself accordingly." It was a good one.

"Oh, Shlomo, I've thought about this very carefully. You just give me a ring when you're ready to pick up this computer, all right?"

"You will hear from me, Mr. Hench, I assure you of that." Shlomo had a kind of nasal, high-pitched voice, not so different from Art's to tell the truth, but when Art spoke, it was sarcastic and smart. Being upbraided by Shlomo was like being beaten about the head and shoulders with a Nerf bat. They should have gotten Father Marek to make the call. He could turn your bowels to water with a single phrase.

"Let me know when you're coming to get the computer, okay?"

The silence stretched on so long that I thought he'd hung up. I was about to do the same when I heard him draw a shuddering breath and let it out in a shaky puff. The line went dead. I pictured him sitting at one of the desks in that buzzing, hushed cubicle farm at Fidelity, trying to intimidate me down a phone, thinking of how the Reverend Sirs would react once he passed on the news.

I felt bad for the guy.

I balanced my checkbook and updated my spreadsheets, took a shower and got dressed. There were new issues of *Dragon, Creative Computing,* and a new magazine that Art had subscribed to after finding an issue at the health food store, *CoEvolution Quarterly,* put out by the same people who did the *Whole Earth Catalog.*

I thumbed through each. An article in *Dragon* delivered four pages of technical notes on designing monsters that were consistent and challenging.

I clipped an ad from *Creative Computing* for an Apple program called "Tax Manager" out of Illinois that promised to automate tax filing, wondering if I could do the same thing with some ambitious Lotus 1–2–3 formulas, and if so, whether I could take out an ad in *Creative Computing* and compete with these Tax Manager jokers. Thumbing further, I found an ad for something called a "Logo Turtle" billed as a "cybernetic toy" that you programmed in "a language for poets, scientists and philosophers." I decided I liked whoever had written that ad.

I flipped through *CoEvolution Quarterly* without landing on anything—the article on farts looked promising but then I saw it was four pages long. A long feature on nonviolent warfare made my eyes glaze over.

Then, right at the end of the magazine, I landed on a short, odd little editorial called "Uncommon Courtesy." The author, Steward Brand, was a hippie icon I was moderately familiar with, and the essay was the kind of hippie thing I expected from him, about practicing kindness. It reminded me of the way Lucille made me feel. Then I came to the part where he proposed founding something called the "Peripheral Intelligence Agency," with three "injunctions":

1. Do good
2. Try stuff
3. Follow through

It was like I was a tuning fork that had just been struck and I couldn't stop vibrating. Do good. Try stuff. Follow through. I'd done plenty of the first two, but not much of the third, and somehow I'd never noticed that fact.

Those two words, in tiny type on cheap newsprint, changed my life, just as surely as my decision to listen to people the way Lucille did. In its own way, it was just as momentous an occasion as the first time I touched a computer.

I'd failed to follow through on MIT. I'd failed to follow through on Process Engineering Models. The accounting and bookkeeping jobs I'd found since I came west were all short-term arrangements, pinch-hitting for someone on vacation or helping with a one-off.

I'd even failed to follow through with Fidelity Computing. I mean, thank God (or whatever) that I had, but there it was.

I stood up. I paced. What was I going to do in this world, in this life, in this moment? All around me, I could see the beginning of a change as momentous as the Industrial Revolution. What was my role going to be? Spreadsheet jockey?

I needed to get out of the house. Art had taken his van that day. It was Friday and he was going to go clubbing in the Castro. He'd told me I was welcome. I could call him at work and ask him to pick me up, but it was only 1:30 p.m. I didn't want to spend the rest of the afternoon in the apartment, balancing my checkbook and packing up the piece-of-junk Fidelity 3000.

I studied the Caltrain schedule magneted to the fridge, did some mental math, and realized I had time for a quick shower and a bike ride to the Santa Clara Caltrain station, where I could get the 2:03 to the San Francisco station in Dogpatch. I sluiced under the shower, grabbed a clean pair of jeans and an MIT Science Fiction Society tee, and hit the door running, shoving all three magazines into my backpack with one hand and fumbling on my key ring for the bike-lock key with the other.

My second Mission burrito experience was even better than the first. I ordered cabeza, thinking sure, I'll gnaw a cow skull, can't be any worse than a hot dog. Turned out to be beef cheek and not brains, but I still gave myself points for adventurousness.

I washed it down with a Tecate and decided I liked it better than Corona, the only other Mexican beer I'd tried. I made a note to sample Dos Equis and Negra Modelo and figure out a favorite. A favorite Mexican beer felt like a pretty sophisticated, Californian thing to have.

Full of beans and cheeks and a little tipsy, I found I still had hours to go before it was time to meet Art in the Castro. Also, I needed to find a pay phone and call him to figure out those details.

But mostly, I just wanted to go back to CF. I wanted to follow through.

5

By the time she'd moved to San Jose to staff the Mission House, Elizabeth Amelia Shepard Taylor was already interested in the Equal Rights Amendment. That was extraordinary, because none of the women in her life—her mother and aunts, her teachers and her girlfriends' mothers—had a single kind word to say about the ERA.

They actually threw Phyllis Schlafly–watching parties at each other's houses, making an occasion of it with Jell-O salads and green bean casseroles. For many years, all that Elizabeth knew was that the ERA was wrong, wrong, wrong. She couldn't say what was wrong about it, but she knew it was bad. Something about tearing down God's calling for women to be mothers, which would lead them to neglect their families and break down the natural roles of men and women in the family.

Her first inkling that this might not be the whole picture came just a week after she moved into the Mission House in San Jose. It was a hurry-up-and-wait kind of assignment. Half her time was spent bailing out the Elders who were away from their mothers for the first time and were struggling to master the basics of laundry, cooking, hygiene, and managing interpersonal conflict (because she was the eldest of eleven, this kind of surrogate mothering came naturally to her). The other half of the time, she was alone in the Mission House, with nothing to do and no one to talk to.

Elizabeth Taylor was not a girl who would sit idle. She'd helped her mother with her prizewinning rose garden back in SLC, and the Mission House had a neglected bramble of old and thorny rosebushes, so she determined to rehabilitate them and so bring a riot of beauty into the Church's outpost in San Jose.

It was as she worked at this labor with tough gloves and a giant pair of shears that she'd sharpened to a guillotine's edge that she met her neighbor, a trim, well-turned-out young blond man with the *tidiest* mustache she'd ever seen. He called out to her over the fence.

"Oh, thank goodness someone is doing something about those poor roses! It was a form of abuse, really. I was ready to call the National Society for the Prevention of Cruelty to Angiosperms!"

Elizabeth had gotten an A+ in AP biology and knew that "angiosperm" was the scientific name for a flowering plant, but she blushed anyway.

"I'm doing my best," she said, with a game smile. "Please don't call the authorities on me just yet!"

He smiled—he had a great pair of dimples on the left side— and winked and said, "I'll give you two weeks, but after that I'll have to think of the flowers. I'm Zion William Menn, by the way. Your neighbor."

"Elizabeth," she said, shucking her glove and shaking his hand. He had nails so perfect they might as well have been manicured.

"Did you just get here?" he said. "I mean, to this—" He waved his hand at the Mission House. "The religious commune or whatever." Now *he* blushed. "Sorry," he said. "No offense. I just don't know much about—"

"That's okay," she said, sensing an opportunity. "I'd be happy to send one of the Elders to explain it if you'd like."

She could tell he wasn't enthusiastic about the idea. It was a feeling she was still getting used to. Back in SLC, she'd been in the majority, and Gentiles had been a curiosity. In her imagination, going on a mission—being in the minority for the first time—would be a contradictory mix of being persecuted for her faith (as years of Sunday school had insisted she was and ever would be) and also being welcomed as a redeemer amid the ignorant and damned.

The reality was different: the secular world wasn't hostile to her faith—it was indifferent. To the extent that Gentiles recoiled from missionary overtures, it was because the prospect of being lectured to by a teenager about God's will was profoundly *boring* and faintly embarrassing. They were embarrassed *on her behalf.* She'd have preferred to be the target of hurled curses and rocks.

"Sure," he said, "that would be nice." He was a well-brought-up young man, and with his faint southern accent, she could almost believe he wasn't lying to spare her feelings.

She gave a mighty hack at one tough rose branch and it came away clean. "There," she said, pretending away the awkwardness. "Got you!"

"I admire your zeal," he said.

"Well," she said, straightening and arching her back and arming sweat off her forehead, "I just got here and I'm still getting settled in. I thought I should make my mark on the place first thing, so the boys here know who's in charge."

"With those shears, they'll never doubt it," he said, and smiled. "Did you come from Utah?"

"Salt Lake City," she said. "My first time out of state."

"Well, let me know if I can give you any tips. I'm an old California hand."

"Have you been here long?"

He showed her that double dimple again. "Three weeks," he said, and laughed.

"Another greenhorn," she said. "It's nice to know I'm not the only one. Where'd you come from?"

"Florida," he said, and put on a funny voice: "You know, where they grow Miss Anita's *beautiful fruits.*" He laughed, and so did she, though she didn't get the joke right away.

Flustered, she blurted out, "Isn't Anita Bryant from Florida? We love her."

His look of shock and hurt only lasted for an eyeblink, and then his face became a mask of treacly sweetness. "Isn't that nice. Well, nice talking to you, hon." He turned to go.

"Wait!" she said. "Wait, please. What is it? I'm sorry, whatever it is—"

He turned back to face her, lips skinned back from his teeth, eyes dark and furious.

"Zion," she said, and it came out in a gasp. "Zion, I'm *sorry*. What did I say?"

He gave her a flat look that went on and on. "You didn't say anything. It's fine."

"No," she said. "Zion, I promise I'm not kidding. If I said something—"

"Look," he said, "you seem like a nice person, but Anita Bryant says people like me deserve to die of AIDS. If you love her, you want me to die. There's other ways I could say it, but that's the plain truth. I don't have any space in my life for nice people who want me dead."

"Oh," she said. "Oh." Something fluttered in her stomach, the place she thought of as her "moral center," whenever the subject came up in Sunday school. "Zion, I'm so sorry. I don't know why I said that. I *don't* love Anita Bryant. I don't even *like* her." And though she'd never let herself think that unthinkable thought, much less say those unsayable words, they were true. They *rang* with truth in the warm California air, perfumed by her sweat and the sap oozing out of the severed rosebush branches.

Zion couldn't hear the truth, evidently. He gave her a skeptical look. "Sure," he said. "No offense taken." He turned away again, starting for his house.

"Wait," she said. "Please." He turned around. He looked older now, or maybe it was just that he looked less open, less trusting. "Zion, I'm sorry for what I said. Where I come from—" She closed her mouth. She'd been about to say something about her family, her faith, her city, three things she loved and believed in more than anything else in the world.

Where had that come from? She shook her head, started over. "There are a lot of people—good people—who hear their own beliefs about the role of men and women in Mrs. Bryant's message. I want to be a good mother and a good daughter, and a *very* good Mormon, but I never liked the way Mrs. Bryant put it. It's just not something I was encouraged to talk about." *Or think about.*

He cocked his head. "Elizabeth, I hear what you're saying, but I don't think you've heard me. Yes, that Bryant woman has awful, disgusting ideas about women, but those filthy notions of hers are positively civilized compared to the things they have to say about men like me." He looked at her significantly. "You know," he said, with a sour smile. *"Faggots."*

His tone made her wince, but *faggot* actually made her flinch. "Oh," she said, again. "Oh." Again. "Zion, I'm so sorry. It's just that—Well, it's just that I've never met a homosexual befo—"

He laughed and she knew he was laughing at her. She didn't like how that felt. She would have shut down and said her good-byes but for what he said next. "Oh, honey," he said. "I *guarantee* I'm not the first homo you've met. I'm just the first one you know about."

And that about blew her mind.

Zion worked in real estate and played tennis. He baked zucchini bread and thought her Jell-O salads were simultaneously hilarious, disgusting, and delicious. He didn't have a boyfriend, but he was dating a couple of nice guys and he thought one of them might be boyfriend material. He was raised Methodist but now he thought he was spiritual, which he eventually admitted meant that he might believe in God but found church boring.

But also, he spent his Sundays visiting sick friends. He had a lot of sick friends. And all of his friends had a lot of sick friends, too. Their parents had disowned them, and their coworkers wouldn't visit them. The nurses wouldn't touch them. Sometimes the doctors, too.

Zion visited sick friends with food, and Elizabeth joined him and sometimes they brought Jell-O salad and sometimes they brought zucchini bread, and sometimes Zion would bake some skunky marijuana from his back garden into it, just to help with his sick friends' appetites.

Elizabeth had a lot of sickbed experience: her four grandparents had forty-six siblings among them, and there had always been someone on the verge of dying when she was growing up. Those sickrooms had been hushed and sorrowful and reverent, the silence broken by hissed arguments between her aunts and uncles about some quack remedy that someone insisted was just the thing for cancer.

Zion's friends had their share of quack remedies—sweetgrass and crystals featured heavily, as did macrobiotics—but that was where the resemblance ended. These skinny men with their facial lesions had beautiful laughs and told wicked jokes, and it was impossible to be offended by the crudity when it came out of the mouth of a dying man, wasn't it?

It was in these sickrooms that Elizabeth got exposed to gender politics for the first time, and while these men weren't above calling each other "bitches" and "whores"—always with a smile, mind—they also had a lot to tell her about the politics of sexuality, and that led her to the politics of sex, and that led her to the library, where she was as at home as she was at any old place, because when you're the eldest of eleven, the public library is more private than any room in your actual home.

And that was how she came to have a discussion with the local bishop about the Church's opposition to the ERA. That discussion turned into a shouting match (he started it, but she was not going to back down, because she'd been exposed to horrors that made a bishop's wrath seem tame by comparison).

After that, Elizabeth Amelia Shepard Taylor never had quite the same relationship with her God, her faith, or her church.

The burrito filled my belly in a way that nothing else I'd ever eaten had managed. It stuck to my ribs and filled my crannies. Sometime in the middle of puberty, maybe around the age of fifteen, I'd grown *hungry* in a way that no meal had ever quite managed to sate. The simple Mission burrito, the size and shape of a bazooka shell, finally filled the gap.

It was coming up on 4:30 p.m. when I rang the doorbell at the front of the old Plaza theater. Elizabeth Taylor—I would never get used to that, but "Elizabeth Ameila Shepard Taylor" was such a genealogical mouthful—answered, looking pleasantly surprised to see me.

She let me use her desk phone to call Art and arrange to meet him at Alfie's in the Castro at seven. Her desk was full of binders and of page proofs, marked up with highlighter and notes written in a looping, neat handwriting in blue ballpoint. I glanced at them a few times while I was on the phone with Art, then kept reading after I put the phone down. It was automatic, and I didn't even realize I was doing it until Liz cleared her throat.

I looked up and found her giving me a bemused look.

"Sorry," I said. "It's just pretty good reading, is all."

She cocked her head. "You're not joking, are you?"

"Not at all," I said. "I taught myself everything I know about computers, mostly from reading documentation." I gestured at the paperwork before me. "I wish it had been half as clear as this."

It was clearly the right thing to say. She beamed. "Well, you are clearly a very perceptive fellow, Martin Hench. When I got to Fidelity Computing, there was practically no documentation at all. I think the Reverend Sirs were worried that if they explained how everything worked, it would become clear how everything was also deliberately broken.

"But I was selling to these Mormon bishoprics filled with hardworking people who were just like my own family, and they were spending money they couldn't afford to get these machines, after seeing flashy demonstrations and hearing all kinds of promises from our reps, who were people they trusted, people they'd known all their lives.

"As soon as they got their computers, well, the reality sunk in. But none of these good people wanted to admit they'd been tricked, especially not by someone they trusted, so they blamed themselves, assuming they just weren't reading the instructions correctly. Eventually, they'd hit a wall and they'd call Fidelity Computing and some patient girl in the phone bank would have to explain things to them.

"A lot of those calls landed on my desk, because I understood things better than most of the girls, and then I started to type up my notes so that everyone would have a set of instructions they could use when it was their turn to get a call, just to get some of that work off my shoulders. The notes got passed around, and people would scribble on them and photocopy them and pass them around again. Eventually they'd land back on my desk and I'd incorporate all those notes into a new draft, based on the real problems our users had phoned in about and the difficulties the previous draft hadn't been able to solve.

"I don't know who first sent a set to a customer, but I got a call from my dad one day to say he'd just gotten a very blurry set, like an eleventh-generation Xerox, and he wanted to know if I could send him a new set. Of course, by then I'd shared my notes with the Catholic and Jewish sides, and they'd been translated into Spanish and Hebrew and Yiddish and were doing the rounds there, too.

"The Reverend Sirs didn't take the news well, not at first,

anyway. They always started from the proposition that anything their people did without asking them was a part of a plot to sabotage the company or take it over. They banned us from using those manuals and made providing a copy to any customer a firing offense. Managers used to walk around the bullpen, confiscating any copies they found and docking the girls' pay in punishment."

"You're kidding," I said. "That's insane."

She cocked her head. "I guess so, but honestly, it's not that unusual as bad boss stuff goes. I've seen a lot worse."

That made me squirm. "I haven't had much experience," I admitted. "The only real job I ever had was working for a doomed software company back east, where my boss was this hereditary shitbird whose daddy bankrolled the company. He was a terrible boss, but I assumed that was about his personal failings, not bossdom more generally. Since coming out here I've only worked short-term contracts, so I guess I missed the worst of it."

"You're lucky. There's plenty of worse boss stuff that's par for the course, and there's plenty more that's even worse that the Reverend Sirs get up to all the time." She sighed.

"So that was it for the manuals at Fidelity Computing?"

She smiled. "Oh no, not at *all*. Those manuals had become the lifeblood of the company. When customers had good documentation, they didn't need to call us all the time to solve their problems. When *we* had manuals, we could solve problems for the customers who didn't have them. It only took two weeks before the Reverend Sirs reversed course and gave us all our manuals back and put a guy in charge of producing an official manual, printed and spiral-bound, that they could sell at an additional charge. I wasn't allowed near the project." She sniffed.

"When we started CF, we knew we'd have to produce good manuals, because we just don't have the people to hold everyone's hands when they run into trouble."

"How'd you start CF? I mean, it must have been a pretty momentous occasion."

She looked at her watch. "I can only give you the short version now. The long version is . . . well, it's long. And messy. But the short version is, I wrote those original manuals, and that meant that I had to be able to understand the thinking that went into the computers and the software that Fidelity Computing was selling. I had to figure that out without their cooperation. I didn't know the phrase 'reverse engineering' back then, but that's what I was doing.

"So I always had these ideas, about how I'd do it if I was in charge, what I could make that would undo all the bad stuff they'd done. Some of it was just mistakes and some of it was downright malicious, but either way, I could always imagine a way to fix what they'd left broken. I guess I just wanted to get out of the documentation business—to make a better system, one that worked so well you didn't even *need* a manual."

I gestured at the papers on her desk. "I guess you've got a way to go."

She giggled. "It's a work in progress. But you'd be amazed at how little hand-holding people need when their computers are designed to be easy to use instead of easy to make money from."

"I'm sure," I said. There was an awkward pause. I became uncomfortably aware that she was an attractive woman and that I was a fundamentally lonely young man. I wondered if she was still religious, and if so, whether that meant that she wouldn't date a Gentile. Then I wondered about the professional ethics of asking a client out on a date. I had never worked for a woman, so it had never come up. I knew that Art sometimes dated guys from the companies he freelanced for, but that seemed different, somehow.

Then I remembered that she wasn't my client. I didn't work for CF. I just wanted to. I really wanted to.

"Do you guys, uh, need an accountant?" It was almost as awkward as asking her on a date.

"Maybe," she said. "We've got a girl who does the books, but she's a bookkeeper, not an accountant. We need to build out some projections and get our payroll under control and get ready for tax season. Last year we were so small, we just used a tax-prep service out of a storefront on Mission. This year I think we probably need something a little more intense."

"I just certified on California tax prep," I said. I'd had a client who needed it. "I have most of it in a Lotus sheet with a bunch of formulas. Just need to tweak it for your specifics and plug in the values. I can give you copies of the sheet on floppies so you can ballpark your tax bill for next year whenever you're thinking about stuff."

She nodded. "I like you, Martin Hench. I have to talk it over with my partners, but yeah, I think we could use some of your time. I'll talk to my partners about how many hours we're looking at per month and maybe you can give us a quote."

"Sure," I said. "That's great. I'm sure I can give you guys a rate that'll work. I, uh, really like what you're doing here and I want to work with you."

She laughed. "I hope you're a better accountant than you're a negotiator."

I shrugged. "I'm a great accountant." I thought of my conversation with Shlomo. "And I can be a hard case when the occasion calls for it. I don't get the impression that you'd take advantage of me, though."

"Don't be so sure," she said. "We're pretty hard-nosed ourselves."

Alfie's was a crazy scene, just crammed with guys dancing and laughing and making out in the corners, but every now and then I'd turn around and catch sight of a guy comforting a crying friend. Art brought a couple of buddies along, guys I'd met around the apartment. They were all in a cruisey mood but they were solicitous of my comfort, checking in with me between dances to make sure I was doing okay before spinning back off into the maelstrom of the dance floor.

Somehow, in the throb of the music and the wild energy of the guys around me, I found a spot of calm, as the events of the past couple of days, my conversation with Liz that afternoon, and the horny guys pairing up all around me swirled together in my thoughts and made me realize how adrift and lonely I had been since coming out west. It left me a little melancholy, but also determined. I was going to have to start dating, somehow, and I was going to have to make a niche for myself at CF. I was twenty-one years old. It was time I figured out what I wanted to do when I grew up. As soon as I had the thought, I realized I'd heard it in my father's voice.

We reeled and stumbled out of Alfie's at 1 a.m., when the bartender turned on the lights and the bouncer started shouting things about not having to go home but not being able to stay here. I had been nursing slow beers all night, while Art and his buddies had been pounding shots and disappearing into the gents' and reappearing with conspicuous sniffles, so I was obviously going to be the one driving Art's van back down to Menlo Park.

All the clubs were spilling out into the Castro when we reached it, and the street had a carnival atmosphere as hundreds—maybe thousands—of revelers thronged the sidewalk and then the curb lanes of Castro Street itself, forcing traffic to a crawl as people darted across the street to give friends sloppy hugs.

My own little group was pretty bombed, and I rode herd on them, keeping them together as we inched our way toward the van. I was looking back over my shoulder to make sure Art and his buddy Rog were still with us when I collided with someone else.

"Oh!" I said, catching the young woman I'd just nearly knocked over and steadying her. "Oh, I'm *so* sorry, honestly! Are you okay?"

It was only then that I registered whose shoulder I was holding—who I had just nearly knocked on her butt: Rivka Goldman, her face ashen with terror.

When she was growing up, Rivka's mother and father were relieved and delighted that she never got into trouble with boys, and not for lack of trying on the boys' part. When the yeshivas let out for the day and the boys spilled onto the streets of Montreal's Outremont, they would egg each other on to saying the most disgusting things to any girls they found on their own, mixing French, Yiddish, and Hebrew to come up with trilingual sexual remarks that were inappropriate in ways that transcended each language's own range of obscenity.

Other girls would pretend shock at these calls and stop to scold the boys, gathering into quarreling knots of teenagers whose performance of hostility was a smoke screen against passersby who might accuse them of impropriety.

Not Rivka. She never rose to the bait, never got into arguments with the boys, never had time for the boys at all. She got all the conversations with men that she needed at home, thanks to her father and her two older brothers and the cousins and uncles she saw at Shabbos dinners.

Girls, on the other hand . . . Well, not all girls. The boy-crazy ones were so boring and predictable, like they were staging private revivals of *Fiddler on the Roof*: "Matchmaker, matchmaker."

But some of the girls, the serious girls, well, they were excellent company. Rivka could spend hours with her best girl-friends, girls like Bina and Malka and Simchah, doing their homework or telling jokes or just sitting quietly and thinking, in companionable silence. They told each other secrets, they cooked with each other, they brushed each other's hair.

And then Rivka's mother came into her room and found her with Simchah.

Her mother's face went so white it was almost green, and she let out a yelp that was like the sound she made once when she burned her hand on the stove, burned it so badly she had to go to the hospital and then wear a bandage for a month.

"Mameh," Rivka gasped. Simchah gasped, too, and pulled the sheet up to cover herself.

"Get dressed, Simchah," Rivka's mother said. "Then go home." Simchah was frozen, eyes so big the whites showed all the way around them. *"Now!"* her mother said. If Rivka hadn't watched her mother's mouth open, she wouldn't have believed that it was her mother's voice she was hearing. Her mother, who was ever the calm eye of the whirling chaos of their household, making that sound of terror and rage? Never.

Simchah jumped and turned her back and dressed in haste, jamming her feet into her shoes without even putting her stockings back on. She left the room in silence and a moment later the front door slammed.

"Rivka—" her mother said, but she couldn't find any words to say after that. The look she gave Rivka said enough. Disgust. Disappointment. Hate, even. The silence was worse than anything she could have said. She closed the door and left Rivka on her own, her world contracting to a pinprick so small and dark she couldn't see a thing through it.

Rivka tried. She cut off Simchah, which meant she had to cut off Bina and Malka, too, which felt like she had cut off her arm, or maybe cut out her heart. She tried to fill that void with the *Fiddler on the Roof* girls, the unserious girls, and she joined them in their boy-teasing. The fact that she had no interest in those boys, none at all, ever, made her so much better at flirting than any of the unserious girls.

She got a reputation, and when her father sat her down to warn her that he'd heard things and he was very disappointed, it was all she could do not to smile. It was working. Then her mother gave her a long, long hug, just out of sight of her father, and she knew she was on the right path.

She'd have been overjoyed, if not for one problem: she was miserable. The girl in the mirror wasn't anyone she recognized, let alone anyone she'd want to sit and talk with. The girls she did sit and talk with were no true friends to her, and she never showed them who she really was, and had no interest in learning who they really were. Bina and Malka gave her awful, hateful looks when she saw them at school or synagogue. Simchah refused to look at her at all. That was the worst part of it.

Inevitably, there was a boy. Moshe Pupa—the boys called him Moshe Pupik and then so did everyone—came from a good family and had nice manners and Rivka's father did business with Moshe's father. The Pupas came to Shabbos dinner and then the Goldmans went to the Pupas for Shabbos dinner and there were many broad hints dropped by Moshe's parents and Rivka's parents.

After one Shabbos dinner, on a nice warm night, the adults announced that everyone should go out and have a walk, because it was such a beautiful night and winter would be here before anyone knew it, and they arranged to walk far enough behind Moshe and Rivka that they were almost walking on their own, a little privacy for the two young people who were not so young that they shouldn't at least be thinking about their futures and who they'd spend them with.

"I'm sorry about this," Moshe said. He looked absolutely mortified, his long face even longer, his big mobile mouth drawn down like a sad clown mask.

"It's okay," Rivka said. "I don't mind, honestly."

"That's nice of you to say," he said.

"I mean it," she said.

"Good," he said.

"Though," she said, "it would be less of a burden if we had a conversation about something more interesting than this."

That got a smile out of him, and then he asked a question that got a smile out of her: "So tell me what you're interested in, Rivka Goldman?"

They talked so much that night that their parents had to pry them apart so the Pupas could get home and go to bed.

Hanging out with Moshe Pupik was a lot nicer than hanging out with the unserious girls, even if they had to do so with the full chaperonage and supervision of their families. They could still go off a ways and talk about, well . . . *everything*.

Moshe was interested in history and he knew so much, things that weren't in the Torah, even things that *contradicted* the Torah, and the way he talked about the past made her feel like the two of them were being transported to a distant land. Best of all was the way Moshe could talk about those long-ago people as if they were real people, the same as the people all around them, but also *different*, both recognizable as part of the great human family and also completely foreign, with values and beliefs and experiences she would never fully understand.

Moshe didn't just talk, he *listened*. Rivka's father's office had sent him home with a terminal so he could log in to the insurance company mainframe and he'd taught Rivka to use it, and ever since, she and it had been inseparable. She was teaching herself Fortran and BASIC out of books from the library. Moshe listened to her describe the worlds unfolding for her, the mistakes she'd made and then figured out, and even if he couldn't program computers, Rivka was a good explainer, and he was *such* a good listener and he thrilled along with her tales of technological conquest.

Gradually, their parents began to give them freer rein, letting them sit in the backyard while everyone else sat inside having cake and coffee, even sending them to the market together to do the shopping. The intimacy of their privacy made their bond even deeper. It was almost as good as the friendships she'd had with Bina and Malka, and Simchah of course. Almost. Some days, she didn't even feel the loss of them.

So it came that one day, Moshe Pupik asked Rivka to marry him. Not *asked her* asked her, not one knee and a ring asked her, but rather, warmed up to the subject. "If our parents say it's all right, if you say it's all right, then I think it's all right, and maybe it would be all right for all of us and—"

The feeling that overcame her then was even bigger than the feeling she'd had when her mother had caught her with Simchah. Shame, of course, because she didn't love him that way and never could, but shame also because she *did* love him, in a different way, and she had let him make the perfectly reasonable assumption that she was who she appeared to be. She had lied to him with every deed and every word, lied to someone she loved, even if she didn't love him like that.

The tears came and wouldn't stop and he stood so awkwardly there in the backyard, amid the rows of her father's vegetable plot. And then he pulled her into a shadow and he did something he wasn't supposed to do: he hugged her. He hugged her and hugged her and hugged her. Not in a bad way, either—not in a way that made her think he was being forward, or presuming that she was the person he had every right to think that she was.

She loved him so fiercely then that she decided that maybe she *could* be the person he had every right to think she was. So she dried her tears and explained them away and disentangled her-

self and said that it was a lovely thing to ask and she felt honored
that he had, and they should talk some more about it.

Her father came to the door then and called them in to say
their goodbyes to the Pupas.

Moshe Pupik wasn't a fool. He knew her well. He was a studious
boy and only had a few close friends, and she was the closest
of them.

"I know you told me we should talk some more about it—" he
began, the next time they stood among the vegetable garden beds.
"And before you say anything, I have something I want to say."

She made herself hold his gaze, because if he was going to
profess his undying romantic love, she was going to be a good
best friend and a good woman and a good *wife* and look him in
the eye when he did it.

"Rivka," he said, and looked away. "Rivka, you aren't like
anyone I've ever met. You're different from everyone around
here." A cold feeling stole over her. He knew. Somehow, he
knew. She'd been so careful. A powerful urge to run inside the
house seized her and it took everything she had to resist it.

"I mean," Moshe Pupik went on, "Rivka, I think maybe,
you're a little like me?"

Her thigh muscles trembled with the effort of not running,
even as her knees turned to jelly with surprise. *Like me?* She
teetered. He steadied her.

"Like you, Moshe? What do you mean?"

He stared squarely in her eyes. "I don't believe in God," he
said. "I haven't believed since I was a little boy." He swallowed.
"I think maybe you don't believe in God, either."

She gasped, then, to her surprise, she giggled. "No," she
blurted. "I believe in God, Moshe. *That's* not what makes me
different."

Now he was sagging. He'd told her his secret, a secret that could separate him from his family and his community forever. Exile. He was her best friend. Did she owe him anything less?

"Moshe," she whispered, "I don't want to marry a man. Any man. I think I want to . . . marry . . . a woman?" She instantly hated how it came out, especially that question mark. But she'd said those words aloud now. She'd never even formed that feeling into words in her own mind.

He looked confused and took a step back from her, letting go of her arm. She wanted to take the words back. She couldn't. Because she couldn't, she decided to give them some more words for company. It was the bravery of a woman in flight, falling from a great height, who couldn't make things worse.

"I'm sorry if you find that disgusting or terrible, Moshe Pupik, but it's who I am. It's how Hashem made me. Remember Hashem? The God you don't believe in? I do believe in Him. He doesn't make mistakes, so I am exactly as I should be." If she said the words fervently enough, she'd believe them.

He said precisely nothing for precisely a hundred years and she died a million times. Then he looked up and looked down and then back at her. "You know, lesbianism was a very common phenomenon in world history. In ancient Greece, it would have been utterly unremarkable."

Lesbianism made her heart thunder. It was a word she'd never spoken, or heard, or read, but she knew it somehow, the way she knew the other forbidden words. Perhaps she'd been born with the knowledge that the word was *treyf.* Is that who she was?

"How about not believing in God?" she asked.

That got him to smile a little. "Atheism? Oh, that's far more forbidden. I'd have been stoned to death, or burned, I'm sure."

"But not today?"

"Oh, no, not today. I just need to change my haircut, get a new suit of clothes, and walk a mile in any direction and no one will care about my feelings about Hashem."

"But I can't do that," she said. "It seems we were both born in the wrong place, but only I was born in the wrong time."

He took her hand. "Times change," he said. "In the meantime, maybe we could keep each other company, here in the wrong place."

Moshe Pupik was a *mensch*.

Letting it be known that they were engaged to be engaged was a *mitzvah* beyond Rivka's wildest imaginings. Overnight, it put a stop to both the disapproving conversations with her mother and awkward conversations with her father, to say nothing of the whispers of the people she met out and about at school and at the market.

But it wasn't to last. Gradually, a new pressure built: to move from engaged-to-be-engaged to simply *engaged*. Moshe Pupik was feeling it, too, and they had many long conversations about whether they could marry, and if so, what that would mean. Would Rivka have his babies? Could he be happy living his whole life with a woman who had no interest in being a *wife* in the biblical sense? Could she be happy in that arrangement?

It was Moshe who found the way out: an advertisement for a job with Fidelity Computing that had circulated at the yeshiva. It promised excitement, professional advancement, a good salary, and it said "Modest, pious women are encouraged to apply."

Rivka's father had graduated to a Fidelity PC at home by this point, as had many of his friends and business contacts. Within the community, Fidelity was known as a Haredic success story (little was said about the other two Wise Men and their faith, though if pressed everyone would say that it was wonderful that Rabbi Finkel had found a way to share the bounty with these important *shkotzim* and their followers).

Moshe had a very serious discussion with her father about his intention to study history at Stanford, where he'd been accepted with a partial scholarship, and how a job at Fidelity Computing would allow him and Rivka to keep up their (chaste!) courtship, averting the risk that his studies would get in the way of the lifelong marriage and family they were both eager to start.

Rivka, meanwhile, worked on her mother, with passionate speeches about the need to follow her betrothed, the importance of having the possibility of work that could help with family finances should they ever fall on hard times (God forbid, but who can know what adversity lurks in the future?), and the excitement of working on Rabbi Finkel's great Haredic enterprise, Fidelity Computing.

She moved to Colma a month after graduating. Moshe Pupik moved out midsummer. They saw each other once a week for Shabbos dinner, at first, then, after Moshe cut off his sidelocks and started going by "Mark," they switched to a monthly lunch, so they could work out a common story to tell their parents on their calls back home.

6

I dropped off all of Art's friends before driving Rivka home. She'd accepted the ride with wooden assent, and sat in silence as we made the drop-offs. The boys' mood was only slightly dampened by Rivka's discomfort—not enough to stop them from boasting and (I think) lying about the action they'd gotten at Alfie's, anyway.

When it was just me and Art and Rivka, she started talking, at first in a dull monotone, and then with more ferocity, and then, finally, with pride.

"The work I did at Fidelity made me proud at first—made me feel like I'd found a way to be a good Jew and a good person and be myself." She got quiet for a while as we jounced down the 280 toward Colma. "I think that good feeling was why I stayed for as long as I did. I knew I was hurting people, that much was obvious very quickly, but I tried not to think about it. The girls I worked with, they were all good girls, but they were also *interesting* girls, like the friends I'd turned my back on. I didn't want to lose them.

"To be honest with you, we put off the decision to start CF for too long. We should have done it the next day, the very next day after we thought of it. The other two, they wanted to. But I held them back. I couldn't lose my friends, not again. I made them wait.

"Now, though? Now? It's the greatest. The *greatest*. The greatest thing I've ever done. Ever. The greatest thing I ever will do. Those people who bought Fidelity Computing computers? They know how great a computer can be, how useful, how *essential*. I don't want to take that away from them! I want to give them *more*. Give them what I promised them, when I was selling for Fidelity. I believed what I told them then. I still believe it. I want to make good on my promise. That's the least I can do. It's what we all owe each other.

"And the other two? Liz and Maria-Eva? They're my sisters now, my *true* sisters. I never lost my faith—not like Moshe Pupik. I love Hashem and I love being a Jew, and I will be a Jew until they bury me. But Liz and Maria-Eva? They understand something about me that's just as important as my religion. It's just as important as the fact that I'm a—" She swallowed.

"That I love who I love. They understand my life's *mission*. If that sounds like a foolish thing that a foolish girl would talk about, so, fine. It's foolish. But it's true. I want to make computers that give people power, not computers that take away their power." She glared at us fiercely. We were in the driveway of her duplex, a run-down sort of place with a sagging staircase and a Trans Am with a DISCO SUCKS bumper sticker in the driveway. The Trans was mostly bondo-colored. "Mr. Hench, I know we must seems ridiculous to you. I know how it is here in Silicon Valley, for men like you. You all want to dream big and make a fortune and change the world. Us three little girls with our funny religious beliefs and our customers in their funny little churches must feel like a joke. A *little* joke. This isn't little for me, Mr. Hench. This is my world, *our* world, and we are *so* serious about it. I'm sure you have many skills we can use, but if you're not as serious as us, you might as well leave now. We are serious people, Mr. Hench. We are *not* a joke. This is a mission, Mr. Hench, a liberation mission. It may not be aimed at the world of *matters*."

We were both watching her, an audience of two. I fished for the right words, but Art knew them. "That's a *great* mission,

Rivka. And you're a great person, I can tell that. I'm proud of you and I'm glad you told me your story. Thank you."

The ferocity leaked out of her, revealing the vulnerability it had masked. "Thank you," she said, in a tiny voice.

"Thank *you*," I said. "I spent the afternoon with Liz, you know. She and I hatched a scheme for me to do work for CF, whatever you need, just to help out. That mission of yours—I think maybe it's mine, too."

By the time we'd dropped off the guys, then given Rivka a chance to tell her story, dropped *her* off, and gotten back home to Menlo Park, it was past three in the morning. Art was sober. We were both exhausted. Thankfully, neither of us had to work the next day. We zombied around each other as we brushed our teeth and got ready for bed.

We were both about to disappear into our rooms when he called out to me: "Marty?"

"Yeah?"

"You serious about working with those girls?"

I didn't even have to think about it. "Yeah. Hell yeah."

He nodded. "Good. Anything you can do to help them, you should do. Plus I get the feeling you could learn a lot from them."

I got up at 1 p.m. the next day. The fridge was empty. I wished I'd saved the other half of Art's burrito. Art didn't need it. He was still snoring. The fridge was empty.

Goddammit, I needed to go get some groceries.

The tough guys were waiting for me. Two of them, in the lobby. One was a big guy, six two, the other was a little guy. If I'd had to put money on one of them, it'd be the little guy. I'd done a lot of fighting in Escambia, it was the way we did it there. When a little guy's got speed and crazy going for him, he's scarier than any big guy.

They both had *kippahs* and the tails of prayer shawls poking out from under their white shirts. They both wore black, belted slacks and black shoes, scuffed.

"Hench," the little guy said. He had just one eyebrow, and it wasn't straight—it went up over his left eye, like a junior Mr. Spock, quizzically peering at the world. He'd had a good nose, once, prominent and proud. Someone had rearranged it for him. Maybe a couple of someones. Now it was a wonder he could breathe out of it.

"Hench," I agreed, hitching a thumb at my chest.

"We're here from Fidelity. To get what's ours."

I nodded. "All right, wait here, I'll go box everything up and bring it down."

"We'll come up," the little guy said.

"No," I said, "you won't." The big guy shifted his weight to his forward foot. On a smaller man, it would have been subtle, but with a guy that size, it was like an earthquake. Seismic.

I didn't want to fight these guys.

Actually, I *did*. The Marty Hench of Cambridge, Mass., wasn't a fighter. For two long years, I'd settled my disputes like a civilized man and my dad had always winked at me and made up an ice pack when I came home with a black eye. I missed my caveman days. I shifted my weight onto my front foot, getting ready to dodge this big son of a bitch's big swing, to get under it and give him one back. The way he was standing, I figured I could get him square in the balls. Some guys won't punch another guy there. Those guys are stupid guys. When a big stranger wants to give you a beating or worse, there's absolutely no reason in the world not to go straight for the groin, as hard as you can.

The little guy put his hand on the big guy's arm, murmured something in Yiddish. Big guy stood down. "We'll come up to the hallway, but not in the apartment," he said. "That way, you won't have to carry everything down."

Little guy had big, innocent eyes and wide-open smile. He should have seemed very nonthreatening. But he didn't. He looked like the kind of guy whose smile would never falter, even after he had you on the ground. Even after you were bleeding. There were guys like that in Escambia. The smilers were a lot worse than the ones who looked serious all the time. The smilers *enjoyed* it.

Big guy cocked his head like a confused dog. I shrugged. I could fight these guys outside the door to my apartment just as easily as I could fight them in the lobby. Maybe the noise would wake up Art and he'd get in on the action. He played in a softball league and kept a bat in his bedroom closet. "Come on, then," I said.

The elevator ride was *awkward*. Big guy murmured something in Yiddish and little guy shook his head impatiently. Big guy looked chastened.

I tensed up when I put the key in my lock, but they stayed put, just a *little* too close to me. I closed the door and locked it. I stuck the Fidelity computer, floppy drives, and printer into their boxes, not bothering with the foam inserts. I put the inserts in a big black garbage bag, then shoved the paperwork on top of the bankers box of floppies and jammed the lid on.

Art was still snoring in his room. I thought about getting his bat, but that felt silly and paranoid. I carried the bankers box with the bag of foam inserts on it to the door and opened it with the fingertips of one hand. Big guy was standing right there, hulking over me. I shoved the box at him and he grabbed it reflexively. "More to come," I said, and stepped back and slammed the door.

I piled the computer and printer box on top of each other and repeated the trick. This time they were ready and little guy tried to insinuate himself between me and the doorway before I could get back, but I was also ready, and I beat him back in.

Now it was just the monitor box and the box with the floppy drives. I put the floppy box under one arm, and positioned it so I could fire it through the crack in the door as I opened it. I did, and I heard big guy curse and fumble with it, and a kerfuffle like they were both trying to keep it from hitting the ground. I seized my opportunity and swung the door wide, shoving the monitor box across the threshold with my foot at the same moment, slamming the door right behind it. I confess that I was enjoying this Three Stooges routine and I was already mid-chortle when little guy got his foot in the door and then big guy's giant paw wrapped around the door and pushed it open.

Now we were staring at each other across the threshold, all of us panting and wide-eyed. Little guy wasn't smiling anymore.

"Mr. Hench," he said, like an angry vice-principal confronting a playground brawler. "That wasn't very nice."

I raised my eyebrows and tilted my head, a kind of facial shrug. He was right, it wasn't, but I didn't owe these door-crasher specials anything like niceness.

Abruptly, little guy snaked out a hand and bunched my shirt in his fist, yanking me down nose-to-nose with him. "Mr. Hench, the Reverend Sirs want you to know that they are very disappointed in your conduct. You had an arrangement with them, one that they were very invested in. Frankly, they're be-wildered, because they made a very *fair* agreement with you. They want you to know how sincere their displeasure is, and further, they've asked me to let you know that if you're think-ing about going to work for those three traitorous *bitches*"—he hissed the word, flecking my face with spittle—"they will take it personally and they will *not* let the matter drop."

He *was* fast. I didn't even see his other hand winding up. And you know, I was right, there is no reason not to sock an-other guy in the balls. It's a very effective move, really.

I lay on the ground in the hallway, gasping and clutching, and watched their ankles recede toward the elevator as they waddled away, under the weight and bulk of the Fidelity computer and documents. The elevator pinged and their ankles disappeared.

Eventually, I got to my feet. I, too, waddled. I waddled to the freezer for a bag of frozen peas that Art had designated the bruise-and-ache ice pack long before I arrived, and which had been thawed and refrozen so many times that the peas were surely inedible at this point.

The little guy had a good arm.

I thought about his good arm and what I'd like to do to it as I sat on the sofa, holding the peas. Finally, they started to thaw and drip, so I put the peas back in the freezer. There was nothing else in there except for a half bottle of vodka, which reminded me that we still needed groceries.

I stood and made my way down to the van. I hardly waddled.

Maria-Eva Fernandez wasn't very religious, at first. Neither were her parents. But when they left Paraguay and made their way to Denver, they enrolled her in a convent school, hoping that religion could substitute for the entirety of the culture they'd left behind forever. There was a sprinkling of other Spanish-speaking kids in the school, which was a comfort to Maria-Eva's parents. They'd spent months coaching her in English before they fled and presented themselves at the Miami airport as asylum seekers, but at seven, Maria-Eva wasn't that interested in English.

For the first two years, the convent school was a place of torment to Maria-Eva. The other Spanish-speaking kids were all Mexican, and they made fun of her accent and shunned her. The nuns were impatient with her slow and uncertain English, and her parents were alternately furious and saddened by her terrible grades.

The summer between fifth and sixth grade, Maria-Eva's parents enrolled her in an ESL class at the Denver public library, with a nice white lady and a group of mostly younger kids, fresh off the boat from Peru, fleeing ahead of Morales Bermúdez's coup and its death squads. They had their own stuff to deal with and commanded the majority of the nice white lady's time between their breakdowns and fights.

No one much cared when Maria-Eva wandered away from the ESL class in the kids' picture book section and took herself on a tour of the library. She was drawn to a strange sound, *blatt-blatt-blatt,* not like anything she'd ever heard. She followed the sound to a group of teenaged boys crowded into a tight knot. She craned her neck and stood on tiptoes to see over them, but they were all taller than her, so she simply shouldered her way through them, the way her parents had done at the bus stops back in Paraguay. The boys gave her looks, but when they saw that she was only a little girl, they grimaced and let her through.

The boys were watching a man, younger than her father, bearded and with long hair and sandaled feet. The man was watching a strange mechanical device, which was making the *blatt-blatt-blatt* sound. It was a printer. She'd seen them, that day they spent at Miami International, being questioned by INS agents and U.S. Customs guards. The man typed some things, the printer chattered, the paper advanced, the boys and the man watched.

The paper was full of nonsense punctuation characters. She thought this must be computer code, the esoteric language of machines. But then it snapped into focus and she saw it for what it was, a drawing of a naked lady, a cartoon with big boobs and a hairy triangle made of commas and semicolons. Maria-Eva gave a squeak of surprise. The man turned around and gave his own squeak, then leapt up from the chair and took Maria-Eva by the arm and dragged her back through the crowd of boys. The man spoke in rapid, angry English that Maria-Eva couldn't follow.

The man got her back to the nice white lady, eventually, and the lady scolded her gently not to wander off. The next day, the man was back, and the boys were back, and she wormed her way back to the front of the clump of boys and peered over the shoulder of the man. Today, he was typing something else—neat numbered lines of words she couldn't understand. The man looked over his shoulder at her, grimaced, and turned back to his typing. Maria-Eva understood this to mean that she would be tolerated so long as the mysterious printer wasn't producing naked ladies, and she set herself to intensely, keenly observing the words on the paper as they scrolled by.

A week later, she was in the seat, laboriously typing out her first lines of code.

That September, the nuns at the convent school all remarked on Maria-Eva's excellent new command over English. Her grades shot to the top of her class, and she was able to handily juggle both her homework and the library computer club, where Dr. Jason Hicks—the bearded guy who brought his portable terminal to the library every day after school—was now teaching her IBM 360 assembly, which she was absorbing like a sponge. Her parents endured her lengthy, excited explanations of the fine points of assembly languages versus BASIC and Fortran, but any technical insights they gleaned were swamped by their tremendous relief at their daughter's newfound English proficiency, social life, and academic accomplishment.

Sister Jean taught sixth-grade math, which Maria-Eva demolished, doodling in her notebook with half an ear cocked to the teacher's explanation of decimals but immediately and perfectly answering any question she was called upon to solve.

Sister Jean was a patient woman, but Maria-Eva's absolute, obvious indifference to her instruction was a distraction for the other kids, who often craned their necks to see what the intense little girl was drawing in her notebooks. The fact that Maria-Eva was equally indifferent to the other kids' attention was, somehow, equally frustrating.

One day, Sister Jean had enough, and confiscated the notebook, telling Maria-Eva that she could have it back after detention. Maria-Eva glared at her with a twelve-year-old's unadulterated fury, and stomped into Sister Jean's classroom for detention with that same look on her face, as exaggerated as a Greek tragedy mask.

"Have a seat, Maria-Eva," Sister Jean said, picking up the notebook from her desk and paging through it. She was evidently looking for something, and, having found it, she carried it over to Maria-Eva's desk and set it down in front of her. "What is this?" she said.

The page was dense with pencil writing and erasures, crossouts and arrows, all surrounding a tight, neat grid of comma-separated number pairs in square brackets.

"I'm trying to figure out how to do an array transformation," Maria-Eva said, still glaring at the nun. She didn't wear the whole outfit, except on school outings, but was still marked out by her large crucifix and a certain nun-ish-ness in lack of makeup, the cardigan and skirt combination. The nuns had a repertoire of teacher faces: stern, coaxing, understanding, coaxing.

But Sister Jean had a new expression: frank curiosity.

"What's an array transformation?"

Maria-Eva had been trying to explain this to her parents for weeks, to the point where they'd forbidden the subject at the dinner table, and so great was her relief at having a willing audience for this explanation that she forgot how angry she was at Sister Jean. The words poured out of her. Sister Jean's curiosity turned briefly to skepticism, as if she was wondering if this was some kind of elaborate child's fantasy, as though Maria-Eva had invented an imaginary zoo of mythological beasts and was now taking her through their care routines.

Then Sister Jean underwent a visible jolt of recognition. "Maria-Eva, please excuse me for a moment."

The convent school afforded its teachers cubby-sized offices for marking papers, silent reflection, and sneaky chocolate consumption. Sister Jean's had a shelf of old textbooks from her undergraduate years—it had seemed wasteful to part with them, though she hadn't consulted them for a decade and they had migrated to a bottom shelf, then had binders of school memos shoved between their tops and the bottom of the next shelf.

Sister Jean excavated them, located her second-year linear algebra text and ran a finger down the table of contents, then flipped to a page toward the end of the book. As she read over the introductory material and the diagrams—grids of numbered pairs—she shook her head. Maria-Eva was twelve.

Twelve.

She brought the book back to her classroom slowly, found Maria-Eva with her head bent over her notebook, her finger tracing over the grid of numbers she'd drawn there.

"This," Sister Jean said, "might help you." She handed Maria-Eva the open textbook, tapping on the relevant passage. "You can take the book home. Please return it when you're done." She stared at the little, dark-haired, serious-eyed girl for a thoughtful moment. "You can go now, young lady."

Mathematics, like chess, is a self-contained system—a world of abstractions that can be manipulated without ever making reference to the real world. Anyone with the right kind of first-rate reasoning ability and a relatively simple set of precepts can build up complicated theories and test them, deepening their understanding and mastery of the subject without having to learn a single thing about the universe of material things that are external to the system.

For a young chess player, this process is greatly eased by the availability of other chess players that they can sharpen their wits against.

For a young mathematician, a computer can fill this role. After all, it only does what you tell it to do, and so computer programming becomes a kind of Socratic dialogue, with the foolishly consistent machine doing *exactly* what you asked of it, forever, until the errors in your reasoning cannot be denied.

That old linear algebra textbook was a trickster's treasure map, revealing pathways that Maria-Eva had not suspected— pathways that seemed to lead to magical lands of power, but that often came tantalizingly close only to veer away into a bramble of complexity and confusion.

Maria-Eva only got a few minutes to use Dr. Jason's terminal every night, when her turn came around, and she used these to probe those brambles for a way through, while the older boys in the club vibrated over her shoulder, awaiting their own turns and making unkind remarks about her code. Unkind because to them, it looked like nonsense.

They were still stuck in BASIC, and her assembly code was gibberish to them. Why were they having to wait while this little girl typed her nonsense programs into the terminal during the too-short periods of access to the IBM 360 mainframe at Dr. Jason's university?

Maria-Eva barely noticed them. She was sharpening herself against the computer. Its rock-hard obtuseness made it a perfect tool for this.

The boy who hurt her seemed nice at first. He'd approached her on her way out of the library after computer club. His name was

Bryan, and he'd stayed late so that he could speak to her after she was done with her customary after-club discussion with Dr. Jason. Dr. Jason answered her questions while he slowly packed up the terminal and coiled up the telephone extension cable that allowed him to bring a phone out from one of the librarians' offices.

Bryan called her name as she left the building, a little sweaty thanks to her convent school shirt, tie, and blazer. She stopped.

"I want to talk with you," he said, "about your program," he said.

Maria-Eva had been sharpening herself against the computer. Her discussions with Dr. Jason had fined down her edge. She'd moved on from scalar operations to vector operations, and they'd been so *easy*! It didn't surprise her that one of the boys from the club would want to talk with her about it.

Bryan knew a place where they could talk, a utility shed behind the library where municipal workers stored bags for the park trash cans and other miscellanea. The door lock was busted.

They were barely in there for a minute when Maria-Eva burst out again, running, crying. Bryan staggered out a moment later, his nose and lip gushing blood and the front of his shirt and pants covered in bright orange. It was paint from the paint can that she'd hit him with. He lost one of his front teeth and his nose was broken. Maria-Eva was strong, and once she'd realized what was going on, fear and rage had doubled that strength.

In Paraguay, there were policemen who did that sort of thing. Every girl knew to steer clear of them. Maria-Eva's auntie had come to their kitchen once in tears. Her mother had held her and wiped away the dirt and iced her bruises and muttered darkly. Maria-Eva's realization had doubled her strength. At least doubled. Bryan was lucky he didn't have a concussion.

She didn't even realize he'd given her a black eye until she got home. Her mother was torn between fury and terror. So was Maria-Eva.

Maria-Eva's faith was grounded in what happened next.

Dr. Jason convened a "meeting" between her and her parents and Bryan and Bryan's parents. Bryan's story was, naturally, an idiotic and transparent pack of lies. Maria-Eva's story was true.

But Bryan's injuries were serious. His parents wanted Maria-Eva's parents to pay for his dental care and emergency room bill. Maria-Eva's parents made it clear that wasn't going to happen. Dr. Jason asked if everyone couldn't just shake hands and make up, with apologies all round?

No one liked that idea. They all left, with Bryan's parents threatening to call the police, the immigration authorities, child protective services. Maria-Eva was suspended from computer club.

Bryan was not.

In retrospect, it was clear to Maria-Eva that her parents were just as heartbroken as she was, in their own way, but it was masked by their cold fury, which Maria-Eva mistook for anger at *her.*

As an adult, she could see it from their perspective—their strange little daughter, who'd struggled so to adjust to this new land, had finally found something she fiercely loved, and she had been excluded from it by white people closing ranks to protect their own. To protect a boy who deserved to be beaten and shamed, not coddled for his injuries.

Sister Jean noticed, of course. Maria-Eva stopped doodling, stopped working out code problems in her notebook, and instead stared with glazed doll's eyes at Sister Jean as she taught, as though sixth-grade math demanded her attention. The slump of her shoulders and the shuffle in her walk told a tale whose broad outlines Sister Jean could guess at. Sister Jean had been teaching girls for a long time, after all.

She caught Maria-Eva at the classroom door and pulled her aside, making her wait until the other students had all filed out. "After school," she said. "I want to see you."

Maria-Eva looked at her with unblinking, unseeing eyes. "Fine," she said, eventually.

Sister Jean couldn't get her back into computer club. Maria-Eva didn't know if she even tried. But what Sister Jean *could* do was help Maria-Eva think about her suffering in the context of her relationship with God, and Jesus, and the Blessed Virgin.

All three had been fixtures in her life, of course, but her relationship to them was like her relationship to brushing and flossing: a set of activities she had to perform at regular intervals. As a little girl, she'd needed cajoling and correction to get them right, and now they happened automatically. She could answer scriptural questions in chapel with the same facility as her answers to math questions, and just as little engagement.

But Sister Jean had found her own vocation when she was Maria-Eva's age, and it had transformed her life and revealed her destiny. Her testimony, plain and heartfelt, pricked Maria-Eva's interest, and then their prayer together stirred something deep in Maria-Eva. She heard something, an irreducible, numinous *something* she'd never heard before, and it was like when scalar operations had snapped into place for her. A subject that had been opaque became transparent. *This is why we pray.*

Being ejected from computer club tore a hole in her life. Sister Jean filled it with faith.

It would be many years before she found a way back to computers again, but she used that time wisely.

7

Art woke up as I put the finishing touches on breakfast: half a package of bacon, a pan of scrambled eggs, sourdough toast. It was about four in the afternoon, and the ache in my balls had receded to the point that I could eat. I wasn't even walking bow-legged anymore, a sight that had drawn stares at the Safeway.

Two plates and half a bottle of ketchup later, Art sat back and said, "I see that shitbox Fidelity Computing computer's gone?"

"Yeah," I said, wincing from the lingering ache in my pelvis. "They sent a couple guys to get it."

"And the frozen peas?" I followed his gaze, and sure enough, I'd left them on the counter, where they'd defrosted in a pool of condensation.

"Ah," I said. "It's a long story."

"I'm not gonna be able to move until I digest that feast," he said. "I've got time."

When I was done, he went and got the softball bat and leaned it in a corner near the front door, next to the heap of sneakers and hard work shoes.

"You're not calling the cops, right? I mean, if you are, we should put the bat away, at least until they've come to take a statement."

"I don't think so," I said. "It'll be their word against mine. Back home, if you called the cops after something like that, they'd just throw everyone in the tank and then drag us all in front of the judge for a thirty-five-dollar disorderly conduct ticket."

"That's how they do it in Alabama, huh? Pittsburgh, they'd call you a pussy and tell you quit whining. I mean, unless you were someone rich and powerful complaining about some blue-collar guy who you got into a shoving match with.

"How are your ladies over at CF?"

The question caught me flat-footed. Here I'd been thinking of myself as some kind of knight errant and them as damsels in distress and I hadn't even bothered to check in on them. "Let me make a call."

It was late on a Saturday and no one was answering at CF, so I left a message on the machine. But now I couldn't stop worrying. I did the dishes, sat down, stood back up, put the peas back in the freezer.

"Why don't you go over to that Rivka's place?" Art said. "Just to put your mind at ease." He ran his hand through his red curls—standing on end the way they always did before he'd had a chance to shower and spend twenty minutes blow-drying them into submission. "My mind, too, maybe. Feels to me like that Rabbi Finkel might have a lot of ways to punish her for her disloyalty."

It took half an hour to drive to Rivka's and it was a struggle to keep the worst out of my imagination. I have a very active imagination.

The bondo-colored Trans Am was gone from the driveway of her duplex when I pulled up, just as the sun was setting. I almost parked in the drive, then thought better of it and circled the block and parked around the corner, then walked cautiously back to her place. There were no sidewalks on these streets, and every time a car went past me I stepped up onto the curb or someone's lawn, resisting the urge to guiltily shoulder-check the car to see if they were checking me out.

I stopped across the street from the house and looked it up and down. The driveway was still empty, the curtains drawn in the upstairs apartment. I stared at those closed curtains for a long time, hoping for a twitch that might provide a clue to whether anyone was home, and if so, who?

Finally, I took a deep breath and crossed the street and ascended the spongy wooden staircase at the side of the building. The doormat was made of frayed, woven sisal; the door was a scuffed dun-colored slab with a peephole and an ancient lock that looked like the kind of thing you learned to pick on your first day at MIT.

I held my breath and strained my ears, but I didn't hear anyone inside. I raised my fist and knocked. Waited. Knocked harder. Waited longer. Finally, I gave the door a hard couple of thumps, just to be sure anyone inside would have heard me.

No one home.

Now what, O White Knight in Dented Armor? Break the door down? Call the police? Go home and tell Art that you have no idea whether Rivka Goldman is still in good working order?

The latter, I guess. Action heroics are for the A-Team, not accountants.

I walked slowly down the stairs, and, just as I turned onto the landing, I found myself falling backward under the furious assault of a flailing, full-body tackle. I tried to get one hand up to fend off my attacker and the other hand behind me to break my fall and spare my skull. I failed at both and an instant later my head *crack*ed off a step riser. My vision blurred and my breath whooshed out of me, and I couldn't draw another one, because someone was sitting on my chest now, and straddling me, and they had something metal in their hand, raised high for a killing strike.

I gasped and bucked, but I was breathless, weak. I tried

to shout, it came out a moan. I turned my face away from the weapon, and then—

"Marty?"

The weight lifted from my chest. My attacker leaned in close. My eyes focused themselves.

"Rivka?" I gasped.

"Marty!" she said. "Oh, no! Are you okay? Oh—" She helped me sit up. I touched the back of my head. It was tender, but the bump was modest. "Marty, I'm so sorry," she said. "I heard the banging at the door, and I thought—"

The weapon in her hand was her door keys, protruding from her fist like a medieval spiked glove. She saw me staring at them and pocketed them hastily. "I took a self-defense course," she said. "A women's course, in the Castro. They taught us this." She blushed. "They also told us to go for the . . . *privates*"—she whispered the word—"but I guess I couldn't bring myself to do that."

"Well," I said, rocking my head from side to side, "I think that's probably good news for me, on balance, but it probably means that you need a refresher course." I massaged the back of my head. "Also, do they have courses for men, too? I could stand to learn a thing or two."

She didn't smile. "Are you okay?"

I climbed to my feet. I ached a little but I didn't feel concussed or anything. "I'm okay," I said. "Good thing those stairs are half rotted, meant the wood was softer than my skull."

"Yes," she said. "My landlord isn't very good about maintenance. I've been looking for another place but things are so busy with work, and I'm almost never here. I'm glad something good came of it at last." She looked away, then looked back at me and folded her arms. "Why were you thumping on my door, anyway?"

I managed a weak smile. "I was worried about you. A couple of tough Orthodox guys from Fidelity showed up at my place and we had a vigorous exchange of our differences. They seemed pretty fussed about what you three are doing and even angrier that I was throwing in with you."

She shook her head. "That's very bad. Come on, I'll get you an ice pack and you can tell me about it."

The wrongness was apparent from the moment her key turned in the lock. From the moment the door cracked open, our noses were assaulted by a noxious wave. We both took a step back and she landed on my foot. I nearly went over backward, but caught my breath.

"Ugh," she said, disentangling herself from me.

I pulled my T-shirt up so it covered my nose and toed the door open a little wider. The stench got stronger, even through the cotton of my shirt. A sour milk smell, but so intense. Like someone bombed a dairy farm and then left the remains in sticky-hot Alabama August sun for a whole day. A whole month.

I turned my face away and gulped fresh air over the landing's railing, then turned back. Holding my breath, I stuck my face into the apartment. It was a wreck: slashed sofa, coffee table stomped in two, the floor and counters of the galley kitchen glittering with shattered glasses and plates. Brown smears on the wall.

A swastika, crudely drawn. It was shit, I was sure. The eight slashed segments swam in the putrid air.

I pulled my head back out of the apartment and gasped some more over the railing. The stench was rolling out of the apartment in waves now, fresh air in short supply. Rivka's face was screwed up in disgust. I retreated down the stairs to the lower landing and she followed.

"What's it like in there?" she asked. She was so pale she was almost green.

I breathed awhile more. "It's bad," I managed. "It's really bad. I think we should go somewhere else and call the police."

She started up the stairs.

"Where are you going?"

"I have to lock up," she said. "All my things are in there."

"I don't think anyone is going to go in there," I said. But she mounted the stairs and slammed the door shut. She came back down with a tight-lipped expression that let me know she'd managed to take a look before she closed the door.

We drove to a 7-Eleven and I bought some trucker bandanas off a rack next to the No-Doz while Rivka dialed 911 from the pay phone out front. We drove back and parked across the street with the windows rolled up until the two SFPD cops rolled up in their cruiser.

Even from across the street, the sour milk smell was noticeable, if bearable. I let Rivka do the talking with the cops, explaining that she'd walked to Shabbos dinner at a friend's house and came back to discover her home vandalized.

"And you?" said the older cop, a white guy with a military bearing and a square chin, surmounted by an impressive nose that made him look more like a character actor than a marquee idol.

"Me?"

"What's your role here?"

"I don't have a role. I was coming by to visit Miss Goldman and I happened to arrive at the same time as her."

He squinted at me. His job was to be mistrustful, but the sensation of being mistrusted still got me hot. I took a deep breath. "Was she expecting you?"

"No," I said. "I was in the neighborhood so I dropped by."

"And how do you know Miss—" He checked his pad. "—Goldman?"

"We are professional associates."

He flipped through his pad. "You work in software?"

"Accounting," I said.

He smirked. It made me hotter, and then a more rational part of my brain kicked in and said, *Hey, you jerk, this guy is underestimating you, which is a lot better than having him overestimate you. What are you getting all freaked over?*

That rational part was pretty smart.

The cop's partner—young, with half the waistline of the senior man, and some kind of styling stuff in his hair that reminded me of how Art's friends looked when they were getting ready for a big night out on the town—said, "Why were you in the neighborhood, sir?"

He was the smarter of the two. I really didn't want to tell these guys the whole story. I mean, I hadn't broken any laws, but it all just felt like a lot of complications that no one needed. "Vietnamese grocery," I said. "Needed to get some Asian cilantro for a stir-fry." I'd read a recipe for the dish in the weekend edition of the *Chronicle.*

The younger guy and the old bull looked at each other and decided they believed me. "All right," the old guy said. "Let's head in."

"You're going to want these," I said, handing out two of the bandanas, still in their plastic packets with hole-punched cardboard tops. I noticed too late that one of them was covered with marijuana leaves. The young cop noticed it, too. "Sorry," I said. "Just what they had at the convenience store."

"I'm sure we'll be fine," the old one said. Rivka handed over her keys. They went up the stairs slowly and the young one opened the door while the older one stood a couple of paces back, legs braced, one hand on his baton handle. The instant the door opened, they both reeled back and retreated to the middle landing, where they tied the bandanas over their faces like cowboy-movie train robbers. Even with the bandanas, they kept their tour of Rivka's apartment to a few minutes and hustled back to us across the street.

"It's pretty torn up in there," the young one said, as the older one gasped for breath. "The smell has to be some kind of chemical agent. We're going to get the Department of Public Health to send an inspector around. Until then, we're going to seal off the building."

"The *building*?" For the first time, Rivka's voice had a tinge of panic. "Not just my apartment?"

"The building," the older cop said. He looked like he was struggling to keep his lunch down. "We don't know what that stuff is, but it's noxious. No sense in taking any chances."

"But my landlord lives downstairs," Rivka says. "He'll be furious."

The older cop shrugged. "I would be, too, but it's not your fault. I'm sure he'll understand."

The younger cop and I locked eyes for a moment in which he managed to convey that he understood that his partner was utterly wrong, and also that it would be a waste of time to argue with him. *Oh well,* I thought. *She said she wanted to move.*

"The DPH boys are quick when it's a chemical spill, anyway," the younger cop apologized. "I wouldn't be surprised if they made it out in the next hour or two."

"Do we have to be here to meet them?" I was juggling the logistics in my head: Could Rivka sleep on our sofa? Could I get her to a friend's place where she could camp out? What would we do for hours?

"Either that or your landlord," the older cop said. "*Someone* has to be here to meet them and let them in."

Rivka sighed. "I will stay here. I will explain to my landlord."

The older cop grunted satisfaction. "That's settled then."

It occurred to me that Rivka had a lot of practice putting aside her comfort and well-being to make older men satisfied.

"What about the property damage?" I said. "What about the investigation? You guys were in and out of there pretty fast. Don't you need to take fingerprints?"

Older cop chuckled. "We'll get you a report and you can have your insurer look into the specifics of the damage. From what I saw, we're looking at a misdemeanor at worst, so I don't think the crime-scene guys will come out for prints. It was probably stupid kids or junkies. Either way, there's no percentage in giving it the crime-of-the-century treatment."

I didn't like this guy. His partner made a face like he agreed with me.

"Miss Goldman, we know it's scary and terrible for you," he said. "But with these petty property crimes, especially when they're random targets of opportunity, there's not really any budget to track down the offenders. Misdemeanor offense, they'll just get supervised release anyway. It's not like any of these kids have any money you can sue 'em for. Just get through it with your insurer, that's my advice. Put it behind you. These kinds of random things, they're like getting caught out in a storm. You get wet, it's no fun, it ruins your shoes, but there's no sense in looking for meaning or revenge. Just move on, just move on."

I was on the verge of asking him whether random break-and-enter artists usually made a point of smearing a shit-swastika on their victim's walls, when that victim was a Hasidic Jewish woman, but I stopped myself. This was Rivka's show.

She stared at the young cop for a long time.

"Unless," the cop said, with no inflection at all, "there is someone you think might be targeting you, personally, here. An enemy or enemies, say." It wasn't a question. This was Rivka's show. I kept my mouth shut.

"No," she said. "No, of course not."

"I'm not insured," she said, after the DPH squad had come and gone. They'd identified the chemical agent as butyric acid, which was harmless except for the smell, which lingered, and lingered, and lingered. "A little drop'll stink up a room for weeks," the DPH woman said through her breather mask. "The load you've got in there?" She gave a mock-shudder. "I'm sorry to have to say it, but I don't think anyone's going to want to live there for a long, long time."

Rivka had thanked her for the news and watched her go and then we piled into my van and she said, "I'm not insured."

"Oh," I said.

"I kept meaning to take out insurance, but I don't really have very much. Just mementos, really. Letters, photo albums. A little jewelry. I put all my commissions from Fidelity into starting CF, and we're keeping every dime we can in the business now, while we get started."

"Well, the good news is that you can probably get all those valuables out of your place and stick 'em in an out-of-the-way spot at work for a couple weeks to air out."

She rustled in the passenger seat as she shifted her weight and adjusted her long skirt. I glanced at her, then looked away to give her tears some privacy. After a while she whispered, "My landlord."

"Well, at least they unsealed his door for him."

The gentleman in question was a long-hair guy with a Led Zeppelin tee and a pack of filterless Camels rolled into one sleeve. He had bought the house with an inheritance and the rent from Rivka's place paid the mortgage. He was a "businessman," whatever that meant.

He'd been disbelieving, then furious, then mean. He'd insisted on going in, wrapping his head in two T-shirts and then hastening out again and glaring at her.

"Looks like you pissed someone off," he said. "That shit on the wall. That's not just kids. It's personal."

"I don't have any enemies," Rivka said. I didn't contradict her. "I don't know why anyone would do this. Honestly." I contained a wince at the timing of that *honestly*. I could see her landlord caught it, too.

"Doesn't look like that to me. I tell you one thing, I'm not eating the lost rent while that place is airing out and getting where I can rent it to someone else."

Rivka compressed her lips until they lost all color. I looked at her, saw how close she was to losing it.

My dad had a way of talking to unreasonable people, just calmly rephrasing whatever they'd just told him, repeating as necessary, until the point was unmissable. It came naturally to me. "It sounds like you're evicting her but you want her to pay rent anyway? That's a pretty good deal for you."

He narrowed his eyes. "Who're you again?"

"Work friend," I said.

He stared at me for a long time.

"All I know is, I'm not going out of pocket on this. It's not my problem."

Rivka was shaking now.

"We can talk about it later," I said.

"I'm sure *we* can," the landlord said. He favored us each with another long, snaky look and then got back in his Trans Am and peeled rubber.

"Charming fellow," I said.

She breathed out a shuddery sigh. "I hate him," she said. "I hate—" She choked. "*This.*" Her balled fists shook.

"How about this. We go to my place, make some calls, check in on Sister Maria-Eva and Liz, figure out where you're going to perch. Maybe we just buy a mattress and stick it in the office for now. You wouldn't be the first high-tech founder to sleep at the office. Art worked one place, they had mattresses in the rafters where exhausted hackers could go to roost after marathon coding sessions. He was forever terrified one of them was going to roll over in his sleep and plummet onto some poor bastard's desk and kill them both."

That got half a smile out of her.

"Before we go, I think we should wrap our faces in as much cloth as we can find and go into your place and pull out all those photo albums and jewelry. Your landlord can try to get the rent out of you, but practically speaking his only move is to pawn whatever he can of yours. So we get all the pawnables out and hit the road. Art's van is roomy."

She sucked up air, inflated her composure, got her chin high. "That's a good plan," she said. "Let's do it."

So we did. Neither of us looked too hard at that swastika. We worked like burglars, filling pillowcases with photo albums, loose jewelry, a silver candelabra, some framed photos off the wall. They *stank,* but not as bad as the apartment, and we stank, too—the butyric acid fumes got into our clothes. We drove home fast, with the fan blowing and the windows rolled down.

I let her have first shower and found some of my sweats for her to wear. Art bagged up our clothes in a trash bag and took them downstairs to the laundry room and we exiled her salvaged precious belongings to the apartment's tiny balcony.

I was working on my second beer when she reached for the phone. "I need to call Liz and Maria-Eva," she said. "Tell them what happened, make sure they're safe."

"Excellent idea. I forgot about that. I feel like an idiot."

She looked at me. "You've had a hard day," she said.

It brought me up short. She'd lost her home, had shit smeared on her walls, walked away from all of her furniture, and she was, to all appearances, concerned about *my* mental state. I mean, sure, it had been an unsettled time, between receiving a reasonably competent beating and walking away from a lucrative contract and into uncertain financial straits. But in the hierarchy of pain and fear, surely my troubles were mere trifles next to Rivka Goldman's.

"I'm fine," I said. "And you're right, we should check in on your business partners."

She left a terse message on Sister Maria-Eva's machine, warning her obliquely to be careful, then called Liz.

After a few confused volleys of conversation, she carried the living room phone into my bedroom and shut the door. Some time later, the door opened. Rivka emerged, drawn, knuckles white on the phone.

"Liz's family has cut her off," she said. "Their bishop called them and told them . . . *things* . . . about Liz and what she was doing out here. Mostly lies, but with some truth, but told in the most awful way possible. They've told her not to contact them again."

"That's terrible," I said. "Man, that's really—"

"That's really typical," Art said. "Around here. Rivka, I think you know it. Go down to the Twenty-First Street Baths, take a survey. I bet you not one guy in five there is on speaking terms with his family."

I stared at him, tried to figure out what he was getting at. Liz wasn't gay. Besides, two wrongs didn't make a right—

"That's what's got you so shook, right, Rivka? Not that your friend is being shunned by the entire state of Utah—it's what you think might happen when they get to *your* family, right?

"I'll tell you what, Rivka. It will be hard. So, so *hard.*" There were tears in Art's eyes now. "I know. But here's the point: *you can survive it.* Here, in this city, you're surrounded by more survivors of that awful business than you would be in any other place on Earth. Sure, some of us are walking wounded, but we are all of us—each and every one—proof that you can survive this. There is no better place on Earth to go through that hurt. So your friend got drummed out of her family? Fine, that says everything about her family that you need to know. And if your family does the same to you? Same to them!

"This is a place where we make our own families, of our own choosing. You can't do anything about your parents and how they'll react when and if they find out who you really are—but you can do a hell of a lot about how *you* react when *they* react. If you spend this time making a new family for yourself, that will mean that you'll always have a family around you, even if the family that raised you turns its back on you.

"Your friend just lost the family that raised her. You're the family she needs right now."

Rivka had tears in her eyes, too. Hell, so did I. I didn't talk to Art much about his folks back home, but I divvied up the long-distance bill and so I knew he hadn't placed a call to his parents in months.

Rivka put the phone back down on an end table and stared at it for a long time. "Can one of you drive me to the city, please? I think I should be with Liz."

"Now you're talking," Art said. "Leave anything you want here, we'll take care of it for you. Also, you've got a sofa to sleep on whenever you need it."

She smiled and scrubbed her eyes with her thumbs. "Thank you, Art." She turned to me. "Thank you, Martin."

"Anytime," Art said. "You ever need family-type help, you just have to ask."

8

To hear Liz tell of it, everything sort of turned around for her after we dropped Rivka off. Rivka bustled around, fixed a dinner of Hamburger Helper and frozen cod cutlets—better than it sounds—with wilted spinach, lit candles, found Liz's cloth napkins and the dark grape juice she kept around instead of wine. The meal that followed was refreshingly normal after all the chaos of her recent life.

After dinner, they tried calling Maria-Eva again. Their lurking unease kept growing. They tried to work on a thorny problem Rivka had been having with a patch to Fidelity DOS that would force it to accept normal floppy disks, but every minute or two, one or the other of them would get a faraway look and they knew they were both thinking about Maria-Eva.

Liz owned a thirdhand Le Car she'd bought from a friend of Zion's when she moved out of the Mission House. Zion's friend was too sick to drive by then, and he just wanted to make sure it ended up in good hands. She'd paid $250 down for it and was paying Zion's friend $50 a month for it for the next year. If he didn't last that long, she'd agreed to give the balance to ACT UP.

As soon as Rivka's door was closed, Liz put it in reverse, backed out of her driveway, ground the gears looking for first, and took off for the Mission and the room that Maria-Eva rented from a family whose son had been sent to Germany by the U.S. Navy.

The family patriarch was a grizzled, lean, short Mexican man in chinos and a loose-fitting T-shirt that advertised an Oakland body shop. He eyed them suspiciously until Liz busted out her best Spanish, then he lit up.

"Maria-Eva?" he said. "*Venga, venga.*" They climbed the stairs to the second-floor apartment over a used-furniture store and piled into a crowded, tiny front room that overflowed with the family matriarch, three kids, a grandmother, two sofas, an easy chair, a constellation of framed family photos, and a twelve-inch TV draped in an icon of the Virgin Mary rendered in embroidery thread.

The TV volume was turned all the way down on a telenovela running off a videocassette. Five sets of eyes looked them up and down.

"*We're friends of Maria-Eva,*" Liz said in Spanish. "*We all own the computer business together.*" Nods of approval all round, and the three kids vacated one of the sofas for them. They sat, awkwardly, and exchanged polite smiles all around.

The kids returned with a plate of conchas the size of silver dollars. Liz took one. Rivka begged off in preference to having a difficult conversation about keeping kosher and cooking with lard. A moment later, Maria-Eva arrived, in sweats, a messy bun, and sleep-gummed eyes.

"Is everything okay?"

The audience turned as one to Liz and Rivka for their reply. Rivka shrugged. "Not really," she said. "They sent a couple guys to rough up Mr. Hench. Then someone broke into my apartment and just ruined it with some kind of stink bomb, and they—" She looked at the kids, fished for a polite way to describe a shit-swastika. "They vandalized the place. Antisemitic vandalism."

Maria-Eva put her hand to her mouth.

"And I heard from home," Liz said. "From my family. For the last time. I'm not welcome there again, they made that clear."

One of the kids whispered to the grandmother, another to

her mother, providing translation. There was a lot of *tsk*ing and sympathetic headshaking.

"You weren't answering your messages," Rivka said. "We got worried and—"

"I had the machine's volume all the way down. I worked late last night and needed the sleep." Maria-Eva had her own phone line, which she used for the work she did with her comrades in Mexico, Nicaragua, and El Salvador. Having her own line made it easier to figure out the long-distance bill and headed off any tensions with her hosts' teenagers. "I'm so sorry that I worried you." She looked at the family. "I'm even more sorry that you're going through all this."

"Thank you," Rivka said.

"We should go to the shop," Maria-Eva said. "If they went after you two—"

"That was our next stop," Liz said. "After we checked on you. People first, things second."

"Agreed," Maria-Eva said. "Give me a minute, I'll get dressed."

While she was changing, the eldest child, a girl of sixteen or seventeen, pretty with a pale pink blazer and streaked hair, shyly asked, "How did you become a, a computer expert?"

Liz beamed at her. "I learned on the job. Do you want to learn? Come by the shop anytime, we'll show you. It's not so hard." She turned to the matriarch, who was scowling a little. "*It's an excellent job,*" she said. "*It pays well, it's safe, and the world will need so many more computer people than we have. We'll treat her well.*"

"Thank you," Mom said, and managed a dubious smile.

They explored CF cautiously, prowling the darkened backstage corridors, projection rooms, and basements with the air of heroines in a slasher pic, spooking at shadows and floorboard creaks. Finally, though, they convinced themselves that the building was empty. They got drinks out of the wheezing, slope-shouldered break-room refrigerator—Maria-Eva materializing a beer from an unsuspected back shelf, the other two sticking to Cokes—and sat down on the piebald break-room sofa.

"Well," Liz said, "I guess they had better things to do tonight."

Rivka opened her mouth to answer, but before she could, there was a building-shaking *thud* and *crunch* and another *thud*, reverberating through the theater's earthquake-loosened structural members.

They leapt up, eyes wide, heads turning from side to side. Maria-Eva snatched up the break room's sole kitchen knife, a blunt thing used to cut birthday cakes, and raced toward the front entrance, where the sound had come from. An instant later, the other two followed.

Someone had thrown a cinder block into the mesh-reinforced glass theater doors at the front of the CF factory. They'd thrown it hard enough to craze the glass and bow the mesh, and the cinder block had cracked in two when it landed, taking a big divot out of the quartz-flecked decorative semicircle apron where the box office had once stood.

Without hesitating, Maria-Eva flipped the deadbolts and slammed shut the doors, nearly braining herself when one of them rebounded off the remains of the cinder block. She emerged onto the Mission Street sidewalk brandishing the cake knife, eyes rolling, head whipping from side to side. A punk girl in a green leather minidress and matching mohawk backed away from the knife, giving a little *eep*.

"Maria-Eva," Rivka said sharply, "put down that knife!"

Maria-Eva was panting, eyes a little unfocused, but she got herself under control. She lowered the knife. The punk girl dithered, wanting to bolt but also consumed by curiosity.

"Did you see who did this?" Maria-Eva gestured at the cinder block.

The girl shrugged. "Not really, but there was a guy peeling down towards Twenty-Fourth Street, just before you came out. I heard the engine and saw the taillights, but that's all." She shrugged. "Coulda been anybody, honestly, so many idiots in muscle cars revving their engines up and down Mission."

Liz explored the damage to the door. It had been her idea to reinforce it, though she'd been thinking about burglars after easily fenced electronics equipment, not this kind of attack. The door had done its job, but it was warped and cracked and full of sharp glass edges and protruding wire ends. It would need replacing.

"I'm sorry about your door," the punk girl said. "That's really shitty."

All three women frowned at the curse word, caught sight of each other, and laughed.

"Thank you," Maria-Eva said. "I'm sorry about the knife."

The girl smiled. "It's okay, you didn't look like the stabbing kind."

Maria-Eva smiled back. "Appearances can be deceiving, you know."

The punk laughed and took off down Mission in a clatter of combat boots and jingling chains.

Rivka announced that she was going to spend the night at the shop, just to keep an eye on things, just because she wouldn't be able to sleep otherwise, for worry about some arsonist or mad bomber. The other two conspicuously failed to point out that things would be worse if someone burned down or bombed CF *with Rivka inside.* They understood what she meant. They decided they'd stay, too.

It wasn't unheard of for one or even two of them to work

so late that they dossed down on a sofa or pulled the camping mattress out of the storage closet, but this was the first time all three of them had been together overnight, and, despite the terrifying circumstances, it turned into something of a pajama party.

Perhaps it was the memory of how CF came to be.

9

The interfaith prayer circle at the 1982 Fidelity Computing sales conference was supposed to be coed, but the men stayed away in droves. It was probably the nuns. Catholic men were nervous around nuns. For men raised Mormon or Orthodox, it was even worse. Maria-Eva always got a lot of personal space at sales conferences, even in crowds.

That was okay with her. She came to see her sisters: Julia Inez, who fled Brazil after her village was targeted by a death squad; Juana Concepción, who performed mass for squatters in Nicaragua and shared her pulpit with Sandinismo organizers who roamed the countryside; and Fatima, whose faith had been transformed by the principle of preferential option for the poor, sending her to rural Chiapas, where she spoke out forcefully and fearlessly against the district officials and their families and the lavish lifestyles they wrung out of the campesinos she lived among.

All three had come to America as asylum seekers and found work with Fidelity, excited by the possibilities of computers as a tool of liberation—a way to link ecclesial communities throughout the poor world and share resources and solidarity. It was through them that Maria-Eva's own faith was deepened into something more than a calling, made into a *mission*.

But Julia Inez, Juana Concepción, and Fatima were not at the sales conference. No explanation was offered for this absence, and all three had sent Maria-Eva letters expressing their excitement at the chance to be in one another's presence once more.

So Maria-Eva's spirit was low as the women of Fidelity poured into the room: nuns, some in habits; Mormon mothers, sometimes with a string of daughters in tow; Orthodox women with their hair covered. They made a point of mingling, despite the awkwardness, and shaking hands or embracing and wishing each other well.

Maria-Eva tried to mingle, she really did, but her heart was breaking. Her daily life was so hard—selling and supporting Fidelity computers by day, then by night meeting with organizers from poor people's movements. Weekends, she worked in a soup kitchen or made home visits. She'd really needed this chance to see her friends again. Their company was the fuel that she burned during the long months on the road.

She couldn't do it. She could work a twelve-hour day and a six-hour night, but she couldn't smile at these women and pretend that her heart wasn't breaking. The Fort Mason Center snack bar provided her with five dollars in quarters and she pumped them into a pay phone by the ladies' room for the next twenty minutes while Julia Inez explained that she'd been fired without warning by Father Marek himself, who'd called her, Fatima, and Juana Concepción in quick succession to tell them that their plane tickets to the sales conference had been canceled and that they were expected to return all company materials by registered mail that day. Father Marek had offered each two weeks' severance on the condition that they not speak to any of their former colleagues.

"But why?" Maria-Eva said. "Why you three?"

Julia Inez's laugh was bitter. "Why? Well, it's not because of my job performance." Julia Inez's territory stretched for five hundred miles all around Denver. She was known by name in every Catholic church in the region and she gave wildly popular training workshops every month in a different church hall. Everyone knew her home phone number and she took support calls at all hours. She'd even been known to give out the number of the motels she was planning to stay in as she drove her territory, when there was someone having a particularly thorny problem.

"So why?"

"Don't be naive, Maria-Eva. You know why."

She did know why. Father Marek had sent a letter quoting Cardinal Ratzinger to all the sales reps, railing against the "Marxist myths" of liberation theology and calling on everyone in the company to be on the alert for "subversive elements" who "seek to destroy the free enterprise system that Fidelity Computing depended on and stood for." It wasn't as if Julia Inez, Fatima, and Juana Concepción had kept their politics a secret—how could they, when the minute they went off the clock for Fidelity Computing they went to work with community poverty groups?

"So how come he didn't come after me? I volunteer, I speak out—"

"Maybe he hasn't gotten around to it. Or maybe he's taking out some of us as examples to the others." She drew in a shuddering breath. "I know I shouldn't hate him, but I do. All three of them. The way they see these people, as sheep to be shorn, they're nothing better than criminals." Another shuddering breath. "I'm glad I'm gone, honestly. At least I'm not a part of that dirty business anymore."

A numbness settled over Maria-Eva then. Whatever she said next, it was automatic. She put the rest of the quarters in her handbag and went back to the prayer meeting and stood against the wall.

That's where Rivka found her, shell-shocked with an expression of nearly comical disgust on her face. She gently asked Maria-Eva if everything was all right, and before they knew it, they were outside in the hallway, huddled close together, muttering to one another as it all spilled out of Maria-Eva, the dam of self-doubt and rationalization broken by Julia Inez's words.

It was as though Rivka was a great stringed instrument and hearing Maria-Eva call out her truth set every string vibrating.

All the doubts that Maria-Eva spoke aloud were doubts that Rivka had privately wrestled with. She'd thought she was the only one. Now, this nun, this emissary from one of the other faith communities of Fidelity Computing, was saying all the secret words she'd never dared utter.

Eventually, Maria-Eva and Rivka sat knee-to-knee in a corner of the Fort Mason Center, in facing armchairs they'd dragged around, eyes leaking, murmuring to one another, whispering confessions of the families and businesses they'd shackled to Fidelity Computing's computers, doomed to pay and pay and pay.

Liz Taylor had observed them leaving the prayer breakfast, and when they didn't come back, their absence nagged at her. They'd seemed like they were in distress, and Liz was the kind of woman who couldn't bear to watch someone else suffer. She found them in their corner, and firmly and compassionately drew them out on the cause of their tears.

She found herself in full agreement with them.

"Why don't we go get some breakfast?" she said. "Since we've missed the prayer breakfast and all. There's an IHOP down the road."

That morning, over pancakes, they planted the seeds of CF.

10

Three Mexican guys were working on the doors when I arrived, replacing the broken glass and then fitting them with a grid of steel bars.

Maria-Eva was overseeing the work.

"Upgrading your security?" I said.

"Someone tried to throw a cinder block through the door last night," she said. I noticed then how pinched her features were.

"Jesus," I said, involuntarily, and she glared at me. "Sorry," I said. I looked at the great divot gouged in the tile in front of the theater entrance. "I'm really sorry." The guys working on the door had moved on to methodically sinking bolts into the frame. "Maybe I could help them? I did stuff like this on a summer job working on a renovation crew back in high school."

Her glare dimmed by a few watts. "That's kind of you, but Chuy and his guys have this covered." The foreman waved at us and went back to his hammer drill. "I have another job for you."

The bankers box on her desk looked very familiar.

"Go on," she said, "have a look."

It was full of purple boxes of floppies. "I think I've seen this movie," I said.

She allowed herself a fractional smile. "These aren't our financials. They're five years' worth of books from Fidelity Computing. We can give you a drive that you can connect to an Apple Two Plus that will read them. I assume you still have the programs you wrote to convert them to Lotus 1–2–3 files?"

I opened and closed my mouth. "Where did these come from?"

She extinguished her tiny smile. "They didn't. We don't have them. We're not giving them to you. Importantly, you won't give them back to us. When you're done, you'll ensure they're not readable and then dispose of them in a way that can't be linked to you or us." She fixed me with a glare that nuns have practiced and perfected for generations. "Is that acceptable to you?"

I withered under the glare, then had to stop myself from chuckling—at myself, not her. She was very, very good. No wonder the Reverend Sirs were so worried about her.

"That is very acceptable," I said. "Matter of fact, that sounds like *fun*."

That fractional smile returned. "All right," she said. "We will pay you your hourly rate, same as the Fidelity Computing."

I didn't say anything, because I liked these women and I didn't want to ask for 25 percent of anything they had. I'd come up with a plausible hourly rate and bill it—

"There's something you're not saying," she said. *Damn, she's good.*

"It's nothing," I said. "That's more than fair."

The smile vanished, the glare returned. I was braced for it this time and didn't let it get to me. "It's fine," I said. "Honestly, it's fine."

"Why don't you let me decide that?"

So I told her about my deal with Fidelity Computing, the bounty they'd put on her life's work. She nodded curtly. "The same deal applies, then," she said.

"Sister—"

She raised a hand, and, impossibly, found more wattage for that glare of hers. "The same deal applies. You go through these financial records, find something that gets Fidelity Computing to leave us alone, and we give you one-quarter of our revenues for the year. There's no reason you should have to take a pay cut just because you changed sides."

"Respectfully," I said, carefully, "I have already scrutinized your finances, and I don't think you can afford that."

She flicked that raised hand. "We also can't afford to be sued into oblivion by Fidelity Computing. You take care of them, we'll take care of you." She dimmed the glare, lowered the hand. "Though perhaps we'll ask for terms. Pay on installments." Her voice was quieter and shook just a little. I got the sense that all that hardcase stuff she was putting on was actually holding her together.

She drew herself up, and the hard case sealed again. "I insist, in any event."

"Then I accept, Sister. And of course, you have my assurance that I will work with you to find equitable terms."

"Thank you, Mr. Hench."

"Thank *you*, Sister."

"I think you'd better not go out the front door, and perhaps we should transfer the contents of this box to some shopping bags."

"I was just thinking the same thing."

Rivka moved in with a friend of Moshe's, an ex-Orthodox woman named Sadie whom he'd met at the Jewish Student Association. Sadie's roommate had flunked out of Stanford and gone home to Cincinnati, leaving her short on the rent. Rivka liked Sadie, and also liked Palo Alto. There were three personal-computer stores within walking distance of the apartment. She also met a law student who sent her former landlord a letter stating that he could keep her deposit to cover last month's rent and disposal of her things.

Art showed Liz his improvements to my little programs for converting SPREADSHEET files to Lotus 1–2–3 and she immediately set about charming him out of a license to them, with an eye to turning them into a fully automated conversion tool that anyone could use. She wanted to bundle it with an improved Apple][+ program that would let you read a Fidelity floppy in an Apple drive; that way people who wanted to leave Fidelity behind could take their files with them.

"That's the goal here," she said. "Get everyone out of the prison Fidelity Computing tricked them into. That *we* lured them into."

Art laughed. "You're going to put yourself out of business," he said.

She smiled. "I don't think that'll happen. Fidelity Computing has a *lot* of customers, and even if we save them all, they'll be *our* customers and we can sell them software, hardware, you name it."

Art smiled back. "I like the way you think," he said. "All the things we've done with computers so far are just for starters. There's so much more to do."

"That's exactly how I see it," Liz said. "Fidelity Computing's whole power trip is based on this weird idea that the PC is fully cooked and all they need to do is take one hundred percent control over how people use computers *today* and they can sit back and open checks for the next fifty years.

"We're not just going to use them to make a little money springing people out of their trap. We're going to use them as a launchpad, to make something so much bigger. A new kind of computer company, one that puts the users first. One that's all about understanding the users, holding their hands, giving them the power to do more in their lives."

Art waved gospel arms over his head and shouted "A-*men* sister!"

"I know you're not religious. I know how people like you think about people like us. Like we're cavemen, believing in magical spirits. That's how the *Reverend Sirs*"—it was a curse on her lips—"think of them, too, you know? That's why they think they can take advantage. For them, their flocks are easy pickings, ready to be sheared.

"But not for me. For me, my faith was a community. It made me stronger. It gave me a moral compass. It—" Her eyes welled over. "Sorry," she said, plucking the last tissue from a box on her desk.

"It's okay," Art said. "My family won't have anything to do with me, either."

He gave her one of his best hugs, and then he cried, too.

As for me, I holed up in our apartment with Art's Apple clone and boxes of floppies and several notebooks and a lot of coffee. I also put a new deadbolt on the door and took to leaving through the fire exit at the back of the building rather than the front door.

The silence from Fidelity Computing was deafening. No one had tried their luck with the CF shop since the Night of the Cinder Block, and nothing else had happened to Rivka, Maria-Eva, or Liz. Every now and then, I'd look up from the notes I was making and think about what the Reverend Sirs might be planning next, and a goose would walk over my grave. I'd shiver and get back to unwinding their finances.

They kept two sets of books. That didn't even surprise me. The Reverend Sirs were presiding over a "network sales" company—a pyramid scheme—and they needed to track how much money they were *actually* making, and how much they were *claiming* they were making.

One of my accounting profs had worked for the FTC when they'd gone after Amway, and he was still bitter that Amway's founder, Rich DeVos, had gotten Gerry Ford to lean on the FTC to shut down their prosecution of his company. Ford had been DeVos's congressman before Nixon's resignation catapulted him into the White House, and DeVos's partner, Jay Van Andel, was the head of the U.S. Chamber of Commerce, the most powerful lobbyist in America, so the FTC buckled.

There was only one problem: Amway was guilty as hell. The company told people that they were selling Amway's products, but really they were selling *the right to sell Amway's products.* Every Amway seller's main preoccupation was finding more Amway sellers, who'd find more sellers, who'd find more sellers. Every time one of your "downline" sellers bought some Amway crap to try to push on their relatives, you got a piece of the action, and kicked a little of that up to your upline, who kicked to *their* upline, and so on.

Anyone who understood exponential math understood that this couldn't work. If you keep doubling the number of Amway salespeople, pretty soon the whole country is full of people who have shelled out for a giant minimum order of Amway junk trying to sell it to someone else who's also sitting on a garage full of crap no one needed.

So the FTC came up with a set of arbitrary rules that it could apply to Amway and conclude that Gerry Ford was right and Amway wasn't a pyramid scheme. So long as bonuses for the "distributors" only kicked in if you sold 70 percent of your inventory, and provided you sold something to at least ten people each month, and provided that the definitely-not-a-pyramid-scheme would buy back your "excess inventory," then you were free. Never mind that all of this was easy as hell to cheat on, and never mind that Amway knew its "distributors" cheated like crazy.

My prof loved to hate pyramid schemes. He brought in a mimeographed set of financial statements from Holiday Magic, a scam that was pretty much identical to Amway except that its founder wasn't buddies with the president of the United States, and showed us how to follow the money and see how the insiders were able to skim extra points, even beyond the vig that got kicked up by their downlines.

A couple of my classmates had family members who were in the Charles J. Givens Organization or United Sciences, and my prof invited them to have the family members come down and give us their sales pitch, on the condition that these relations allow *us* to give them our pitch for why they were getting scammed. Knowing what I did about how pyramid schemes worked, I could see that their pitches were pathetic, but I could also see how someone who didn't know any better could get sucked in. A couple of my dumber classmates actually nodded along from time to time.

Then it was our turn. We showed these people how a pyramid scheme could only ever produce riches for a small number of people at the very top of the pyramid, mostly off the backs of everyone else caught up in the scam.

We showed them our mathematical models. We had printed out spreadsheets on overhead transparencies and we pulled down the screen at the front of the classroom and went through them line by line, the way we'd been taught to do when presenting an audit, aiming for an audience without any accounting or math training. We paused often to check if they had questions. We brought in case histories of other pyramid schemes and showed how they always went the same way.

When we finished the first of these, the classroom was filled with a palpable sense of accomplishment. We'd done it! We'd talked a nice lady out of her membership in a destructive cult! We'd saved her!

And then. She smiled at us and thanked us for our time and said, "I know you're all just trying to help, but you just don't understand. The Charles Givens method is a tested, effective way for everyday Americans to build wealth ahead of inflation, to provide for their families and their future. I know you mean well, but I'm afraid you just don't understand the Givens method."

And she packed up her samples—videotapes, books, and mimeographed self-study materials—thanked us again, and left. Our classmate—her niece—looked like she was ready to cry. Our prof looked grimly satisfied.

The second time around, we were better prepared: We'd taken the time to understand Givens's pitch. We'd produced charts showing how his claims about real-estate investing couldn't be true. We found an interview with his former editor at Simon & Schuster where she called it all a "scam," and called Givens "a fucking idiot'" and a "psychopathic liar."

It bounced off our classmate's cousin without making a mark. The nice fellow smiled at us and told us that we just didn't understand. The classmate looked furious. Our prof just nodded.

The final time, when our classmate's grandmother came in to pitch us on their vitamins and diet bars, she spent as much time talking about how nice the United Science family was, how selling for United was more than a way to benefit your friends and neighbors, it was a way to join a community who would always be there for you.

That was a revelation. This sweet, lonely granny was turning her friends into cultists and turning cultists into friends. Of course she wasn't going to be dissuaded. When she left—once again telling us that we didn't understand—our prof looked at us for a long moment, then he paraphrased Swift: "You cannot

188 ◄ **cory doctorow**

reason someone out of something he or she was not reasoned into."

My classmate thanked us for trying.

The Fidelity books documented how the Reverend Sirs and their trusted lieutenants worked a precise formula that was supposed to retain sellers and customers in the system. For sellers, it was simple enough: when a seller's numbers dipped too much—so much that they might quit—Fidelity Computing would cut them a break, reapportioning the way their downline sales were booked to give them more money. It wasn't like the seller would *get* that money, but their debts to their own uplines and Fidelity Computing would be reduced so that they were once again able to make their minimum payments from their sales. That meant they wouldn't accrue penalties for a while—most of the debts on Fidelity's books were from penalties for missing a minimum, which then made the debt bigger and the minimum bigger.

If you didn't read the books closely, you might go away with the impression that Fidelity Computing had some outstanding salespeople, some competent salespeople, and some poor salespeople, and that the system was forgiving and fair enough that even the worst salesperson never got into the kind of debt that turned other pyramid schemes into scandals.

But if you read them carefully, if you cross-referenced payments that were listed on one sheet as commissions, on others as bonuses, and on a third as debt forgiveness—a tally they diligently reported to the IRS and took a deduction on—the real picture came into focus.

Fidelity Computing was a con. The numbers were all fake. If you were in the Reverend Sirs' charmed circle, the numbers always worked out such that you got a fat check every month.

If you weren't, you got chicken feed, or slid deeper and deeper into debt. Whenever that debt got so bad that you might walk away—or call the attorney general's office or the *San Francisco Chronicle*—they loosened the screws. It couldn't have been more crooked if it was a poker game with a marked deck where half the players were working with the dealer to fleece the other half.

It took me days to figure this out. The tricks they pulled would have been really hard to detect if you were just using ledger books and pencils. Even SPREADSHEET wouldn't have been able to make much sense out of the financials. With a maximum of only 256 rows, Fidelity's SPREADSHEET books were split out across multiple files. If anything, it would have been harder to untangle the books with SPREADSHEET than with paper ledgers.

But once I had all the data in Lotus, with its cap of 2,048 rows, I peeled it like a banana. I was able to determine who was in the charmed circle and who was the sucker at the table. I was even able to determine when they were in a hurry to cheat: I turned the payments into strings, then calculated the frequency distribution of the number one as the first, second, and third digits.

Benford's law predicts that 30 percent of numbers will start with a one. Seventeen percent of the time, the second digit will be a one, and so on. Anytime you ask your stupid brain to make up numbers, it will violate Benford's law, because our brains want made-up numbers to look "random" and not start with a one 30 percent of the time.

Once I'd crunched all the Fidelity financials through my Benford's law checker, I was able to compile a list of which sellers were getting fake payouts. A little fiddling split that group into two chunks: sellers whose payments were greater than the median quarterly commission, and sellers whose payments were less.

Guess what? The people with fake payments *above* the median were *way* above the median—they were being showered with money.

And guess what else? The people with fake payments *below* the median were *way* below the median: their paydays were measured in pennies, so small that they slipped deeper and deeper into debt every quarter, until someone at Fidelity took pity on them and gave them a little boost so they could still afford to stay in the game. Why not? Again, all that debt was just penalties and interest and interest on penalties. None of it had been borrowed from the Fidelity company, so forgiving the debt didn't cost Fidelity anything. In fact, thanks to those tax breaks for debt forgiveness, Fidelity *made* money by forgiving these imaginary debts.

I made a list of goats—people who were getting shafted—and angels—people who were getting rich—and printed it out to share with CF.

I never did find out how the *San Francisco Chronicle* got onto the CF story. I think it helped that they had a new Latino beat reporter who was working the Mission. The *Chron*'s tech reporting didn't usually feature the likes of CF.

But there'd been a string of stories about the labor conditions in the *maquiladoras,* the factories on the Mexican side of the U.S.-Mexican border. Someone must have thought that CF would make a nice contrast with that story.

The reporter was a nice Puerto Rican lady who'd been poached from a New York paper, and she wrote a glowing two-page spread for the weekend edition of the paper. Anyone who read the story would understand three things:

1. CF was a fast-growing, high-tech company;
2. It was owned by women and employed women;

3. Its business was selling computers, software, and peripherals to people who felt "trapped" by their earlier technology choices.

The words "Fidelity Computing" did not appear in the paper, but the photos clearly showed some Fidelity 3000s and their printers and hard drives, instantly recognizable thanks to that weird, glowing violet plastic casing, somehow even weirder in black and white.

Anyone who was trapped with a Fidelity computer couldn't miss the meaning of the story.

Fidelity Computing made terrible computers, but they had a very sophisticated financial operation. The business with their sellers was only half the story; they also had a whole operation devoted to *buyers*.

Take those printers: the weird sprocketing they installed in them made them jam-prone, and eventually they would need service. Naturally, Fidelity wouldn't provide parts to anyone except their authorized service depot.

I discovered a whole sheet devoted to doing calculations for these depots. If a customer came in with a busted printer, they'd be given a quote within forty-eight hours. In reality, it only took a minute to come up with the quote, because all the printers were busted in the same way: the nonstandard sprockets were too widely spaced, which produced frequent jams. The jams stressed the motors that advanced the rollers, and either the gear teeth would snap or the motor would burn out.

But even though the diagnosis and repair were easy, the delay was important to the hustle. It gave time for the repair depot to check in with the head office and find out how much of the oddly sprocketed paper the customer had ordered, and when.

The Reverend Sirs had a toy mathematical model they'd built to estimate how fast their customers burned through printer paper, and they combined that with their sales data to figure out how much paper each customer likely had on hand.

The more paper you had, the more fixing your printer would cost—because someone who'd invested a lot of money in over-priced special printer paper that only worked in a Fidelity printer would be willing to pony up more to keep their printer going. If they thought you were out of paper, on the other hand, they'd charge you just a hair over cost, and offer you a deal on five reams of paper at a discount.

The whole business was the mirror image of how the Reverend Sirs kept sellers on the hook.

They had beheld the spreadsheet and found in it the means by which they could carefully titrate the amount of positive reward and punishment they could mete out to both sellers and buyers. They were playing them like an angler plays a fish.

This was only possible because they had computers. The sole bright side was that their computers were so awful that they capped how much of this sort of thing they could get up to. There's a limit to how much malice you can wring out of a 256-row spreadsheet.

The *Chronicle* article ran on Saturday. At 9 a.m. Monday when Liz opened the CF shop, all the phones were already ringing. Up until that point, all of their sales had come through personal connections and word of mouth: Liz, Rivka, and Maria-Eva had called up their old customers and taken them through their product offerings. The business had built slowly but surely, as word got around that there were better ways to get more out of your Fidelity 3000 for less money.

But the *Chronicle* feature blew open the market. They were no longer reliant on satisfied customers chatting at church or temple or synagogue. Everyone in the Bay Area who read that piece called everyone they knew who had a Fidelity PC. The timing couldn't have been better: Sunday night was when Mormon boys on missions called home to SLC, it was when Orthodox boys studying at Stanford or Berkeley spoke to their mothers, it was when Mexicans who'd come to the city in search of work out of the fields of the Central Valley made brief, expensive calls to their families. It was when I called my own parents, and I couldn't help but brag a little on it, and my father was volubly, surprisingly impressed, and I was doubly surprised by how good that left me feeling.

So the phone started ringing at 9 a.m. and didn't stop. Liz and Rivka grabbed some of the factory women who had a good handle on the product line and got them to work the phones while they took a quick inventory. Maria-Eva, meanwhile, went down the street to a pay phone to call Pac Bell and order four more phone lines.

They booked orders until 7 p.m., working those phones until their throats were sore and their tongues were dry. Liz had scheduled a lunchtime meeting with Art to talk about the software contract he was working on, but when he arrived, she press-ganged him into going out for lunch bags of big, fat Mission burritos and big plastic cups of oatmeal and cinnamon horchata drink—and then put him to work on the phones while she ate.

At seven, they turned on the answering machines and went to work packing orders. They'd been reluctant to ask any of the factory women to do this, because it was clear that they were going to be out of inventory in a day or two and they wanted to ramp up production while they could.

I came by at eight with a case of Anchor Steam for me, Maria-Eva, and Art, and a couple of pizzas. We packed orders until our lower backs screamed and then kept packing until all the bubble wrap was gone. That was 2 a.m. Art and I slept in the back of the van while Rivka, Maria-Eva, and Liz dossed down in their office and break room.

The next day, we did it all over again.

Art had a friend who had worked at Commodore when the PET took off like a rocket. He agreed to come by early the next morning and talk to CF's owners about how to weather a storm like this. I met him in the doorway as I arrived for my three-times-delayed appointment with Maria-Eva.

We took over the break room—every other space in the building was being used to assemble new parts, pack orders, or answer calls—and I walked her through my analysis. I'd printed it all out and organized it into a tabbed binder, the way I'd learned to do in my audit class, and I was pretty proud of how official it all looked.

Maria-Eva tore into it with gusto. She was *damned* smart, and absorbed the implications of my charts and tables quickly, asking intelligent questions. It had taken me two weeks to assemble the report, and she digested it in less than an hour. Maybe that's because I'm so good at making difficult things easy to understand, but my money's on Maria-Eva's analytical skills.

The first question she asked me after she put the binder down on the scarred, ringed coffee table was "How long would it take you to turn this into a business plan?"

I just stared at her.

"Oh, no," she said, and laughed. "Not like that. Oh!" She laughed harder. "No, we're meeting with some investors from a family that sold their father's chain of office-machine stores. They have good connections with manufacturers and shipping companies and they're looking to spend their money on something that has more of a future than IBM Selectrics and account books. It just seems to me that the information you've just presented could be a very efficient sales-lead generator. All those people, the sellers and the customers, getting cheated by Fidelity. We just go to them and offer to help them out, and they become our customers and our sellers."

"That's . . ." I ran out of words. "It's very clever," I said.

"You think it's unethical," she said.

"I—" Did I? "I don't know that it's unethical. I mean, the only unethical part is that the Fidelity data I analyzed is—" I bit down on *stolen*.

"Accurate? Damning?" She stuck her chin out and busted out that nun glare. I made my spine as stiff as I could manage.

"All of that," I said. "You're right."

"I am," she said.

"She is," Art said, as we navigated 280 traffic that night. "She's *smart,* Marty. This is a *good* plan."

I shrugged.

"You don't think so?" He unrolled the passenger-side window and put one foot up on the rearview mirror. Traffic was stuck solid.

"I guess so. Look, they're clocking up a lot of sales right now, but that's just publicity from the *Chronicle* article. What happens when that peters out? I mean, how much money can there be in supplying parts and software for someone else's computers?"

"Oh, Marty, baby. I knew you were only skimming *Creative Computing.* Don't you remember Carterfone?"

"No, I don't remember Carterfone. Lemme guess, it's a phone that asks you to turn down your thermostat and put on a sweater."

"No, dope," he said. "It's a gadget. Or it *was* a gadget. Late fifties. It was a way for ranch hands to get phone calls when they were out on the range—a kind of walkie-talkie you plugged into your Western Digital phone handset that would relay your calls to a radio you wore on your belt."

"Sure," I said. "I could see how that would be useful."

"It was," he said. "It was also illegal. Remember, Ma Bell had a monopoly on plugging things into the Bell System, and Carterfone didn't bother to ask AT&T before opening up shop. The Bell System sued, and Carterfone won. That was the crack that split open the Bell System: after that, we could make all kinds of stuff, modems, PBXes, answering machines, fax machines . . ."

"Okay, good for Carterfone, but I just don't see—"

"I know you don't. So I'll tell you. Try to keep up."

"Asshole," I said.

He thumped his ear. "Sorry, I didn't catch that. Having some problems with my left ear. No mind. What made Carterfone possible?"

I shrugged. "Engineering? Finance? Little green fairies? Phlogiston?"

"Fine, I'll give you a hint. This gadget, it worked like an acoustic coupler."

I'd coveted one of those all through college, especially a Novation CAT. It was like a cradle for one of your standard phones, with a speaker in one cup and a mic in the other. You dialed a computer somewhere else with the phone, listened for the warbling song of the modem on the other end, and then slammed the receiver down into the coupler's cradle, so the coupler's speaker was nuzzled against the phone's mic and vice versa. The phone and the receiver would then screech at each other, the noises leaking faintly out of the coupler's rubber gasket like distant cricket song.

"I hate it when you're cryptic, you know that? I can't figure out your riddles, I gotta concentrate on the road."

He just snorted pointedly and jerked his chin at the red

brake lights stretching to infinity before us. I chewed on the problem.

"Okay, give me a hint."

He grinned. "The Carterfone worked like an acoustic coupler. It was made in 1959. They're making acoustic couplers today. Both of them work just fine, though. Why is that?"

"Because of—" I thought hard. The sun was in my eyes. The brake lights shimmered. "I dunno. Because the phone receiver fits it."

"Aha!"

"Aha?"

"Yes, Watson, aha. You know my methods. Apply them."

"I *hate* your Sherlock Holmes shtick."

"*Apply them,* Watson."

Ooh, he was smug. Now I wanted to figure it out. *The phone receiver fits in it.*

"The phone receiver fits in it?"

"Yes, it certainly does, doesn't it?"

"It does."

I thought.

"You're going to strain something," he said. "The Carterfone was made in 1959 but if you got a new phone today, it would still work."

"Right," I said. "It's a standard Western Digital phone. My parents had one in their kitchen when I was kid. Rented another one when we got to Alabama. Familiar as an old friend. An American icon. Naturally it fits."

"You are *so close.* You're just a prisoner of your own cramped imagination."

I smacked my hands on the wheel. "Fine. Enlighten me, oh wise and perspicacious one, what am I missing?"

"I'll give you another clue. I have confidence in you. You will get there, eventually."

"I'm going to clean the toilet with your toothbrush."

198 ◄ **cory doctorow**

"Here's your clue: Why aren't there phones that *don't* fit?"

"Because—" *Ding.* "Because there's only one phone manufacturer."

"See! You're smarter than you look, my old *ami*. Yes, there's only one manufacturer, a division of Ma Bell. Western Digital. They had the monopoly—the *legal* monopoly—over equipment that could be coupled to the Bell System. That was one of the big issues in the AT&T breakup."

"I didn't pay attention to it," I said. "I was in high school."

"So was I. But *I* have priorities. For more than half a century, one company controlled all the equipment that could make or receive or route a phone call. The Bell System imposed standardization on the whole kaboodle. That meant that Carterfone could make a gadget with a pair of standard-sized cups on it, and *know* that *every single phone in America would fit it.*"

"Aha," I said.

"A-*ha*," he agreed.

"So what?"

"So, schmuck, that's the interoperator's advantage! You've got this Goliath that's created an any-color-you-like-so-long-as-it's-black policy on the whole nation, and that means that you can know exactly what's out there and how you can plug into it. Every time the Bell System sells a standardized Western Digital phone, that's another potential customer for a Carterfone. *Now* do you see?"

Traffic jerked forward, giving me a moment to think about it. "You're saying that every Fidelity Computing computer sold is a chance for CF to sell their drives and printers and paper and whatnot."

"The game is afoot, Watson!"

"I really hate it when you do that Holmes thing." But I was smiling.

He was right. When you put it the way he did, it was easy to see how this whole thing could work.

"Every time Fidelity Computing sells a product, they create an enemy. They have to, because they're rip-offs. Every time CF sells a product, they create a friend, because they're un-ripping-off the people who got screwed by Fidelity."

"Exactly," he said. Traffic was moving now. Good. I wanted a beer and a baloney sandwich.

"And meanwhile, CF is learning to build a really good computer, one piece at a time, by doing the opposite of what Fidelity does. Anytime they don't knock it out of the park, the customer will blame Fidelity. Anytime they get it right, they'll get the credit. They're basically getting a free, unlimited R&D budget courtesy of Fidelity's angry customers. And by the time Fidelity is dust—"

"They'll have built an entire PC company up," Art finished as I hit our off-ramp. "It's the Ship of Theseus of computer companies!"

"Right on!" I said.

"You have no idea what the Ship of Theseus is, do you?"

"It's Greek," I said.

"It is Greek," he said.

I pretended to be occupied with driving.

"You need to take some humanities classes, Watson. The Ship of Theseus is a hypothetical ship that gets replaced one piece at a time: first the sail, then the mast, then the floor—"

"The deck, I think you'll find." I briefly reveled in the feeling of having corrected him.

"The *deck*," he said. "The hull, the oars, the—I don't know—the ship's parrot, whatever. Eventually, there's nothing original left. Is it still the Ship of Theseus?"

"Right," I said.

"Well, is it?"

I shrugged. "Sorta," I said. "Is that the right answer?"

He grunted. "Actually, it is."

I smacked the steering wheel. Our apartment building hove

into view. My mouth filled with saliva at the thought of a baloney sandwich and an Anchor Steam. "Got it."

"Those ladies are building a better Fidelity computer, one part at a time. When they're done, there'll be nothing left that the Reverend Sirs would recognize. Will it still be a Fidelity PC?"

"Nope," I said. "Because they'll hire good lawyers to make sure it's not."

The sandwich was delicious.

11

My college graduation suit had once been my high-school graduation suit. Though it had only been worn twice, it was five
years old and looking pretty seventies when I put it on for the
meeting with Maria-Eva's investors. I'd had it dry-cleaned after
graduating, but I hadn't bothered to ask the cleaner to take in
the belled cuffs. It'd need cleaning again after the meeting. I'd
get the legs narrowed then.

Or maybe not. Those *lapels*. I looked . . . Well, I looked like
a guy who never, ever wore a suit.

"Don't start," I said.

Art looked back into his cereal bowl. "I didn't say anything."

"Don't say anything about straight guys' fashion sense."

He mugged at me. "Wouldn't dream of it." Then he looked
me up and down, snorted ostentatiously, and muttered something.

"What's that?" I said.

"Nothing," he said. "I literally just went *rhubarb rhubarb* because I had to say *something*. Next paycheck, we're going to get
you a decent suit. Every adult needs at least one."

"Fine. But please let's not become the kind of gay-straight
roommates where the gay one takes the straight one out for
makeovers."

"Furthest thing from my mind, buddy."

"Because I know how you dressed back east, Arthur Israel
Hellman. I have photos."

"I hear you," he said.

"Remember the coat? The long one that looked like a flasher's raincoat? The one you wore every day for six months?"

"I remember it," he said. "You make an excellent point, Martin Aloysius Hench."

"My middle name is Harold."

"Whatever you say, Aloysius."

When I got to CF, Maria-Eva, Rivka, and Liz were in a dervish, neatening up the place from top to bottom. The investors were due in half an hour and they'd already tidied the break room and their office to within an inch of their lives. I pitched in to straighten out the shipping area and then moved on to the workbenches.

I'd just straightened the last soldering gun in the last row when the doorbell rang. I put on my jacket and straightened my tie and accompanied Rivka and Liz to the office while Maria-Eva got the door.

The investors were a pair of brothers in their forties, with suits even worse than mine. They passed out business cards with the name of their father's former business on it and new phone numbers written in pen on the back. I tried not to judge them: I didn't have *any* business cards. On the other hand, weren't these guys in the office-supply game?

Pleasantries. Doughnuts. Coffee. Herbal tea for Liz. Pleasantries. Liz handed out the investor kits she'd run off on a modified Fidelity printer and bound in neat folders.

"Thank you, darling," one of the brothers said. His name was Benjamin Kohler, and he was the older one, with a paunch and wet lips that he kept unconsciously licking. He was a grown adult who still went by Benny.

They paged through the paperwork for a moment, then turned to me. "Marty, you want to tell us what we're looking at?" That was Benny's little brother Ted, skinny with a high

forehead and an easygoing way about him. I got the impression
that he was the good cop to Benny's bad cop.

I looked at Liz. She'd predicted this would happen. *They
want to talk to a man,* she said. *Put on a suit, come to the meeting.*
She shrugged.

"Fidelity Computing is selling about two hundred thousand
computers per year. That's not much, not compared to, say, Apple. They sold a million Two Pluses last year. But it's still a big
market. They have an effective sales operation, and there are
about a million machines out there in the field today.

"Fidelity doesn't have Apple's volume, but it doesn't need it,
because Apple doesn't have Fidelity's *margins.* Those margins
are our opportunity. We can let Fidelity bear all the expenses of
creating a demand for our products and then we can swoop in
and take advantage of it."

The Kohler brothers looked at each other, then back at me.

"Run that by me again," Benny said.

The Kohlers weren't all that bright.

"You see, the Fidelity product line is a trap." I explained how
Fidelity's bait-and-switch worked, something I'd gotten good at.

"We sell the adapters to free their customers from this trap.
Want to import someone's Lotus 1–2–3 files into their SPREAD-
SHEET program? We can do that. Want to throw away your
Fidelity computer and buy an Apple and use your SPREAD-
SHEET files with Lotus? That's us. Want to buy cheap floppies
at J. K. Gill—"

"Or Kohler's," Ted said. He was starting to get it.

"Or Kohler's," I said. "We've got you covered. Want to adapt
your printer to use regular paper? Or plug it into a different
manufacturer's computer? We'll sell you the software and the
adapter."

"But do people want this? It's all so confusing." Benny had a
good confused face, like a mutt experiencing snow for the first
time.

Liz, Maria-Eva, and Rivka had been growing visibly impatient through this exchange. Even though Maria-Eva had appointed me designated hitter for this meeting, it was clear that they were better situated to answer these questions than I was.

"It may seem confusing," I said, "but I think Maria-Eva could explain what it's like from our customers' perspective."

Benny actually rolled his eyes. To his credit, Ted sat up straighter and aimed his attention at Maria-Eva.

"I oversaw the Catholic market for a large territory that included San Francisco for three years, and booked over half a million in sales. I dealt with some individuals, but mostly worked with community leaders who acted as my sales agents."

The dollar figure made an impression on the Brothers Kohler. Benny stopped rolling his eyes.

"Our customers aren't technologically sophisticated, but they care about money. They have to be cost-conscious because they are not wealthy. Every penny counts. Fidelity wouldn't be able to sell to them at all except that they use trusted religious networks to market to them.

"Because these people don't have any money, Fidelity doesn't have any competition. No one else is trying to sell them computers. That's a huge marketing advantage. I saw it firsthand. Because these people *need* computers. They use them in so many ways for their businesses, and their kids love them.

"Fidelity Computing has built a captive market. Most of my customers had very little English. You can't go into a convenience store and buy a Spanish computer magazine. They get all their information from Fidelity and its sales reps. Not the sales managers like I was, the reps who work under us, who recruit their friends and relatives to sell for them. They're the only source of information on computers for these customers, and they're helpless without them."

Benny pursed his lips. "So how are *you* going to reach these customers?"

Maria-Eva's serene smile was like a Renaissance saint's. She reached under her chair and got out a second set of documents in their own three-ring binders. Clipped to the top of each one was a nondisclosure agreement I'd copied out of a Nolo Press book, *Be Your Own General Counsel.*

"Gentlemen, I hope you don't mind signing these before we go any further."

Rivka was the one who figured out how to structure the sales book, creating charts showing, rep by rep, how much we stood to make by bringing them over, then clustering them by value, region, and sales channel (Jewish, Catholic, or Mormon). She even sketched out plans for marketing to Protestants, on the reasonable basis that they were the largest religious group in the USA. The Reverend Sirs had tried repeatedly to crack their market and failed, but Rivka had her own ideas.

Liz turned those charts into a timeline, with revenue projections by the week, month, and quarter: we recruit this many sales reps in the first week, who sell to so many customers in the second, and so on.

Maria-Eva sold it. In quiet, calm, even stern tones, she explained how the Reverend Sirs had sown the seeds of their own destruction, ripping off sales reps and their customers, setting family members and friends against each other. She told it like a Sunday-school Bible story, and it had a *great* ending: three women, pure of heart, ventured forth and redeemed these people, liberated them from bondage, and were rewarded in both the Kingdom of Earth and the Kingdom of Heaven.

I practiced my listening on her, that deep listening I'd learned from Lucille, and I discovered just how *eloquent* she was. Her words were so plain that they seemed incapable of hiding any untruth. She made me want to convert my own paycheck into stock in her company.

When she finished, the Brothers Kohler were poleaxed, slack-jawed, stupefied. I emptied out the elderly Mr. Coffee that was still brewing and reboiled the kettle for Liz's herbal tea.

I handed cups around. The factory had come to quiet life while we talked, and Maria-Eva took the guys for a tour. As soon as they left the break room, I traded looks with first Liz, then Rivka.

"She's *good*," I whispered.

"The best," Liz said.

Rivka slumped and mugged and fanned herself with both hands. She looked sixteen years old, gangly and nervous. "I think we sold them," she said. "Do you think we sold them?"

"I think they're sold," I said. I'd gone out on my share of Process Engineering Models sales calls and none of them had been as convincing as Maria-Eva's closing pitch.

"Thank God," Rivka said.

The words had barely escaped her lips when my vision went blurry and the room seemed to warp. My inner ear went crazy. The walls seemed to shake. It was only when my coffee cup fell off the table and spilled all over the carpet tiles that I realized it was an earthquake. A millisecond later, I was under the table, having teleported there without passing through any of the intervening space. Or at least, that's how it felt. One instant, I was sitting on a folding break-room chair, wondering if I was hallucinating, then in the next instant, I was prone beneath the low coffee table, trying to coil my legs under it, my spilled coffee soaking through my one white shirt, my one tie—wide and striped and never untied once after my dad knotted it on my graduation morning—and my graduation suit.

When the rattling stopped and my heart rate returned to normal and I figured out that the cold, wet feeling on my chest was the coffee, I thought, *This sale better go through, I need a new suit.* When the sound of my giggle reached my ears, it snapped me back to reality.

I climbed out from under the table. Liz and Rivka were balled up on the sofa, seat cushions over their heads.

"Get back down there!" Liz said. "There might be after-shocks."

I dived back under the table as the floor rumbled and shifted again.

After an eternity in a puddle of cooling coffee, I heard Liz say, "Okay, I think it's all right now."

We dusted ourselves off, checked ourselves for injuries, then went off to survey the damage.

It was minor, thankfully. The factory girls were experienced with quakes, and had immediately sheltered under their work-benches, along with the Kohlers and Maria-Eva. Everyone on the factory floor had been scared when a piece of the ornate proscenium molding around the disused movie screen had top-pled to the ground and shattered into plaster fragments, but no one had been hurt.

Apart from the molding, the only losses were a few dented boxes that fell off the warehouse shelves—the contents were fine, thanks to the packing peanuts—and a few soldering irons and multimeters that took hard knocks and would need some maintenance before returning to service.

Maria-Eva organized a gang of the factory girls to sweep up the damage, and Liz led the Kohlers back to the break room, which Liz had tidied up.

"Well," Liz said, "that was quite a finale for your grand tour, I think you'll agree."

Benny—pale and shaken—muttered something inaudible, but Ted smiled and shook his head slowly. "That was a good one, all right. You never get used to 'em, do you?"

"I wouldn't know," I said. "That was my first."

Ted slapped me on the shoulder. "Well, that was barely a

dish-rattler, but I suppose it still qualifies as your initiation into the California lifestyle. Wait'll you catch a real wave, brother, then you'll know you're alive."

"Unless you're dead," Benny grated.

"Yeah, that's always a possibility. But hell, it's the Golden State. We're optimists here. That's what I find so exciting about what you all have done here. So much optimism. So much smart gumption. Really, it's inspiring. I can't wait to be a part of it."

Benny rolled his eyes. Ted saw it and elbowed him. "Come on, sourpuss, let's get you back to the ranch. We'll talk to you folks soon, all right?"

Liz recovered first. "Let's plan for tomorrow," she said. "We can certainly wait until then before we talk to anyone else."

As far as I knew, there wasn't "anyone else" waiting to write a check to CF, but I was quick on the uptake and so was everyone else on our team. We all deadpanned it. The Kohlers, on the other hand, were rotten poker players. Benny and Ted exchanged a series of urgent glances that could be easily decoded:

We gotta get in on this with a good offer or we're going to get in a bidding war!

Shut up, kid, before you give the game away!

Don't let this opportunity pass us by!

Don't give away the store!

We all studiously pretended not to see it and kept the Mount Rushmore impression up until the boys were safely out the door and on the way back to their cars, then we exploded in whoops and hollers and hugs.

The next day, the Kohlers cut the girls a check. A really, really big check.

The money was good news. It paid everyone's late rents and checking overdrafts—the founders had been living on promises and good thoughts for weeks, plowing everything into paying for the inputs to make the products to fill the orders that were pouring in. All the factory girls got a five percent raise and a bonus worth a week's pay for anyone they recruited to work for CF.

But the biggest checks were written to Fidelity sales reps who flipped. CF focused its recruiting in the states where noncompete agreements were illegal, starting at home in California, while picking off reps whose tenure with Fidelity predated the change to its standard contract that incorporated a hairy, bowel-loosening noncompete drafted by the kinds of attack lawyers who didn't need to get their templates out of a Nolo Press book.

The last thing we needed was to get tangled up in a lawsuit with Fidelity.

Oh, yeah, right. We were *already* in one of those.

Nominally, my compensation—a quarter of CF's annual turnover—was tied to making the suit go away. That had been the whole point of going through their books with a fine-tooth comb. But then Maria-Eva had her brain wave about using my research to mount a frontal assault on Fidelity's business. That plan had worked out so well that the fact that we—they—were being sued by the Reverend Sirs faded into the background.

Later in life, when I'd had occasion to be sued a few more

times, I came to recognize the strange toll it takes on your psyche. On the one hand, a lawsuit is a very urgent matter, because so much is at stake, and the lawyers have so much advice about what you mustn't say and who you mustn't say it to.

On the other hand, the gears of law grind s-l-o-w-l-y, with weeks and months going by while judges request briefs, lawyers write briefs, judges review briefs, hearings are held or canceled or delayed. Nothing is happening and everything is happening and everything—*everything*—is at stake.

I knew that we were playing with fire. Obviously, the financial data Maria-Eva had slipped me had been stolen by a mole inside Fidelity. She never mentioned this and neither did I, but Maria-Eva, Rivka, and Liz were so plain likable and the Reverend Sirs were so habituated to using fear as a motivator that it was easy to imagine that some of their former coworkers back at Fidelity would be batting for Team CF.

I had destroyed leaked data—I mean, *really* destroyed it. I'd wiped the floppies with a magnet, then put them into a foil roasting pan and stuck them in the oven at 500 degrees for an hour. Even with all the windows and doors wide open and every fan in the house blowing out the patio, the apartment was too toxic to breathe in after just a few minutes, and I barely made it back in to turn off the oven, holding my breath and racing out again, stuffing a towel under the front door and retreating to the van in the parking lot, watching our open balcony door for telltale black smoke that would tell me that the floppies had ignited.

That was the last time I used an oven to get rid of floppies. Even after I'd cleaned the oven three times, it was useless. Just preheating it would fill the apartment with an unbearable stink. The one time I tried to cook some frozen pizza, it came out tasting like burning tires.

But the data? That was *gone*. I hauled the pan of congealed plastic slurry and the cardboard bankers box down to Half

Moon Bay, wrapped in three thicknesses of contractor bags, and threw it into a landfill myself.

Rivka found another apartment. Liz got used to not talking to her parents and even managed to make contact with one of her sisters, who called her collect every Friday at 4 p.m. from a pay phone to catch her up on her family. I did the company's books. Art gradually shifted from consultant to contractor to head of software development, putting together a whole suite of tools for migrating data.

It was his idea to release these as shareware.

The initial release included WiseFloppy (drivers for Apple computers to interface with Fidelity floppy drives and vice versa), 3-Lotus-3 (convert SPREADSHEET files to Lotus format), and StarWord (convert WORD PROCESSOR files to WordStar). He designed a basic label for each one and had two hundred of each made at our duplicating house, which were divided among the twenty-five CF sales agents Rivka was managing, with encouragements to make more as needed.

Word filtered back that this concept was difficult for the field agents to grok, so we had the copy shop on the corner make a couple of thousand copies of a one-page sheet explaining that anyone could copy these disks and hand them around, but if you used them, you were on your honor to send a check for five dollars to CF headquarters.

That did it. Checks started to roll in. Cash, too. Sometimes the envelopes only had three or four dollars, along with an apologetic note. Other times, it was twenty. Once, a hundred. They evened out. It turned out that marketing to ardent churchgoers by appealing to their sense of morality was good business sense.

I can't say for sure, but I think it was the shareware that tipped the Reverend Sirs over the edge. In retrospect, it was a genius move on Art's part. All those people who'd been suckered into thinking that they were "small business owners" because they were downlines for Fidelity's pyramid scheme had a come-to-Jesus (or Moses) (or Joseph Smith) experience the first time someone handed them one of those disks. Something about loading up the shareware and then, poof, saving hundreds or thousands of dollars could make you realize that Fidelity Computing's "business" was a scuzzy *hustle*.

It was the kind of thing we all hated yuppies for, a business founded on predation, a three-card monte game with pretensions of legitimacy. The floppies raced through the Mormon, Catholic, and Jewish user groups like a wildfire (we learned later that the Reverend Sirs likened it to a virus, which I thought of again years later the first time someone used the term "going viral" in my presence). The five-dollar checks rolled in. We thanked each buyer with a personal note and a catalog for the latest CF product line. When they sent us sales inquiries, we fulfilled their order via the sales agents we'd poached away from Fidelity.

We were devouring them from within. Their sales force was becoming our sales force. Their furious customers were becoming our grateful customers.

It must have driven the Reverend Sirs to distraction. That was a funny thought, at the time.

The old Plaza movie palace was pretty sturdy to begin with. After the cinder-block incident, Maria-Eva had overseen the reinforcement of all the doors, and then once we started to keep serious inventory on the premises, she bought a halfway decent burglar alarm.

We even talked about a night watchman, but decided it was an expense we didn't need. Rivka was adamant that every spare dollar be rolled into additional production: new workers, more stock, upgrades to the warehouse and fulfillment system. She had worked with me to build a financial model that showed that every dollar we put into production turned into two dollars in profit within six weeks, provided the orders kept rolling in, and the biggest determinant of new orders was the happy customers we shipped goods to in timely fashion so they could go and talk us up to all their friends.

I did a lot of that: built models to test Rivka or Maria-Eva or Liz's bolts of inspiration about how to expand the business. None of them had ever thought of starting a company before, but they all had that habitual computer user's sense that decisions should be evaluated by probing the data.

In between doing all that, I kept the books, made sure the payroll went out on time, kept on top of invoices. Oftentimes, I'd find myself working after hours, after all the factory girls had gone home and the warehouse staff had cleared out and locked up, and it would be me alone in the office, or maybe with one of the three founders, or Art if he'd come into the office that day.

I kept a bottle of rum in my desk drawer, old Puerto Rican stuff, brown and mellow, and once I'd saved my work, I'd pour two or three fingers into a glass and retire to the break room sofa with a Bloom County book, kick off my shoes, and unwind for a bit before heading out for a burrito.

The night the Reverend Sirs kicked off the next salvo in our war, I was just finishing up *Loose Tails* when the burglar alarm went off. I leapt up from the couch, spilled my drink, and jammed my feet into my shoes. I looked around the break room for a weapon and hit on that one blunt, sad birthday-cake knife. I snatched it up and stepped out of the break room into the theater's downstairs landing, by the bathroom doors.

The building only had four entrances: a loading bay, the two main auditorium fire exits, and the front doors. I crept upstairs, the burglar alarm clanging so loudly that I couldn't tell whether there'd be anyone waiting for me in the old theater lobby.

I hugged the inside wall of the staircase and slid one eye out from behind cover, peering intently around the darkened lobby. The front door was locked and intact. Quietly, I ascended to the projectionist's booth, which let me see the whole auditorium at once. I hit the overhead lights and flooded the main space with light. If there was anyone hiding there, they were doing an excellent job of it. I watched the space for a long moment, panting, holding my blunt kitchen knife, before I crept back down and down again, using the service corridor to pop up behind the screen, where I could scope out the loading dock and the rear exits. All still securely locked.

As I made my rounds of the place, I grew more confident. I killed the alarm and had a good look around the warehouse space and all the other nooks and crannies (those old movie palaces had a surprising number of stockrooms, film-storage areas, maintenance rooms, administrative spaces, and miscellaneous closets).

Finally, I retired back to the office, called the alarm company and gave them the password, left a message on Rivka's answering machine telling her not to worry if the alarm company had left her a message of their own.

Then I poured another two fingers of rum, kicked off my shoes, and went back to the sofa with Bloom County. False alarm or no, it would have felt like dereliction of duty for me to just abandon my post at that point.

I was halfway through the book—and laughing heartily—when the alarm went off again. This time, I didn't spill my drink and I stopped to lace my shoes up before turning off the alarm and doing the rounds again. Nothing. The alarm company apologized profusely for the inconvenience of two false alarms and promised to send a technician around the next day. I left another message for Rivka and thought about leaving, but something niggled at me—I hit the sofa again and read some more.

I was nearly finished with the book when the alarm went off for a *third* time. Sighing, I heaved myself off the sofa. I didn't bother with the knife. I made the rounds and then called up the alarm company and snippily informed them that I was turning off their defective gadget right now, and expected to have their technician on the doorstep the next morning at 9:00 a.m. *sharp.* They were satisfyingly contrite.

This was back when I thought of myself as a Computer Guy. I knew about computers, and I was an accountant, so I did accounting for computer companies. A decade later, I'd specialized, and become a *Security* Guy. Not that I became a cryptographer or anything, I never had the math for that, but security *thinking* became essential to my job. I wasn't just reconciling numbers: I was doing battle with people who were trying to deceive me. I started reflexively asking myself "Is this a trick?" and, eventually, "How would *I* trick someone with this?"

Once I became a Security Guy, a series of false alarms would have set off my *real* alarm. But for a Computer Guy, a system that kept malfunctioning was just another annoying bug in the code that I didn't have time to figure out.

Art had mentioned that he was meeting some friends in the city and that they were going to get dinner at a place called Maggie's in Noe Valley. I'd been in the Bay Area for two months and I'd gotten a pretty thorough orientation in the Mission burrito landscape and a cursory look at the Castro's bars, but apart from that, I was a San Francisco virgin. I hadn't even been to Alcatraz, or ridden a trolley. Hell, I hadn't been to Chinatown. I *loved* Chinese food.

I checked the pocket-sized city atlas in my backpack and figured out how to get to Maggie's and headed out. It was nearly seven, but I figured if I walked quick, I'd catch them.

It was a great night to be out and about in San Francisco. Dolores Park was caught in the twilight moment between the day shift of the dog-walkers and the night shift of drug dealers and their customers. A group of well-turned-out, shirtless men played frisbee. On one hillside, a group of beautiful women were packing up their picnic blanket.

They sent a jolt through me. I hadn't had even a semi-romantic discussion with a woman since Lucille at the motel. I'd dated in college, squeezing some romance in between hanging out with the computer freaks at the Newbury Street Irregulars, long hours crunching for Process Engineering Models. Despite the fact that spreadsheets and computers took up the lion's share of my time, thinking about women had taken up at least half my brain.

Something about coming west made me turn off that part of my brain. Maybe it was Rivka and Liz and Maria-Eva's chaste ways, or the inappropriateness of even thinking of any of the factory girls that way. Maybe it was the intricate financial puzzles I found myself defining and solving. Hell, maybe it was the fact that Art had stopped pretending to have any sexual interest in women—back when we'd roomed together in Cambridge, he'd made a point of bringing up the opposite sex pretty regularly. It must have been camouflage. Poor Art. What a way to live.

Whatever the reason for my monkish demeanor, the sight of these three women shattered it. There in the setting sun, painted with pink-orange, moving languidly, laughing and chatting as they packed up, they riveted me. Months of repressed sexual energy was unleashed all at once. I literally broke out in a sweat.

One of the women—short, with a pixie haircut and a kind of preppie polo-and-capris look—caught me looking at her and planted a fist on her hip and stared right back at me, a stern expression on her face. I held up my hands in a reflexive, apologetic gesture and she broke out the biggest, sauciest smile and flapped her hands at me in an oh-go-on-you gesture. Were we flirting? We were flirting. I was flirting. I didn't think I knew how to do that. Apparently I was a natural.

I waved at her and set off up the hill toward Noe Valley. It seemed like every woman I passed between Dolores Park and Maggie's was more beautiful than the last. Looking back on that moment, with the benefit of hindsight, I'm a little embarrassed, but I'm also struck by just how much of my young adulthood was consumed with these sudden passions, moments when common sense and perspective fled and left behind these overwhelming urges to just find someone—not just someone to screw (though yeah, that), but someone to pair off with. The months where I'd been free from that urge had left me with so much headroom to think about other stuff.

At least the majority of my swift and overwhelming currents were romantic, and not violent. I'd tried not to think about the fight I'd had with the two goons who'd shown up to repo my Fidelity 3000 PC and its accessories, but my mind kept going back to it of its own accord. Whenever I thought of those two guys, I'd find myself spinning off into ultraviolent, cinematic reveries in which I pummeled them and stabbed them and even shot them. I hated these thoughts, but they kept coming back.

The checkstand at Maggie's was staffed by another woman I found rivetingly gorgeous, though today I couldn't tell you what she looked like. She brought me back to Art's table and he and his pals greeted me and made space. They were all part of Art's core group of nerd-gays, in better shape and better-dressed than most of the guys we'd hung out with in the Newbury Street Irregulars, but still recognizably of the tribe.

"Sit, sit," Art said, and passed me the bread basket and the remains of a tray of oysters on ice. I sucked down the last two oysters with nose-burning horseradish, then buttered the sourdough with a thick coat of unsalted butter with sage. I ordered a cheeseburger from the waiter and guzzled the wine Art had poured me in the meantime.

"We're just talking about Mabuhay Gardens tonight," he said.

"What's that?"

"It's a venue. The Mab. In North Beach. We're seeing a show there."

My burger arrived. Art ate one of my fries. He reached for another and I slapped his hand, then I felt bad and scooped a handful onto his salad plate. "Who's playing?"

Art's friend Lewis—they'd stopped dating but were still tight—grinned and said, "Ever hear of the Dead Kennedys?"

Ugh. "Punker music?" I'd sold my collection of Led Zeppelin, Jethro Tull, and Creedence LPs before leaving Cambridge, but there was plenty of that on the radio. My nighttime excursions to the Castro with Art had introduced me to disco and I could see its virtues. But punk? Everyone back east who'd listened to that kind of thing seemed to be engaged in an elaborate put-on, pretending that they liked being hammered with noise even as they slam-danced their bodies into strangers. Ugh.

Art socked me in the shoulder, but not hard. "Free your mind and your ass will follow, boychick. The DKs are a local fixture, like Rice-A-Roni. Every San Franciscan needs to hear them play at least once."

"How many times have *you* seen them?"

He drew himself up and pointed his nose at the ceiling. "Never! Tonight I become a true San Franciscan! Bar mitzvahed with Jello Biafra!"

"Jello—"

"Biafra," he said, and the guys snickered. "That's what the singer calls himself. He ran for mayor!"

"Came in third," Lewis said. "I voted for him."

"Have *you* seen them?" I asked. As far as I knew, Lewis loved disco with the heat of a thousand suns and hated all other music. The one time he'd been over for an ACT UP meeting and I'd put on *Dark Side of the Moon,* he'd given me a fifteen-minute lecture on the shortcomings of pretentious album rock. Not even my weird trivia about how the album lined up perfectly as the soundtrack to *The Wizard of Oz* would sway him.

"I love 'em," he said. "They're not one of these ponderous metal bands like Led Zeppelin. They have a sense of humor. They're pissed off as hell and they don't care who knows it, but they don't take themselves serious. Their shows have an amazing vibe."

"I'll bet. Getting maimed while slam dancing."

Trey, another one of Art's pals, leapt in. "I felt the way you do, believe me. But the mosh pit is amazing. Yeah, you're jostling into all these other people, bodychecking them and whatnot, but no one is trying to hurt anyone. It's like a leather scene without the leather. Strictly consensual. Plus the music is great. It's not the kind of thing I'd play on my stereo, but when I'm dancing? Forget it."

"You should come, buddy," Art said. The waiter set down my burger. "Burn off that calorie-bomb." He'd gotten body-conscious since we hit the West Coast, even going to the gym three times a week. He was turning into a five-foot tall Charles Atlas ad. I was starting to feel flabby by comparison.

I thought about it. It had been a crazy week: exceptionally busy at the office, then those three false alarms, then the sudden reawakening of my libido. And hell, I'd never expected I'd like dancing my ass off at gay discos, but it was turning into one of my favorite pastimes.

"What the hell," I said, draining the wine. "TGIF, right?"

The Mab was a columnated building in North Beach, ringed with a dense crowd of chain-smoking, laughing, shouting, *raucous* punks in leather jackets, safety pins, and jingling chains. I felt out of place in jeans and a long white Indian cotton shirt I'd picked up in a flower power kind of mood. My no-cut shaggy haircut was similar enough to the cuts on many of the guys waiting to get in, but it felt like their hair was like that on purpose, whereas mine had grown over my ears because I hadn't found a barber yet and kept forgetting to try one out.

But no one gave me or Art or his friends any kind of funny looks. Someone even passed me a joint, which I took a hit off and passed on, while Art beamed approvingly from the sidelines. Art and his friends found a niche with a group of gay guys they knew from the bar scene. They didn't quite abandon me—I'd have been welcome with them—but they had a shared experience that I didn't share. I mean, I had helped Art stitch a square for the AIDS quilt but I still felt like an imposter in the group. How do you say "I'm not gay" without making it sound like you are worried that someone will hit on you, rather than worried that someone will think you're trying to get a free pass into a group that you don't belong to?

Plus, my libido was back.

After months of not even thinking about being around women in a romantic, sexual way, it was suddenly all I could think about.

And there were a *lot* of attractive, interesting women in that crowd. I found that shaved heads were unexpectedly sexy. There was something swanlike about the line from a leather-clad shoulder up the back of a skull, a line that continued all the way to some green spikes or a floppy mohawk.

Another joint came around and I passed it on to the woman beside me—short, with a jingling leather jacket, stompy boots, and piercings up both ears and in one nostril—and held her gaze for a moment as I did.

"Thanks," she said, and toked hard.

"You're welcome," I said, coughing a little.

She coughed a little, too, and the ice was broken.

"I'm Marty. This is my first punk show, ever. I just moved here."

She smiled wider. "I'm Pat," she said. "I've been to a *lot* of these shows. You're going to have a great time, I promise."

And just like that, we were friends.

Pat seemed to know everyone, from the doormen and the bartender to half the audience. I got the impression that about three-quarters of these people came out to every DK show and had become a kind of family. I suddenly missed the Newbury Street Irregulars. Being part of a scene was just so *great.*

"That's the mosh pit," she said, pointing at a spot in front of the stage where some of the burliest bruisers in the crowd had gathered and were milling around, giving each other jokey body checks and practicing a dance step that looked like a high-stepping silly walk straight out of a Monty Python sketch.

"That's definitely varsity-level stuff," I said. "Right?"

"Hell no," she said, and bodychecked me hard enough that I staggered back a couple of steps. She had a low center of gravity and it gave her an advantage. "You *gotta* slam. At least once." She checked me again. I found that being batted around the increasingly crowded club floor by this tiny woman gave me an erotic charge. I mean, in the mood I was in, an issue of *Vogue* would have carried an erotic charge, but Pat was the real deal.

"Uh, okay, but—"

"You won't get hurt. Probably. I mean, not beyond a couple bruises." She gave me another hip check, and I got another little thrill. "Maybe a broken nose. Worst-case scenario, you lose a tooth. Or two teeth."

"I can't tell if you're joking?"

She pointed at her nose, which was proud and bladelike and had a cute bump in it, but not the sort of bump you get from a broken nose. Then she gave me a dazzling smile that showed off a front tooth that had the sweetest little twenty-degree tilt that caused it to nuzzle up to the tooth next to it in a kind of bony cuddle.

(Yeah, I was feeling it.)

"See? Face intact. I've been doing this for years. I'll protect you, have no fear."

The emcee came out and announced that the lead singer and bass player for the opening act had been arrested and that the headliners would be coming out in ten minutes. Which is how I ended up in my first mosh pit, at my first Dead Kennedys show.

They were *great*. The frontman, Jello Biafra, was a skinny guy with high cheekbones and charisma that just radiated off the stage. He came out in a black sleeveless tee and a cowboy hat and, after a crowd-pleasing opener ("Nazi Punks Fuck Off," which was a sentiment that crowd roared its approval of), he gave us all a breather while he orated for a bit, talking about the Reagan administration, the situation in Nicaragua, and the official indifference toward AIDS.

He had a kind of nasal, wise-guy delivery, like a world-weary streetfighter who's seen it all and lost a thousand scraps but refuses to be cowed. It made me want to stand up and salute.

Not literally. Literally, I wanted to keel over and die. My first adventure in the mosh pit had been a blur, again, literally. I was ping-ponged from one body to another for what couldn't have been more than a minute but which felt like an eternity. As I pinged and ponged from one body to the next, I experienced a kind of disembodied high, as though I was floating above the melee, watching as more skilled players than me caught me expertly and slingshotted me back and forth between them.

When the final chord crashed to a halt and Jello screamed that last "Unless you think!" over the crowd, I found myself coming to rest in a wobbly stance, steadied by Pat's hands on my shoulders.

"How'd you like it?" she shouted over the crowd's cheers.

"It was—" Words failed me.

"Yeah, it sure was," she said, and spun me around to face Mr. Biafra for his between-songs rap.

By the time Jello had wound up the audience with his spiraling, profane, hilarious rant, I was ready to dance again. Dance? Mosh? Was there a difference? I could do the Electric Slide and they'd taught me a box step in PE, but I'd never really cottoned on to what *dancing* meant until that night.

When the lead guitarist and bass player hammered out the opening bars for "California Über Alles," I started to spring up and down on my toes, and Pat shoved me from behind, sending me back into the pit, and I *danced*.

By the time intermission came around, I was wringing with sweat. Jello had stripped off his tee—carefully replacing his Stetson, screwing it down on his sopping hair—and so had some of the guys in the mosh pit, turning them into slippery meat slabs. I careened into one of them and nearly ended up skidding right off his sweaty chest and onto the floor. The guy saved me from being trampled under a forest of combat boots, catching me by the armpits and righting me, making sure I was okay and then shoving me back into the chaos.

I never felt more alive.

Pat was just as sweaty as me, her mascara smeared into a black, high-sheen racoon mask. She grinned crazily at me and asked me how I liked it.

"Holy . . . *shit*," I managed.

"That's about what I figured," she said. "You need two glasses of water and a beer. So do I."

That was the best plan I'd ever heard. "Can I buy?"

She cocked her head, looked me up and down. "Only if you get ideas," she said, and grinned.

We were halfway to the bar when I realized what she said. "Did you say 'only if I *get* ideas'? Or was it '*don't* get ideas'?"

She broke off from waving at a friend in the crowd to hip-check me. "Get the shit out of your ears, fella. A girl doesn't like to repeat herself." Then she pinched my ass. Hard. But nice.

After the show—two encores, including a song called "Too Drunk to Fuck" that was a predictable crowd-pleaser—I found myself standing in the middle of the rapidly dispersing mosh pit, soaked to the skin, ears ringing, body a welter of not-unpleasant aches. I'd been kicked in the face by a stage diver in huge Doc Martens (he'd screamed an apology as he crowd-surfed away), and I thought I might have a bit of a black eye on the way.

I felt great.

Then I noticed that Pat was nowhere to be found.

Through the course of the evening, we'd exchanged a few more words, but mostly, we'd exchanged a lot of *contact*. She really knew how to work that coiled, low-to-the-ground energy, and she was obviously aware that the big guys in the pit were reluctant to lay into a tiny woman, which gave her all the openings she needed to take them out at the knees.

Whenever she caught my eye, she'd do something—wink, touch her tongue to her lips, bodycheck me into a stranger. I had been under the distinct impression that this was a form of flirting, and that it was headed for something more than flirting.

Staring around the half-empty club and not finding her, I decided I'd been engaged in dickful thinking—self-delusion driven by my newfound horniness. I shrugged and stepped out into the cool night air and the thick tobacco and clove-cigarette and weed smoke to see if I could find Art.

I found him just as Pat found me. I was about to ask him how he liked the show—he'd clearly enjoyed it from a safe distance and emerged far more sheveled than I was—when I got body-checked from behind. I caught myself before I fell into Art, but it was a close thing, and Art was visibly alarmed.

I turned around and spotted her, face washed, hair brushed back, and makeup repaired. She looked amazing, her leather jacket unzipped and showing the straps of her gray wife-beater, hand-decorated with a shaky DKs logo.

"There you are!" she said.

"Here I am," I agreed, conscious of Art and his friends, all staring at me with varying degrees of bemusement and curiosity. "Pat, meet Art, my roommate, and this is Trey, Lewis, Bart, and José." The boys all made their pleasantries. Pat gave them all a broad wave and a "Hi, howdy, Marty's friends!"

Then she turned to me. "You busy? I want to get doughnuts. Dancing makes me hungry."

Art leaped in. "Funny, Marty was just talking about how much he wanted doughnuts and we were trying to let him down easy because we all want to go straight home. Maybe we could release him into your custody?"

Pat socked him in the shoulder. "I like this guy," she said. "This guy? I like. Yeah, you should absolutely put him in my custody. I'll see to it that he stays on the straight and narrow."

"Poor word choice, honey," Lewis put in.

She rewound the conversation and laughed at herself. "You're right. Marty, I'm going to keep you on the extremely queer and wiggly. You boys okay with that?"

"Do I even get a say?" I asked, looking from Art to Pat and back again.

"Seriously?" Pat said, and she instantly transformed into a more serious version of herself, like a switch-flip. "Seriously, yes, you get a say." Then the goofy smile was back. "But I hope you'll say yes."

"He'll say yes," Art said.

I mock-glared at him. "As a matter of fact, Arthur Hellman,

my answer is . . ." I let the pause stretch. "Shit, who am I kidding, of *course* my answer is yes."

Forty-five minutes later, the #20 Muni bus disgorged us at Twentieth and Folsom and we staggered to Mission Street and Hunt's Donuts, "open 25 hours," and filled with a night crew with saucer-sized pupils and a psychedelic, drunken, stoned gabble that harmonized nicely with my still-ringing ears.

We collected two styrofoam coffee cups, a maple glaze, and a chocolate from the sneering counterman and snagged a booth under a "Don't sell it here" sign, still warm from the two streetwalkers who'd just vacated it and wobbled out on their six-inch heels.

"I've been thinking about this thing you're doing," she said. On the bus, I'd given her an abridged version of CF's origin story, skipping over the part where I analyzed stolen internal documents to help them raise outside capital. I was worried that I'd bore her with a bunch of nerdy stuff she wouldn't understand without a lot more explaining, but she followed it really well.

Finally, she revealed that she was a freelance Unix programmer who'd come to San Francisco from New Jersey.

"My mom was a coder at Western Electric, Dad used to chair Usenix meetings. I grew up listening to Dennis Ritchie lecture on C data structures." She smiled. "Oh, scrape your jaw off your chest, Marty. You know that programming was *invented* by a woman, right?"

"Ada Lovelace," I said, like a student hoping for a good grade. "I know. That's not the part I was impressed by—" She frowned. "—though it's *very* impressive. It's just, you know, Bell Labs. We used to drive out to North Andover twice a month just to go through their dumpsters. And you grew up in the *headquarters*? I mean, that is *so* cool."

She nodded. "I know I'm supposed to pretend that it was totally boring to grow up with supernerds in New Jersey, but it *was* cool. All the Bell Labs brats played together, we used to challenge each other to write code. Our house had three phone lines, so that Mom and Dad could both run acoustic couplers and keep their terminals connected."

"Jesus. It's like the promised land." I thought for a moment. "Nerdvana."

"You didn't just make that up."

"No," I said. "It was a saying from this club I used to belong to." Which led me to a potted history of the Newbury Street Irregulars, and from there into Process Engineering Models, and into CF.

Now we sat over our doughnuts—she'd ripped them in half and swapped, so we each had half of the other's doughnut— under the "Don't sell it here" sign. She licked chocolate off her fingers and spooned sugar into the bitter coffee.

"You should support the Apollo," she said. "Apple is a lost cause. The future is Unix shells."

I'd only ever read about Unix shells in *Creative Computing,* and Apollo workstations were so far out of my price range they were like mirages, but I was half in love with her and deeply impressed with her technical knowledge. "Oh, yeah, totally," I said.

She cocked her head. "You don't know anything about Unix shells, do you?"

I shrugged. "Not really. But I hear they're amazing. Powerful."

She nodded. "Super powerful. I'll show you. I've got a baby network of two DN100s at home, just to test out networking ideas."

I didn't have to pretend to be impressed. I actually choked on my doughnut. "*Two* DN100s?" That was like having a spare Rolls-Royce for odd-numbered days. I had been slam dancing with this woman. She was either such a genius that she was already rich, or such a genius that someone rich had sent her home with two scientific workstations with enough power to outclass my whole lab at UMass Boston.

She lowered her eyelids to half-mast and nodded coolly. "Two. Wanna see?"

I spent the next three hours absorbing Unix lore in her small Mission apartment, up three flights of stairs in a painted lady on Van Ness. It smelled of sandalwood incense, and its walls were decorated with xeroxed punk gig posters and a big, framed Grateful Dead poster. It was something between a loft and an efficiency, one big room with a kitchen in one corner. There wasn't a bedroom corner—she slept on a futon-sofa in the living room that she hadn't bothered to fold up into its couch configuration that morning, which left the two of us sitting side by side on her unmade bed, which smelled of her, in an enticing and spicy way.

Sitting on a beautiful woman's bed, with a beautiful woman, at three in the morning, after hours of intense flirting (including multiple hours of being body-slammed by her in the most pleasant way imaginable), on the eve of the triumphant return of my libido—sex should have been all that I could think of.

But instead, I was obsessed with her Apollo DN100s. They had huge, cubic, high-resolution color monitors perched atop a main computing unit the size of a bar fridge, and they whirred like jet engines. There were two, side by side, easily accessed from her sofa (that is, her bed, which, once again, we were sitting next to each other on). She took me through their paces, extolling the virtues of their twin Motorola 68000 processors, losing me in a low-level description of how one processor handled the main compute process and the other handled faults, seamlessly fixing code as it ran, in crashproof choreography.

When I finally worked up the nerve to ask her how much they cost, she didn't bat an eye. "Thirty-five thousand dollars."

I was about to say something—*holy shit* or *motherfucker* or *Jesus fucking CHRIST*—when she added: "Each."

I had priced out a car the week before—juggling access to Art's van was getting complicated—and I'd been sticker-shocked by the $2,500 price tag on a year-old Ford Escort, a tiny, boxy car that accelerated like a tortoise and handled like a tank. The computer under my fingertips was worth *fourteen* of those cars. My dad was a big man in a big oil patch, and even during the big oil crisis his annual salary wouldn't have paid for one of those beauties.

I took my fingers off the keyboard like they'd been scorched. She laughed.

"It's okay," she said. "It's not mine and you can't break it. Here, let me show you what a Unix shell can do."

Yes, we eventually stopped playing with Unix and started playing with each other.

I'd gone to bed with five women in my years in Cambridge, and only one of them had opted for a second bout. My impressions of sex were of a hasty fumble with someone I desperately wanted to impress and please when I had *no idea* how to do either.

Pat didn't let me wonder. She told me, with all the directness of the mosh pit, what she liked. When I got it right, she told me. When I got it wrong, she told me. And then she made me tell *her*, and when I said I didn't know what I needed, she told me that I had best figure that out because how could anyone else make me happy if I didn't know something that basic.

Then she took pity on me and made some excellent and imaginative solutions that made me self-conscious at my inexperience at first, then made me self-conscious about how I was in no way able to offer comparable suggestions to her, and then finally made me nearly *lose* consciousness as some of those suggestions turned out to be unexpectedly excellent ones.

When it was over, I lay in the glow of those two $35,000 Apollo workstations and felt her breath on my chest and watched the dawn creep up her windows.

"Do you seriously think we should make tools for people migrating from Fidelity Computing PCs to Apollos?"

She breathed out a soft laugh and nipped at my earlobe. "Of course not. That would be insane. I was just fishing for an excuse to boast about these amazing computers I get to keep around the house."

"Why *do* you have these? I mean, what do you do with them?"

"Oh," she said. "Well, nothing much these days. But I *was* working on a really cool CAD/CAM package that would have let different kinds of people both work on the same model, over a network. So like, you could have a structural engineer and an electrician and a plumber all tweaking a single model, all in real time."

"That sounds incredible," I said. "Like science fiction, even. Those files must be huge. I wouldn't even want to move them around, let alone modify them. And then there'd be the problems when you had simultaneous, contradictory changes, and—"

"Yeah, that's about right. Unfortunately for my boss, he didn't figure that out until *after* he'd spent a million bucks of some rich Japanese investors' money. He says we're 'retrenching' and he's put me on half salary while he looks for money. I'm supposed to be working part-time working out some gnarly bugs."

"That's rough," I said.

"Not really," she said, yawning. "I'm not doing any work, I get seventy thousand dollars' worth of badass computers to keep at home, and if that loser never pays me, I'm keeping 'em. Plus I can sleep in until lunchtime and no one will bug me about it."

I thought about my next working day, at CF. I didn't have formal hours—technically, I was a "consultant" and came and went as I pleased—but they'd wonder where I was. I asked if I could use Pat's phone and I called to leave a message on the machine, but it didn't pick up. Oh well, I tried.

When I got back to Pat's bed, she was already asleep.

13

Pat had a bachelorette's fridge—half a lemon, two eggs of indeterminate age, a six-pack of Tab, and a nearly empty pint of Safeway vanilla ice cream in the freezer—so we decided we'd go get tacos. Why not? It was 2 p.m.

We put away three each at La Cumbre, then grabbed a sack of six more to go and walked over to CF. She'd quizzed me on the business all through lunch and I had a half-formed thought that maybe I could get this hotshot programmer to come on contract with CF and attain heroic status after she rewrote everything or created a dozen new programs beyond Art's shareware.

I carried the sack of tacos in one hand and she slipped her hand in the other. We strolled down Mission, the midafternoon sun just perfect, the skin-to-skin contact even more perfect. I led her to the door and took my hand back to fish for my keys.

But the door was still deadbolted, which was weird, since the first person in that morning should have unbolted it. I knocked and cupped my hands over the glass to peer around the lobby. Usually one of the factory workers would be in there, going to or from the bathroom or just having a break and a chat. It was empty.

I hit the doorbell, but no one came. I hit it again after half a minute, as a sense of foreboding stole over me. That turned to alarm when I realized I couldn't hear the bell ringing inside the building.

"Shit," I muttered. "Let's go around back."

The loading dock had a gate and a door, and the door had a deadbolt that opened from the outside. That was how I'd left the night before, when I'd locked up and headed to Maggie's. A lot had happened since then.

More than I knew.

We circled the block and entered the alley that led to the old theater's rear entrance and loading area. I found the right keys and unlocked the metal safety door and then took a deep breath and opened it.

The factory *stank*.

It wasn't more butyric acid, thankfully—more a smell like nail-polish remover. It was overpowering and I got an instant headache. I fumbled for the light switch but the lights wouldn't come on.

"Marty," Pat said, "this doesn't feel right."

"No," I said, "it doesn't." I swallowed. "But I'm going to go in anyway. Hold the door open so I've got some light, okay?"

You see, I knew there was an earthquake kit on some utility shelving just a few steps in from the door, a big stamped-metal shelving unit where we kept coffee supplies and spare work gloves and birthday party decorations. The earthquake kit had a flashlight. A flashlight would let me move around inside the windowless, blacked-out theater box and figure out what, precisely, was going on here.

The slice of light from the open door illuminated a long, slanting rhombus of scuffed wooden floor, but beyond its sharp lines, the room was in perfect blackness.

I followed the light to its edge and then crossed over the terminator, eyes straining to make out details. I shuffled slowly, in a straight-armed Frankenstein march, feeling for danger—or for the shelves—and it's a pity I was holding them out at shoulder height, rather than sweeping them at knee height, because if I'd been doing that, I might have encountered the fallen shelving unit before it took me mid-shin and sent me face-first into a jumble of coffee supplies, spare work gloves, and birthday party decorations. I didn't knock any teeth out, because the bridge of my nose absorbed all the punishment when my face hit the edge of the shelf.

"Are you okay?" Pat called from the doorway.

"Ow, fuck," I said, with characteristic eloquence.

"Marty?"

"I'm okay?"

"Was that a question?"

I got to my feet. My face was wet. I tasted blood. My shins hurt. A lot.

I staggered back to the slash of light from the door, and then back out.

"Jesus," she gasped, and rummaged in her purse for a crumpled ball of Kleenexes, which she pressed to my face.

"Ow, fuck!" I said.

"You said that already. Your nose is bleeding."

I put my fingers to my nostrils.

"Not there," she said. "You've sliced it open across the bridge." She lifted the tissues. "It's shallow but wide. I've seen worse in the mosh pit. I don't think you'll need stitches."

The middle of my face was a hot blob of pain surrounded by a salad-plate-sized region of numbness.

"Come on," she said. "Let's sit."

The loading dock had a ledge that some of the factory workers would smoke on. I sat down on it and yelped.

"What?"

I gingerly rolled up my pant legs and discovered twin horizontal bruises under my knees, each of them seeping a little blood where the skin had broken.

"Ugh," she said. "Poor guy. What did you trip over?"

"Shelves," I said. "Someone had knocked the shelving over. I was heading for a flashlight. Someone really did a number on that place. No one's in there. I don't think we should try to get in today, either."

"Yeah," she said. "That is a bad, bad scene."

Apparently we missed the cops by five minutes. If we'd eaten our tacos a little faster, we would have been able to talk with the detective who debriefed Rivka, Sister Maria-Eva, and Liz.

Rivka had been the first one to arrive that morning. She'd flicked the switch a few times, then locked up again and walked around the corner to a smoke shop and bought a penlight and a package of AAA batteries. By its light, she had explored the factory floor, which stank of the acetone that had been splashed over every circuit board on every workbench. Whoever had done it had brought gallons of the stuff and they'd used some kind of big awl or pick to systematically puncture every box on the warehouse shelves before pouring a big glug of it onto the floppy drives, printers, and other components inside.

The power was out throughout the building, but before Rivka could go and flip the main breaker, Liz arrived and called out to her from the doorway. They were debating whether to try to turn the power back on when Maria-Eva arrived and insisted they call the police first.

Maria-Eva was right. Someone had turned off the main breaker, removed all the fuses, inserted pennies into the screw holes, and then loosely screwed the fuses back in. If they'd powered the box back up, the power would have come on . . . at first. Then, sometime not long thereafter, the otherwise indestructible box would have burst into flames, or possibly exploded.

The cops showed up with big cop flashlights, the kind that doubled as billy clubs and took six D batteries, and then retreated quickly with orders for no one to enter until the Department of Public Health had come and gone.

236 ◀ **cory doctorow**

Maria-Eva figured out that Rivka was having flashbacks to what happened to her apartment, and whisked her off to walk around Dolores Park while Liz waited with the cops for the DPH and told all the factory women who arrived to go home and wait for a phone call before coming back, assuring them that they would get their paychecks as usual on Friday.

They came, they inspected, they left. The acetone fumes were bad enough that no one should go into the place until someone had aired it out, which meant opening the doors and getting big industrial fans in to create a cross-breeze, while removing anything acetone-soaked from the premises. Before they could do that, they'd need an electrician who was rated to work in hazmat conditions, and before *that* could happen, a police hazmat team would need to do an evidence sweep.

It was an extremely efficient piece of sabotage, in other words. Not only had the saboteurs destroyed all of CF's stock and its business records—before they'd sabotaged the power, they'd used some kind of big magnets to wipe all the floppies in the office—but they'd sent the building itself into a kind of bureaucratic limbo, where the cops couldn't come until the electrician did his job, and the electrician couldn't do his job until the cops were done.

That's where I came in. After calling everyone's phone numbers and getting machines, I finally had the bright idea of calling my own machine and picking up my messages, which were a procession of increasingly distressed messages from Maria-Eva, who must have fed several dollars in quarters to the corner pay phone in between waiting with the cops.

That's how I found that everyone had decamped to Zeitgeist, a grimy beer garden on Valencia. It was an odd choice for three pious, religious women, but I guessed that Maria-Eva was ready for a beer, and Rivka had brought her own kosher sack lunch anyway.

"I love their burgers," Pat said, and with that, invited herself along. Why not?

Maria-Eva was on her second burger and her third beer by the time we arrived. Pat ordered cheeseburgers for both of us and then surreptitiously offered around our sack of tacos, which were a lot colder and less appetizing than they had been when we'd arrived at CF.

"This is my friend Pat," I said. "She's a really good coder," I added, as all three of the CF founders looked from her to me and back again. It wasn't like I was going to tell them I'd spent the night having carnal knowledge of her—and it wasn't like they hadn't figured that out for themselves.

"Marty's told me about your company," Pat said, coolly un-selfconscious. "It's impressive."

"It was," Maria-Eva said. She ran down the situation while we waited for the burgers and sipped our own beers. Pat made disgusted noises of increasing intensity, and when Maria-Eva was done, she let fly with a string of curses that were impressive even by the standards of the oil-patch kids I hung out with in Alabama. By the standards of, well, for example, a nun, it was off the charts.

But it made all three of the CF women smile, then giggle, then laugh. Rivka ended up doubled over, tears streaming down her face. Pat wound down eventually and chugged her beer. "Seriously, that is *fucked up*," which set poor Rivka off again.

Maria-Eva clinked beers with Pat, and Liz and Rivka joined in with their root beers.

Pat finished her beer and set the glass down on the graffiti-carved picnic table with a wild *clunk*. "Well, let's get you going again, right?"

Pat's boss was Leon Boudin, an optimist with a good line of patter. He'd been offered admission at Caltech, MIT, and Princeton, but after reading about the Arpanet project, he'd turned them all down for UCLA, where his long-simmering love affair with high-performance computing had boiled over. He ignored the profs who tried to talk him into getting a master's and instead talked a rich family friend into letting him pitch a wealthy Japanese investor on his computing idea.

He had finagled access to UCLA's Prime Computer workstations, and when he learned that one of Prime's founders, William Poduska, was starting a new workstation company called Apollo, Leon sent him a fan letter that was practically a love note. Poduska rewarded him by adding him to the press list, and soon Leon was receiving fat envelopes of marketing materials for the forthcoming DN100.

Leon's silver tongue, combined with those marketing materials and some testimonials from his UCLA profs, was sufficient to extract one million U.S. dollars from one starry-eyed Japanese investor who was obsessed with the idea that young American men possessed an entrepreneurial zeal that his own stuffy countrymen couldn't match.

A year later and the whole million dollars was gone, and the integrated CAD/CAM software Leon had hired Pat to work on was on "hiatus," and its offices—a floor in a century-old, renovated brick factory building at the bottom of Potrero Hill—were sitting empty as Leon tried to figure out how to break his lease.

Leon was frankly relieved to hear that CF was interested in a short-term sublease while they negotiated with their insurer over the damage to their old movie theater. Though Potrero Hill was a twenty-minute walk from their old Mission digs, it might as well have been in a different city: whiter, straighter, and wealthier.

The women who worked in the factory now made a point of packing lunches rather than going out for tacos, and they went home from work in groups, ready to close ranks if some old white guy decided to start shouting about "greasers" needing to "go back where they came from."

But the building had a better loading dock, a freight elevator, and easy access to 80 and the 101.

Unexpectedly, the hardest-hit casualties of the attack were the Brothers Kohler, specifically Benny, who thrashed around looking for some way to blame Rivka, Liz, and Maria-Eva for the damage, even though they had insurance and even though they had installed a top-notch burglar alarm that somehow failed to go off, despite the fact that the burglars had simply taken a pry bar to one of the fire exits at the back of the theater.

I kept my mouth shut about that for the whole time the Kohlers were in Pat's old office, berating the supremely calm Sister Maria-Eva, who gave them a hard nun-face while Benny raved. Eventually, Benny ran out of steam and then Ted talked him all the way down off the ledge. They wrote a check. Of course they did—they'd already committed to the money, they were just moving it up a little to cover the gap while the insurance adjusters ground their slow way toward the inevitable payout.

Recovering the order book would have been impossible, except for Rivka's daily practice of backing up all her working files to floppies and bringing them home every night. As it was, all we needed was a couple of Apples and a copy of Lotus 1–2–3 (which I supplied, after Art slipped me a floppy with a tool to break the copy protection) and they were literally and figuratively back in business.

Took two weeks, tops.

Would have taken longer, except for Pat. She was a dervish: setting up workbenches, finding deals on used computers, even automating Rivka's lifesaving backups based on all the problems they hit as they got set up again. She called it a "living will"—the instructions needed to keep CF running even if Rivka, Maria-Eva, and Liz got hit by a runaway trolley. She presented it to the Kohlers when they came over for an inspection, separating the fanfold printer paper with dancing hands, making it into a juggling act that wowed Ted.

Benny was impressed by the living will itself and tried to talk Pat into starting a "commercial living will" business working his family stationery store's customer list, selling each of them an annual planning session. I thought it was a pretty good idea, but it was clear that Pat was completely uninterested in devoting even ten seconds more of her life to that kind of work: the fact that it was work for CF had made it worth doing. As a technical challenge, it wasn't worth another second's thought.

When Benny pressed her, she busted out some pretty salty language, seeming to enjoy Benny's purpling face. She got as far as "I wouldn't fuck that business with your dick and him pushing—" when I stepped in. Luckily, Ted thought it was a gas.

As for me, listening to Pat swear was hands-down the second-most-erotic experience of my life. The most erotic was what happened those nights I stayed over at her place, which became more and more frequent until Art started to make "jokes" about advertising for a new roommate because he was getting lonely all the way down there in Menlo Park.

The jokes were half serious. It was less than a month, but it felt like a lifetime. Living in the heart of San Francisco, with a beautiful woman, going to punk shows and getting six kinds of shit knocked out of me and then going back to her place for an altogether more pleasant form of physical contact—it got to me.

All the people I'd been before—the kid in San Diego, the high schooler in Alabama, the college kid in Cambridge—they faded into distant memory. My self-image was transformed, and I became a new man—I became a *man*—with a mate and a city and a tribe and a real, grown-up job.

For a charmed month, I shuttled between Pat's place and the new, temporary Potrero Hill headquarters of CF, stopping at the laundromat to drop off a wash-and-fold in the morning, juggling the bundle of still-warm laundry with a sack of burritos and a six-pack of beer on the way back. In between, I crunched numbers, building the models that helped Maria-Eva plan the sales strategy and identify struggling reps who needed support; that helped Rivka plan the inventory and production; that helped Liz manage the payroll and shift schedules.

I went to war with the insurance adjuster, keying his figures into Lotus 1–2–3 and revealing their miserly deficiencies and shaved corners, and wrung from him an extra 17 percent, which Liz celebrated by bringing me a six-pack of my favorite Anchor Steam beer. That it was Liz's gift made it especially sweet, given that she would no sooner drink beer than Rivka would order a BLT.

Pat came to work with me, or didn't, and she would just sniff around, paging through the product plans while she nodded in time with the sound leaking out of her Walkman headphones, then staring out the window, or going for a walk around the block—sometimes coming back with a fragrant box from Goat Hill Pizza—and then commandeer someone's computer and page through Art's code and start twiddling it, fingers keeping time with her bobbing head and the tinny thunder from her headphones. After a few days of this, she'd hand Rivka a floppy with a new version number—3-Lotus-3 1.3—and a scribbled list of improvements and new features.

Liz insisted on paying me, and I booked it in the company financials as an advance on my commission. But we all knew that was a shuck. I was a salaried employee in everything but name, the CFO of a successful start-up.

After their final shove, the Reverend Sirs had observed the women of CF bounce back and had decided to call a truce. We hadn't heard a peep out of them in weeks, and Liz's contacts at Fidelity told her that the company's internal seething fury had simmered down. Even when a new rep defected from Fidelity to CF, it barely rated an announcement from Bishop Clarke, let alone a furious memo from Father Marek.

I had wandered the country, from San Diego to Alabama to Cambridge to San Francisco, a jewel of a city with a picture-postcard harbor. I rode the cable car, I took the ferry to Alcatraz, I ate a lobster roll on Fisherman's Wharf and pretended it was as good as the ones I used to eat in Boston.

One night I tried to go for tiki drinks at Trader Vic's—I was working my way through the *Bay Guardian*'s Best of the City list—and took a wrong turn and found myself in a bar in the financial district where I quickly realized that *every table was full of computer programmers,* all talking about the hot companies they were working at, the products they were developing, the millions that were sloshing through the streets. I realized that I had my own pan out in that river of gold. CF had just experienced its third consecutive month of one hundred percent growth, and every day, we hired: factory workers, sales reps, warehouse guys, and junior programmers to work under Pat and Art.

I ordered Anchor Steam after Anchor Steam and got progressively drunker, on the beer and the talk. Not the talk. The *buzz*. The sense that there was *so much money* out there that I could just pull it out, like a bear grabbing salmon out of a stream.

Pat wasn't with me. She wasn't interested in Trader Vic's, called it "a racist colonial fantasy with sugary drinks." I sloshed out of the door and poured myself into a taxi and rode back to her place with the window open and the heavy, cold, fog-drenched air whipping past my face. It was so intoxicating, I think I was even drunker when I got to her place. I stumbled up the stairs and let myself in—she'd given me my own key after the first week—and found her shuttling back and forth between her DN100s, making $70,000 worth of computers whirr and dance to her tune.

"I *love* this town!" I declaimed, as I staggered into the apartment.

She rolled her eyes. "It won't love you back, you know. San Francisco is a fickle bitch."

I shook my head so violently that it threw off my balance and I flopped onto the bed/futon. "I love it," I said. "Sincerely. I found a place tonight and they were all *computer programmers*. By accident! I found a place full of my people, just by accident! Now I know how Art feels, all his life he was surrounded by people who couldn't understand him and then he came here and there's so many people who just *get it*, you know?"

She took her hands off the keyboard. "Baby, unless you want to fuck a compiler, that's a terrible analogy. You have a hobby, not a sexual orientation."

"That's what you think," I said. "Maybe I *do* want to fuck a compiler. I mean, they are fucking *gnarly*. The brains it takes to make one of those, shit. Shit! I *do* want to fuck a compiler. Can we have an open relationship?"

She snorted and hammered at the keys for a while. I drank in the sound, willing the room to stop whirling around my head. Finally, she gave up on her machine-gun typing.

"You're not entirely wrong," she said.

"About compilers?"

"About this city. Look," she said, and tore a piece of flip-chart paper off the huge pad she kept leaning against the breakfast nook. She used two pieces of masking tape to mount it on the wall, covering the Grateful Dead poster. She uncapped a marker and sketched a shape, a kind of elongated, irregular oval, with a narrow opening on the left side, toward the bottom. "What's this?"

I focused on it, willing my drunken brain to make sense of it. It was naggingly familiar, but . . .

"Here," she said, "more clues." She drew a couple of dots inside the oval. I cocked my head left, then right.

"All right, some more," she said. She slashed three vertical lines across the oval, and drew another circle in the middle of one of them. "Come on, now, don't make me give it away."

"It's . . . Ugh. It's right on the tip of my mind."

"All right," she said. "Final clue." She drew a series of scalloped horizontal lines, inside the oval and to the left of it. The light dawned.

"It's the San Francisco Bay," I said. The dots were the islands: Alcatraz, Angel Island, Treasure Island. The lines were the bridges: the Bay Bridge, the Golden Gate, the Dumbarton.

"Finally," she said. "We'll make a Californian out of you yet," she said.

"You're from New Jersey," I said. "I was actually born in San Diego."

"All the best Californians were born somewhere else," she said. "As you have just demonstrated. Back to the geography lesson now: this harbor has a lot of obvious military value, right?"

"Sure," I said. "You can put a fort or whatever at the narrow harbor mouth and blast away at anyone who tries to get at the city."

"Exactly. That's the Alcatraz story, it was a fort. Spanish-American War, Civil War. It's why we had all these shipyards here, why the navy was such a big deal."

"Right," I said. The harbor cruise captain had recounted some of this over the distorted speaker.

"Right. So where you have the navy, you have sailors, and where you have sailors, you have gay guys. Those guys, when they were discharged here in the city, a lot of them stayed. It made San Francisco the gay capital, and soon lesbians and gays from all over America moved here, looking for a place where they could be themselves."

"I didn't know that," I said. "The U.S. Navy made San Francisco gay?" I giggled. The beer was still working its way through my system, clearly. My dad had enlisted in the navy, but was washed out after they found his heart murmur at his end-of-training physical. I wondered how he would feel about that bit of intelligence.

"Yup," she said. "Insert salty seamen joke here." I snorted.

"Now for the bonus round. Apart from ships and homosexuals, what else is the navy known for?"

"Uh," I said. "Hang on." I thought about it. "Barnacles. Rum. Grog, which I'm pretty sure is different from rum. Keelhauling. Cannons."

"The plural of 'cannon' is 'cannon,'" she said. "You're not even warm. How about radar?"

"Radar," I said. "Sure."

"A little reverence, please. Radar was an amazing accomplishment, and its development required a huge electronics industry. Caltech, Stanford, Berkeley—why do you think we've got so many top electrical engineering programs in-state?"

"Oh," I said, affecting a broad Boston accent, "I don't know that I'd call them 'top programs.' Now, MIT is a top program. You have to be *wicked smaht* to get into MIT."

"You flunked out of MIT," she said.

"You're from New Jersey," I rebutted.

"Enough," she said. Then she snapped her fingers, sat down at the keyboard of one of the DN100s, and made the keys clatter. A few minutes later, she looked up and nodded. "Where were we?"

"New Jersey," I said.

"*Radar.* My point is, why do you think we've got all this high-tech in the area? It starts with the navy. And why are we the Queer Capital? The navy. The navy, which is here because of that—" She gestured at her diagram. "Geography begets strategy, strategy begets sociology and industry. So when you talk about coming here and finding your people, the way Art did when he came out west and then came out, you're not wrong."

I grinned. "You say the nicest things."

She waggled a bitten-nailed finger at me. "You're not right, either. Because Art came out west and came out, and he didn't just find his sexual people, he found the people who loved computers, too. Whereas you—"

"Whereas I only found computer people. Sure. Art's definitely getting the better end of this deal, I get it. But my point still stands: *I love this town.*"

"And my point still stands: it won't love you back. San Francisco has had gold rush after gold rush, and each one was a disaster. Nearly everyone went broke. The city was mobbed and everything the locals loved about it was destroyed. Sometimes it even burned down. They chopped down all the fucking redwoods. This gold rush won't be any different, mark my words."

I was still trying to think of a rejoinder when she was struck by another bolt of inspiration and went back to making machine-gun noises on the keyboard, and long before she finished, I had fallen asleep, fully clothed and mouth full of residual beer that spent the night turning into a disgusting, sour paste that coated every tooth and my tongue by morning.

CF was doing so well that it was possible to forget that we were being sued. Even the Kohlers didn't mind the hefty lawyers' bills on every financial statement I prepared for them. In fact, when Rivka proposed that we hire Pat full-time to explore designing a CF PC—one that integrated the ideas she'd been exploring on those twin DN100s—it was *Benny* who insisted that we take more money than we'd asked for. We never did payroll Pat, instead paying her whenever she bothered to invoice us for whatever sum she named. It was always less than what she was worth, but I couldn't convince her to take more.

Benny had the same fever as me. Our revenues were *still* doubling, and we couldn't buy enough parts to keep up with orders for modified floppy drives that could read one of Fidelity's gimmicked floppy disks, or get enough sprocket replacements to produce the kits for converting their printers to take normal paper. We bought out Leon Boudin's lease on the Potrero Hill space and I started negotiations to take over the ground floor as well, so we'd be able to relocate the shipping area and load up the trucks without having to move everything down that slow-moving relic of a freight elevator.

Art still came by, but he was barely needed by then. All of his code had been rewritten by Pat, and she had hired some of her former AT&T brat pals to maintain it long-distance, airmailing floppy disks back and forth across the continent. I missed him, but only when I wasn't running around doing eleven things at once, which was always.

One night, I came back to Pat's apartment to find her gone, which wasn't that unusual. She kept weird hours that let her see every Dead Kennedys show—and every other show—in town. I made myself a cheese and cold cut sandwich, brushed my teeth and folded down the futon and smoked one of the pre-rolled joints that she kept in a mint tin on her bookshelf, a habit that she'd imparted to me, which I found absolutely indispensable for finding sleep quickly.

I barely roused when she came in and padded around, brushing her own teeth, fishing the joint out of the ashtray and finishing it, sliding open the window to admit the night fog and the distant hiss of car tires. She slid under the blanket next to me and nuzzled my neck, waking me up in the nicest way possible.

"Hey, babe," I said, turning to kiss the top of her head, which smelled of a cocktail of sweat, smoke, and beer. "You go to a show?"

"It was amazing," she said. "MDC opened for the Angry Samoans. My ears are still ringing."

"That does sound great," I said. "MDC?"

"Millions of Dead Cops," she said.

"Not really."

"I bought you a T-shirt."

I threw my arm over her and gave her a one-sided hug. "You always know just what to get me."

As I drifted back to sleep, I felt a sense of warm satisfaction pour over me, thick as syrup. I had a great woman, a great job, a great apartment, in a great city. I'd confronted the worst the world had to throw at me and I'd overcome it. I'd come west for gold and I'd found a mother lode. I was going to be rich. I was going to change the world. I was going to go to punk shows and get the stuffing knocked out of me and wear MDC T-shirts to my corner taqueria and then come home and play with $70,000 worth of computers. I had it all figured out.

That's what I thought.

14

That was Wednesday night. I spent Thursday processing payroll and cutting checks, and Friday was payday, the day we ordered in pizza, the day the warehouse guys and the factory women all knocked off at 3 p.m. and any sales reps who were in town came over to see the operation. Rivka, Maria-Eva, and Liz all made a point of shutting down their own work and coming down to the factory floor, and Pat joined nearly every week. My role was to pass through the group handing out pay envelopes and playing Santa Claus.

I was halfway through when one of the factory women, Mariela, tapped me on the shoulder. "Visitor, Mr. Marty," she said.

"Uh," I said, shifting the box of alphabetized envelopes to my other arm. "Sorry, can you ask Rivka or—" I looked around to see who else from management was in sight. "Can you ask Rivka to get the door?"

"For you," Mariela said. She was one of our youngest hires, the daughter of someone who'd been with us since the beginning. Barely out of her teens, with tailored blouses and her hair in a big, blow-dried sculpture.

The box of pay envelopes was still more than half full. I craned my neck to check the wall clock. Three forty-five. No one would leave before four thirty. I thanked Mariela and hustled to the door.

Shlomo Spinka did not look good. He stooped. Behind his wire-rimmed glasses, his eyes were bagged and red. He startled guiltily when I opened the door and checked both shoulders before he extended a shaking hand. His grip was weak and warm and wet.

"Shlomo?"

"Mr. Hench." He looked over both shoulders again. "Can I speak with you?" The *privately* was unsaid but it didn't need to be said.

"Come in," I said. The ground-floor warehouse was empty— the guys were all upstairs, eating pizza—and I led him to the area in the back where there was a card table with an overflowing ashtray and a few folding chairs.

Shlomo pulled out a pack of Marlboros and lit one, giving me another chance to see how badly his hands shook.

He stared at the cigarette, put it down carefully. "You think you understand so much, but you don't, you know." His voice was as nasal as I remembered, but there was a gravity to it this time.

"Shlomo, brother, I'm getting worried here. You look like you're having a hard time. There's no reason we have to be enemies. There's plenty of room in this world for both CF and Fidelity Computing. Competition is good for us both. Keeps us sharp. It's—" Then words came up from the base of my spine and exited my mouth without traversing my brain. "It's the American way."

"You don't understand," he said. A few tears leaked down his cheeks.

"So explain it," I said. "Honestly, I'll listen. Come on, guy, we can work this out. Did they fire you, or—"

"Shut up," he snapped. "You don't understand *anything*."

You said that already. I waited. Watched as this little guy—Art would have called him a *schmendrick*—mustered his courage.

"You think that Fidelity Computing's business is just the Reverend Sirs and those girls in the field, the ones who sell the product. You think that if you hire those girls, steal our customers, that the worst thing that happens is that three old men will get angry at you."

"I don't think that's the worst thing. They might sue us. They might send two tough guys to punch me up a little and kick me in the balls. They might destroy our factory. They might break into Rivka Goldman's apartment and poison the air and smear a shit-swastika on her wall."

He'd been looking at his hands, but now he gasped and looked straight into my eyes. If he wasn't shocked, he was a master of method acting.

"That didn't happen," he said.

I shrugged. "The Reverend Sirs don't like to be thwarted, I suppose."

He gave a hollow, mirthless laugh. "You don't understand anything. You think that the men you've angered are the Reverend Sirs."

I catch on. Eventually, I catch on. "You're saying that the buck doesn't stop with the Reverend Sirs."

He looked me in the eyes again for an uncomfortably long time, then he slowly shook his head.

The secret to Fidelity Computing was its close-knit faith communities, the religious bonds of trust that enabled Fidelity to recruit women who'd draw on their friendships to sell to their husbands and their husbands' friends. It was the greatest marketing scheme ever devised, built on the folktale of the faithful helping the faithful.

For religious people who already made a point of doing business within their community, the idea of a faith-based computer was a double blessing: you could spend money with a fellow parishioner, and master the intimidating and complicated world of computers at the same time.

No need to patronize a fast-talking computer salesman—Fidelity salespeople carried VHS cassettes with commercials for Crazy Eddie, a New York computer salesman whose pitch confirmed every fear the customers had about how they'd be treated if they braved the digital waters on their own.

The formula was an instant success. Sales ballooned and the company's factory in Provo struggled to keep up with orders, even after they found a factory in Taiwan that would put together the subsystems and send them to the U.S. for a final assembly.

The Reverend Sirs probably could have gone to a bank at that point, taken out a loan to cover the capital costs of their expansion. But why would they? There were wealthy men in each of their congregations, and those wealthy men had friends, and before you knew, it, a syndicate of investors had come together to—

"You're saying that Fidelity isn't just a way to separate poor parishioners from their money by selling them gimmicked computers. It's a way to share the wealth with 'community leaders' in the Reverend Sirs' charmed circle."

Shlomo adjusted his glasses and then wiped his hands on his pants. Then he took his glasses off again and cleaned them on the tails of his prayer shawl and reseated them. He looked around the warehouse, at the floor, at his hands. He opened his mouth. He closed his mouth.

"Mr. Hench." He spoke softly, like he was tasting each word. "The . . . gentlemen . . . that invested in the company are . . . not . . ." He took off his glasses again, got his sweaty fingers all over the lenses again, cleaned them again, wiped his palms again. "They are . . . They . . ."

"They're what, Shlomo? They're mobsters?"

He shrank back. "Not mobsters, no!" He thought for a while. "They're, I suppose, well, they're *gangsters*." He expelled the word like it was a chicken bone he'd been choking on. I wanted to thump him between his shoulders to see if he'd dislodge anything else.

"All right," I said. "Gangsters." The word ricocheted around my mind: *gangsters*.

"They expect a certain . . . return . . . on their investments," Shlomo said, looking off into space, contemplating the vast, uncaring universe. "Last week, the Reverend Sirs told them that they could not expect their next payment in full." He put his hands under his armpits and hugged himself. "He told them why."

I turned that over. "Shlomo, these three women have come in for a lot of hard-guy stuff. You're saying that this was these mobster—" He held up his hand. "Sorry, *gangster* associates of the Reverend Sirs?"

He wiped his hands again. This time, he left visible streaks on his gray wool pants. "No, Mr. Hench. No, you've misunderstood me, I'm afraid." Wipe, wipe. "I'm saying that all of that was what the Reverend Sirs did because they didn't want their gangster investors to get involved."

He ripped his glasses off his face and let them clatter to the table, then looked at me with those red-rimmed, liquid brown eyes. "Mr. Hench, don't you understand? All of that was the Reverend Sirs' version of gentle persuasion. What comes next will be *terrible*."

Shlomo's thousand-yard stare reminded me of the GI Bill guys from Vietnam who had attended classes with me, the sense that something had been seen that could never be unseen. A finger of ice crept up my spine.

He put his glasses back on. "There was a man who stole," he said. "A trusted man. Well-placed. On the Catholic side of the operation, though that didn't matter, the investors are . . . *interfaith*." A mirthless bark, then, so dry it fell like a puff of dust. "The Reverend Sirs couldn't call in the police, because that would have raised questions about the way the money was handled. The investors found out.'

"It was a sizable sum.

"The man . . ." He swallowed and then stood abruptly. "I need to go," he said, and began to speed-walk out of the warehouse, getting turned around and finding himself in a dead end of high cargo shelves stacked with boxes. I cornered him and spread out my arms.

"What happened to the man, Shlomo?"

For a second, I thought he'd rush me. But then he sagged.

"The police identified him from dental records," he said. "It took some time, though. Some of his teeth were gone."

I dropped my arms. Shlomo shuffled past me like a sleepwalker.

"To your right," I said. "The exit is to your right, then your left."

He stopped and turned around. "Thank you, Mr. Hench."

"Thank you, Shlomo," I said. "I know you didn't have to tell me this."

"I did it for the girls," he said. "Rivka, Elizabeth, the sister. They are good people, I know. What's coming next—"

"I'll tell them, Shlomo. You've done your part."

He nodded and then resumed his shuffle. I heard him thud into the exit door's crash bar, then heard the door close itself and click shut.

I went back upstairs and handed out the rest of the paychecks.

Pat knew something was wrong, of course. We walked up Potrero, stopped so she could talk with the bouncer at A Little More, the lesbian bar on the corner, who sported a sleeveless Lydia Lunch tee that showed off her ripped biceps and her linked-Venus-symbols tattoo. I stood off a ways, smiling absently at the women who drifted in, dressed and eager for Friday-night clubbing.

Pat broke off and joined me. We resumed our uphill walk. "Danni says you could come in with me some time, so long as you behave yourself."

"That's nice," I said.

She didn't reply. We trudged uphill, and Pat handed dollar bills to the three guys who'd pitched tents on the sidewalk in front of SF General. They'd appeared a couple of weeks before and Pat, ever curious, had stopped to talk with them, learning that they were all ex–mental patients who'd been thrown out on the street when Reagan repealed the Mental Health Systems Act. Two of the guys had tardive dyskinesia, which you got after years on schizophrenia drugs, and it was why they kept twisting their faces into gargoyle masks, sticking out their tongues, pursing their lips.

When I'd first gone past them, I'd assumed they were either tripping or trying for some kind of shock effect, and Pat's explanation left me ashamed. The fact that she remembered to keep some singles in her pocket to help the guys out—and that she remembered their names and spoke with them whenever she passed them—made me feel like even more of a heel.

Once the guys—Liam, Bob, and Jay—were behind us and we'd turned onto Twenty-Fourth Street, Pat stopped walking abruptly and stood in front of me, hands on my biceps, staring intensely into my face.

"Are you going to tell me, or am I going to have to guess?"

"I'm sorry," I said. The Friday-night crowd streamed around us on the sidewalk. Someone hip-checked me as they squeezed past. Pat's small, strong hands stabilized me. "When we get home, okay? It's not something I should talk about in public."

She stared into my eyes, like she was trying to see through them into my brain, and I stared into hers. They were wild, those eyes of Pat's, as full of chaos whether she was coding, moshing, or hissing dirty words while we slammed into each other at home. Meeting that searching gaze, I felt a little slip of the fear Shlomo had put into me. God, she was a good woman.

"Okay, jerk, I'll wait until we're home. But it had better be good." We took a few more steps. "Do I need to buy a six-pack for this news?"

"Maybe a bottle of tequila," I said.

"Oh, shit," she said. "All right, tequila."

It was mezcal, actually, a clear liquid that poured thick but went down as mellow as a bourbon. The clerks at the liquor store on our corner doted on Pat, knew her from her regular beer runs, and when she made a theatrical announcement that she needed a bottle of tequila to help her recover from some heavy news, they sprang into action, eventually bringing a bottle of Tehuana down off a high shelf. She peered at the dancing woman in a Oaxacan peasant dress on the label and then gave it the nod, handed the bottle back, and struck a perfect replica of the Oaxacan dancer's graceful pose. That won her a laugh from the clerks and earned me a sizing-up glance that left me feeling distinctly wanting. These guys definitely thought she was out of my league, and I wasn't about to argue.

I drank one shot of the mezcal quick, while I puttered around the kitchen nook, putting together a plate with crackers and some of the zesty cheddar I'd bought from one of those grocery-store free-sample ladies at the Safeway. She'd served it on crackers with sprigs of peppery watercress, and I'd bought some of that, too. It was a little wilted, but I rinsed it and picked off the saddest-looking leaves, then arranged it with the cheese.

Pat poured out two more shots of the mezcal and then looked this way and that at the cracker plate. "I'm impressed," she said. She ate one in a single bite, dribbling crumbs on the table, chewed thoughtfully, sipped the mezcal. "Very impressed." She slid the plate closer to herself. "You're going to want to make another one of these for you."

So I did, and by the time I got back, she had a copy of *Maximum Rocknroll* open on the table, spotted with crumbs. Her plate was empty. I gave her half my crackers and sat down and sipped my mezcal and ate a cracker. I didn't taste either.

"I got a visit from one of the guys from Fidelity Computing tonight," I said.

"Yeah?"

"He told me that things are about to get bad." I told her about Shlomo. She sipped her mezcal and picked crumbs off the newsprint and nibbled them. When I was done, she poured more mezcal.

"It's bullshit," she said.

"What's bullshit?"

"All of it," she said. She rolled her eyes. "God, can't you see you're being played? These dirty priests tried everything, the girls beat 'em anyway, so now they're sending this guy out to see if you can convince them to just surrender, right when they're about to just destroy these three old guys."

"Pat, you didn't see this guy—"

"No, I didn't, and isn't that strange? Like, he knows Liz and Maria-Eva and Rivka. He worked with them. And yet he came to you. Why do you suppose that was? You think it was some kind of Orthodox thing, he thought they might be on the rag and didn't want to catch period cooties?"

"Maybe it was *because* he knew them. Maybe he didn't want to look them in the eye and admit that he'd been working for crooks all these years and he'd known it. Or hell, yeah, maybe it's because he's an ultrareligious male chauvinist pig. I don't know why he came to me, Pat, but I saw him and—"

"And he was very convincing. Okay, so he's a talented actor. Maybe he majored in theater at the yeshiva. Maybe he's got a

258 ◄ **cory doctorow**

gift. But come *on,* you think he's *mobbed up*? This is Silicon Valley, Marty, not Jersey. Take it from a Jersey girl."

"Fine," I said. "I don't have any proof, I admit it. I just have the word of this guy who I don't trust as far as I can throw up." She smiled. What a smile she had. I hated arguing with her. She was a lot smarter than me, and faster, too. "But what if he's not lying, Pat? What if he's not lying and the next thing that happens is worse than anything that's happened so far? Don't you think we should have a plan for that? Take some steps to improve our safety?"

"And what if the whole point is to *make us come up with those plans* so we can't do business because we're too busy putting bars on all the windows and paying security guards to watch the door? Marty, you're pretty good with computers and you're a great accountant and you screw with a lot of style, but you *don't understand anything about security.*"

"And you do?" popped out of my mouth before I could ask more about how I screwed.

"Of course I do. I grew up in Bell Labs, fella, which makes me a fully paid-up member of the military-industrial complex. I attended my first war game before I went to my first school dance. They're trying to force us to play blue team."

I must have looked confused.

"You know, blue team? Defenders. Right now, that's them. We're the attackers. They've built these fortresses, incompatible file formats and stupid games with printer sprockets and floppy controllers. The red team—that's us, the attackers—we just need to find *any* exploitable hole in their strategy. To defend, they need to be perfect, to have no holes.

"So if they can get us to change sides, to see *ourselves* as the blue team, then we've got the hard job and they've got the easy job. This is a tactic, Marty, an old one. If we fall for it, that's on us."

She stared intently at me, lips compressed, eyes stern. I couldn't help it, I giggled.

That earned me a cuff upside the head, but also a smile.

"I love it when you go all military-industrial. You're a punk-rock hacker drill sergeant."

That made her laugh. Oh, what a laugh. "Okay, great. So we're in agreement."

"Are we?"

"We are," she said.

"What have we agreed?"

"We've agreed that it's bullshit and we're not going to worry about it."

"We're not," I said.

"We're *not*."

"Are we going to tell Liz and Maria-Eva and Rivka?"

"Absolutely not." She barely waited for me to get the words out of my mouth. "Those girls have more on their plate than they can handle already. You wouldn't be doing them any favors."

"But if it turns out that it's for real—"

"It's bullshit, Marty, come on. I mean these three guys are already a bad joke: 'A priest, a rabbi, and a Mormon bishop walk into a Silicon Valley bar.' But throw the *Mafia* in? Take it from a Jersey girl, that is *not* a Mafia operation."

"But if—"

"If, if, if." Her stern face was back. She slapped the table and made the remaining crumbs jump off the page of her *Maximum Rocknroll*. "Jesus, Marty, do you have any *idea* what kind of strain those girls are under already? Do you ever bother to check in with them to find out what's going on in their life?"

"Of course I do. I see them every day."

That made her unexpectedly angry. She glared at me. "Okay, so tell me, how are things with Liz and her family?"

"Uh," I said. "A couple of her siblings are still talking to her, I think, using a pay phone, and—"

"No," she said, biting down on the word and plowing on before I could continue. "Liz's father found out about that and he beat those kids within an inch of their lives, then made them write Liz letters telling her that she wasn't welcome in their lives anymore. They mailed them to her in a box with every birthday and Christmas gift she'd ever given them."

"Holy shit," I said.

That made her even angrier. Her being angry at me was making *me* angry at *her*. Before I could get a lid on that, she spat, "I suppose you know all about Liz's bishop?"

"Bishop Clarke?"

"Who? Oh, the Reverend Sir? No, not that asshole. Liz's bishop back home in Utah. He's a part-time bishop, full-time dentist. Put braces on Liz's teeth. He also excommunicated her."

"He *what?*"

"Yeah." She glared at me, then started again, talking like she was explaining something to a child—or a fool. "Liz sent him her tithing check as usual—"

"Her *tithing check?*"

She shook her head. "Liz sends—sent—ten percent of all her earnings from CF to her bishop. Tithing. Except he returned the last one, with a brief note telling her she had been excommunicated *in absentia.*"

"You're fucking kidding me—"

"*Do I look like I'm kidding?*" Her face was stone. "Marty, I know you try to be a decent guy, but you are in your own little world here. You act like you're in a hot technology start-up."

"Gee, I wonder why?" I said, channeling my dad's best sarcastic tone, the one that could reduce my mom to tears. "Could it be because we're a start-up, that's doing tech, and growing by hundreds of percent?"

"CF isn't just a hot tech start-up, Marty. It's a lifeline, and not just for Liz and Rivka and Maria-Eva. You know the factory girls?"

I got up from the table and took a step back, hands on my hips. "Of course I do."

"Name them."

"Of course!" I said again. I started rattling them off, ticking them off on my fingers: "Lucia Acosta. Tanya-Luz Alvarado. Anna Alvarez. Romina Ayala—"

"Alphabetical order." She snorted and rolled her eyes. "Names on paychecks. Can you tell me *anything* about them? What about Romina—where's she from?"

"Mexico—"

"El Salvador. Civil war refugee. Father was in the FMLN. They butchered him in front of her. Then they came for her. She escaped, naked, into the woods. She's got a mother and a grandmother and a bunch of siblings left behind, she gives every penny she can to a lawyer who's trying to get them status so they can come, too."

I was momentarily stunned. "Jesus." I fished for something else to say.

She didn't give me a chance. "How about Tanya-Luz. Where's *she* from?"

I tried to picture her. Dark eyes, shining hair, round face. A smile when I handed her the envelope on Fridays. Did she wear a pin? "She's got a dead baby," I said.

"Marty, *what the fuck?* What are you *talking about?*"

"She wears a pin, a picture of a baby, in a gilt frame."

"That's her *granddaughter.* She's obsessed with the kid. The kid who is *not* dead."

"Fine," I said, "so I haven't gotten to know the factory girls as well as I could. I don't speak the language, we're growing fast—"

"What about Rivka?"

"What about her?"

Now *she* was on her feet, arms crossed over her chest. "Marty, goddammit, you *really* don't know?"

"What?" I said, a sinking feeling competing with the rising blood filling my fists, my cheeks, my ears.

"She almost quit," Pat said. "How could you not know about this?"

"I don't know! How could I know about any of that?" I wanted to say something, but I didn't know what. I swallowed. "How come *you* do?"

"Because I *listen*, Marty. I pay attention. I know you want to be a caring guy, I can tell that matters a lot to how you see yourself, but you're so wrapped up in your own trip that you miss the clues. Didn't you notice anything different about Maria-Eva?"

I barely registered her question, because my brain went into vapor lock when she said *I listen*. Didn't I listen? I mean, wasn't that the skill I'd learned from Lucille, that full-body, full-brain listening?

And it didn't help that Pat was still talking, and *I wasn't listening to her.*

"—death squads murdered like six of her friends in Nicaragua, and she only just found out about it last week. These were other nuns, they tied them to trees and bayonetted them, left them there for the locals to find, like a message, don't fuck with the Contras—"

"What?"

"Maria-Eva's got a lot going on, Marty. The reason none of this shit with the Reverend Sirs touches her, she's deep into some *real* struggles that make them look like *kindergartners.* She doesn't like to talk about it, but she will, if you *just fucking* listen, and you *should,* because it does her good. Those murderous bastards are *our* bastards, after all—they're the 'good guys' who are working to keep the commies out of the region. No one's going to tell you about the bayonetted nuns on the six o'clock news, though. Maria-Eva's got a line on something that no one else is gonna tell you about."

"I thought I was a *good listener!*"

She *whooped* with laughter. It was clearly involuntary and maybe she regretted it, but both of those facts made it so much worse. I turned and picked up my backpack and, for some reason, retrieved my toothbrush from the bathroom.

"What the fuck are you doing?"

I didn't trust my mouth. Maybe it was the mezcal.

"Are you . . . *leaving*? Because I *laughed at you*? Because I don't agree that you're a *good listener*?" She was very good at sarcasm. She was better at it than me. She was better at it than my dad.

She'd been brought up among very smart adults, and had learned to hold her own with them at an early age. I'd been turned loose in the fields of Alabama while my dad chased the American dream in an oil field and my mother chased domestic perfection around our split-level home. I hadn't had a conversation with an adult as an equal until I dropped out of MIT. I was out of my depth in that room, and my stupid mouth wanted to say something that would prove just how out of my depth I was.

I stooped to tie my shoes at the door and my backpack, slung over just one arm, flopped forward and whacked me upside the head. I fell over, literally fell on my face.

"Oh come *on*," she said. "Be an adult, Marty."

"Look," I said, and my voice cracked and I swallowed as hard as I could, then did it again. "*Look*. Fine. You're right. I'm a shitty listener. I'm a self-centered asshole. I don't know what's going on in anyone's life except my own and that makes me a fucking meathead. Fine, I *accept that*. But you know what? I'm *still right*. Those people are in danger and they deserve to know about it."

I sat on the floor and tied my laces, then climbed to my feet, holding my head and wiping tears from my eyes.

"Okay," she said. She looked at me with pity and contempt and I couldn't believe how much I hated her, especially because I couldn't believe how much I loved her. "Fine, Marty. Maybe you're right, maybe I'm wrong. And yeah, you're an asshole. So you go wherever you have to go, do whatever you have to do."

She shook her head hard. "Maybe I'll even talk to you when we're done."

I stared at her, wanting to say something even worse than what she'd said to me, like *What makes you think I give a shit if you ever talk to me again?* But my wise brain stilled my foolish tongue for once and I said nothing.

I should have been drinking in a last vision of her, in her great Mission apartment with its humming minicomputers, short and wiry and tough, smart and sexy and loving. Instead, I got an out-of-focus, tear-blurred image haloed in reddish black. A voice whispered *You don't have to go. You can apologize to her and beg for her forgiveness and spend the night in that bed next to her again.* I ignored the voice.

"Goodbye, Pat," I said.

The walk to the Twenty-Second Street Caltrain station took the best part of an hour, giving me ample opportunity to sober up and regret my choices. The train took another forty minutes, and by the time it arrived, I had numbered those choices and placed them in order based on how much I regretted them. When I put my key in the lock of Art's apartment, where I still paid half the rent, I was ready to declare the whole Marty Hench project to have been an unmitigated disaster and scrap it.

15

Art shook me out of bed the next morning at nine.

"Come on, cowboy, up and at 'em." He was dressed in perfectly aged denim jeans and a tight polo shirt, and he'd gotten a new haircut since I'd last seen him, something preppie, requiring a substantial amount of gel to maintain structural integrity. It looked good. It also completed his transformation: no one would mistake him for the wild-haired, redheaded weirdo I'd met in an MIT dumpster looking for fanfold paper that had only been used on one side.

"It's Saturday," I said.

"I know," he said. "I've got a brunch date in the city and I don't plan on being late for it, and I don't want you spending your whole day moping in bed."

I sat up, realizing as I did that I was fully dressed. Well, all the boxers and tees I liked to sleep in were up the peninsula, in San Francisco. In Pat's apartment.

"I like the haircut," I said.

He grinned and primped it. "I know it's a little shellacked, but my barber swore it would flatter me, and three guys bought me drinks last night."

"I'm not surprised," I said. "You're a fox."

He smiled again and then got serious. "Pat asked me to make sure you were okay."

"I'm okay."

"Are you, buddy? To hear Pat tell of it, things are pretty intense right now."

"I'm okay." He gave me a skeptical look. "*Really*. Thank you, thank Pat, but I'll be okay. I just, I dunno, I just took my eye off the ball and got beaned by it. I'm gonna get my focus back, concentrate on what matters."

He looked at me with that relentless Art-ish skepticism, like a wise-guy remark in gaze form. I was out of practice with that look, but I braced myself and powered through it.

"Okay, Marty. You gotta be you, I guess." He started to leave my room, then paused in the doorway and looked back at me. "You know I'm your buddy, right? I love you. You're my brother. I will be there for you." He swallowed and gazed upon me with placid Californian serenity. "I just wanted you to know that."

This wasn't the place for a wisecrack, but oh God did I want to let fly with one. The sincerity was so intense it almost hurt.

"Thanks, Art" is all I managed to mumble. If I could have said, "I love you, too," I would have, because it was true. But I couldn't say it. I still don't know why.

It was Saturday. I could take Caltrain back to the city, or go find something to do in the Valley. I'd heard good things about the Winchester Mystery House. Pat and I had planned to go.

I could call Pat.

Nah.

I could call home. They wouldn't be expecting my call until Sunday, but I could call them a day early, right?

Then I thought about trying to explain Pat—or any of it, really—to my dad.

Nah again.

I had to speak to *someone*. Not Art. Not my parents. Not any of the CF women. My brain was vapor-locked, chasing itself in circles. I tried talking to *myself*: "Hench, pull yourself together.

You're an adult male, you're doing a man's job, master your god-damned emotions."

I paced. I tidied. When I moved a stack of unfiled—but meticulously paid—bills off the desk in my room, I found Lucille's last letter. It was over a month old. God, I was a shitty pen pal. A shitty friend. A shitty *person*.

I reread Lucille's last letter to me. Like all our correspondence, it was lighthearted, a little flirty, full of book reviews, movie suggestions, and inconsequentialities. It ended, as ever, with her usual sign-off and postscript: "Love, Your Lucille. PS: Don't ever forget that you've got a friend in Sacramento."

I untangled the phone's long extension cord, ran it from the living room, down the hall, and into my room, and then I dialed Lucille.

"Martin Hench, what a surprise! I thought perhaps you'd fallen into the San Andreas Fault."

"I'm sorry, Lucille. Work has been—" I groped for words.

"These are your computing ladies?"

"Yeah," I said. I must have put something into that word, or maybe it was just her excellent listening skills.

"Marty, you can tell me about it. I've got—" She paused. "I've got four hours until I need to start preparing dinner for some people who are coming by tonight. And if need be, I can chop vegetables while we talk."

So I told her. Not about the violence, or Shlomo, but the shape of things, the pressure-cooker life of a fast-growing computer company that nevertheless danced on the brink of destruction. Then I told her about Pat. I told her about the fight. I thought I was being fair to Pat. Certainly, I made myself sound like an asshole.

But then she said, "Marty, do you know what my secret to a happy life is?"

All my banter had run out. I blurted, "You mean how you

listen? Lucille, that's no secret, it's your winningest attribute, out of a crowded field."

I heard the smile in her voice. "Okay, thank you Marty, yes. That's my secret. Listening."

I waited to be sure she was done, trying to listen the way she did. "I learned it from you. Ever since we first met, I've been listening *so hard.*"

"Marty," she said. Her tone was gentle, but it was firm. "Great listeners aren't born. They're made. It takes practice. It's very admirable that you're trying to listen better—"

Each word pierced me, from the kindly *admirable* to the damning *trying.* "Dammit, I *am* listening, I'm a *great* fucking listener."

She didn't say anything, but then, she didn't have to. All I had to do was listen to *myself.*

"God*dammit,*" I said, finally.

"You'll get better at it, Marty. And you get points for trying, honest! That's not a put-down. I'm not patronizing you. Most people don't even try."

Part of being a good listener is leaving some silences. She paused to let me think about what she'd said. I paused to think about it.

"I'll work on it," I said, finally.

"I know you will," she said. "You're a good man, Martin Hench, and I love you."

She was the kind of person who could lay down those "love you"s and you knew she meant it. I felt very lucky to have the love of someone like her. I also felt ashamed of myself, and very, very stupid.

"All right," she said. "That's that, and I just realized I need to get some spices for tonight's dinner, so I should run down to the market."

"What are you making?"

"Cauliflower and crispy bacon soup, a big salad with apples

and walnuts and pumpkin seeds, and oven chicken. I stuff the cavity with whole oranges and onions and serve it with potatoes that I roast in a pan of duck fat until they're so dark they're *just* about to turn black."

"Wow."

"Make time for the good things in life, Marty. Friends and food. Good wine. Laughing.

"Love."

I swallowed hard. "Thank you, Lucille."

She let the pause hang there for a while.

"Love you, Marty."

"I love you, too, Lucille."

I was hungry. I wandered into the kitchen and discovered that Art had gone on some kind of health kick, and the fridge and cupboards were full of *ingredients,* as opposed to the ready-to-eat freezer meals and pasta we'd lived off in Cambridge and continued our love affair with in California. I found a bowl of brown, scaly ovals on the counter and realized they were *avocados.* Art had gone native.

Pat hated cooking. I pulled down Art's copy of *The Moosewood Cookbook* and paged through it. We had all the ingredients needed for apple-cheese pancakes. The author's hand-lettered note said, *This recipe makes enough to satisfy four reasonably hungry sorts.* As I grated the apples and beat the batter, I realized I was more than reasonably hungry.

Fifteen minutes later, I had a stack of pancakes and a spattered stove and countertop. I reached for a cloth with one hand and a pancake with the other, intending to wolf it down one-handed while I wiped up the mess.

Then I stopped and rooted around the cupboards. Yes, there were the lemon-yellow vinyl placemats, as cheerful as an airport Moonie. There were the disposable paper napkins saved from a Chinese delivery meal. I polished a knife and fork on a kitchen towel and laid the table like it was Friday-night supper back in Alabama, then I spooned some strawberry jam into a little ceramic dish that we used to use as an emergency ashtray back when smokers dropped in on us in Cambridge, and squeezed a couple of oranges by hand into a glass, fishing out the seeds with a teaspoon.

I sat myself down at the table with a carefully arranged plate with three pancakes on it and picked up the gleaming cutlery and cut a perfect, dainty chord across the circumference of one of the pancakes, swirled an artful curlicue of jam atop it with the tip of my butter knife, then took a bite. As my teeth pulled the morsel from the fork, I tried to engage the kind of attention to tasting my food that I'd watched Lucille devote to listening.

It was a revelation. The texture of the pancake—crisp on the outside, soft on the inside, viscous jam atop—was complex and satisfying in a way I'd never noticed and now couldn't stop noticing.

Keeping my attention on the food through my slow but inexorable engulfment of enough pancakes *to satisfy four reasonably hungry sorts* was hard at first, but it got easier, and expanded to encompass everything that contributed to the experience: the way the sun made the placemat glow, the motes of dust that sparkled in that sunbeam, the little bits of pulp in the orange juice that burst between my tongue and the roof of my mouth.

I finished breakfast and did the dishes and cleaned the counter in a bemused fug. Then I threw *The Moosewood Cookbook* in my backpack and grabbed the keys to the bike I shared with Art and cycled to the Duca & Hanley grocery store. There I picked out the ingredients for Cossack Pie, Gado-Gado, and Vegetable Stroganoff, before turning to the dessert section and stocking up on the inputs for Finnish Whipped Fruit Puddings and Maple-Egg Custard.

It didn't all fit in my backpack, so I ended up riding home with tripled-up paper bags hanging from each handlebar, and I had to walk the last half mile with one bag balanced on the seat after all three sets of handles gave way. I didn't mind. It gave me a chance to think about the food I was going to cook.

Art boggled when he got home and saw the *gado-gado* on the table, a spicy, honeyed peanut stew I served with a mix of carrot sticks, quartered hard-boiled eggs, steamed green beans, and shredded cabbage. I'd precisely squared off the placemats and cutlery and cleaned the glassware.

"Holy shit," he said. "Heartbreak clearly agrees with you, buddy." Then he added, "Shit, sorry, that was probably in bad taste."

"It's okay," I said, though it wasn't. I'd only thought about Pat about twelve thousand times that day, and it had been at least six minutes since I'd last thought of her. "But you're on dish duty now."

He looked relieved. "I will. Uh, but I'm gonna leave them to soak? I'm meeting some friends at the Boot Rack after dinner."

"Fine," I said, though it ended up taking a heroic act of will not to clean up afterward. But he was true to his word, and when I got up the next morning, the kitchen was spotless—and all the leftovers were gone. Then I noticed an extra pair of size 12 Timberland hiking boots by the front door—just as a big guy with an impressive mustache and a pair of tighty whities and nothing else emerged from Art's room and waved sheepishly to me before disappearing into the bathroom. I shrugged and got down the cookbook and started planning brunch.

I decided I'd make banana bread—there were a couple of mushy bananas on the counter I'd spared from the trash can during my cleanout—and those Finnish whipped fruit puddings. The banana bread was just cool enough to eat when Art and his friend—Brant—rolled out of bed and into the kitchen. They were just putting away their second slices—dripping with unsalted butter and dusted with cinnamon—when I decided the fruit puddings were chilled enough. Despite their complaints about being too full to eat another thing, they ate two each.

The entire experience was fantastically satisfying, especially their effusive praise and Brant's insistence on doing the dishes, during which time Art and I reclined with coffees and hands over tight bellies and experienced a great and peaceful satiety.

That afternoon, I took Art's van down to Kepler's Books and bought *The Joy of Cooking*, *The Better Homes and Gardens Cookbook*, and, off the new-release table, *The Cook's Illustrated Cookbook*. I went home, made a list, and then went back to Duca & Hanley and bought so many groceries I had to write them a check to pay for them all.

First thing Monday, I called Rivka (thinking *she almost quit* and wondering when that was and what *almost* meant and what the circumstances had been) and told her I wasn't feeling good and I'd be working from home. The backpack I'd gone home with *did* have a box of floppies with the day's work on it; my computer at the office had two floppy controllers and four drives, which let me make a backup of my work as I went, and take it home with me every night, just in case there was another disaster. That had been Pat's initiative and she'd easily smoothed over the Kohlers' feathers when they'd seen the expense on the monthly expense report I prepared for them. Offsite backups were a bargain, and she'd hung a sign over the office door that read "Did you take your backups?"

Rivka assured me that they could survive for a day or two without needing me on the premises.

I'd forgotten how productive working from home was. Without the distractions of Rivka and Maria-Eva and Liz, and (especially) Pat, I was able to get through everything I had planned for the day in under two hours. I made a batch of Julia Child's hot scones and then used them as the basis for her avocado/bacon sandwich, and made a note to buy some paprika.

I'd cooked and tidied from two meals, done a full day's work, put a load of laundry in the machine, and finished all of my work duties and it was only one thirty in the afternoon. Pretty soon, I was going to start thinking about Pat.

I got out *Cook's Illustrated* and started working my way through Four Cheese Lasagne with Artichokes and Prosciutto.

I dropped by the office on Wednesday to swap some floppies. Maria-Eva looked up from her intense conversation with Pat and sprinkled a wave at me. Pat cut her eyes toward me and then away. She sat wooden-faced until Maria-Eva recommenced the discussion, then her face animated again, like something out of a mime act. I went home and built a very slow-burning mesquite charcoal fire in our balcony grill, then put on the ten-pound brisket I'd driven Art's van to Yuba to buy from a family-owned ranch I'd read about in a *Mercury News* profile.

By 8 p.m., the brisket was tender enough to cut with a fork and Art was hungry enough to skip the fork altogether. I served it with mashed potatoes and green beans, and a yellow vinegar barbecue sauce. Art brought home some bourbon, and not just Jack Daniel's, which is where my own experience with brown liquor started and stopped. After half a beer, I let him pour me two fingers over ice and then discovered a minor miracle as the burn of the booze and the burn of the fiery sauce and the meat's natural gravy all landed in my stomach at the same time.

I made a mental note to find out more about brown liquor.

Art promised he'd do the dishes the next morning. Honestly, I didn't care if he held up his end of the bargain. Washing dishes was the kind of mindless activity that let me stop thinking about Pat. See also: doing CF's books. See also: cooking. See also: driving 170 miles to Yuba to buy a brisket.

At least I'd have leftovers.

Art did the dishes. I ate some of my homemade granola over the yogurt I'd cultured overnight in the oven in a big glass jar with a cheesecloth tied over the mouth, kept warm and fertile by the pilot light.

As I washed up my breakfast dishes, I thought through the work I had teed up for the day: work on the quarterly numbers for the Kohlers, double-check the cash flow for our major suppliers' next round of invoices, make a backup of the work I'd brought home . . .

I was just ticking all this off when someone rapped authoritatively at the door. The building's front-door buzzer had been busted for a month and the super had solved this problem with the simple expedient of duct-taping over the lock so it no longer closed. That made life easier when the postman delivered a parcel, but it also gave me a brief case of the willies, as I remembered the tough guys the Reverend Sirs had sent to my apartment before.

I looked over at the block of kitchen knives and decided that was overkill.

"Who is it?"

"Messenger, package for Mr. Hench?" The voice was squeaky and uncertain, and looking through the peephole I spied a kid barely out of his teens, fuzzy mustache doing very little to make him seem older. He was holding a brown manila envelope and looking nervous.

I opened the door. "I'm Hench," I said, holding my hand out. He gave me a clipboard to sign, then swapped it with the envelope in a practiced gesture and ticked a two-fingered salute off his forehead as he spun on his heel and headed for the stairs.

My name was neatly lettered on the outside of the envelope, block caps, blue ballpoint. The envelope itself was slim, but there was something rigid in there, sliding back and forth. I set it down on the kitchen table and stared at it again. No return

address. Was that normal? No one had ever couriered me anything before, not in my entire life.

I took a breath, got my thumb under the flap and opened it
up. One sheet of paper. One floppy disk, in a paper sleeve. A
blank Fidelity label.

I turned the sheet of paper over.

>Mr. Hench
   I am very sorry for my actions. I can no longer be a party to them.
When you speak to Rivka, please tell her how sorry I am.
                                                        > Shlomo

Blue ink. Block letters. I set the paper down. Maybe Shlomo
just blew town and this was his parting gift.

I didn't think so.

I was pretty sure that Shlomo Spinka had killed himself.

Two. That's how many suicides I'd lived through. Two.

Billy Tayloe, part of a fine Alabama family, always grinning
during basketball games where he never excelled but nevertheless had the best time of any of the players on the court.
I watched him from the bleachers, sometimes ran into him at
parties. We weren't close, but we weren't strangers.

He did it with his dad's service revolver on a Sunday night
and we all found out about it by lunchtime on Monday. I was
one of the ones who said, "He always seemed so happy," though
even as I said it, I had to admit that I barely knew the guy and
only saw him at games, the odd party, and that one year we
were in algebra together, but I sat behind him and only ever saw
the back of his head. How happy does the back of someone's
head look?

The other one was Miz Grimshaw, who lived on our block and
had home help come by three times a week to hold her arm as

she hobbled to the corner and back, getting some air and sun. She kept a pristine 1957 Lincoln Continental in her garage, though she hadn't been able to drive it for years; her home help kept it in good running order and took it out to buy groceries once a week. There was enough gas in the tank for Miz Grimshaw to laboriously attach her garden hose to the tailpipe and run it into the driver's-side window and tune the radio to a classical music station.

I didn't know anything about her, not even enough to pretend that she always seemed so happy. After, I found out that there were three different cancers eating her alive, and the pain was literally unbearable.

Shlomo's floppy disk had a single WORD PROCESSOR file and two SPREADSHEET files. Out of cowardice, I started with the SPREADSHEET files, plugging a gimmicked CF floppy drive into my Apple so I could read them. I ran the first through Art's program to translate it to Lotus and opened it up.

As it opened and populated, a tremor rattled through my bones. There'd been a time on that Monday morning when I'd heard something really bad had happened to Billy Tayloe, but not what had happened, when I'd known what it would be but hadn't confirmed it yet.

That time, maybe between 9 a.m. and 11 a.m. when the lunch bell rang, had been an eternity. Over and over again, a voice had whispered in my head: "He killed himself." The knowing and not-knowing was actually worse than the knowing, when it came. The actual knowledge happened once and then it was all aftermath. The not-knowing? That happened every five minutes for hours.

I looked at the spreadsheet. It was called SPECIAL_CON-SULTANTS. Four columns:

- CONSULTANT
- TARGET

- DATE
- AMOUNT

The CONSULTANT column was just initials: DD, JB, RHA. The dates were all in the previous week. The amounts started at $1,000 and went up to $6,000. The targets were initials, too: RG, MF, ET, a few more, then MH.

I recognized MH: Martin Hench. Then I recognized the other initials: Rivka Goldman, Maria-Eva Fernandez, Elizabeth Taylor. That unlocked PC: Pat Currie.

The knowing/not-knowing feeling made me shake again. Names. Dollar figures. Shlomo, and that WORD PROCESSOR file. It was called FINAL.

Dollar amounts. Initials. FINAL.

I quit Lotus, converted the file, and found my Apple Writer floppy. I typed ctrl-L, then F-I-N-A-K. The program said FILE NOT FOUND. I typed CATALOG and confirmed the file was called FI-NAL. Noticed I'd mistyped it. Typed it again. Just before I hit Enter, I saw that I'd typed "FINAK" again. I corrected it. My hand shook.

FIDELITY COMPUTING IS A CRIMINAL ENTERPRISE.

I HAVE KNOWN THIS FOR FIVE YEARS AND YET I CONTINUED TO WORK FOR THEM.

THE COMPANY'S LEADERS AND INVESTORS ARE CROOKED, VIOLENT MEN. THEY HAVE HURT PEOPLE. I SAT BY WHILE IT HAPPENED. I PRAYED FOR GUIDANCE. I PRAYED FOR WISDOM. I PRAYED AND I PRAYED AND I PRAYED.

MY PRAYERS WERE NOT ANSWERED.

LAST WEEK, I LEARNED THAT THE COMPANY HAD PAID THREE MEN TO COMMIT ACTS OF TERRIBLE VIOLENCE. LAST WEEK, I LEARNED HOW MUCH MONEY THE THREE RELIGIOUS LEADERS WHO ARE THE FACE OF FIDELITY COMPUTING HAD PAID THEMSELVES AND HOW MUCH THEY STOOD TO MAKE FROM THESE ACTS OF VIOLENCE.

```
    I CONSIDERED GOING TO THE POLICE. I DID NOT. I KNEW
ABOUT THE CRIMES THE COMPANY HAD COMMITTED AND I DID
NOTHING. FOR FIVE YEARS, I DID NOTHING.
    HOW COULD I GO TO THE POLICE AND DENOUNCE MY
EMPLOYERS WHEN I SHARED THEIR GUILT?
    I HAVE MET THE MEN WHO WILL CARRY OUT THESE VIOLENT
ACTS. THEY ARE VICIOUS AND MERCILESS. I COULD NOT SIT
BY AS THEY CARRIED THEM OUT.
    I COULD NOT.
    G_D FORGIVE ME.
    SHLOMO SPINKA
```

With shaking hands, I quit Apple Writer and swapped in the Lotus disk, and opened the file called DISPERSALS.

Row upon row, the green numbers marched down through their boxes, recording the sums that the Reverend Sirs had taken from Fidelity Computing. All told, it was just a little more than eight million dollars. Some of it had been wired to fictitious suppliers that were little more than a gateway between a bank account and an anonymous company in Delaware. Some of it had been converted to real estate.

It turned out the Reverend Sirs collectively owned their factory building, through a fictitious landlord that the company remitted sky-high monthly rent to. It turned out that all the *furniture* in the Fidelity Computing facility was owned by a leasing company that was, again, jointly owned by Rabbi Yisrael Finkel, Bishop Leonard Clarke, and Father Marek Tarnowski, and that leasing company charged enough to buy a new set of furniture every other month.

They were looting the place.

The company's cash reserves were nearly zero. Their bank liked them: Wells Fargo had extended them a line of credit that they drew on whenever they had a cash-flow crunch. They had a lot of those. The Reverend Sirs were greedy gentlemen.

Unwinding these numbers was marvelously satisfying, a perfect distraction, like a crossword puzzle that's easy enough that you get all the answers quickly, but not so quickly that it's no challenge at all. I barely even thought about Shlomo Spinka for a good fifteen minutes.

Of course, then it all came rushing back and I felt like my chest was being squeezed and squeezed, air coming in sips and my blood roaring in my ears.

I picked up the phone and called CF.

I'd waited too long. It was 5:15 p.m. and no one was answering the phone. That didn't mean that everyone was gone, of course, but Rivka, Sister Maria-Eva, and Liz had a pact that they would clock off at five, in the name of preserving their mental health. Rivka and Sister Maria-Eva stuck to it. Liz loved to chat and if no one else was around, she'd pick up. So either no one was there, or one or two or three of them were there. Hell, maybe Pat was there. She sometimes worked late and she *never* answered the phone.

I thought about those three CONSULTANTs, DD, JB, and RHA. Were they the tough guys who'd come by to get my Fidelity 3000 back and then kicked me around a little? I didn't think so. Shlomo knew about those guys already. They didn't worry him.

Art was on a contract job, second week there, and I didn't even remember which one. He'd been pulling long hours, though not mattress-in-the-rafters hours. Maybe he'd be back soon with the van.

I checked the Caltrain schedule. Rush hour. Trains every fifteen minutes. I could ride my bike to the station, wait as the train crawled up the peninsula. Maybe the CONSULTANTs weren't even on the job yet. Maybe I had all the time in the world.

Maybe it was too late.

I left a message on Maria-Eva's answering machine. I could call the police. I probably should. Isn't that what normal people do when they get a suicide note, evidence of millions in financial fraud, electronic proof of payment to CONSULTANTs to injure their friends (or worse)?

But every time I tried to imagine that call, my imagination failed. *Yes, Officer, yes, Shlomo Spinka. No, I don't know where he lives. No, I can't prove he's hurt himself. Where's my evidence? Well, it's on these floppy disks. I use this special customized disk drive created by a Marxist nun, an Orthodox Jewish lesbian, and an excommunicated feminist Mormon to read the files. You can see here in this spreadsheet, all the money is there in green and black. What's a spreadsheet? Oh, Officer, you've come to the right place. No one can explain a spreadsheet like me. Pull up a seat, Professor Hench's Introduction to Financial Software class is in session!*

And probably I wouldn't even get that far. The waves of re-remembering were coming fast and hard: Shlomo dead. The CONSULTANTs, gunning for my friends. For Pat. Pat. Shlomo. Dead. CONSULTANTs. The Caltrain schedule. The police. The spreadsheets.

I began to do the most extraordinary thing. I paced into the bedroom and put on my jacket and shoes, gathered the floppies and the letter, then headed for the door. Then I stopped, turned, took off my jacket, extracted the floppies and the letter, went to the phone, lifted the receiver. Finger in the dial-hole. Stop. Rack the receiver. Put on my jacket. Shoes. Floppies. Letter. Door. Stop. Turn. Jacket. Floppies. Letter. Phone. Stop.

Stop. Stop. *Stop.*

I was crying. I couldn't stop, and I couldn't stop crying. What the fuck was I supposed to do? I had thought myself so mature, so cool, an adult living an adult life, and here I was, acting like a teenager who's wrecked the family car and doesn't know whether to call the police, the garage, or his mommy.

I sat. I breathed. I couldn't breathe right. I got a paper bag from the kitchen, tried breathing into it, the way they did on the sitcoms. It was the wrong kind of bag, a big grocery sack, not a lunch bag. It didn't work. I let it fall.

I would go to the Caltrain station on my bike. I would ride the train to the city. I would find the girls and I would warn them. That's what I would do.

Shoes.

Jacket.

Floppies.

Letter.

Backpack.

Keys.

Door.

That's when Art came home.

"Holy shit, Marty, what's wrong?"

Breathe. *Breathe,* Marty, and tell Art what's going on. He has the van. *He has the van.* You can go right now.

"We need to go," I said. "We need to go *now.*"

Art looked at me like he was wondering whether I needed to be sedated. "Where do we need to go, Marty?" he asked, gentle, like you'd talk to a kid who woke screaming from a nightmare. Like you'd talk to a crazy person who cornered you on a sidewalk.

"To San Francisco," I said. "We have to warn them." I forced a deep breath. It was hard, because I wanted to pant, there just wasn't enough air left in the world right then. "To San Francisco, right now." I was panting. My mouth was so dry. I tried to swallow, couldn't. "I'll tell you on the way."

Again, he gave me that look.

"*Please, Art.*"

I watched him decide I wasn't losing my mind.

"Let's go."

16

The traffic crawled. By the time I'd told him the story, we had barely cleared San Carlos.

"Marty," he said, changing lanes to get around a fender bender on the 101, "has it occurred to you that this Shlomo guy might be socially engineering you? Maybe his bosses have run out of tactics and they asked him to run a psyop on you so you turn into a headless chicken, spook the CF ladies, disrupt the business?"

I wasn't hyperventilating anymore, but I could still hear my blood in my ears. The traffic was so slow. I let myself ponder Art's question, let it distract me. Distraction was good. "I thought that when Shlomo came to meet me, last week. I thought that maybe he was just a great actor. That's why I let Pat talk me into keeping quiet about it. She thought he was trying to psych me out, too."

What did it say about me that all the people who knew me best thought that I was prone to being psyched out? I got stuck on that for so long that Art actually looked up from the road and snapped his fingers in front of my nose.

"You okay, buddy? Stay with me here."

"Sorry," I said, feeling a flush crawl up my face, my ears, my scalp. "Sorry. I thought maybe Shlomo was acting. When I read the letter, I had that thought again. Even when I saw that first spreadsheet, with the CONSULTANTs and the amounts and everyone's initials."

"They're pretty easy props to produce," Art said, changing lanes again, leaning on the horn.

"Yeah. But what about the other spreadsheet? What about DISPERSALS? What is the point of sending me evidence that the Reverend Sirs are looting Fidelity?"

"It's a convincer," Art said. He hit the horn again. The guy in the next lane leaned on his horn and Art wiggled the wheel, sending the van over the lane markers into a space that wasn't nearly big enough for it. Art ignored the blaring horns and inched his way into it, then used his new position to stage an attack on the next lane, where things were moving faster.

"It's a convincer," he repeated. "Doesn't cost Shlomo anything to make it, and it makes the whole thing seem more real. You take the whole package to your CF friends, they freak out, maybe leak the data to some of the religious freaks who buy Fidelity stuff, try to get a rumor started. Then the Wise Men show that it's a fabrication, pin it on the girls, who look like conspiracy-peddling sore losers. Costs them a lot of business."

He brought the van up to the bumper of a slow-moving K-car and hung there until it changed lanes, then he closed the distance with the car ahead of him. "That's a much better plan than hiring hit men or whatever. Hell, it's what I'd do."

Art was always so convincing. It calmed me down some. I thought over his points. "You make a lot of sense," I admitted.

"See?" he said, as we crossed the San Mateo line and traffic sped up, and he goosed the van, making its engine roar. "No need to freak out."

I interrupted him. "You make a good point, *Art,* but there's one thing you haven't considered."

"What's that?"

"*They're not you.* I've met the Reverend Sirs. They're not the kind of people who come up with subtle ways to trick people, not when there are brutal ways to scare them within their reach. They're vindictive, short-tempered, and used to getting their own way. It's just not . . . It's not their *style.*"

Art snorted. "Not their *style?*"

"No. Not their style. Laugh if you like, but what if you're wrong?"

He concentrated on driving. Traffic was getting thicker again. The 101 at rush hour was a stupidly hard video game in both directions. "Yeah, that's not a bad point. But what if you're wrong? What if you panic the CF girls and Pat and that just helps the Three Little Pigs?"

My turn to snort. "I like that." The fact that Art had conceded that I had a point calmed me down to where I could think again, no longer buffeted every minute or two by a fresh stab of fear and realization. "Liz, Maria-Eva, and Rivka are adults—women, not girls. They have the right to make up their own minds."

"And Pat?"

I grimaced. "Pat's already made up her mind, but I have a duty to tell her anyway."

We stopped at Rivka's new place on the way to the office. It was an apartment in a painted lady in SoMa, up three flights of stairs. I left Art to circle the block for parking while I pounded up the stairs and thumped on her door.

I heard cautious shuffling beyond the door, saw the shadow of her feet in the crack at its bottom. "Yes?" she called.

"It's me, Rivka, it's Marty."

"Oh, Marty—" The light from under the door switched off, and her fingers fumbled with the latches and chains and the door swung open, Rivka hidden behind it.

The apartment was dim. I took a cautious step inside.

"Rivka?" She was a shadow, half hidden behind the door. Once I'd crept far enough inside, she closed it. My eyes adjusted to the dim. She was hunched, one arm held close to her side. It was too dark to make sense of her face, but something was wrong.

"Rivka?" She turned and walked back into the apartment. Walked? Shuffled. One leg dragged. "Rivka, are you okay?"

The living room was a shadow box, gray with black rectangles. She moved around the coffee-table rectangle and settled slowly onto the sofa rectangle, letting out a hiss as she did. Cloth noises as she drew a blanket around herself.

"Can I turn on a light, Rivka? I'm afraid I'm going to trip over something and break my neck."

She made a noise in her throat. I waited for her to give some other sign, then pawed the wall for the switch. I flipped the switch, filled with dread at what I was about to see.

She had the blanket pulled up to her chin. Above it, her nose was askew, nostrils packed with bloody tissues. One eye was swollen shut. The other leaked tears.

"Rivka, *holy shit*—"

She worked one hand out from under the blanket, held it up to silence me. I bit down on my words. She breathed heavily, swallowed. Breathed again. Opened her swollen lips. One of her front teeth was gone. "They put me in a van," she said. "Outside the factory. One man behind me, pushing, another man inside, grabbing. As soon as the door was closed, they hit me—" She touched her eye, flinched. "The van started and I fell over backwards, hit my head. I tried to get up and they kicked me and told me to stay down."

"Rivka—" She silenced me again with her hand, groaned a little with the movement.

"We drove for a while. Maybe a long time. I don't know. It felt like a long time. Then we went up some ramps. A parking garage. Then the van stopped." Her tone had been steady, but on *stopped*, it broke. She breathed heavily for a time.

"Please can you bring me some water, Marty?" she said, her voice barely a whisper.

"Of course," I said, practically jumping to my feet, grateful for something to do.

She held up that hand again, winced. "And a little glass of wine, please."

"Of course," I said again. Her kitchen was spotless. The wine was in a cupboard. Manischewitz, sweet, with a screw cap. It was next to a candelabra and a box of white Shabbos candles. I filled a large tumbler with water from the tap, running it until it turned cold, then found a little juice glass and filled it with wine. I was about to carry them out when it occurred to me to look in the freezer. I found a bag of frozen peas and another bag of frozen broccoli. Out of hands, I stuck one under each arm and carried out the glasses. I handed her the frozen bags first and she whispered *thanks* and I turned my head as she fished under the blanket and got them situated. Then I handed her the wine, putting the water on the end table at her elbow.

She drank off half the wine in a series of pained sips and shivered. She dug under the blanket for the frozen peas and pressed them to her mouth, then her swollen eye. She closed the other eye. "Once we parked, the driver climbed into the back and they hit me. They took turns. I tried to shield myself, to curl up, but when I did, the two who weren't hitting would hold me. They hit me in the face, then the stomach, then my breasts, then—"

She broke off. Shifted the frozen peas back under the blanket. Didn't open her eye. "They hit me, Marty. For a while, I thought they would kill me. They didn't say anything to me, but they talked to each other. 'My turn,' they'd say. Or they'd talk about how ugly I was, how it was no loss that I was a dyke. They used so much bad language. They laughed.

"They hit me."

She drifted off and I thought maybe she'd passed out. But then she set down the wine glass beside her and groped for the water. I put the water in her hand. She drank.

"They hit me. I stopped feeling it. You know what, Marty? That was scarier. I thought my soul was leaving my body. But then they switched who was hitting and the new man knew how to hit me so I'd feel it again. I almost felt grateful then, because if I could feel it, then my soul was still attached to my body.

"All that time, they didn't speak to me. Not until the end. Not until I couldn't see out of my eye, not until I'd spat out my tooth, not until every part of me hurt. Then one of the men grabbed me by the hair and dragged me to my feet. I couldn't even stand. He had to hold me up by the hair. He shook my head and kept saying, 'Rivka, look at me, look at me Rivka.'

"Once I looked at him he said, 'You need to get out of the computer business. You and your—'" She cut off, sipped from her water. "He used bad language to talk about Maria-Eva and Liz. Terrible language. Not just them, he said racist things about the factory workers, used words for Mexicans I don't want to repeat. He said, 'Get out of the computer business. You were warned before. This is your last warning. Take the—'" She winced. "'Take the f-word hint. You won't like what happens next. We will destroy you.'

"Then he shook me by my hair some more, shook me until I thought my scalp would come off, shook me until I thought my eyes would fall out of my head, kept saying, 'Look at me Rivka.' I looked at him. I think I'd seen him before, at Fidelity Computing. A gentle-looking man." She smiled, showed her missing tooth. Winced. "Isn't that funny. Gentle-looking man. He said, 'Do you believe me, Rivka? Do you believe I will destroy you?'

"I nodded and he smiled. His smile was gentle. 'I'm glad, Rivka. It was very stupid of you to do this to yourself. No one wanted to hurt you, but you made us do it. I'm glad you're not going to make us destroy you. You go and talk to your friends, make sure they understand.'

"I guess he wanted me to say something out loud and when I didn't, he got angry, because then he punched me very hard, right in the stomach, and I threw up and then I breathed in some of the sick and choked and he dropped me, waited for me to stop gasping and then he kicked me in the ribs. 'Rivka, tell your friends and make sure they understand.'

"This time I said 'Yes,' and that must have satisfied him, because he left me there on the floor and they drove me home. Lying on the floor of the van, I saw there was a toolbox, with a hammer, and the whole drive I kept thinking about how I could grab that hammer whenever we got to where we were going, grab the hammer and use it on whichever one came for me, smash him wherever I could reach, then smash the others, hit them with that hammer over and over, a whirlwind, a demon, unstoppable. I planned it all out in my mind, every move. I knew where the two men were in the back, followed the engine sounds as the driver got us up to the curb, and then as he put the van in park, I did it, I grabbed for that hammer. I knew which one I'd go for first, and where I'd hit him—the side of his knee, and then, as he fell, in the ribs or the head, whichever I could reach.

"I grabbed for the hammer. I was going to kill that man. I grabbed for it, and my arm didn't move. I was so badly hurt, here—" She touched her shoulder and whimpered, shifted the ice pack to it. "—that my arm barely twitched. I don't think the man even noticed. The man I was set to hit got up and yanked the door open and then he and his friend rolled me out of the van onto the curb, throwing my purse after me. It hit me in the head. I was too hurt to make a sound.

"They drove off. I lay there for a long time before I managed to roll onto my stomach, and then I got up on my knees and got my good arm under me. Then I got to my feet, and got my purse over my shoulder so I could dig through it for my keys. Then I came up here. That's what happened to me, Marty." She had some more water, and then dabbed gingerly at the tears that streaked her cheeks with her blanket.

"We need to take you to the doctor," I said.

"No," she said. "Not now. I don't want to move anymore. Marty, you don't know what it was like coming up here. How it hurt me. I want to lie here and put ice on my body and take aspirin."

"Rivka, you *need* to see a doctor. You could have—" *Organ damage? Broken bones? A concussion?* I didn't want to speak the words, lest I conjure these things into existence. "You could be very hurt."

"I am very, very badly hurt, Marty. I have earned the right to decide what to do about it. Thank you for your concern, but no. No, Marty."

Someone cleared their throat behind me and we both jumped. It was Art, who emerged from the shadows of the hallway. "Sorry," he said. "The door was open."

I felt purely idiotic. Here I was, lecturing Rivka about her safety and I hadn't even locked the door behind me. Idiot, Marty. Idiot.

"Rivka," Art said, pulling up a chair next to me, "I think Marty's right about seeing a doctor. I have seen plenty of guys get beat up around here. Fag-bashing, I mean. Comes with the territory. Seeing a doctor goes with the territory, too."

Rivka let out a groan: half pained, half exasperated. "I don't *want* to." She sounded like a little girl. Like they'd beaten the adulthood out of her. I wanted to hug her. I wanted to run to Pat and make sure she was okay. I wanted to leave town and never come back.

"I know you don't, I know." Art's voice was as soft as a parent's comforting a sick child. "But you have to. We'll do it this way, how about: you rest up there, take some aspirin. I'll stay with you while you recuperate, get you a cold washcloth so you can clean up, then, when you're ready, we'll get an ambulance. Can you do that for me?"

Rivka peered at him through her good eye. "I'm not a baby," she said. "I can take care of myself. I can make my own decisions."

"No," Art said. "You're a grown woman who's been beaten within an inch of your life. And you're a grown woman who has friends who love you. And you're a grown woman who has the wisdom to know that when you're injured, you need medical attention."

She was silent for so long. If it wasn't for the tears that dripped off her cheeks, I might have thought she'd gone to sleep or passed out. Finally, she drew a pained shudder of a breath. "Thank you," she said.

"It's only what every friend owes to every other friend," Art said. "We love you, Rivka."

She choked out a sob, then gasped in pain. I half rose from my chair. I couldn't stand to just watch her there. Art grabbed me by the arm and whispered, "I'll try to call the others. *Go.*"

I left.

Art told me where he'd parked, two blocks away in a spot that was barely inches longer than the van, and as I inched back and forth, hauling on the steering wheel, I tried to formulate a plan, mixing together the proximity of Maria-Eva's, Liz's, and Pat's places and my guess at how well each one could protect herself.

But it was all a show I was putting on for my own conscience. I knew where I would go first: Pat's place. All that mental cartography and working out the Traveling Salesman Problem in my mind was just to justify that decision.

I parked in a fire lane half a block from Pat's place. The Mission parking-enforcement cops would give me a ticket, but they wouldn't clamp or tow me unless I stayed for at least thirty minutes. I slammed the van door, locked it, and pelted down the sidewalk to Pat's door, dodging pedestrians, feeling like I would never arrive, like I was trapped in one of those nightmares where obstacles kept appearing between me and my destination.

I fumbled for my keys as I ran, and yanked them out—scattering coins from the bottom of my pocket—as I pounded on the doorbell. I jammed the key into the keyway and turned it, twisting the doorknob and then grabbing the keys back and charging up the stairs. I let myself into the apartment, shouting "Pat!" as I came through the door.

The apartment was dark and empty. I slapped the lights on, expecting to see wrecked furniture and Pat, unconscious or worse, but the place was empty and smelled a little stale, like no one had been in in a while. I stepped on something: her mail, piled up behind the mail slot.

I staggered back and leaned on the wall. Pat was away. I didn't know where she was, but then, neither would the CONSULTANTs. I yanked open the kitchen drawer where she kept her take-out menus and fished a pen out of the spiral binding of one of the notebooks she kept by her DN100s and bent over the kitchen table—

—and stopped. What would I write? PAT BEWARE FIDELITY HAVE HIRED HIT MEN TO TAKE YOU OUT? Where would I post it? The door to her apartment? The CONSULTANTs would see it before she did. The downstairs entrance? The *neighbors* would see it before she did. Either way, I'd create chaos and risk.

Okay, Hench. Think this through. If the CONSULTANTs get here before Pat does, they'll see the note and tear it down. But maybe Pat gets here first. Where can you leave the note where she will see it, but they won't? I pictured Pat coming through the door, blending the memories of dozens of actual homecomings. She'd stoop for the mail and stick it on the pile on the end table by the shoes, drop her keys on top of it. Slam the door with a backward kick, reach back and twist the deadbolt. Go into the kitchen for a glass of water, then—

—back to the sofa, where she'd sit down at whichever DN100 she'd been using last. She had a whole notebook full of big rendering and compiling jobs, work that would take hours, and she always made a point of setting up at least one computer, if not both, to run through them while she was out.

I sat down at the keyboard of one DN100 and typed "emacs" and hit return, and then struggled to remember all the text-editor shortcuts. My brain refused to cough up any of them; all I could conjure up was Lotus macro syntax—like trying to speak French and having all the words come out in Spanish.

Forget it. I hit Caps Lock and:

PAT: THREE WM ARE SNEDING MEN TO HURTS YOU. THEY BEAT RIVKA BAD ANS ART IS TAKIN HER TO HOSPITAL. GET OUT. LEAVE MESSAG EON MY MACHIEN.

I stared at the typos, decided I didn't care enough about them to remember my Emacs keybindings. I added:

LOVE, MARTY

And then realized I didn't know how to change it to just "MARTY." My stupid subconscious. I moved to the other DN100 and replicated the message, making exciting new typos this time as my hands shook and cold sweat coursed down my back. I hesitated a moment, then typed another LOVE, MARTY, but it came out LVOE, so there was that.

I headed for the door and slapped the lights off, then turned them back on again. The CONSULTANTs wouldn't know that Pat was religious about turning the lights off, and if she got back and saw light under her apartment door, she'd be on full alert.

I sprinted back to the van. There was a ticket under the windshield wiper, which I dropped between the driver and passenger seats before peeling out and making a screeching left onto Seventeenth, toward Liz's place.

I so badly wanted to be waiting outside of Pat's place, watching for the CONSULTANTs in the white van, coiled to leap out with Art's tire iron in hand. I actually signaled a turn that would have taken me back to Pat's place, actually changed lanes, before signaling again and carrying on.

17

Liz lived in a Noe Valley triplex, uphill, just off Thirtieth Street. I angled the van's wheels into the curb and yanked the parking brake, then raced around the van and opened the rear doors and shoved aside all the kipple and trash, rolled up the matted carpet and yanked open the spare compartment and grabbed the tire iron. I had the presence of mind to put it under my jacket and hold it flat across my torso with one arm, rather than charging down Thirtieth while brandishing it.

I pelted up the first flight of stairs, then paused to get my breath and get out the tire iron. I padded up the second flight to Liz's door and stood outside it for a moment, looking for signs of forced entry. Then I put my ear to the door. Faint music.

I rang her buzzer, heard it ring inside her place, heard muffled voices, footsteps. I leaned back from the door just as it opened. Liz took me in. I must have been a sight.

"Marty?" she said. "Oh my heck! What's wrong?"

What I wanted to do was shout at her for opening the door without looking through the fisheye or putting on the chain. What I did was take a step back, lower the tire iron, and say, "You're safe?"

She took a half step back, and her expression changed from surprise to concern. "Marty, what's going on?"

I heard a noise from below and imagined that it was the stealthy ascent of the CONSULTANTs, following in my footsteps. That would be a hell of a timing coincidence, but I couldn't shake the feeling.

"Let me come in," I said. Seeing her concerned expression

turn to fear, I added, "Please, Liz. Something really bad is happening."

She bit her lip and looked at the weapon in my hand. I could have put it down to calm her, but then I wouldn't have had it.

Instead, I spoke quickly. "Rivka's hurt. Fidelity is gunning for you, all three of you." I swallowed. "And Pat." Another sound from below. I jumped. "Please, let's get inside."

Liz nodded once, convulsively, then stepped aside and I followed her in. I closed the door behind me and shot the bolt and the chain.

"Everything okay?" A man's voice, from deep in the apartment. It was furnished in thrift-store chic, with Indian blankets on the walls and a worn Persian runner in the hall. He emerged a moment later, and a moment after that, I placed him. Zion, Liz's old neighbor, who'd come to pizza night once at the new factory. Neat mustache, tight white tee, perfectly cuffed 501s with wool socks. "Oh, hi, Marty," he said, then noticed the tire iron. "You have a flat?" he asked in a tone that made it clear he didn't think that's why I was carrying it.

I set the tire iron down, leaning it against the wall next to the door. "Liz, you need to leave here. We need to find somewhere for you to go. It's not good, it's really bad, it's—" and then I realized I was crying, my breath hitching in my chest. Zion got to me first, putting his arm around my shoulders.

"Come on, buddy, let's sit down and talk about this." My heart thundered and my chest tightened at the thought of sitting down. I had so much to *do,* I hadn't even warned Maria-Eva yet, and then there was—

Pat.

"I'll make tea," Zion said. "Chamomile, I'm afraid. Liz doesn't stock the strong stuff." He smiled. He was fantastically handsome, like someone out of an underwear ad. A distant part of me suggested that I should introduce him to Art. Art liked 'em pretty.

"Sit," Liz said, taking my arm, leading me to the sofa. "Come on, Marty, you have to calm down, start making sense. You're in a lather."

I was. Literally. Cold sweat was drying on my back and legs, and there was dried spit in the corners of my mouth. No wonder Zion and Liz were more worried about me than about whatever warning I was failing to deliver.

"Last Friday, you remember I got called away from pizza night for a while?"

She shrugged. "Maybe. I was paying attention to the pizza, mostly."

"Did you know Shlomo Spinka?"

She tried to place the name, then her eyes widened a little as she did, then a little more as she noticed the past-tense question. "From Fidelity Computing," she said.

"It was him on Friday. He wanted to warn me—wanted me to warn you."

"If he wanted to warn me, then why didn't he—" She rolled her eyes. "Oh dee, of course. What a load of bull." Liz's sanitized profanity cut through my panic and I smiled a little. She saw and smiled back, a little relieved, and I realized she'd laid it on thicker than usual because she knew it amused me. Liz really was one of the good ones. "What did he want to warn me about, then?"

"The Reverend Sirs—" She groaned. The CF women hated that term. "—Shlomo said they have backers, bad men. Impatient men. Men who get a cut of what Fidelity Computing brings in, who aren't going to sit on the sidelines as that cut goes down because you're cutting into their business."

Zion set down a steaming earthenware mug on the coffee table, fragrant with chamomile. "Are you talking about some kind of Mormon mafia?"

Liz snorted.

"He didn't call it that. I got the impression it wasn't just the Saints—that each of the Wise Men had their own heavy hitters backing them." I looked at them. They were clearly telling themselves a story: ole Marty Hench was spooked by the kid from Fidelity and now he's foaming at the mouth, let's calm him down and—

I slowed down my breathing, lowered my voice, made myself speak each word slowly. "He was seriously scared. Yeah, he didn't want to tell you because you're women, but he also didn't think you'd believe him. That's why he came to me."

"Because he thought a man would see the truth," Liz said, rolling her eyes again.

"Or because he thought a man would be more gullible?" Zion suggested, and they shared a smile.

"I didn't tell you. Pat thought it was all bullsh—" I caught myself, looked at Liz. "She thought it was a psych-out. She told me not to bother you guys. Said you had enough to deal with." I looked away, embarrassed anew at how little I knew about what Liz had been going through. "I thought she was wrong. We had a fight about it." I swallowed. "I left." The gravity of my departure slammed into me, the thought that the last words I said to Pat might be the angry ones I'd blurted out on my way out the door. I swallowed again.

"But then, today, a courier rang my doorbell." Both Zion and Liz leaned forward at that. Couriers were the stuff of mystery novels. They were treating this as a juicy tale. I needed to get them to take it more seriously than that. I told them what was in Shlomo's envelope.

"More psych-out," Zion said. "Has to be. He's just yanking your chain. It's amateur dramatics."

Liz nodded along. They were talking themselves into it. First Pat, then Art, then these two. Why was it so hard to accept the truth? Why was I the only one who could look at this situation and see what was going on? Maybe it was my accountant brain: I'd inputted all the values into my mental spreadsheet and there was the total. Spreadsheets don't lie.

(Spreadsheets lie like hell. I could write a book, *How to Lie with Spreadsheets*. The practicum would be the stolen Fidelity files that we'd destroyed. But *my* spreadsheets don't lie.)

I wanted to shout at them. I kept swallowing, swallowing the screams.

"They beat up Rivka. Beat her half to death."

That started to get through to them. "They hauled her into a van, right outside of the factory. Drove her to a parking garage. Smashed her ribs, her arm, her face. She can't see out of one eye, it's so swollen. Barely talking." I looked from Liz to Zion and back again. "They told her why they did it. They told her that it was Fidelity Computing, and that this was her last warning." Look to Liz. Look to Zion. Back to Liz. "Liz, I'm not overreacting, you are *underreacting*. Shlomo sent me spreadsheets showing how much the Reverend Sirs were skimming, and he sent me another sheet, showing how much they'd paid these men to come for you three and Pat. He sent them to me in an envelope containing his suicide note. I can't say it more plainly than that."

I swallowed again. My mouth was so dry. My throat was so dry. I sipped the tea. It didn't help.

"Yes I can, actually. We need to get out of here fast and hide somewhere because there are violent men coming to beat you and anyone around you within an inch of your life. They want you to shut down CF, and they will keep coming for you until you do, because Fidelity isn't just a scam, it's a criminal enterprise that feeds up to an even bigger criminal enterprise, the way your old salesgirls for Fidelity fed up the chain to the regional reps who fed up to the Reverend Sirs."

"Marty, what are you talking about?" Liz sipped her tea, then set it down. Her mug rattled on the coaster. Some tea spilled on the coffee table.

"Liz, I'm telling you that there's another layer above the Reverend Sirs. They're not the top of the pyramid scheme. There's another layer above them, made up of bad, violent men who are very upset with you. They're coming for you. Physically coming for you. To hurt you. Badly. You need to get out of here. You need to hide."

"Hide? Marty, come on. We'll go to the police," Liz said. Zion snorted.

"Liz, I'm not saying this makes any sense, but I'll tell you this: if you go to the SFPD and tell them that you're being hunted by shadowy Mafia dons who pulled the strings on a scam run by a Mormon bishop, an Orthodox rabbi, and a Catholic priest, they'll laugh you out of the station house."

"Not if we show them Rivka," Liz said. "Marty says she got beaten up badly. Maybe so badly she needs to go to the hospital, right? So we show them Rivka and—"

"Rivka's a dyke, Liz. A *homosexual*." Zion's eyes glittered. "You tell the cops your queer lady friend got six kinds of shit beaten out of her, you know what they're going to say? 'Yeah, queer-bashing is up this year. Again. Whaddaya want us to do about it? Maybe you should tell your friend not to flaunt it so much, lay low.'"

I gave him a grateful smile, while my heart raced. I still hadn't spoken to Sister Maria-Eva and we were still *talking*. Drinking *tea*.

"Liz," Zion said, standing up and shrugging into his denim jacket, "how about this: Why don't you come over to my place? Just for a couple nights. I'll stay on the sofa and you can take the bedroom." He stared at me, then looked back at her. "Better safe than sorry, right? It'll be like a pajama party."

She looked from Zion to me and me to Zion. "What about Maria-Eva?"

"I left her a message," I said, "but I'm headed to her place next."

She stood up and grabbed her handbag. "I'll just get a few things from my closet," she said.

"I've got a box of fresh toothbrushes," Zion called after her. He gave me a handsome smile. "You know," he said, "for unexpected guests." He winked.

"Thank you," I said.

He got a serious expression. "I don't know if you're nuts or what, but someone went after Rivka, right?"

"Right," I said. "Look," I said, "I've got to—"

"Get out of here," he said. "I promise I'll get her to my place safely and then have her leave a message on your machine."

Maria-Eva's landlord—the family papa—kept the chain on the door when he cracked it. When he saw it was me, he unchained the door and opened it. Once I was in the vestibule, I saw that he was holding the largest, sharpest machete I had ever seen. It was so menacing it practically *hummed*. I approved.

"*Venga,*" he said, and led me up the stairs.

The living room was empty, the TV silent. Papa called out something in Spanish that I couldn't follow and suddenly there was the sound of people moving around, from behind the closed kitchen door. A moment later, the far living room door opened and Maria-Eva appeared. She was dressed in jeans and an SFU sweatshirt, her hair down, looking ten years younger than she did in her usual long dresses and hair pulled back in a severe bun. She had a gym bag in one hand.

"You got my message," I said.

She nodded. Her cheeks were hollow, her eyes sunken, her lips pressed together so tightly that they almost disappeared.

"I also heard from Liz," she said. "I'm going to meet her at her friend Zion's place."

"I like that plan," I said. Maria-Eva didn't need any convincing. She knew what people like the Reverend Sirs were capable of, including what kinds of men they could find themselves in business with.

"I can drive you," I said.

"Good," she said. She turned to the papa, spoke in low, fast Spanish. He listened seriously, nodded, and then put one large hand on her shoulder and stared into her eyes for a long moment.

"Let's go," she said.

Zion had relocated since Liz's Mission House days, snagging a cute little bungalow in the Outer Sunset. I drove out of the Mission with my shoulders up around my ears, compulsively checking my mirrors. By the time we got to Golden Gate Park, the tennis racket between my shoulders had unstrung itself and I'd relaxed my grip on the wheel.

At a red light, Maria-Eva said, "Your roommate called me before we left. He said to tell you that he was taking Rivka to San Francisco General."

"That's good," I said. "She didn't want to go."

"He said she was badly hurt."

"Yes," I said. I tried to think of what to say next. I wanted to reassure her, but I had nothing reassuring to say. If I'd said, "I'm sure she'll be okay soon," it would have been a lie. Finally: "I'll visit her after I drop you off."

"Good," she said.

Rivka was asleep by the time I got to SF General. Art let go of her hand and tucked it back in, smoothing the hospital sheet. She did look better, a little. Bruised and brutalized, but with the blood washed away and her hair combed out, she seemed peaceful. On the mend.

Art didn't say a word until he was behind the wheel of the van. "Home?" he said.

I shrugged. I was about to say that I wasn't tired, couldn't possibly sleep, when I realized I could barely keep my eyes open. "Yeah."

I nodded off before we hit U.S. 101. I dozed fitfully with my cheek on the passenger window, then let Art lead me up to the apartment. I was about to collapse into bed when I was struck by an urgent thought. I got out my phone book and dialed Zion's number.

He answered in a sleepy voice.

"Sorry, Zion, this is Marty. Can you put Liz or Maria-Eva on?"

"They're asleep," he said, making it a pointed remark.

"Sorry. I'm sorry, really. But can you wake one of them up?"

There was a long pause, a sigh, then a clunk as he set the phone down. I heard him padding around the house, heard a door squeak, a murmur of conversation, footsteps getting closer.

"Marty?"

"Liz?

"Yes, Marty."

"Liz, you can't go in to the shop tomorrow. No one should."

Another long pause.

"Yes," she said. "That's probably right." She sounded more awake.

"It's definitely right."

"Yes," she said again. "Oh *flip*. How do we let the staff know?"

"That's what I was calling about. None of you should go any-where *near* the shop tomorrow. I will go first thing in the morning and catch Angel when he comes to open, send him home. Then I'll stay and tell all the rest of the staff, as they arrive. Then I'll go, and bring the employee files with me, so we can contact them once this blows over."

"*Flip*," she said again, with feeling. Mormon swearing was funny at first, but honestly, it was all in the tone. Now, I just heard it and mentally substituted *fuck*. "Yes. Yes, okay. That's what you'll have to do. Crud. Crud, crud, crud." A long pause. "Be careful."

"I'll be careful," I said. "You be careful, too."

"We will be."

I set an alarm but I didn't need it. Tired as I was, I was more worried, and that worry had me up and at 'em at 5 a.m. I showered and gobbled down a bowl of Art's health-food granola, grabbed my keys, and headed for the van. Then I turned around, drove back to the apartment, retrieved Art's softball bat, and got back behind the wheel.

I puttered around CF, spooking at creaks and noises. When Angel the caretaker arrived at 8 a.m., I sent him home again, exacting a promise from him that he wouldn't come back until we called him, making a promise of my own that it wouldn't be too long and that his paycheck would arrive by mail to his home address by Friday. I implied that the building inspectors had found some emergency in the wiring, and he nodded sagely and headed home.

The factory women and the warehouse guys started to show up in ones and twos around 8:45, and I got my patter into a practiced groove. By the time the last few people straggled in, I was able to smoothly turn them around and get them out the door in under a minute.

I grabbed a cardboard box out of the warehouse and used a tape gun to assemble it, and then started pulling hardcopy HR files out of Liz's filing cabinets, working methodically while my mind wandered to how I would go about cutting the paychecks from home.

I was working my way through the bottom drawer of the filing cabinet when I caught a flicker of motion in my peripheral vision; I was squatted down on my hunkers in front of the filing cabinet, awkward and vulnerable.

Something—a bow wave of air from the rushing body, a rustle of clothing—made me aware of the rush, and I rolled away,

304 ◄ **cory doctorow**

flailing to gain my feet even as my attacker landed a glancing
blow on my shoulder, making my arm numb.

Struggling to my feet, I saw him and I realized I knew him:
it was the little guy who'd come to my apartment door, the one
who'd landed such a fast and competent punch square in my
nuts.

He was holding a softball bat. I recognized it. It was the bat
I'd brought from the apartment and left leaning at the reception
desk before heading into the office to retrieve the files. *Nice going, Marty.*

He gave me a cold and terrifying smile, swishing the bat
at me a couple of times, his smile broadening when I flinched
back. But then he flung the bat away, sending it end-over-end
into the wall, where it left a dent before clattering to the floor.

"We gonna have a fair fight, then?" I gasped.

He snorted and reached into his back pocket, coming out
with a knife that he flicked open with a showy, practiced move.
It had a blade as long as a man's palm, and some small mecha-
nism gave a metal *snack* as it locked into place.

"Fuck no," he said. He stamped forward with one foot, feint-
ing, laughing as I flinched again. He did it again, with the other
foot, and laughed harder. I swung my hand behind me, found
the office chair I expected to find, grabbed it, swung it in front
of me like a lion tamer.

He cocked his head. "That's not gonna help you," he said.
His voice was just as I remember: nasal, cruel, mad. Even after
all the fighting I'd done in Escambia, I never quite got over my
hesitation to inflict pain on another person. This man had no
such hesitation.

A curious clarity overcame me. This man would hurt me
badly, or even kill me. Hesitation or no, I had to do something.
He made the knife dance a little S curve, watching my eyes. I kept
my eyes steady; then, without windup, I charged him, chair first,
aiming center-mass.

I might have made it, if not for the injury to my shoulder. But he'd gotten a good blow in with the bat, and when he grabbed the chair with his off hand and twisted it, my left arm gave out. He followed through on the movement, twisting further so I overbalanced and went to my knees. I sensed him coming for me from behind and mortal terror got me into a runner's crouch and then propelled me forward, racing heedlessly across the small office, leaping onto the visitor's chair and toppling it behind me as I launched myself off it toward the wall, smacking into it with my palms—pain jetting through my injured shoulder—and rebounded, dragging myself sideways so I just missed him as he came up behind me.

Now I was behind *him* and I kicked out hard at his leg. I missed the knee, but caught his shin and knocked him off-balance, which let me get a desk between me and him. He turned around and sized me up behind the desk, his smile getting even bigger. He used his free hand to adjust his yarmulke and smooth the front of his white buttoned shirt, then took a quick step toward the desk, slashing out at my chest with the knife.

I leaned back and he used the moment to knock the desk over, and I went over with it. I cracked my head on the floor and in my swimming vision, I saw him daintily step over the fallen desk, dress shoes crunching over the litter of fallen papers, kicking a stapler into a corner. He leaned over me, his knife arm pulled back for a strike, the tip of the blade aimed straight at my gut. His arm pistoned forward and—

—he went over sideways. In no particular order, I registered: a searing pain in my side, a sick cracking sound, the sight of the softball bat connecting with his head, then Pat's war face, her winding up with the bat for a second swing, another meaty cracking sound, a groan from the fallen man.

My vision and thoughts cleared and I understood that I'd been cut, that Pat had just brained the man who did it with Art's softball bat, that she'd given him another across his shoulder blades, and now, yes, she was leaning over me, the bat still close by—she was better at this stuff than me, clearly—pressing her hand to my side, applying pressure to the wound, the feeling like a tongue probing a missing tooth, a raw nerve sensation.

"Pat?" I said.

She lifted her hands from my side, peeled up my shirt, had a good look, replaced her hands. "Just a graze," she said. "Stitches, maybe, but nothing serious."

"Pat?" I was truly in fine form.

"Marty," she said. "Okay, Marty. Let's get the fuck out of here."

"I need to bring the files," I said.

"Marty, I don't think you're engaging with the urgency of this situation."

I opened my mouth to object, closed it. "You're right, I'm not." I let her help me to my feet. Blood soaked my shirt, my jean jacket, the waistband of my jeans. "But if we take the files, we can make payroll this week."

"Yeah, all right."

"It's that box there," I said. It had gone over on its side and a few of the manila folders had slithered out. She shoveled them back in while I leaned on the filing cabinet, hand pressed to my side. She hoisted the box up onto one shoulder and got her other shoulder under one of my arms and got me into the cargo elevator.

We rode down like that, my arm around her, smelling her smell, feeling the tickle of her hair on my chin, feeling her breathing and heartbeat. The moment lasted forever, and was over in an instant. God, I'd missed her. The feeling was a physical ache, throbbing in counterpoint with the beat of my heart and the pulse of pain from my side.

She went out of the building ahead of me, and it was then I realized that she was still carrying the bat. She held it casually at her side, swinging it like a cane as she walked to the van, peering at the parked cars and in the doorways. Then she hustled back to me and got her arm under my shoulder again.

"Quick as you can," she said.

I headed for the driver's side, but she steered me to the back doors.

"Keys."

I handed them over.

She got me and the box inside, then: "Stay there." She slammed the doors, locked them.

I assumed she was going around to the driver's side, but after a long moment, I realized she'd gone somewhere else. I crept up to the porthole-shaped window and peered through it, watched her head back into the office.

Time crawled. I stripped out of my jacket and peeled off my shirt, gasping when I lifted my arm. The slice wasn't deep but it was long, running shallowly across my whole gut and then biting deeper across my side, the curve like a stroke from a calligraphy pen.

It seeped a steady ooze of blood, and I balled up my shirt and applied pressure to the deepest part of the cut, sneaking looks out of the porthole from time to time, trying to resist the urge to look and expose myself and failing, repeatedly.

After a million years, Pat emerged, this time with the guy who'd attacked me with one arm over her shoulder. I nearly bolted for the door and raced to her, shirtless and bleeding, but I quickly grasped that he was stumbling like a drunkard, barely conscious, and I watched her lay him out on the sidewalk against the building, facedown. She yanked his jacket off and draped it over his head, then stepped back and observed her work, head cocked.

I understood at once that she was trying to determine if he could pass for an unconscious homeless person, and grasped her strategy. Leaving an unconscious, concussed thug in the CF offices would raise questions, eventually. Leaving the same man

308 ◄ **cory doctorow**

facedown on a Potrero Hill sidewalk would buy us many, many hours before anyone even checked in on him.

I wondered if that delay would be enough to turn a concussion fatal. My blood-soaked shirt squished in my hand and I decided I didn't give a single, solitary shit.

She crossed the street, a cool customer, bat at her side, and unlocked the driver's-side door and slid behind the wheel. Her hands shook as she got the key into the ignition, but not much.

I let her pull out into traffic, waited until the jolts and revs told me that we had merged with 101 traffic, and then I shrugged gingerly back into my jacket and climbed forward into the passenger seat.

"You okay?" she said. She had a white-knuckle death grip on the steering wheel, and her clenched jaws bulged.

"I'll live," I said, and assayed a weak grin. She turned to look at me, saw the grin, didn't return it.

"Thank you," I said. "I know I could say more, and I will, but in the meantime, thank you."

"You're welcome," she said, downshifting and swerving into a gap in traffic. She drove like she slam-danced.

"Also," I said, and swallowed. My side really did hurt. She looked at me again. "Also, sorry. Sincerely. Sorry."

She started to say something, but I held up my hand, which was red with my own blood. "One sec," I said. "One more thing. I'll figure out how to thank you properly later, but I'm going to say sorry properly now. I was an idiot. I was a child. I was a fragile man-baby who let his ego get the best of him."

"Okay," she said. "That is entirely true. Also true is that I was wrong about the situation, and you were right, and that was a pretty consequential error in my judgment. Plus, you took a big risk to send me a warning, and who knows, maybe that saved me from the same treatment Rivka got."

"You heard about it, huh?"

"I checked in with Liz, and when I didn't get her, I tried Zion. They told me you were planning to go by the factory alone the next morning, which seemed like the kind of dumbass thing that might get you into trouble, so I came by to see if you needed any help."

"I guess I needed help."

That made her smile. Oh my heart, she had a hell of a smile. "I guess you did."

"I love you," I blurted.

Her hand flew off the gearshift, socked me in the shoulder, and returned to the gearshift in a blur. "Don't be an idiot," she said.

My mouth opened and no words came out of it.

"Of *course* you love me," she said. "What the fuck do you imagine we've been doing all this time, Marty? But this isn't the time or the place."

I notice you didn't say that you loved me back, I didn't say. I decided she'd implied it.

"Ow," I said.

"Don't be a baby." She changed lanes again and the van surged forward. "I barely tapped you."

"I'm a wounded man," I said.

"You'll live," she said.

"This isn't the way to the Outer Sunset," I said.

"No," she said.

"Aren't we meeting the others?"

"Yes," she said.

"Zion lives in the Outer Sunset."

"They're not at Zion's place. They're headed to Palo Alto. Zion's driving."

"Are *we* going to Palo Alto?"

"Yes."

The traffic was clearing. We passed SFO and merged onto 280 and she put the hammer down.

"Why are we going to Palo Alto?"

"Because I heard clicks on the line when I was talking to Liz."

"Clicks."

"So I took a cab out to the Outer Sunset and I called my own number."

"You did."

"Marty," she said, "I don't need the call-and-response, okay? Just shut up."

She'd called her own number, using the avocado Western Electric kitchen extension over Zion's countertop, vigorously waving the others to silence while she clamped the headset to her ear. After three rings, she had it: a Nortel DMS-100 switch, the ring sound as distinctive as a friend's voice. She hung up and dialed a service number she knew by heart, entered a string of numbers from memory, then dialed Zion's number, which he'd scribbled on a kitchen pad for her at her hissed insistence.

Now she heard a busy tone—naturally, she'd just used Zion's line to penetrate the switch that handled her home phone, then used it to call back to Zion's phone—but a few keypresses lowered the volume of the busy tone. She held her breath, pressed the phone to her ear, and yup, there it was: *click, click, click.*

She hung up the phone. "All right, that phone is tapped, which means that someone knows you're all here and wants to know who you're talking to and what they're saying."

Zion made a skeptical face, looked from Liz to Maria-Eva, and the look turned scared.

"My phone is tapped," he said.

Pat ignored him. She was thinking. "You all need to get out of here and I need to get Marty."

"Can't go to the office, can't go home—" Maria-Eva ticked off on her fingers.

"Moshe Pupik," Liz said. "Rivka wanted me to call him."

"I don't know who that is, but sure," Pat said. "Where is he?"

"Stanford," Liz said. "Palo Alto."

"Great," Pat said. She pointed at Zion. "You've got a car, right?"

"I do," he said.

"Great. Don't call this guy at all. Just go. Liz, give me his address. From now on, we don't use phones, all right?"

Liz and Maria-Eva nodded, and after a moment, Zion nodded, too.

18

Moshe Pupik was taking it well, all things considered. He was mostly worried about Rivka and kept asking when he could go visit her.

"I keep telling you," Pat said, "you can go once we've figured out what we're doing."

"What *are* you doing, though?" He'd started off calm, but now he was starting to lose his cool. The fact that there were five of us crowded into his dorm room didn't make this any easier. His roommate had already come and gone three times, and the third time, he'd left muttering about bringing the RA down to evict us. Moshe Pupik had followed him out into the hallway for a furious, whispered conversation.

We all looked at Pat. Pat looked at me.

"Goddammit," I said, and then felt bad when Moshe Pupik flinched. He might be a heterodox historian with religious doubts, but he still wore a yarmulke. Liz and Maria-Eva glared at me.

"I need to think," I said.

"So think," Moshe said.

"I need to walk and think."

"Who's stopping you?" he said. "You've got one of my shirts balled up and taped to your side, and another one on top of that. So go already." The shirts were gray athletic tees with Stanford logos, and there was no way either would be fit for Moshe Pupik to wear again. There just wasn't any way to get out that much blood.

I stood up with ginger care and let myself out of the crammed dorm room. I stopped in the hallway for a moment. I was hoping that Pat wouldn't come after me, but I was also sad that she didn't.

I took the elevator down to the ground floor, and as I stepped out of the car, I caught sight of the RA's office, the line of pay phones, and I was transported with perfect fidelity back to my dorm at MIT, to those two conversations with my dad: the one where he put the fear of God into me, and the one where he confessed that it had all been a bluff.

I must have been rooted to that spot for some time, because a young man touched me on the arm and asked if I was all right.

I snapped out of it and lied to him, saying I was, transfixed anew by how *young* he was. He was surely just a normal freshman with a bit of a baby face, but he seemed to me to be a literal *child*. It felt like I had been a seventeen-year-old MIT freshman only recently, but I was twenty-two, and five years had gone past. The interval between my freshman year and now was the same as the interval between my twelfth birthday and my freshman year.

Five years. A lifetime. I wasn't that person anymore.

I thanked the very, very young man and hobbled out into the Palo Alto sun.

Maybe it was the blood loss, maybe it was the stress, maybe it was the confused and awful feelings I was having about how I'd screwed things up with Pat, but I found myself with a swimming head, a restless mind that wouldn't alight on any idea.

I had Fidelity Computing dead to rights: they were stealing from their employees and their customers, rigging the game so that the Reverend Sirs always won. I could prove it. Who would care, though?

The FTC wasn't going to do anything about this pyramid

scheme, not after they'd given Amway and all its copycats a Get
Out of Jail Free card. Anyway, who did I know at the FTC?

Fidelity's employees and customers? Sure, they'd be furious,
but what could they do to the Reverend Sirs, call for their ex-
communication? Take them to small-claims court? If I wanted
to inflict paper cuts on those three, I'd send them a box of
printer paper.

Besides, even if I put Fidelity Computing out of business,
that wouldn't stop their backers from coming after me and
my clients. It wouldn't send the CONSULTANTs back to their
kennels.

The cut in my side hurt like fire. I sat on a bench, hand
clamped over Moshe's blood-soaked tee, pressing hard, almost
enjoying the scorching raw-nerve feelings that arced across my
torso, down to my foot, and up to the nape of my neck.

"What do you think they're worth?" The voice made me
jump, and I hissed at the feeling of my wound splitting open
again, the rush of hot blood over the skin of my abdomen and
resoaking the blood-stiffened waistband of my jeans.

I don't know how long Liz had been sitting next to me on the
bench before she spoke. Judging from how much *she* jumped
when I did, it had been a while and she had made the natural
assumption that I was actually seeing her, rather than staring
straight through her.

"You okay, Marty?" she asked, softly.

"I'm okay," I said. "Moshe's got a friend here who's premed
that's going to check me over, but the cut's not deep, it's just
bloody."

"Did you disinfect it?"

"Vodka," I said. "Pat pulled over at a gas station next to a liquor store then called me a big crybaby as she poured it all over
me and I begged for mercy."

That got her to smile. She looked like such a *Mormon*—
clean-cut, wholesome, a face full of caring lines and planes that

she could arrange into so many different configurations, all of them full of concern. It was a face you'd be hard-pressed to slam the door on, even if you didn't want to hear about the exciting possibilities for your own salvation.

"What were you asking me, Liz?"

"I wondered how much Fidelity is worth. Fair book value."

"Why, are you going to buy them?"

"Not me, but what if the Kohlers did? They could borrow some money, give them a big lump sum now, owe them the rest, and we'd pay it out of their revenues over the next five years, say."

"You want to *merge* with Fidelity Computing?"

She giggled. "Call it a hostile takeover. I was just thinking, we take it over, fix the engineering, get better software, stop playing games with the hardware, play it straight with the sales reps, both the ones in-house and the field reps marketing to their communities, and—"

"That is a *profoundly* weird idea." She started to say something but I held up my free hand, which was covered in dried blood. "I didn't say it was a bad idea, just a weird one." I thought for a moment. "I can't give you a precise figure, you understand. I didn't look at the books that way."

"Guess," she said. "Make an educated guess."

I thought about it for a while. "Okay, assuming five times annual turnover, I'm going to say, eleven million."

"Huh," she said. "That's more than I thought."

"Well, I ballparked it based on the fair book value, like you said. I included all the money the Reverend Sirs are skimming, all the accounting tricks, and I also assumed they'd get out of all the dirty real-estate deals they're in, where they're paying three hundred percent more for warehouse and office space than they should be."

"So they'd be a profitable business if they weren't a scam?"

"Liz, they're a scam *because* they're a profitable business.

Hell, even if they stopped gouging on consumables and parts, they'd still be turning a good profit. There's a hell of a lot of hands in that cookie jar."

She rearranged the angles of her face, transforming into an astute businesswoman. I could almost hear the adding-machine keys clicking in her head. "All right, let's park that for now. What about driving *them* out of business?"

"I thought that was the idea already?"

"Well, *eventually,* but I'm thinking something immediate. What if we cut our prices, lost money on every sale, so that you'd have to be out of your mind to buy anything else from Fidelity. What if we bulk-bought Apple computers and sold them at a loss to people wanting to trade in their Fidelity systems. All-out war."

"I don't understand, Liz—what are you asking me?"

"How much would we have to spend before they ran out of money? We have investors who want to run a business. They've got, I don't know, *gangsters* who just want to show up every week or two and get a giant sack of cash. Let's say that if Fidelity Computing was losing money, they'd lose interest—or, at the very least, that they wouldn't hand over their own cash to keep Fidelity afloat. How much money would we need to make that happen?"

"Jesus, Liz—" She winced. "Sorry. I mean, 'Holy moly, Liz.' That's bananas. I don't even know how I would begin to calculate it—"

She made an impatient gesture. "Okay, break it down. What if we just gave away our current inventory, or you know, sold it at half off. Assume that this triples our sales rates. How long until we run out of inventory?"

"Uh . . ." I thought hard, picturing the cells on the sheets I'd pored over. "I wouldn't swear to it, but I'm thinking two weeks. Three, maybe."

She shook her head. "Not long enough. No one is that impatient. What if we kept ordering supplies, using cash on hand, to produce new inventory and fulfill orders?"

I shrugged. "This is the kind of question that spreadsheets are good at coming up with answers to but dumb meat-brained humans suck at. Maybe two more weeks. Maybe four?" I shrugged. "I have my disks in the van, I can run the numbers if you want me to."

She nodded absently. "If we get another chunk of cash from the Kohlers, skip a couple rent payments, we might hold out for two months." Her lips moved as she bargained with herself. "Let's go back."

"To the office?"

"No, to the dorm room. I want to talk to Maria-Eva. Then we'll get Rivka on the phone."

"I don't think Rivka will be in any shape to answer her phone."

"Well, in that case, we'll have to act on her behalf. Maria-Eva and I are a quorum, anyway. Our bylaws are set up to allow any two of us to act if the third can't be reached."

"You know that if this doesn't work, you're going to go broke, right?"

She looked at me, and none of her wholesome maternal lines and planes were in evidence. She looked like an avenging angel. "I'm not in this for the *money,* Marty. I'm doing this to *atone.* For years, I was part of a scam that preyed on people who trusted me because of my faith. I helped trap those people. I stuck a tap into them and let those criminals hook it up to a drainage hose that's sucking them dry. I have a duty to those people, Marty. A debt. I owe them this."

My side was oozing again. My vision kept going out of focus—not blurring so much as defocusing, like I'd lost the subroutine that kept my eyes on the most important thing in sight.

I must have been quiet for too long, because she said, "I hope you understand this, Marty. I didn't think it would be a surprise to you, or I would have made it explicit earlier."

"What?" I snapped back. "Oh, no, I guess I knew that. Don't tell the Kohlers, though—they're definitely in this for a return on investment."

That brought back her smile and all those maternal lines and planes. "I hear you, brother. Let's go find Moshe's premed kid, shall we?"

The premed kid thought I needed a couple of stitches but in the end was persuaded to just stick me together with skin glue, and then, when she couldn't find any, used a half-dried tube of Krazy Glue that Moshe Pupik kept in the top drawer of his dorm desk.

"You'll have a smaller scar if we sew you up," she said, as she snapped on a pair of disposable gloves and laid out alcohol and wipes on a sterile towel she took out of a sealed envelope.

"I don't mind," I said. "Anyone who gets as far as seeing my bare torso will already have fallen prey to my winning personality and charm." Moshe Pupik's almost-a-doctor friend rolled her eyes and cleaned away the crusted blood with antiseptic. I hissed and Pat took my hand. I had an audience, a whole sea of faces crowded around, watching me get glued together. I squeezed Pat's hand. "Sorry about your shirt, Moshe."

"*Shirts*," he said. "Two, and counting, because you're going to need a third one, I suppose." He gave me a stern look that melted into a weak smile. "It's okay. I'm just glad you're all right. Rivka always said nice things about you." He swallowed. "I hope she's okay."

Zion squeezed his shoulder. "She was fine when we left her. 'Resting comfortably,' the doctor said."

"Doctors," Moshe Pupik said, and waved his hand.

"He seemed like a trustworthy sort," Zion said.

"He was cute," Liz translated.

"That too," Zion said.

"He had a wedding ring," Liz said.

"You checked?" Zion said.

"He was cute," Liz said. We all laughed. The almost-doctor glared at me: "You opened the wound again."

"Sorry," I said.

"Now you *will* get a gnarly scar."

She was right. Pat squeezed my hand. It was worth it.

"It's punk as fuck," Pat said. We were at a vegetarian restaurant that Moshe Pupik had recommended, finishing our bean burgers and tofu scrambles. "I mean, who cares about the money, right? That only matters if it's part of making people's lives better."

Maria-Eva and Liz both nodded minutely. Both of them had professed that they were committed to Liz's plan, but both of them had also immediately turned pale and solemn as soon as they did so. Maybe they were fully committed to blowing up CF if that's what it took to destroy Fidelity, but some part of them had to be thinking of all they'd built, of the workers who'd be out of a job, of the customers who trusted them.

The restaurant door opened and Zion came in, followed by a puzzled-looking Art Hellman. They spotted us and parked themselves in the extra chairs we'd requested from the teenager at the podium.

"He's a stubborn customer," Zion said, giving Art a friendly look and a shove on the shoulder.

Art pretended to be offended. "It's just all this cloak-and-dagger nonsense—can you just use the phone like a normal person?"

"Not if that phone is connected to a Nortel DMS-100," Pat

said, around a mouthful of eggs and tofu. "Not unless you want bad guys listening in on it."

Art gave her a look like he wasn't sure if she was kidding. She squeezed more hot sauce on her tofu out of a red ketchup bottle and forked up another mouthful, then held his gaze.

He shook his head. "I think you'd better tell me what the hell is going on."

He was pretty skeptical right up to the point where I hiked up Moshe Pupik's borrowed shirt—yet another gray Stanford Athletics tee, he had a drawerful of them—and peeled back the bandage to show him my glued-together torso.

"Jesus," he said. "You should go to the cops."

I looked at Maria-Eva and then at Liz. We'd had this discussion several times already.

"They're not going to treat it as a conspiracy," Liz said. "They'll treat it like isolated harassment and attacks. They're not going to put a cop at the door to the office or stake out our apartments."

Maria-Eva took over: "At least, not until something much, much worse happens."

Art winced. He hadn't been able to stop thinking about Rivka, had been calling SF General and pestering the floor nurses for updates.

"So these are desperate times and you've devised a desperate measure. But how are you going to make it work? What's going to happen when you start showing up at your office again to fill these deep-discount orders?"

"That's the part we're trying to figure out," Maria-Eva said.

"That's why I brought you here," I said. "You're a devious sort."

He nodded. "Thank you. Well, how about this: We move you all somewhere safe—somewhere that you can't be found. We get outside movers to relocate your inventory, get it to a storage locker or something, a big one with a loading bay that you can use as a temporary warehouse. You get your orders on the answering machine and pick them up from wherever you're hiding out, call the warehouse guys and tell them what orders to dispatch the next day. It's a little slower than if you were all under one roof, but you're also discounting below cost, so no one will mind too much. Fast, good, and cheap, pick two, right?"

We all stared at him. Well, some of us stared, the rest of us gaped. He shrugged. "What? None of you have ever planned how you'd run a business while living underground?"

Liz drummed her fingers on the table, staring up and to the left, thinking it through.

"How do we get checks?"

Art said, "Oh, that's *easy.* You just go to a Realtor and ask them about empty houses on the market. Figure out which one has been up for sale for the longest time, and ask the post office to forward your mail to that address. Pick it up once a day, *carefully,* making sure you aren't observed. If there are a few empty houses, then you pick the one that is best sited for scoping out at a distance. That wouldn't work against cops, they'd just make the post office tell them where the mail was being forwarded. But it'll work on thugs."

"You have really thought this through," Liz said, marveling.

"I used to fantasize about disappearing," he said. "Back in Cambridge."

"Why did you want to disappear?" I asked.

"So I could start over and be someone else," he said. The look of absolute sorrow came and went so fast that I nearly missed it. But if you knew him as well as I did . . . Ever since we'd come west and Art had come out, I'd been struck from time to time by how it must have been for him to live in the closet. I had an idea that it wasn't very nice, but that look—

I gave his shoulder a squeeze and he patted my hand. "It's

okay, buddy. Live and learn. Plus, I got all this amazing trade-craft out of it. Speaking of which: no one has asked about *depositing* the checks yet."

"All right," Liz said, "tell us about depositing the checks."

"Well, if I was the bad guy, I'd order something and then try to follow the money."

"Good strategy," I said.

"There you go, right from the horse's mouth," Art said, gesturing at me. "The CPA agrees.

"So you've got to get the money into your account. You bank at Wells Fargo just like everyone in San Francisco. Who can resist those adorable stagecoaches on the checks? It's the romance of the West.

"Wells Fargo's got branches all over the state. Wherever you're hiding out, you won't be more than an hour from a branch. But this isn't enough, right, Marty?"

"Right," I said, slowly, thinking it over. "Because they'll get the check back from their bank, and it'll have a stamp from the branch giving the location. They'll intercept you there."

"Exactly. That's how a CPA *does it,* folks. So you need to deposit the checks at a more distant branch. Actually, at more distant *branches.* You need to map the locations of every branch within a day's drive, put them in a spreadsheet, and then randomize the list. Never go to the same branch twice, and don't go to them in any order—don't draw a bull's-eye by going to the closest ones first, then working your way out."

"You'll still get a bull's-eye—randomizing the order won't change the fact that you're at the center of the pattern," Pat said.

Art nodded, "That's true, but this isn't supposed to last forever, just for a couple months, until the money runs out."

"Okay, conceded," Pat said. "Proceed."

Art shrugged. "There's not much more to say, honestly. Go into hiding. Use a dead drop for checks. Set up a secret warehouse. Burn through all your available cash and credit, and hope the other guys go bust before you do."

"Will they?" Pat said, and everyone looked at me.

I spread my hands. "Look," I said, "I got all of an hour with Moshe's friends' Apple to look at the spreadsheets on my floppies. They're a month out of date."

Pat glared at me. "Stop hedging. Just give us an estimate and your error bars."

"Maybe," I said. She balled up her straw wrapper and threw it at me. "Sorry," I said, "how about 'probably'?" She reached for Liz's straw wrapper. I held up my hands. "All right, here's the story. They run very, very lean, taking every dime out of the business they can without actually killing it. They've got a line of credit at their bank but they like to keep that running close to max, too, I suppose so that they can keep the handouts flowing to these tough-guy investors.

"They're the wild card. If they are willing to reverse the money flow out of Fidelity, then they could stay in business indefinitely. That would be the smart call—they've taken millions out of the business and they could get billions more, if they are willing to provide some patient money."

"These guys don't strike me as patient money," Pat said.

"No," Maria-Eva said. "These type of men are rarely patient."

She'd been handling this better than any of us. It was a reminder of when Pat and I had our blowout, of Maria-Eva's other life with the dirty wars south of the border. For her, finding out that thugs had beaten someone she loved near to death was an experience she had to cope with every month. Sometimes more often.

"Maybe the top men could be persuaded to be patient, the very clean-handed, respectable fellows who bankroll this thing. But they won't even hear about it—they will have handed it off to someone with dirty hands, and that person will hesitate to give disappointing news to their patrons. They'll just try more terror, more violence."

We were all silent after that.

"Whatever hiding place we find, it has to be good," Maria-Eva said. We nodded solemnly. I went to find a pay phone.

Don't ever forget that you've got a friend in Sacramento.

19

Lucille met us in the elementary school parking lot half an hour after the final bell rang and all the kids had dispersed, except for a few older students who were fooling around on the swings.

She sashayed across the parking lot, headed straight for the van. I rolled open the side door and jumped out. Her smile was radiant, her hair messy and glorious under the kerchief. Her hug was amazing. Her *smell* was amazing. Once she'd squeezed me carefully, picking up right away on my care for the wound in my glued-together side, she let up and took a good look at my face, her smile just as beautiful as I'd remembered. She had some new crow's-feet and they made her smile even better. She was fantastically sexy.

"You've grown up some," she said. "Got some . . . *gravitas*. It suits you." She surprised me with a quick kiss, which made me self-conscious, especially about Pat, even though we were still officially unofficial and stuck in a no-man's-land.

"Lucille, these are the women I told you about," I said, turning around to point out the whole crowd, who'd piled out of the van. "That's Sister Maria-Eva, that's Liz—they're two-thirds of the computer company I mentioned." They nodded solemnly at her. They'd spoken to Rivka's doctor from a pay phone at a roadside burger joint and had been quiet and sad ever since. "And that's Pat, she's—"

Pat snorted. "I'm along for the ride," she said. "Nice to meet you."

Lucille looked from her to me and then to her and then to me and then to her. "I don't know you, Pat, but you give a hell of a first impression." Pat scowled and Lucille laughed. "A *good* first impression. I'm going to say, huh, brilliant, funny, and driven. Also fun at parties. Also fun *after* the parties. Am I right?"

Pat tried not to smile. "I think you'd better ask someone else," she said.

"It's true," Art said, stepping out of the van.

"This is my roommate, Art," I said. "And yeah, it's true."

"Lucille," he said, "I've heard so much about you. You were all Marty could talk about after he arrived."

She mimed primping her hair. "Well, I'm glad to hear I made an impression." She took stock of us. "Folks, I don't want to rush you along, but honestly, that van looks a little serial-killer-y for an elementary school parking lot, and I imagine you're anxious to get some food and get settled in."

Everyone nodded. Art patted his van like he was worried Lucille was going to hurt its self-esteem.

"Food first? Or rooms? I've got Ben to agree to give you the long-term rate for two motel rooms, which normally you'd have to commit to a month for, but he understands your plans aren't firm. I spoke to Gretchen, who's cleaning today, and had her give them an extra sprucing. They're not fancy, but they're sanitary."

"I'm hungry," Maria-Eva said. Everyone nodded.

"Perfect," she said. "I was hoping you'd say that. Let's go to my place, it's close by. I'll take shotgun and give you directions, Art."

"Don't you have a car?" I asked.

"Oh, I like to walk," she said. "Sharpens my appetite."

Her house was like her: warm, good smelling, messy, and comfortable. There was a no-breed mutt that needed walking, and she handed the leash to Art. There were two cats who demanded dinner, and she handed Pat a can opener. She took me, Maria-Eva, and Liz into the kitchen and handed us aprons and put us to work chopping and prepping for dinner.

"Everybody helps," she said, probing the back of her freezer. "No such thing as a free dinner."

Soon there were red onions and garlic slow-cooking in shimmering oil in the bottom of a giant pot, which she set me to stirring. Every time I pronounced them done, she sniffed at them and made another stirring gesture.

Finally she cracked a whole tray of brown ice cubes into the pot. "Venison stock," she said. "Local hunter saves me his bones. I brown 'em in the oven, then cook 'em down with celery and carrots, parsley and bay leaves and freeze them. Normally I just use one or two at a time in a red sauce, but for company, I'm willing to give up my whole stash."

The smell that permeated the kitchen once the frozen stock cubes melted was indescribable, a rich, earthy, *brown* smell. It would be years before I learned the word *umami*, but when I did, that was the meal I thought of.

To this, she added the liquor from a cooling pot of black beans from her back burner, tossing in a whole peeled orange. She gave a handful of different dried chilis to Maria-Eva along with a mortar and pestle and got her to grind them. There were at least eight types. Liz was set to work slicing fresh chilis into the finest mince, and Lucille reminded her no fewer than six times not to touch her eyes, nose, or mouth until she'd washed her hands twice, and even then, not.

I picked up the stirring duty, which came with frequent exhortations to stir slowly, dig deep, bring the stuff from the bottom up to the top, don't dare let anything get scorched.

The smell got even *better.*

Pat and Art finished their animal-care duties and drifted into the kitchen to sniff the pots. Lucille chased them out and showed them where the placemats and plates and cutlery were and had them set the table. She sent Art back out for beer, and then handed Pat a salad spinner and a load of spinach and bent her to the sink to wash it twice, smacked her hand when she tried to snitch some of the chili, and then as penance sent her into the living room to work over a cutting board on the coffee table with Art to chop fresh tomatoes and soft farmer's cheese for the salad. Lucille made the dressing herself, using mustard and oil and vinegar and more mysterious herbs she took off a drying rack that I'd mistaken for an ornamental dried grass display.

Finally, she came by and dipped a deep-bellied soup spoon into the chili I'd been stirring, brought it to her lips, blew across it, closed her eyes, and put the spoon's bowl in her mouth, holding it there for a moment while she breathed slowly through her nose. She stood like that for a moment, then snapped her eyes open and pointed at me. "Keep stirring," she said, and grabbed a wicker-wrapped chianti bottle off the counter and pulled out the cork and made ready to empty it into the pot.

I yelped "Stop!" and physically interdicted the bottle before she could upend it over the pot.

Fist on hip, brow furrowed: "Martin Hench, you'd better have a damned good reason for interfering with my creative process."

"Liz," I said. "No booze for her."

I watched the light dawn. "Right!" she said. "LDS. Sorry."

"Hey, Liz!" she called over her shoulder. "Come here a sec, would you darling?"

Liz peeked cautiously around the kitchen door and Lucille beckoned her close. "How much chili you think you can eat?" she said. "Make it a generous estimate. Two bowls? Three?"

Liz looked from Lucille to me, and then I pointed at the wine bottle. "Before we add the final ingredient," I said.

"Oh!" She blushed a little. "It's fine," she said. "Really, you don't have to make a special allowance for me. All the alcohol will boil off anyway, and I'm a lot less of a stickler for this than I was a few months back. You know, recent events and all."

Lucille flapped her free hand at her. "Girl, I don't cook it until the alcohol evaporates, that's a waste of good booze. Come on, it's no problem. Two bowls? Three? Tell me."

"One?" Liz said.

"Two," Lucille said. "*No one* ever eats just one bowl of my chili. Plus one more for leftovers tomorrow." She grabbed a pot down off a wall hook and snatched a ladle out of a pot next to the stove and dropped four large dollops into the second pot. "Right," she said, and emptied the wine into the big pot. "Stir, Marty, stir!" she said, as the wine glugged into the chili.

I had stirred in the wine; she turned the heat down and had me keep stirring for another two or three minutes, then tried another spoonful. "That's it," she said. "Cut, print, check the gate." She turned her head to the kitchen door. "Bowls! Bring bowls!"

The chili was incredible. The beer was cold. We went through two and a half sourdough loaves and then, as we sat and talked and burped and rubbed our distended bellies, we picked at the remaining half loaf and used it to scour the bowls of every last drop of red-brown chili gravy.

Lucille looked over those sparkling bowls and said, "Well, I can tell that none of you enjoyed that, not one bit." We did the dishes and stashed the leftovers in Tupperware which Liz showed us all how to burp, citing her long experience of aunts' and cousins' Tupperware parties: "It's the original group salvation project—all you need to do is get ten friends together, put them in your downline and you'll all get to heaven together."

Then we all piled into the backyard, where we unfolded

330 ◀ **cory doctorow**

lawn chairs and sat in a rough circle, breathing the cool, green-tasting night air, listening to the cricket-song and watching the stars wheel overhead and the moon come up.

"Thank you, Lucille," Pat said. She was a silhouette in a chair, just a few inches away, close enough that when the wind blew right, I could smell her familiar, delicious skin. "If you'd asked me this morning, I would have sworn that there was no way this day could end on a good note, but you've proved me wrong."

Out of the dark, Lucille gave a satisfied grunt. "I'm not going to say that every problem can be solved with good food and good company, but they don't hurt, and there are plenty of situations where they can get you further than you'd imagine."

"Amen," Art said. I heard him crack another beer.

Then there was a little hand in mine, a hand whose shape I knew in the dark and solely by touch. I gave Pat's hand a squeeze and she gave mine a squeeze. A shooting star went by and we were all looking at just the right spot of the sky to see and we all went *ooh* together, and Pat and I squeezed our hands together hard enough to hurt, just a little.

"We're never going to top that," Pat said. "Bedtime."

Art glugged and belched. "Someone else had better drive to the motel," he said.

"I'll do it," I said.

"Shotgun," Pat said, quietly and swiftly.

Lucille gave us each long, soulful hugs on the way out the door, told us where to find her spare key in the morning so we could set up shop in her living room, and waved to us as I got the van into gear.

It was a short drive and no one felt the need to talk. Every time I merged right and did a shoulder check, I caught Pat's eyes and then I caught my breath.

Lucille had given us three motel-room keys that she'd negotiated for with the owner. Her promises of special attention from the maids showed. One room had two battered Rubik's Cubes, one on each end table for the single beds. Another had a *Dallas* board game on one of the twin beds. The third had a double bed with a much-loved Cabbage Patch doll resting its head on the pillow. Some chambermaid had raided her kids' toy stash to add homey touches to the rooms, which also all smelled of disinfectant and furniture polish.

Maria-Eva and Liz took the Rubik's Cube room. Art took the *Dallas* board game. I was about to join him, but he rolled his eyes at me and gestured with his chin at Pat, who was standing at the door to the Cabbage Patch room, looking expectant. I made a little thank-you gesture with the fingers of one hand and rushed to join her.

I had never stayed with anyone long enough to have make-up sex. It proved to be strangely wonderful, a heady, contradictory mix of mutual familiarity—Pat had never been shy about telling me what she wanted and how she wanted it, and I'd been an eager student—and trembling excitement, almost like a first time, because I had subconsciously concluded that I would never hold and taste and smell and touch that body again.

We exhausted each other, and then lay sweating under the beady glare of the Cabbage Patch kid—Anastasia Kenneth, according to her frayed name tag.

We murmured to each other about how sorry we were, how foolish we'd been, how sincerely we forgave one another. Then she started to cry, silently at first, then louder, building to sobs.

"Oh, Pat," I said, shushing and rocking her. "It's okay. It was my fault anyway. I'm sorry."

She snuffled up her snot and pulled back to look at me.

"That's not what I'm upset about, Marty. I think I might have killed that guy."

Oh. "Uh, would it help if I told you that I snuck off and called 911 when we stopped on the way to Moshe's?"

"You did?"

I shrugged. "Yeah."

"They wouldn't have called 911 for you."

"Yup," I said.

She kissed me, then she started crying again. I held her tight. She fell asleep mid-cry, face resting on my chest, and then I stayed awake and felt her breathing against me until the rhythm of her breathing put me to sleep, too.

We all met up again for hungover breakfast at a diner down the road, filling a booth and talking in quiet, strained voices. Sometime in the night, the charmed circle of Lucille hospitality and cooking had evaporated, as we confronted the reality of our situation—we were playing chicken with Fidelity Computing, seeing who could bankrupt the other first, and what's more, Fidelity were playing the game as a full-contact sport, with blades and bats and firebombs. Guns couldn't be far behind.

"Okay," I said, after we'd paid the check. "Art, let's get a move on."

We had a mission: go back to the city, rent a storage locker to use for an alternate warehouse, get the inventory moved in, and then really crunch the numbers to estimate how long CF and Fidelity could hold out, and tease the numbers to figure out how to eke just a few more hours out of it.

Pat held my hand as we walked to the van, and she pulled my face down to hers for a hard kiss before I climbed in. "Be safe," she said. "There's no one around to save your ass this time."

Art, overhearing, said, "I'll take good care of him, don't worry."

She jerked her chin at him dismissively. "Who's gonna take care of you, shrimp?"

Art had all of a quarter inch on her, so he stood up on tip-toes and looked down his nose at her. "I can handle myself," he said. She snorted. "Lace your shoes up tight, in case you need to run."

"Excellent advice," Art said, and hugged her. Then I got another quick, fierce hug while he circled the van and climbed into the driver's seat. Pat let go and yanked open the passenger door.

"Take care of each other."

"You know it," Art said, and gunned the engine. A minute later, we were back on the road.

I'd liberated the self-storage section of both the San Francisco and the South Bay Yellow Pages before we headed to Lucille's, and as Art merged with the morning commute traffic, I attacked them with a ballpoint pen, circling numbers and consulting Art's pile of fat road atlases to check freeway access. Once I narrowed it down to four possibilities, I got Art to pull off at a gas station and we hit the pay phones in parallel, asking about rates, availability, and the permissibility of a couple of daily loading/unloading efforts. That narrowed us down to two possibilities, one of which was on our route, and we pulled off the highway just before Rockville and meandered through the streets and past an enormous cemetery before pulling up to Mudgett's U-Store.

Mike Mudgett himself greeted us, his florid cheeks at odds with his laid-back demeanor. He was unfazed by our need for a temporary shipping depot and led us to a pair of corner units, one small, one large. "You can keep your inventory in the big one and then pull it into this little one to pack up and label," he said. "That's what the last bunch did."

Learning that he wasn't the first person to get the brilliant idea of using a storage locker as a shipping depot seemed to sting Art. "What were they shipping?" he asked.

Mudgett's eyes narrowed and he looked at us for a long time. "That's not something I had any reason to inquire about," he said. "And for that matter, it wasn't anything I was going to ask you about, neither."

"That suits us fine," I said, quickly, before Art could object. Let him assume we were shipping dope or stolen goods—it would explain our squirrelishness and the fact that we were renting by the week. I handed over cash right then, locking it in for two weeks, with another week's security deposit. I folded his handwritten receipt into my wallet; I'd add it to the company books once I got to my Apple][+ and got to work.

We detoured into the city so that I could visit Rivka while Art called Lucille's place to let them know where to send the inventory. He joined me by Rivka's bedside a few minutes later. She had been asleep when I got to her, but she roused when he came in and looked up at both of us, groggy behind her pain medication. I picked her glasses up off the bedside table, one arm broken off and mended with surgical tape by a nurse. I carefully put them onto her face. She focused on us, and something that might have been a smile crawled up the corners of her swollen mouth.

"Hello," she croaked. I passed her the half-full plastic cup of lukewarm water and helped her get the straw into her mouth. She got a little bit of water in her mouth and swallowed painfully.

"How're you doing, gorgeous?" Art asked. He managed to

make it cheerful, not forced. I wished I could manage that trick.

Another tiny smile. "I'll live," she said.

"You certainly will," Art said. "I spoke with the floor nurse and she's very impressed by your recovery."

Rivka closed her eyes for so long I thought she'd fallen asleep, then she snapped them open and skewered us on a look that came from a million miles away.

"They're not going to stop," she croaked. "They're coming for all of us."

"They'll have to find us," I said, then pulled up a chair and leaned close to her ear and whispered an abridged account of everything that had happened since we'd parted ways. Her eyes kept closing, but when I trailed off, she cracked them open and made an impatient twirling gesture with one finger.

"It's insane," she said. "It's an insane plan."

She wasn't wrong.

"You should just leave. We should all just leave. Give up, go somewhere else, do something else."

"You can still do that after you go out in a blaze of glory," Art said. "After you inflict some financial pain on them. That's not a bad plan B. And plan A might be a long shot, but if it works, we'll destroy them."

She sighed. "That won't stop them."

Art shook his head. "We've just got to give them a bigger problem than you—a problem like bankruptcy. Once they go bust, their investors are going to switch from coming after you to going after the Reverend Sirs."

"They've got a lot of cash salted away," I said. "Shell companies in the Caymans that own real estate up and down the Rockies, lots of ski resorts and gas stations. Those nest eggs are bound to capture the Wise Men's investors, once we let them know about it."

She sighed again. "You keep thinking that they're businessmen, that they care about money more than they care about revenge."

"Well, they *have* a lot of money," I said. "You don't pile up a lot of cash by focusing on anything *but* cash."

She closed her eyes and made that twirling, impatient finger gesture again.

"It's a long shot," I said, feeling bad about arguing with this badly injured woman in her hospital bed, but unable to stop myself. "But if we pull it off, I think the odds are good that they'll become each other's problems."

"The odds," she said, and swallowed. I gave her another sip of water. "You know what you're betting, right?"

If Moshe Pupik hadn't arrived at that moment, I might have kept arguing. As it was, I gave her hand a squeeze and Art and I said our goodbyes, leaving Moshe Pupik stricken and grave at her bedside.

Once we got home, we worked quickly, boxing up our computers in heavy cartons we taped together, padding them with our clothes and toiletries, saving us from having to pack suitcases.

"I'm supposed to go to a client site this afternoon, and Ryan offered to put me up in his guest room."

"Ryan?"

"A guy I know." Art blushed a little. "A guy I know *well*. I'll give you his number and you can leave me messages on his machine."

He took me to the San Jose airport and I put my computer box on a luggage trolley and wheeled it to the Budget car desk and rented a midsized, nondescript sedan, then I headed to Potrero Hill and circled the CF offices twice before parking a ways off and settling in to wait for the movers, hunched down across the street from the office, wearing a ball cap and sunglasses. I felt like a kid playing superspy, until I spotted the bloodstains on the sidewalk, on the spot where Pat had dragged the thug she'd clobbered. A discarded surgical glove next to the stains memorialized the ambulance crew that came after I put in my phone call.

Spotting that glove transformed my self-conscious feelings of silliness to equally self-conscious feelings of paranoia.

The movers arrived after an agonizing delay, and the slice across my belly ached the whole time I spent unlocking the doors and getting them inside, only abating a little as I walked them through the warehouse and gave them instructions on the job: move everything, even the shelves.

The foreman sucked his teeth and shook his head as he confronted the rows of shelves, stacked high with finished goods and parts, some in boxes, some in neat piles. He was a broad, short, powerful Mexican guy who spoke lightly accented English to me and rapid-fire Spanish to his crew of half a dozen guys.

"This is a two-day job, boss," he said.

"I need it done in one," I said. "Your Yellow Pages ad said that rush jobs were a specialty."

"We can do a rush job, but I'll need to get more guys. That's a lot of packing." He left that hanging.

"Okay," I said. "Get more guys."

"They don't work for free, boss."

In the end, I promised him twice what we'd negotiated, with more overtime for them to set up the shelves and unpack at the storage unit, no matter how late they'd have to go.

I looked up and down the street, twice, before scuttling into my rental and putting down the pedal, racing back to Lucille's with my cardboard box full of clothes and floppies and a computer.

Lucille had just come back from work when the movers called to say they'd arrived at the storage locker. I got up from the living room sofa, where I'd been working, hunched over the coffee table where I'd stuck my Apple, plugged into an extension cord I'd requisitioned from an end-table lamp that hadn't been using it.

I rubbed my lower back and accepted a warm hug from Lucille, then scrubbed at my burning eyes, dry from the desert air.

"I'm going to go make sure they're okay," I said. "It'll take an hour or so to get there. I'll call once I'm settled in."

Maria-Eva came in from the kitchen, where she'd been perched all day, phoning every salesperson and important account, letting them know about the new discounted rates. Liz was back at the motel, monopolizing their phone line, taking orders.

"Do you need help?" she said. She looked as tired as I felt.

"Stay," I said.

"Take Pat, at least."

"No, we can't afford to miss any calls."

"We can afford it," Maria-Eva said. "You're too tired to drive on your own."

I started to object, realized I couldn't even form a coherent sentence, and just nodded. She was right. I drove to the motel with exaggerated care.

Pat answered the door in panties and a T-shirt, leaving it on the chain at first and peeking through a crack. "Sorry," she said, "phone's been ringing so hard that I haven't had a chance to dress or shower. Keep your distance, you don't want to smell me."

Just like that, my exhaustion lifted. I gathered her up in a tight hug, breathing deeply. She was *funky,* in a good way, smelling of sex and girl and Pat, in that order, a smell that reached up through my nose, took hold of my central nervous system, and *yanked.*

She pulled back and caught my eye. "Uh-oh," she said. "Whoa there, tiger. We've got urgent business to attend to."

She was right. I let her go. "I'm going to Rockville to supervise the movers," I said. "Maria-Eva says I need a navigator to keep me from nodding off at the wheel. Wanna come on a road trip?"

She yawned and stretched her arms over her head, twisting from side to side and making my engine rev harder. I was *wide* awake now, at least temporarily.

"What about the orders?"

"The sister has this crazy idea that if I die on the road, it'll limit our ability to fill those orders."

"She's got a point," Pat said. "Maybe we can stop for burgers or something. I'm starved."

"Burgers are a great idea," I said. "Let's go."

"I need to shower first," she said.

"You most certainly do *not*," I said, and waggled my eyebrows at her.

"Pervert," she said, but she smiled. My heart melted, my breathing quickened, and a muscle two inches below my belly button twitched. How had I been stupid enough to walk out on this woman? Jesus, Hench, for a smart guy, you're quite a fool. "Okay, let me put on pants then."

"What a shame," I said. "Like draping a sheet over the Venus de Milo."

"You keep that up," she said, picking up her jangling, chain-draped combat fatigue pants from the floor. "That is just fine."

The movers arrived in two trucks, three guys in each cab, but when they rolled up the cargo doors, eight more guys climbed down and milled around while I met with the foreman and took him for a walk around the storage locker.

He spoke rapid Spanish to a couple of guys and they produced tape measures and started calling out numbers, comparing them to a clipboard with a sheet of paper with dense markings in pencil. I peeked at it and realized that they'd drawn a diagram of the warehouse setup before they'd dismantled it and now they were figuring out how to re-create it.

"It won't all fit, boss," the foreman said.

Well, of course not. I'd only estimated the floor space. I rolled up the door to the smaller storage space I'd marked out as my office and the measuring team got to work.

"Gonna be tight," the foreman said. "But okay." They got to work. Pat went for pizzas. I stayed out of the way and thought about spreadsheets. The sun set. The shelves were assembled. Boxes flew out of the trucks in bucket brigades, and I was called upon to make executive calls about which ones would go where. Pat came back and had better ideas. The guys shrugged and moved stuff some more. I ate the last slice of pizza. The guys emptied one truck and turned it around in a series of tight, fast maneuvers and got the headlights on, shining into the garage. The boxes flew out. The guys grew visibly tired, but didn't flag. I went for a couple of cases of beer. By the time I came back, they were done.

I wrote the foreman a check. A case of beer disappeared into the back of each truck. Pat produced a roll of twenties and gave one to each guy, and I wished that had been my idea. You can trade money for beer, but it's a lot harder to turn beer into money.

"It feels ridiculous to say this, but watching those guys unload tired me out."

Pat merged onto 80 and maneuvered the rental all the way into the fast lane and put the hammer down. "You just had a near-death experience. You've been running flat out for *days*. I think you're just exhausted because you *stopped* for a couple of minutes. You're not tired—you're just *noticing* that you're tired."

"You're right," I said.

"Course I'm right," she said.

Hardly anyone spoke at dinner that night. Lucille did her best, but she was at heart a listener, and we were all out of talk. We'd spent a day getting set up for a game of chicken, and it had worn us down—and we hadn't even started the race.

20

It only took four days for the Kohlers to figure out that something was going on. Maria-Eva was supposed to be checking the answering machine at the office a couple of times per day, but the new prices had brought in a flood of orders, and every time she hung up Lucille's phone, it rang again. By the time 6 p.m. rolled around, she was cooked and just purely forgot to pick up the messages, which is how she missed three calls from the Kohlers—the first two breezy messages from Ted, the third firm and alarmed, from Benny.

She discovered the messages the next morning, and she called them probably right around the time that Benny and Ted were arriving at the empty factory in Potrero Hill, letting themselves in with the keys they'd insisted on. They saw the empty warehouse, even the shelves gone. They saw the empty factory floor, the soldering irons cool and abandoned. They saw the office, a mess of scattered papers, upturned furniture, and file-cabinet drawers yawning open and empty.

They had every right to be alarmed, of course. By the time they called their receptionist and picked up their messages, including Maria-Eva's call with her temporary number, they were convinced that the people they'd invested so much of their capital in had absconded with it and that they had lost their shirts.

The thing is, they weren't precisely wrong.

It would have been better if laid-back, friendly Ted had

called, but naturally, it was Benny who had the operator break in on Maria-Eva's call with a customer.

Of all of us, Maria-Eva was the best person to take that call. She was used to picking up the phone in the middle of the night and learning that an old friend had gone missing, or been murdered, or horribly violated or beaten. Benny swearing a blue streak up and down the line, calling her a "rip-off shit" and a con artist and a crook and promising to have her arrested and deported, barely registered.

She calmly waited for him to run down, taking it with so much equanimity that he broke off mid-rant to say, "You better not have hung up on me, bitch!"

"I'm still here, Benny," she said, and now it was his turn to fall silent. Evidently, he'd thought that he was swearing down a cut line, not calling a nun a bitch.

"Oh," he finally managed. He wasn't done, but he'd lost his momentum. Ted said something indistinct in the background and Benny must have covered the receiver to answer, so Maria-Eva was treated to an extended, muffled family squabble. She waited patiently for it to resolve, going over the fat spiral notebook where she'd been taking orders so that I could hand them off to the guys we'd hired by asking Mudgett for recommendations. I didn't think they were stealing, and so far they'd proved adept at reading part numbers off an order sheet, finding them on the shelves, packing them into larger cartons, and labeling them for shipping. I took them down to the UPS depot every afternoon at 4:30 p.m., arriving just before they closed down at 5:00.

Finally, Ted came on the line: "I'm sorry about that, Sister."

"It's okay, Ted. I'm sure you two were worried. I should have called you earlier, but things have been a little unsettled around here."

"That seems to be the case, all right." Benny made a rude

noise, so close that Maria-Eva could tell that they had put their heads nearly next to one another, with the handset in between, so they could both listen in. "What is going on, Maria-Eva?"

We had done extremely well, all things considered, flying by the seat of our pants but not losing altitude. But in all the hurly-burly, we had completely forgotten to think about what we would tell the Kohlers. For so long as we had been sending them big monthly checks, they'd been happy to let us just run the show without a lot of elbow-jostling. I'd come to think of them as just another line item in our cost structure, a cell on the spreadsheet I used to calculate our monthly outgoings.

In the absence of any plan for dealing with the Kohlers, Maria-Eva did what came naturally to her: she told the truth.

I'm the first to admit that it was a pretty outlandish story: three religious criminal syndicates forming an alliance, not merely to destroy the business but to maim or kill its princi-pals. But Maria-Eva was no stranger to accounts of spectacular violence in service to the pettiest goals. Once you'd repeatedly told the story of nuns tied to trees and bayonetted to death by jeering Contras acting on behalf of a landlord whose peasant fruit pickers were demanding that he pay all the money he'd promised them before they brought in his crop, CF's tale of woe came easy.

"Marty tells us that we have a fighting chance," she said. It wasn't a lie, because she believed it. She believed because I'd told her so.

However, I *had* been lying. I hadn't taken orders. I couldn't name more than four of the Ten Commandments.

And we *did* have a chance. Not a *fighting* chance, but a chance, nevertheless. The fact that I was thinking of this in terms of whether *we* had a chance—that I had become my own client—had a lot to do with my decision to lie to a nun (and the rest of the group). I calculated that our chance, small as it was, depended on our continuing on even when the odds were stacked against us.

In other words, I'd decided that it was in everyone else's best interests to be kept in the dark.

In hindsight, this was a mistake.

To Ted's credit, he was obviously horrified on our behalf, volubly concerned with our safety, making noises about money not being as important as our precious lives. Benny conspicuously did not join in to this part of the conversation, and once it was over, he demanded to know how he could get in touch with me. Ostensibly, this was because Benny wanted to review the finances. In reality, it had more to do with the fact that I was a man. Benny didn't like talking business with women.

Mudgett had a phone in his office at the storage locker, a grimy rotary-dial Western Electric number from the 1940s, heavy as a boat anchor, infused with decades of cigarette smoke. He had grudgingly allowed me to give the number to Maria-Eva and Pat in case they needed to reach me in an emergency.

But Mudgett made it clear he was doing me a favor. When Benny demanded that I be found and put on the line, *right now*, that violated the spirit of our arrangement. Mudgett was a man of few words, but he'd served on a navy ship in the South Pacific and he knew some doozies. He favored Benny with a short selection of this highly specialized vocabulary and firmly hung up the phone. When it started ringing again, Mudgett unplugged it. There wasn't anyone he *needed* to talk to, after all.

I didn't know any of this. I found out two hours later, when Benny and Ted showed up in their maroon Mercedes 380 SEL, the V-8 rumbling as they prowled through the aisles of Mudgett's self-store until they spotted the rolled-up door and the guys moving boxes in and out of the locker next to my temporary office.

346 ◄ **cory doctorow**

The engine revved once more before Benny killed it and they both got out, jamming their fists into their lower backs and groaning. I had somehow forgotten about their existence—until that moment. Their sudden appearance made me feel like I was in a waking nightmare, an anxiety dream in which my dad came home in the middle of a party I was forbidden to host and walked in on a scene of debauchery, while I made weak excuses and watched my life slip away.

I got up from my perch—one of Lucille's kitchen chairs, jammed up against a large cardboard box holding a defective monitor for a desk—and did my own ritual to placate my lumbar spine.

"Ted, Benny," I said. My voice only quavered a little.

Ted gave me a wave. Benny folded his arms and scowled. It occurred to me to wonder whether this good Kohler / bad Kohler routine wasn't something premeditated and mutually advantageous. It would have been smart to pull on that thread but it got away from me.

"How long until you're broke?" Benny said.

I could have begged and apologized, but my months in Silicon Valley had evidently rubbed off on me because I blurted, "That depends on how much more you invest."

Benny was so surprised he forgot to scowl. "You have got to be—"

"The proprietary data I've seen from Fidelity gives them another month at the outside. At the rate we're going, we'll be out of inventory in three weeks."

Benny remembered to scowl again. "This is some kind of fucking—"

I had no idea how much they knew, but I hate playing dumb and if they caught me lying to them after I'd kept them in the dark, we'd be cooked. "Once Fidelity folds up, we can buy out their inventory—we'll need it, we'll be fresh out by then—and bring the factory back up to full capacity to modify them. We'll have lots of back orders, and that'll give us time to tool up our own lines, making new from scratch. That'll have a very favorable cost basis and I'm betting Kohler Brothers has some OEM relationships we can capitalize on. Fidelity is a sick, weak enterprise, a scam masquerading as a computer company. It will eventually die anyway—we're just helping it slip away quickly."

"The nun said you had more time left than they did," Benny said.

"It's not an exact science," I said. Not a lie. "Who goes first is a coin toss. Depends on how optimistic you are about our error bars." I swallowed. "Depends on you two. You can make it a certainty."

"So what, you want us to loan money to a business that's selling goods for less than cost?"

"Selling stuff for less than it costs just makes you a hot ticket in Silicon Valley. This is the land of the loss leader." My joke fell flat. Benny took on the facial expression of a model in a Pepto-Bismol ad. "Benny, look, you ever heard of Z-DOS? No? How about DR DOS? You know why? Because every time someone tries to sell a version of DOS that's better than Microsoft's product, they slash the prices they charge companies like Dell and Compaq for MS-DOS licenses."

"Sounds illegal to me," Benny said. "Isn't that what the DOJ nailed IBM for?"

"Benny, the DOJ did *not* nail IBM. Ronny Reagan called them off. Big Blue's bigger and more profitable than ever. It's a new day in America, haven't you heard? The DOJ and American enterprise are best friends now. Everyone's doing it.

"Look, they've got impatient capital and bad products. We've got good products. Add some patient capital and we'll drive them into the ground, take over their customers, make them happier than Fidelity Computing ever could, and rake it in."

Benny looked like the director had just asked him to convey the sensation of acid jetting up his esophagus. "Sounds like a load of hooey to me," he said. "These fuckin' technology dorks keep saying they've repealed the law of gravity. My family was running a successful business before any of these dorks were born, and they did it by charging *more* for what they sold than what it cost them. How the fuck does anyone plan on making money if they lose on every sale?"

"We make it up in volume," I said. That, at least, got a faint grin out of Ted, who'd been hovering in his habitual cringe in Benny's shadow, off to one side and slightly behind him. Benny snorted. "Look, Benny, the idea isn't to lose money forever. It's to *strategically* lose money to get rid of a competitor. Microsoft does it to get rid of companies that have better products before users can find out about them.

"We're different, though. We want to get rid of a competitor with worse products, who tries to preserve their leadership by sending thugs to beat the shit out of their rivals."

"Why wouldn't they just come and beat the shit out of you to stop you from doing this, then?"

"Because," I said, trying to keep the exasperation out of my voice, "they can't find us. We are *hiding*. That's why the factory was empty, remember?"

He grunted. I had him there. Ted nodded a little encouragement at me and gave me a thumbs-up that Benny couldn't see or pretended to ignore. "So why won't these guys just raise more capital and try to outspend *you*?"

"Because they're *already* bleeding out. They ran a crooked business, and it depended on a captive market of customers who *had* to pay extortionate prices for everything. They took so much money out of the business that without those huge margins, they couldn't keep the lights on. They *could* have cut off the flow to their investors, but we've already seen how their investors deal with disappointment. So instead they've drained their reserves, shredded their cushion, and shaved their margin of error to the bone.

"Gentlemen, we're losing money because we're discounting good products below cost. *They're* losing money because they have terrible products that no one uses voluntarily, and we're providing the escape hatch those customers need to free themselves from their commercial prisons. Fidelity Computing has a criminal enterprise. We have a business. They only succeed where their customers have no choice. We succeed because their customers choose *us*. I don't know how I can make this plainer. We are in this to win this."

"And all you have to do is avoid getting beaten to death by their thugs." Benny was starting to look like the after in the Pepto commercial, after the slow and soothing pink ooze has coated the cutaway diagram of his digestive tract.

"That's all we need to do, all right," I said. "We don't have to do it forever. Just for a while."

"How long?"

I shrugged. "Couple weeks. Three at the outside. Their payables are a mess. They've been stiffing their suppliers to get free cash flow. They're two months late on their rent. They skipped their last payment for the leases on their commercial vehicle fleet. Next week, it'll be payroll. This is a business in substantial distress."

"You know this because you looked at their books, huh?"

"Yeah, that's right."

"And how do you know you can trust these books? How do you know they didn't send you those books to trick you into driving yourself out of business?"

"Because," I said, my voice hoarse, "the man who delivered those files to me killed himself not long after." Rivka had clipped the obit out of the *San Francisco Chronicle*, where he was one among a long list of young men with elliptically described causes of death. I swear Benny was about to ask me if I'd seen the body myself, but Ted put a restraining hand on his brother's arm.

"Jesus, Marty, that's hard." Benny barely managed to paste on an unconvincing scowl.

"Thank you, Ted. Look fellas, I'm sorry we didn't manage the communications better. You don't have to believe this, but the honest truth is that we were just so distracted, maybe 'panicked' is a better word, that it just didn't occur to us. With Rivka in the hospital, all the moving, and my wound—"

"Your *wound*?" Benny said.

I hiked up my shirt. The slash was scabbed over and still sometimes oozed a little around the edges. I'd been wiping it down with Neosporin twice a day, according to Moshe's almost-a-doctor friend's advice. There was some nasty discoloration around it, and I'd ripped it open a little during one of my nighttime adventures with Pat. It had come at a very intense juncture, and I hadn't even noticed until I saw the blood on the motel sheets. Pat had sworn that she wasn't due for weeks and then I'd noticed the weird, wet feeling on my abdomen and taken a peek.

"Holy shit," Benny said. I was perversely proud that I'd managed to flap the unflappable Benjamin F. Kohler. Ted actually turned a little green.

"—so it just got lost in the shuffle. I'm the first person to say that wasn't right. You're our investors, you have every right to know what's going on, especially when it is something this drastic, and dramatic. All I can say is that it wasn't deliberate, it doesn't reflect any lack of respect for you, or duty to you, and we're all profoundly and sincerely sorry."

Sometimes, when the other guy keeps pushing and pushing and pushing, you can win by just not pushing back. Sometimes, surrender is the path to victory.

After I'd walked the Kohlers through the spreadsheets, crowded close behind my cardboard box desk (now sagging), they'd agreed to cough up enough operating capital to let us make two more weeks' payroll, agreeing that our top priority had to be keeping the skilled staff happy so that they would be available once we reopened for business. We structured it as a loan, and I personally signed for it, because they didn't have time to drive all the way to Lucille's place and get two nonhospitalized company officers to sign the note.

It was a *lot* of debt, but I was confident in my spreadsheets. Shlomo had made a senseless, terrible sacrifice, but I wasn't going to let it go to waste. I had the data.

I felt smug and victorious the whole drive back to Lucille's, still feeling the solemn handshakes each Kohler brother had delivered in turn. I was a smooth talker, all right.

21

Any day now, Fidelity Computing would cease to be a going concern. Any day now. It had to happen. There was no way that they could keep going. Between missing rent, missing payroll, and stiffing their suppliers, they'd have to cry uncle.

This was obviously true to me. The Reverend Sirs disagreed. Maria-Eva's contact inside the company told us that they were still making payroll, but that the company cars had all disappeared and they were using contract haulers to bring their shipments to the depot, with no sign of the company trucks.

Meanwhile, we were counting the dwindling pennies. Lucille sat me down one night and told me that the manager at the motel couldn't be held off any longer and asked in a roundabout way if there was enough in the company checking account to pay him. I wrote the check. The pile of pennies got smaller.

The problem wasn't orders. We had *plenty* of orders. Our "seasonal sale" had brought in more business than we could handle. That was the problem. With inventory going out and no factory producing new goods for sale, we were running out of things to sell. I'd saved a little money by consolidating the remaining stock into the small locker I was using for my office, and that meant that I got to watch the shelves grow more bare by the day, even as my sheets of back orders grew longer.

Shortly after eating lunch on the fourth Tuesday since I hired them, Mudgett's shipping guys let me know that they were out of *everything* we had on order. I paid them for the rest of the week and sent them home and thanked them for their service.

If anyone happened to order any of the few items we had left on the shelves, I could handle it.

I pulled down the rolling doors and snapped on the big pad-locks. I'd bought them from a specialist locksmith who swore they could be relied on to protect thousands of dollars' worth of inventory. Now they were vast overkill. I threw the few pack-ages the guys had parceled up in the back of the rental and drove back to Lucille's, stopping by the UPS depot en route to drop them off.

I got back to find Lucille seated at her kitchen table, run-ning over her lesson plans, Liz in the kitchen, taking orders on the phone and scribbling furiously in a fat spiral notebook, and Maria-Eva and Pat going over her twin DN100s, which Art had driven up from San Francisco that day.

"Isn't this a cozy domestic scene?" I said, forcing a jolly note into my voice.

Everyone looked up at me and then went back to what they were doing before I got there, except Art, who stood up from his perch on an ottoman covered in a Navajo rug and gave me a hug. "Good to see you, brother," he said.

"You too," I said. "How's life in the big city?"

He sighed. "Well, we're gonna have to hire a cleanup crew for the apartment, I can tell you that much."

Art had been staying with a sometime-boyfriend whose roommate had moved out unexpectedly, transferred to Tokyo after getting headhunted by Sony. Art had been dipping into our apartment every week or so to pick up the mail and any-thing else he needed. The first few times, he'd been on high alert, looking for suspicious cars in the parking lot and strang-ers in the lobby, but by the third week, he'd let his guard down, not even realizing that he'd forgotten to scope the scene before walking in until he was in the van, driving away with a pile of bills and junk mail on the passenger seat.

The fourth week, he was distracted enough that he didn't

even notice the scratch marks around our door's keyway until he found himself having to jiggle and shake his keys to get the door open. Those scratches put him on guard for what he found inside, but even so, it took him a moment to close his mouth and start breathing again, whereupon he stepped back and closed the door.

"It smelled just like that stuff you brought back from Rivka's place, and everything was trashed, just totally trashed. I remembered what you said about the county sending in its hazmat team when you called them for Rivka's and I decided there was no point in hanging around, waiting for them, so I just closed the door and left."

He'd promised Pat he'd swing by her place and get her mail, which a neighbor had been taking in for her, and he'd been putting it off. Now he regretted it, and filled with dread, he drove up to the city to pick up her spare keys and mail from her neighbor and let himself into her apartment.

"They hadn't set off any stink bombs, at least," he said, "but they sure did a number on those gorgeous, innocent Unix boxes." That was when I realized that Pat hadn't taken the cases off her DN100s to reveal their innards for Maria-Eva—they were assessing the damage.

"Oh, no," I said, and rushed to peer in.

"I think we can salvage one working system by cannibalizing parts from both of them," Pat said, stone-faced. "This one wasn't on when they pissed in it, so it just needs a good clean." Which explained the smell, and the fact that they were both wearing dish gloves. "This one still has a good monitor and keyboard, at least."

"You're home early," Liz said, peeking out of the kitchen.

"Well, about that."

While I walked them through our remaining inventory (or lack thereof) and the state of our finances (ditto), Art mixed drinks, working from Lucille's limited selection to offer us a choice of either White Russians or Black Russians ("I like vodka, and one of my students' parents gave me a giant bottle of Kahlua").

"How much longer can Fidelity hold out?" Art said, after we'd shared a morose toast and sipped at our drinks.

Maria-Eva said, "I spoke to my friend today. They just told everyone they'd had a problem with the check writer and that payday would be delayed."

"Can I just say that I'm proud that at least we've kept paying our people?" I said it to head off any proposal that we try to eke out a few more weeks by kiting our payroll. If we were going to lay people off, we should lay them off—not string them along. Everyone nodded solemnly. I guess I didn't need to say it, not to that crowd. They weren't the stiff-your-workers types.

Art drained his White Russian and wiped the cream out of his mustache. "I call that a near-death experience," he said.

"Yeah," Pat said. "We're getting to be experts in those around here."

"Well," Liz said, "the Kohlers aren't going to give us another dime. They're already calling me six times a day to find out when we can pay them back on that bridge loan." She sipped at her strawberry milk—Art had found Lucille's Quik stash and made sure that Liz had a faith-appropriate drink. Then she thumped her spiral-bound order book. "The real shame is that we have so many orders backlogged. If we could fill a quarter of them we'd be sitting pretty."

We'd agreed early on that we wouldn't cash any checks for orders unless we could fill at least 50 percent of the items. The whole point of CF was to rescue people who'd been preyed on by scammers. We weren't going to turn into scammers ourselves.

Art got a faraway look I'd last seen back in Boston, when we'd been hypnotized by an issue of *Creative Computing* and making plans to turn in our resignation to Nick Cassidy III and Nick Cassidy II.

"You've got detailed assembly manuals, right?" he said.

"Yeah," I said.

"The kind of thing any skilled computer nerd could make sense out of?"

"They're better than *that*," Liz said. She and Rivka had designed them together, drawing detailed schematics and diagrams, with instructions in Spanish and English. Every one of the women in our factory kept a binder full of their documentation on her workbench and referred to it often.

"How big are we talking here?"

"How *big*?" Liz snorted. "Art, I never had you figured for a size queen." That made Lucille crack up. Liz had clearly been spending more time with Zion than I'd figured.

"I mean, could we fit one in a FedEx box?"

"Of course," she said. "Where are you going to send it to? It's not like we can make these things in Japan, the shipping would kill us."

"I was thinking more like Cambridge, Mass.," he said.

There had been some turnover among the Newbury Street Irregulars since we'd come west. Some of them had gone west as well, and we'd run into them in bars or even at Dead Kennedys shows. Some had graduated and gone to work up and down Route 128, too busy with grown-up love and jobs and even kids to keep showing up at the old clubhouse. But computers kept getting faster, cheaper, and more interesting, and the Irregulars didn't lack for members.

In fact, it was so crowded some nights that there was talk of closing off membership and starting a waiting list. The diehards *hated* this idea, because they had spent their whole lives being picked last for sports teams and being passed over by bouncers behind velvet ropes. They were shopping for a bigger space, two or three times the size, with room for everyone.

One of those diehards was Joe Axelrod, whose whole family worked in the tech industry in one way or another. He had actually quit a hardware-design job and was making a tidy living scouting employees for his family members' employers, collecting the finder's fees that every hot new tech company was paying as they scrambled to get on board the money train.

Joe had already been looking at new potential locations for months, so when we pitched him on setting up a temporary factory, he knew just the spot: the former location of the Free Store, which had been evicted after one too many bounced rent checks. The landlord had been sure that he would find another tenant immediately, but months had crawled by and he was desperate for a short-term rental.

We still had plenty of credit with our own suppliers—in fact, we'd gone so long without placing an order that they were getting antsy. They'd started to factor our large—and steadily rising—orders into their own business plans. I negotiated net ninety-day terms with them and let them know we'd shifted manufacturing to Massachusetts. They didn't blink an eye. In tech, you chased talent and money all around the country. They expedited shipping, and within a couple of days there were trucks showing up at the back of the old Free Store, where Newbury Street Irregulars unloaded them and set to work following Liz's documentation. We started by filling orders for the simplest, highest-ticket items, using a Lotus 1–2–3 macro I'd whipped up to get us the most bang for our buck.

We didn't tell Joe much about *why* we needed this done, and he hadn't asked. He was not a big-cash-economy kind of guy—more of a banker-of-favors and knower-of-people. A decade later, he'd reinvent himself as a top-tier VC with an address book so comprehensive it crashed the first generation of Palm Pilots. He made millions doing exactly what he'd been doing all along: collecting people and favors, and connecting them.

I spent a lot of time on the phone with Joe over the next

two weeks as he got the Irregulars on task and started shipping inventory. At one point, I asked him how he'd talked so many of the members into doing free factory work and he'd laughed down the line.

"You kidding? Every one of these yahoos wants to design something that gets built and shipped to people someday. I had to beat 'em off with a stick! They're taking notes and meeting afterward for long sessions to discuss how to improve production."

At first, I'd worried that we'd end up stiffing our suppliers, but I was able to make minimum payments to them, keep up rent, and payroll—but only just.

Rivka got out of the hospital and Moshe Pupik moved her into his dorm room, after a long heart-to-heart with the RA. His roommate moved in with a girlfriend, and Moshe spooned chicken soup for Rivka until she was strong enough to get on the phone with Liz and Maria-Eva for long strategy calls, picking their brains for sales leads. They'd caucus for hours, then get off the line so that Liz could plug in the fax machine and send more orders to Boston.

It shoulda worked.

22

Lucille had the patience of a saint, but even a saint's patience can wear thin. Five and a half weeks into our takeover of her humble home, she served me with notice.

"Marty, you and your friends are wonderful and I don't have any doubt that you're doing something important here. If you tell me that you truly don't have anywhere to go, I'll find some way to keep making it work but—"

"Lucille," I said, "it's fine. Honestly, it's fine. You've been more than fair. More than more than fair! If there's a maximum of fairness that one human being can show, you've blown through it and come out the other side—"

She waved me to silence and refilled her wineglass. I'd noticed her affinity for Napa cabernet sauvignons and I'd been dipping into the company funds to pick up a bottle for her every couple of days—more often on the nights where we hung out and drank it all.

"Yes, I'm a good-natured slob. Thank you, Marty, I appreciate it. You have all been tremendous fun to play host to. I don't suppose I'll ever get closer to all the high-tech madness you're getting up to down there in the city. Just watching Pat and Maria-Eva fix that fancy computer up was an education. But I'm a simple woman, Marty. I teach children and meet interesting men in bars and sometimes bring them back here for a little recreation."

"Oh," I said. "Jesus, I'm sorry, Lucille. God, we must have been really cramping your style on that front—"

Again, she waved me back to silence. "It's okay, Marty, honestly. Sure, I can get a little horny, but this is far from the longest dry spell of my checkered career. Bottom line, though, is that I'm a hermit. I like people—in small doses. You folks are welcome anytime, of course, every one of you, but for a shorter visit under more pleasant circumstances."

I'd been Lucille-style listening, really giving this all my attention. It worked. "You don't need to feel guilty about this, Lucille. Honestly. No one is going to be upset with you. Honestly. We owe you."

She gave me a sad little smile. "I'm always gonna feel a *little* guilty asking people to go before they're ready." She brightened a little. "But I'll get over it." She drained the wine. "How long will you need? Is a week enough time, or—"

"Lucille, we can be gone tomorrow."

She looked surprised. "That soon?"

"We're mobile," I said. "At this point, all we need are phones and a couple of computers and a fax machine. Even after we thank the Boston folks and bring our San Francisco workforce back into the factory, I expect we'll never get back to the old normal. First thing I'm going to do is invest in some modems so I can dial into the office from home."

"Better get one for Pat's apartment, too," she said.

The wine must have gotten to me. I blushed.

"I really like her, Marty," she said.

"Me too," I said. "I know this is crazy, but there're times when I feel like maybe she's The One, you know?"

"You could do a lot worse," she said. "I never saw the point of marriage, but it seems to make a lot of people happy."

We stared across her kitchen table at each other, a little wine-warmed. Maybe it was talking about Pat and getting my blood going, maybe it was her talk about getting horny, maybe it was the wine, but I was suddenly overcome with an awareness of just how beautiful and sexy she was, a sensation that sent me swimming back to that night in the motel, back before all this started.

"You're really fantastic, you know that?" I said. Or, blurted. It just came out.

Lucille laughed, and she *was* fantastic. What a laugh. "Thank you, Martin Hench. I believe I *do* know it. It took me a long time to figure it out, though. You're pretty fantastic yourself, even if it seems you don't know it yet. You're all tremendous people." Before I could say anything else, she stood up and said, "When I meet a group of special people, I like to *feed* them. How about we get down to the grocery store and pick up some cowboy steaks and fixings for fresh slaw and corn? You can clean the grill and I'll show you how to barbecue."

It was a fantastic meal. We took turns toasting Lucille, and my friends did me proud, digging deep to bring forth sincere words of praise and recollections of moments of Lucille's compassion and insight.

The moon was more than halfway across the sky when we cleared the picnic table in Lucille's backyard and did the dishes and went back to the motel to sleep. As Pat and I snuggled under the sheets with our Cabbage Patch doll, I made a sleepy joke about how much I was going to miss little Anastasia Kenneth. I felt Pat's smile against my bare chest and drifted off to sleep balancing the books in my head, factoring in the final motel bill.

There are motels everywhere, but not all of them have the kind of dedicated phone lines in each room that you can use with a fax machine. We stopped at four motels before hitting on the Bona Nova motel in Vallejo, where they had just upgraded their PBX and were excited to learn that there were "tech executives" checking in with their very own fax machine. I even gave the on-duty manager—who was the owner's brother-in-law—a demo, faxing an order to Joe in Boston. The manager was appropriately impressed, and doubly so when Joe faxed back the previous day's shipping and production numbers.

We didn't have much to unpack. Maria-Eva found a laundromat and used the rental to visit it and run a load for all of us, while Liz caught up with her sales leads and Pat coaxed her DN100 to life and commandeered our room's desk to work on some Unix utility programming. I told her I was going out for sandwiches and asked her if she wanted to come. After she failed to hear me twice, I repeated myself more forcefully and she focused on me long enough to snap, "Look, I'm in the zone here." I got the sandwiches on my own.

I ate mine on the bed, watching Pat's bare arms and neck tendons flex as she delivered flurries of keypresses in short bursts, rocking her head from side to side as she worked. When at last she came up for air and said, "Did you mention sandwiches?" I handed her the ham and Swiss on dark rye and broke out the little styrofoam take-out pot. She cocked an eyebrow at it: "Mustard?"

"Guacamole," I said. "They had some kind of Mexican fusion thing going on and I knew your weakness for avocados, so . . ."

She kissed me hard and flopped down next to me on the bed and began to fill it with rye crumbs and avocado smears.

"I gotta make a call," I said. "I didn't want to disturb you before when you were in the zone, but—"

"That's fine," she said.

When I didn't move toward the phone, she said, "What?"

"I, uh—"

She narrowed her eyes at me, but I could tell she wasn't really suspicious. "You calling your other girlfriend or something?"

I snorted. "If only. No, I'm going to call the Kohlers and let them know what's going on."

I had been putting it off since we'd tapped Joe to start building for us. At first, I told myself that I was just waiting to see how it all worked out before I involved them. Then I rationalized that there was nothing amiss about keeping *good* news from our investors—dishonesty lay in hiding *bad* news.

The reality, though, was that I knew they wouldn't be happy about it.

Not happy about it? Hell, they'd be furious.

It wasn't that we'd found a temp workforce on the other coast that was willing to do the job for free. Hell, Benny never met a wage bill that he didn't want to shoot in the head and bury in a shallow grave. Benny wouldn't be angry that we'd found a free workforce—but he'd be *volcanic* when he found out that we were paying for our San Francisco workers while they sat idle.

Any argument I could have mustered about the need to keep on skilled labor had just been devastated by the ease with which we'd brought a new workforce up to speed—without even having to meet them physically. Never mind that those new workers were elite engineering students at the world's most selective technical university, who could expect to graduate and make a hundred times more than we were paying our workers. Benny would insist that we fire every last one of the women from our factory, every one of the men who worked the warehouse—all of them.

So I'd kept it to myself.

So long as Benny had been able to phone me every day at Lucille's or the motel, I could maintain the fiction that we were just stretching the last of our capital in a bid to outlast Fidelity Computing. But if Benny were to discover that we'd skipped town without updating him . . . Well, it had taken a miracle to get him on board the last time we did that. I didn't want to gamble on a mulligan.

"So I've got to call them, and they're probably gonna yell at me, and I'm probably gonna have to grovel," I finished. "And I just didn't want to grovel in front of the woman I love."

"I like weak men. They're sexy and easy to dominate," she said. She crossed her arms at the head of the bed, then uncrossed them to brush crumbs off her sleeveless Black Flag T-shirt, and crossed them again. Then, she crossed her eyes. "Call away."

It was Ted who picked up, and I breathed a sigh of relief, covering the receiver and mouthing *Ted* at Pat. "Sorry to bother you, Ted! This is Marty Hench from CF. I'm just calling to fill you on all the latest developments, you know, a kind of sitrep." I could hear the nervousness in my voice, and see it reflected in Pat's dubious scowl.

"First of all, I want to assure you that our finances are sound. Better than sound, even. As of today, we are actually turning a small profit, even though we're still engaged in our temporary below-margin selling event." I hated this euphemism, but I hated "selling at a loss" even more.

"That's just *great,* Marty, Benny's gonna be very happy to hear it." Ted was such an easygoing, good-natured slob—a million miles from his cynical asshole brother.

"I also wanted to update you on our coordinates—we've had to move on from our previous location, but I've got some new numbers you can reach us at." I read from the bedside pad that I'd scribbled on.

"And one more thing, Ted, just to let you know that we've resumed limited production. We've found a temporary workforce on the East Coast and—" I let my mouth go on autopilot, strongly implying that we were paying some temps from MIT without ever actually *lying,* because a lot of those kids were at MIT, and they were temps, and my assurances that they were an affordable expense was true, because *working for free* is the most "affordable expense" of all.

Ted had a few questions, which I fielded expertly, staring into the middle distance, mind in the world of the spreadsheets. Maria-Eva's contact at Fidelity had phoned her with some new bank balances and I'd been itching to input them into my model of Fidelity's finances to game out how much runway they might have before they crashed and burned.

Finally, Ted was satisfied and promised to fill Benny in. I reached over Pat to rack the receiver on the bedside phone, and she bit my earlobe and wouldn't let go, and then one thing led to another and we were both busy for a while.

Once we were done, she twined her fingers in my hair and said, "I find it weirdly exciting to hear you spew business bullshit, Marty. It's like I'm cheating on you with a corporate drone."

"I knew you secretly craved a company man," I said. "Some guy in a blue tie from IBM who wants to have two point three kids with you."

She made a gagging noise. "No thanks," she said. "I'm not *that* kinky." We enjoyed the silence for a while. "I was surprised that you told him about Joe," she said. "I thought that was a secret."

"Well, I just told him about it in broad strokes. The Kohlers know we were running low on inventory, so I had to reassure them, let them know where the new cash flow was coming from."

"But you told him Joe's name," she said. "You think that was wise?"

"I didn't tell him Joe's name," I said.

"Uh, yes you did."

"I told him Joe's name?"

"You told him. First and last. It kinda stuck out."

I'd been in my fog, thinking about my spreadsheets, eyes focused on the middle distance. On autopilot. Tired. It would be fine. Surely, it would be fine.

23

I can't say for sure how close we came. We lasted another week in that motel, long enough that I started juggling invoices to our wholesalers to keep the parts coming in to Joe and his Junior Woodchucks.

I'd like to think that we nearly made it. The plan was a crazy one, but it was a good one. The whole situation was crazy, after all—crazy times call for crazy plans, surely.

Surely.

Liz and I were early risers, so we'd taken to doing the breakfast run together, hitting a Denny's or an IHOP off the freeway and coming back with a sack of takeout that we'd eat in either our room or the room she was sharing with Maria-Eva, while we all planned out the day's strategy.

We parked outside of my room and juggled the food and the room key, keeping up our chat about a customer who had a complicated order that we couldn't quite fill, and that's when Ted got out of his car and hailed us.

"Ted," I said. "Uh, it's nice to see you."

"Sorry to drop by out of the blue like this," he said.

"That's okay," I said. I mean, what else was I going to say? There he was, mild as milk, standing and smiling at us with that affable, easygoing smile.

Ted just kept smiling that smile. Liz made a tiny, annoyed sound, and then smiled at Ted in the way I privately called *Mormon nice.* "We have pancakes for everyone, Ted, and we're about to have a breakfast meeting. Would you like to join us?"

"I wouldn't want to take anyone's breakfast," he said, smiling that aw-shucks smile again.

"There's plenty," Liz said, with such an accurate facsimile of cheerfulness that I almost believed it.

Normally, our breakfast meetings were easy affairs, the scrape of plastic cutlery and squeak of styrofoam take-out containers counterpointed by chewing and murmuring about the day's tasks. With Ted at the tiny motel table, a strained near silence descended on us.

Finally, the last of the coffee was poured and Pat stole the piece of bacon I'd been saving, then, on seeing my dismayed expression, split it in half—the sharp *snap* of a truly crisp rasher—and shared it with me.

"Well folks, I have to say, I'm impressed," Ted said. "Really. You've gone very far with this thing under what I think we can all say have been some challenging circumstances." He smiled at us like a proud uncle.

"That's why I came out here, you understand. Benny wanted to do this by phone, but I figured, we owed you an in-person conversation."

They were going to call in their note. Of course. My brain went back into spreadsheet mode, calculating a repayment schedule based on bringing the factory back online. If we all took a serious pay cut, made some layoffs, we could offer them a pretty aggressive buyout, take back their equity at, say, 135 percent of face value, over two years and—

"You understand that we have an investment to protect. This is our family business, you understand, the capital our father and his brothers built up and—"

Let's say we placed big orders with all our suppliers today, called our major accounts and let them know the sale was over but offered them bulk discounts if they placed an order this week, brought the factory back online on Monday and—

368 ◀ **cory doctorow**

"Now, those three Reverend Sirs, they were horrified when we told them about what you'd experienced, what poor Rachel had been through—"

"Her name is Rivka," Sister Maria-Eva said. She was quicker on the uptake than I was. I was still figuring production cash flow in my head. She had already spotted the double cross.

"Rivka," Ted said. "Of course. How's she doing?"

"She'll live," Liz said.

Ted squirmed. "Well, good. That's good. I mean, thank God for that. Right?" I was catching up. Last to do so. "The thing is," he said. "Well, the businesses are so complementary. You've made some key improvements on their designs, corrected some of the mistakes they made early on, but they've still got the superior sales and support network. So it's—" He fished for a word. "It's *synergy*." Having found *le mot juste,* he beamed his simple, open smile at us. I was still at sea. Maria-Eva was not.

"You sold us to Fidelity Computing, Ted," she said. To an outside observer, her flat tone might have been mistaken for neutrality. For all of us, it was a warning sign. We all shifted minutely away from her.

"We sold *our* stake to them, yes," Ted said. "It's synergy."

"You said that," Pat said.

Ted's smile flicked off like it was on a switch. "Miss," he said, "would you mind excusing us? You aren't a founder, you aren't an employee, and I think it would be best if you would give us a moment alone here." When Ted stopped smiling, all those simple, open lines collapsed into a hard expression that made *Benny* seem like the friendly one.

He could have played a movie serial killer with that face, that transition. From good-natured slob to dead-eyed killer in a blink.

Calling Pat "Miss" was a tactical blunder. Patronizing her, a greater one. Asking her to leave her *own motel room*?

"How about you go fuck yourself sideways with a brick?"

she said, speaking in a convincing imitation of Ted's mild and friendly cadences, pasting on an eerie facsimile of Ted's hayseed mask.

Ted blinked slow, like a lizard. I waited to see if he'd make the catastrophic error of looking to me to deal with my unruly girlfriend, but some survival instinct saved him that day.

One more slow blink. "The price war was destroying a lot of capital. Just putting our money in a big pile and setting it on fire. Once we fold CF in with Fidelity, we'll be poised to set a more sustainable margin for the combined product line."

He looked from Liz to Maria-Eva. "And so you know, we made sure you'd maintain your independence. Publicly, CF will continue to run as an independent business, with its own sales force and product line. On the back end, we'll coordinate engineering and product planning. Fidelity will release a product, then, after a decent interval, CF will sell a complementary product. We get two shots at the same customer, and we can even use Fidelity's sales records to pinpoint the sales calls for CF. That way, everybody wins."

"Except the customers," Pat said, and Ted made an elaborate show of not hearing her.

"Except the customers," I repeated.

Lizard blink.

"The customers," Ted said, "get a high-quality product, which improves over its lifespan. There aren't many products that you could say that of."

"The product gets better because the first version you sell them is deliberately crippled," Liz said.

"The up-front limitations finance the development of new products," Ted said. I wondered if he would serve as spokesman for the new company, but of course, those duties would fall to the Reverend Sirs. No one sells a scam like a man of God.

"Not interested," Liz said.

"Not me either," Maria-Eva said.

Ted shook his head minutely, pursed his lips in a disappointed way. "I'm afraid that's not how this works," he said.

"You only own thirteen percent of the company," I said. It was 12.8 percent, but I rounded up.

"We are owed a substantial sum in a convertible note," he said. "And we have transferred title to both to Fidelity Computing, in exchange for an equity stake. Like it or not, CF is now a division of Fidelity Computing. You can figure out how to resolve your differences of opinions with those guys and stay on to make great products and lots of money, or you can go to—" He paused, checking his tongue. "You can find other ventures to participate in. Bottom line: we're your business partners, they're our business partners, and that means that you and they are going to have to play nice."

Art had a friend who was a top tech lawyer, a perfectly sweet guy who could turn into a vicious attack dog when his clients needed him to. I was already mentally summarizing the situation for a memo addressed to him, and thinking about where we'd get the cash for a retainer, when Maria-Eva broke in.

"Thank you for coming in person, Mr. Kohler. You're right, it was better that you told us this face-to-face."

Ted made the mistake of trying to stare down a nun, then looked away.

Liz and Maria-Eva looked at each other for a long moment.

"Well then," Liz said.

"Yes," Maria-Eva said.

Ted might have had the cunning to trick me into thinking he was the easygoing, nice half of the Kohler brothers, but that didn't mean he was truly quick on the uptake. He was still putting on his hard-guy face and glaring at the two founders as they stood up from the table.

"Where are you going?" He said it *after* Maria-Eva had gone out the door, Liz almost out, too. Liz stopped and gave him a smile that never went past her dimples.

"We're leaving," she said. "It's your company now. These rooms are booked on the company credit card, so we'll just leave you to settle the bill. Goodbye, Mr. Kohler."

Mormon nice.

Pat was already up and packing her things in the ragtag collection of shopping bags we'd accumulated. She'd got as far as unplugging her beloved Unix workstation when I stood up to gather my meager possessions.

Ted Kohler stood and interposed himself between the motel dresser, where I stood, and the bags I'd arrayed on the bed.

"Marty, be reasonable," he said. "There's plenty of money for all of us to make here."

"Ted, I know you're the kind of guy who likes to talk man-to-man"—Pat snorted at that—"and that's why you are trying to have this conversation with me instead of those two women, who are actual equity shareholders in CF. I'm just a hired accountant."

"You work for the company," he said. "They trust you and—"

"I'm a *contractor*, Ted. I'm not even an employee."

"You could be," he said. "We need smart finance people like you, and we could make it worth your while—"

"Respectfully," I said, "you cannot make it worth my while. Leaving aside the fact that I wouldn't work for those crepuscular God-botherers for *any* sum, you've just let your technical talent walk out the door. You're not going to make a single product that any of their old customers will want to buy, not without them. And that's *before* they go out and warn every one of those customers—and their sales reps—not to go near you and your new business partners under any circumstances."

He actually *sneered*. "They're not going to trash their own business. They're shareholders."

"Yes, they each own a small percentage of this new abomination you've created. They're not going to see a dime from it, though, because that is not a viable business, because they are not going to participate in it. They are the only truly productive elements of either Fidelity or CF, and without them, you've got nothing."

"So what're they going to do, go wait on tables?"

"No," Pat said, "they're going to go talk to my headhunter and get a job that pays ten times more than they were paying themselves. They started an entire PC company, you jackass. They can write their own ticket."

"We'll sue," he said. "Sue them, sue anyone who hires them. They're under noncompete."

I actually laughed. "Fella, noncompetes aren't enforceable in California. It's in the state constitution. Didn't you know that? Hell, I'm from *Alabama* and I knew that."

His scowl twisted into a snarl, his hands balled into fists, and for a second, I thought he was going to swing at me. Pat must have thought so, too, because she was suddenly between us, chin raised, deep into his personal space, with all the rough grace of a slam-dance veteran. "Time for you to go, pal," she said.

He tried sticking his chin out, too, but he wasn't as good at it as she was. "I'm paying for this hotel room," he said. "It's my room. I'll stay if I want to."

She got right up to him, eyes boring into his. "Either your whole body leaves in the next three seconds, or your whole body leaves minus your fucking teeth in the next thirty seconds. Your choice, dickhead."

He looked like he wanted to swing at *her* now, and I was about to step in when she put both hands on his chest, braced her chain-draped, calf-high combat boots, and *shoved* him, using her low center of gravity to excellent effect. He shot backward, windmilling his arms like a Looney Tunes character, and went down hard on his tailbone, an instant before the back of his head made contact with the motel door hard enough to make a dent.

"Ow, *fuck*," he said, hands on his head.

"*Out!*" Pat said, and stamped one jingling boot in his direction. He scrambled awkwardly to his feet and pawed at the doorknob. As he left, I saw her winding up to kick him square in his narrow ass and I pulled her back. "Not in the back, darling," I said, heart thudding, trying for a Nick-and-Nora bantering tone. "It's not sporting."

She turned to me, eyes flashing, ferocious and strong and glittering, bared small teeth. She was frightening in her full flight, but also, holy shit, was she ever *sexy.*

Her chest heaved. Mine too. She grabbed the back of my head and pulled me down for a kiss, then broke off and kicked the door shut with a bang and pulled me to the bed.

We checked out twenty minutes later, grinning like horny teenagers.

Ted's car was already gone.

24

In retrospect, the plan was obviously flawed. Even if we could have driven Fidelity Computing out of business, we'd have carried over a giant load of debt. Half of our factory workers had been smarter than us and they'd gone off and found other jobs, treating those paychecks I dutifully mailed out to them as a long and uncertain severance pay. If we'd started up again, we'd have struggled to fill orders, needing to hire and train a fresh round of workers.

I'm a forensic accountant, not a CFO. Yes, I can build models as well as anyone and predict cash flow, but my real skill is to look at someone else's models and spot their errors—or, more often, their deceptions. I never signed up to be CF's finance guy—at best, I was supposed to be their bookkeeper and competitive intelligence analyst, combing through smuggled Fidelity spreadsheets to find their crimes and misdemeanors.

You know what got Fidelity Computing in the end? This is great. Waves of PC clones tore up their business far more efficiently than we ever could have. Turns out that the combined sales forces of Gateway, Dell, Compaq, and Acer were much better at convincing people to give up their purple Fidelity computers than we ever would be—and that held true even for Orthodox Jews, Mormons, and devout Catholics.

The Kohlers and Fidelity Computing should have disappeared at that point, but they hung on for one more caper. I learned about it in the papers, when the California attorney general raided Fidelity Computing's offices and confiscated three truckloads of merchandise.

These weren't PCs, though. They were cash registers.

When Fidelity's business started circling the drain, the Kohlers and the Reverend Sirs had hunkered down to save their business, which had accumulated sizable debts and which had some extremely impatient, violent men who had grown accustomed to taking very large withdrawals whenever they needed some pocket money.

This is where the Kohlers and the Reverend Sirs discovered some of that legendary "synergy" that made Silicon Valley such a hotbed of innovation. It turned out that both groups of men knew large numbers of small businesspeople who were desirous of a highly specific kind of cash register: one that would add an extra couple of percentage points to every sale, tack on a sales tax, and produce two register tapes and two end-of-day reports reflecting two different counts.

For a dry cleaner or a Wendy's franchisee or a watchmaker turning over a million bucks a year, squeezing three percent, tax-free, out of your customers was an easy sell, provided the customer didn't mind committing a *lot* of very serious felonies.

It worked. For a while. The Kohlers and Fidelity found lots of small businesspeople who loved the convenience and accuracy of their funny cash registers, and were even able to branch out into selling funny time clocks and payroll systems to their lineup.

In hindsight, this isn't surprising. There's never just one ant. Once a business is willing to steal from its customers and from the taxman, a little wage theft is a no-brainer.

It was the wage theft that got 'em. One of their customers—a discount jeweler in downtown LA—skimmed the wages of his receptionist, whose son was on a full-ride scholarship to UCLA Law, where he was specializing in labor rights. He grabbed that loose thread and yanked, and one of his profs was an ex–U.S. attorney and still had some friends, and one thing led to another, and then one day I turned on KRON4 to watch the news and there were the Reverend Sirs being led away in handcuffs, their merchandise disappearing into California Highway Patrol vans.

Joe later told me that they asked *him* to build the damn things for them, even had *Nick Cassidy III* put a heavy arm on him, try to convince him that this was the best thing for the Irregulars. Joe told Nick Cassidy III to fold his floppy disk until it was all corners and then insert it where it would do him a world of good.

Today, Nick Cassidy III is a top-tier VC with a good firm on Sand Hill Road. He's considered a genius.

I kept tabs on Maria-Eva, Liz, and Rivka for a few years after that. Zion found Liz a job at Compaq in their hardware-design department and collected a fat finder's fee that they used as a down payment on a condo in the Marina.

Maria-Eva went to Mexico, then made her way to Nicaragua. She disappeared for a while, and we got worried, but then Liz let me know that she'd got a late-night, crackly call from Buenos Aires, Maria-Eva reassuring her that everything was fine and she was safe. Much later, I found out about the time she spent in detention in the south of Nicaragua, close to the Costa Rican border, in a hellhole that the CIA knew all about and did nothing to prevent.

Rivka ended up in Israel, running the technology for Shulamit Aloni's campaign for gay rights. She and her parents didn't speak for nearly twenty years, not until 2003, when they came to Toronto to attend her wedding, to the woman she'd lived with in Haifa for decades. Moshe Pupik was her best man.

I never made the mistake of actually joining a company again. From then on, I stopped pretending I was a finance guy and stuck strictly to being the *anti*-finance guy—the guy you called when you wanted to catch the finance guy red-handed.

Anti-finance guys don't have steady work, but we also don't have any long-term responsibilities. You call me up, tell me about the job, and then I make the call. If I take it, I get 25 percent of whatever I recover. It pays well. Paid enough for my mother's funeral, when the fast-moving leukemia got her a couple of years later. A lot of the oil wives went that way.

And it was enough to pay for my dad's care after his stroke, just a couple of weeks after her funeral. He wouldn't let me move him to San Francisco, so I flew out to Alabama twice a year to sit with him and tell him about my adventures, waiting while he laboriously ground out questions. They were shrewd questions. He wasn't a fool, my old man. He lasted seven years in the home, though the last two were bad.

I miss him.

I don't get emotionally involved with clients. Maybe I'm working for a company, or for an investor, and maybe that person is something like a friend, but not while I'm on the job.

One thing I never, ever, ever do is get romantically involved with anyone remotely connected to any client. I explained this thing to a delightfully vulgar client one night after an extremely frank offer came at the end of a long session going over the spreadsheets she'd paid me to analyze and she'd said, "Oh, that's the deli rule."

"The deli rule?"

"Don't get your meat where you get your bread."

(She renewed the offer some time later, when a sufficiency of time had passed since our professional entanglement, and I took her up on it, and I was glad I did. Delightfully vulgar, she was.)

I practiced the deli rule assiduously after that.

Pat and I lasted for a while—longer than either of us would have imagined. We both liked going to Dead Kennedys shows, and we made a good team in the pit. We got to be tight with Jello Biafra's roommate, a racoon-eyed, razor-tongued tiny woman from Montana, and we spent a lot of time at their place, eating potluck dinners and experimenting with some laboratory-grade substances.

We eventually figured out that we were better tripmates than lovers, and then she took a job with an encryption start-up inside the Beltway and disappeared into a world of secrecy for a decade. When she reemerged, she was married and had a rambunctious little girl whom I got to meet when she came to San Francisco for an RSA conference. We still keep in touch, sporadically.

I knew Art Hellman before he was Art Hellman. We made great roommates. We had both grown tired of our little apartment and wanted a life in the city, so we went in together on an amazing place on Russian Hill. That had the added advantage of putting our last known address behind us, and we stopped looking over our shoulders for CONSULTANTs and other thugs on the Reverend Sirs' payroll.

But of course, we weren't hard to find.

They found us.

Art had settled in with a new modem company, working out the kinks in their compression algorithm, a gnarly sort of problem that required that he simultaneously debug their custom circuit boards, the acoustic properties of their carrier signal, and the compression system itself. It was the problem he was born to solve—and it was way, way over my head.

At a certain point, he hit a wall. He'd hack on the problem all day, come home ferociously angry and frustrated, and I'd cook some dinner, and he'd slowly unwind while we ate together and made small talk and drank a couple of glasses of wine.

Then we'd pile the dishes in the sink and go for a walk, down

Russian Hill to Washington Square, then back again, while he talked through the problem and I hung on for dear life and tried to follow along. Every once in a great while, I'd be able to suggest a possible avenue of attack, but really, just having someone listen patiently to him while he verbally worked through the problem was useful. Me, I liked the company and valued the exercise.

We were practically on our doorstep when they jumped us: two big guys in tracksuits who'd been waiting in a pickup truck, who sprang out and blocked us, fore and aft.

"Hench," the one in front of us said, and the one behind us gave me a little shove.

Art didn't hesitate. *"Bashers!"* he shouted. *"Gaybashers!"* A couple of guys had been hospitalized the week before, so his confusion was understandable, but I didn't think these two were—

"Bashers!" he shouted again.

The guy in front of me swung, but I'd been taking self-defense classes, and I slipped under his big, slow fist and got a knee in, missing his balls and hitting his thigh. Art grunted behind me and gave a loud, angry yell. *"Baaashers!"*

The guy had me in a clinch, and I could smell his sweat and the Big Mac sauce he'd spilled on his shirt and I burrowed my face into his arm, trying to bite him and also to avoid his face punches, catching them on the forehead instead of in my nose.

I had a mouthful of tracksuit and maybe a little skin that I was biting down hard on, and the guy's arm was around my head, so I didn't hear the approaching footsteps, but a moment later I was free and the guy was on the ground, surrounded by four extremely fit young men with the kind of well-groomed mustaches and lumberjack shirts I'd learned to think of as *Castro Clone.*

Three more were helping Art out, or, more precisely, had dropped Art's attacker and were methodically going over him with Kodiak boots, and a moment later, my attacker was down and getting the same treatment.

The guys were nicer than I would have been, avoiding spine, balls, face, and kidneys, making it hurt without making it permanent, and they moved with grace and speed.

The men on the ground cried out, squirmed, tried to grab at the kicking feet and got their fingers mashed for their trouble. Eventually, our saviors relented and two men lay on the sidewalk, whimpering.

"You okay?" said one of the rescue party, a blond with a deep southern drawl.

Art moved his hand away from his eye to reveal an incipient shiner. He opened and closed the eye a couple of times. "I'll live," he said, and gave Mr. Deep South a winning smile.

"I'm fine," I said, patting myself down. "Fine."

One of the other guys, also blond, tall, and broad, said, "You're bleeding, sir," and pointed to a spreading stain on my shirt. I lifted the sticky cloth to reveal a shallow slice, bisecting the still-tender scar from my last knife wound, turning it into an uneven X. I touched it gingerly. "Not deep," I said. I marveled at the new wound. "X marks the spot, I guess." I was giddy, almost giggly. I looked around and spotted the knife, an ugly clasp knife with a cheap handle, lost in someone's flower bed. I started to bend to pick it up but now I could feel the slice and I thought better of it. The big guy handed it over to me.

The two guys on the ground were stirring, and the one who'd called my name got to his hands and knees.

Suddenly, my giggles gave way to fury. I wound up and kicked that motherfucker with everything I had, square in his ass, sending him face-first back onto the pavement, sanding the skin off his chin and lips. I was winding up for another kick, this time in the beautifully exposed target between his splayed legs, when Art caught me, assisted by the big guy. I struggled against them, then relented.

"Fuck off," I shouted at the guy on the ground, who was groaning and just beginning to get back to his knees. "Both of you, fuck off." Art shot me a wounded look. "Not you," I said. "Those assholes."

The one who'd gone for Art was on his feet now, staggering to his friend and helping him into the pickup.

"We've got your license plate number," one of our rescuers said. "Drive safe now."

The one whose face wasn't a bloody mess put the pickup in gear, stalled on the slope and rolled back, then, after two more tries, managed to get rolling.

"Tourists!" another rescuer shouted, and that broke the tension and we all cracked up.

We thanked the guys, who were all from the same choir group and who had started their nightly patrol around the neighborhood after their practices when those two poor guys had been beaten up the previous week. Art offered to make them tea or pour them a glass of wine, but they were adamant that they had to keep up their patrol (but one of them gave Art his phone number).

We said our goodbyes and watched them power-walk up the steep hill, joking and laughing with each other, disappearing with a trail of song behind them.

"Let's get you patched up," Art said. "I've got some superglue in the kitchen drawer."

We turned toward the steps leading up to our front door, and that's when I saw the big guy's front tooth, knocked loose when I'd kicked him. It made my stomach do a slow roll, but I pointed it out to Art and made him get it for me. It wasn't the whole tooth, just a broken-off half, bloody and sharp at the line where it had cracked.

For years afterward, I flinched whenever I met someone with a broken front tooth, but as far as I know, I never saw those two guys again. The Kohlers and Fidelity Computing were indicted the following week, and I suppose their "partners" decided that they'd better lay low.

382 ◂ **cory doctorow**

By the time the trial finished—plea bargains all round, no jail time for anyone, because "white collar" crime isn't really a crime—everyone seemed to have forgotten my role in the whole affair.

But I never did.

The Dead Kennedys broke up in 1986. That same year, Microsoft went public. It was the starter pistol for a new race whose finish line was the West Coast tech scene.

That was the first year I truly felt like a San Franciscan, finding myself grousing about the awful computer people who were piling into the city, ruining its character. In so doing, I was continuing the brave tradition of centuries' worth of my forebears, who'd voiced the same complaints about the gold miners, sailors, hippies, and queers who just didn't understand the authentic character of San Francisco, which was the character of the city when *I* arrived.

My favorite restaurants closed in droves, replaced by yuppie places that I refused to eat at on principle. Oh, I could afford them. There was no shortage of demand for the services of an expert in untangling the cack-handed scams of tech's amateur con artists. But I hated the company.

epilogue

About a month after Pat decamped for DC, I found myself confronting the brown butcher's paper in the window of the great little Mission crepe joint we used to go to for Sunday brunches. It had shut, and somewhere behind the glass and brown paper, someone was getting ready to open the kind of place specializing in wine spritzers and *nouvelle cuisine,* dishes like "smoked chicken with plums and kiwis in a raspberry coulis."

I was unaccountably angry at that hypothetical smoked chicken, fists and jaw clenched. What the hell was I doing here? Was I really going to spend the rest of my life as a spreadsheet jockey? Was that even a job? I had just turned twenty-five, but I felt *old* compared to the kids flooding into the city.

They were the new pilgrims. Did they stop outside of Sacto *like they're standing on the diving board and taking a couple test bounces before they make the leap?* Was Lucille welcoming in a new crop of searchers there on the outskirts, smiling at them with that incredible smile, listening to them with that amazing focus?

I decided to find out.

Once I got the idea, I leapt on, determined to move before I could chicken out. I threw an overnight bag in the trunk of the 1985 Honda Accord I'd paid $8,999 for two months earlier. I got as far as Davis before it occurred to me to call her. I pulled in at a truck stop.

"Marty, what a treat to hear your voice," she said.

"Hey," I said, suddenly thick-tongued. "Uh." I should turn

around. "Uh, hey, Lucille, I was just heading through Sacramento and I wondered if you'd like to have dinner with me?
While I'm passing through town?"

"I would like nothing better, Marty. Is Pat with you?"

"Uh." My tongue got thicker. "She moved. To DC. For a job."

"Oh," Lucille said, with a curious lilt in her voice. "Well, I
suppose congratulations are in order. You'll have to tell me all
about it. When do you expect to get in?"

"I'm about an hour away," I said. "In Davis. But if you're busy,
I could get a cup of coffee and—"

"Nonsense," she said. "Come straight to my place, and I'll
have figured out dinner by then."

She figured out dinner, warming up some excellent shepherd's
pie she'd made the day before and opening a bottle of Charles
Krug pinot noir.

The food was delicious, but I barely tasted it, because she
was wearing a filmy green blouse and a perfume that was more
citrus than flower, and it mixed with her own smell in a way
that made me a little dizzy.

She listened so well, and I must have told her everything, from
the Dead Kennedys breakup to the yuppie restaurants to the
fraudsters I'd caught. She told me about her students and their
parents and the pilgrims who'd passed through town on the way
to seek their fortunes in the latest gold rush.

"They're so young, Marty. I must be getting old."

"You're not old," I said, the words tumbling out like they
were racing ahead of my filter. "You're beautiful."

She smiled then, and didn't say anything, and I realized
something about her listening—she didn't just listen to the
words, she listened to the *silences*.

I listened to the silence, too. Her breathing. A dog-walker
outside her front windows. A nighttime raptor looking for din-

ner, calling in the sky overhead, Dopplering like a jet. For a moment, I thought I could hear her heart, thudding in her chest.

But it was mine.

The next day was Saturday and she didn't have to teach, so I cooked her breakfast while she slept, still remembering my way around her kitchen. I made Moosewood apple–cheese pancakes from memory, then brewed coffee, opening her bedroom door so the smell could lure her out.

She was even more beautiful in the morning, tousled hair and eyelids at half-mast, and she slid into my arms and pressed every part of her against every part of me for a hug that went on and on and on.

"Thank you, Marty," she said.

"Thank you, Lucille," I said.

We're still friends, all these years later.

acknowledgments

I am grateful—as ever—to the usual suspects here, whose support is usual, but whose importance to my life is extraordinary: my wife, Alice, and my daughter, Poesy; my parents, Roz and Gord Doctorow; my agent, Russell Galen; my editors, Patrick Nielsen Hayden and Mal Frazier; my Wunderkind publicists, Elena Stokes, Brianna Robinson, and Kayla Slusser; and my Tor publicist, Laura Etzkorn.

I am also profoundly grateful to the booksellers and librarians who made the tours for the four books (!) that preceded this one over the past two years (!!) such ringing successes. As a recovering bookseller, page and cataloger, I salute you and offer my most sincere and enduring thanks.

I am grateful to everyone who has talked with me about my favorite spittle-flecked, overexcited hobbyhorses: DRM, adversarial interoperability, hacking, tinkering, reverse engineering, and the like. An incomplete list: bunnie Huang, Tom Jennings, John Gilmore, Limor Fried, Phil Torrone, Seth Schoen, Cindy Cohn, Cooper Quinton, Mitch Kapor, Voja Antonic, John Park, Mitch Altman, Liz Henry, Danny O'Brien, Emmanuel Goldstein, and everyone else who has ever discovered the wonders of letting the magic smoke out of a circuit board.

I want to thank all the enthusiastic readers of my newsletter, *Pluralistic.net,* whose kind feedback made it possible for me to shout into the void without feeling quite so self-conscious. If you don't read *Pluralistic,* give it a try. It's free as in beer (costs nothing) and free as in speech (licensed Creative Commons

Attibution 4.0, so you can give it away, sell it, adapt it, etc.). There are no ads, tracking, or other enshittificatory nonsense.

Finally, I am grateful to Framework, for making the greatest laptop I have ever used. What a fucking *wonder* this thing is. I spent the lockdown years in my backyard hammock, hammering out *nine* books on a Framework, while listening to Talking Heads 5.1 Downmix on endless repeat.

about the author

CORY DOCTOROW (craphound.com) is a science fiction author, activist and journalist. He is the author of many books, most recently *The Lost Cause*, a solarpunk science fiction novel of hope amidst the climate emergency. His most recent non-fiction book is *The Internet Con: How to Seize the Means of Computation*, a Big Tech disassembly manual. Other recent books include *Red Team Blues*, a science fiction crime thriller; *Chokepoint Capitalism*, non-fiction about monopoly and creative labour markets; the Little Brother series for young adults; *In Real Life*, a graphic novel; and the picture book *Poesy the Monster Slayer*. In 2020, he was inducted into the Canadian Science Fiction and Fantasy Hall of Fame.